Praise for the

NIGHT SEEKER

"Ms. Galenorn's exceptional insight into supernatural mythology is readily apparent and her added mixture of new lore produces a stunning urban fantasy world . . . a perfect blending of carnal passions, electrifying action, realistic characters, and stark betrayal. . . . If you enjoy noir urban fantasy that stretches all your boundaries, then Yasmine Galenorn is the author to buy and her Indigo Court is the series to read." —*Smexy Books*

"A complex tale . . . Filled with action and plenty of lethal road-blocks, readers will enjoy trekking the dangerous Galenorn mythological world." —*Genre Go Round Reviews*

"This richly inventive series is full of dark characters who face difficult and sometimes virtually impossible decisions." —*Night Owl Reviews*

"This steamy addition to the Indigo Court series blends justice and sacrifice in order to help the greater good . . . Galenorn has created a multifaceted world full of adventure and passion!" —*RT Book Reviews*

NIGHT VEIL

"A thoroughly engrossing series . . . Once again, Galenorn creates a magical world of both ethereal beauty and stark horror." —*Bitten by Books*

"An en   of the best
at Othe   bble to the
climati   *nd Reviews*

continued . . .

"Will have the reader turning pages long after bed time . . . a perfect read for any fantasy lover." —*Fresh Fiction*

"Excitement at every turn . . . a great read for those who love paranormal romance, and a fantastic read for all the Yasmine Galenorn fans out there!" —*Night Owl Reviews*

"Non-stop action from beginning to end." —*Romance Reviews Today*

NIGHT MYST

"This is an amazing book. The story flows and rushes and the author makes constant incredible mind pictures . . . Lyrical, luscious, and irresistible." —Stella Cameron, *New York Times* bestselling author

"An adventurous, fast read that had the right mix of tension, passion, and tenderness." —FlamesRising.com

"Puts a unique twist on the paranormal world, leaving the reader begging for more. Yasmine Galenorn's imagination is a beautiful thing." —*Fresh Fiction*

"A great start to a new series." —*Smexy Books*

"This is the first in a new urban fantasy series and I am definitely looking forward to the next one . . . There is great worldbuilding here and that is one thing that I love about Ms. Galenorn's books." —*Book Binge*

Praise for the Otherworld series

"Yasmine Galenorn creates a world I never want to leave." —Sherrilyn Kenyon, #1 *New York Times* bestselling author

"Chilling, thrilling, and deliciously dark—Galenorn's magical fantasy is spectacularly hot and supernaturally breathtaking." —Alyssa Day, *New York Times* bestselling author

NIGHT VISION

An Indigo Court Novel

YASMINE GALENORN

BERKLEY BOOKS, NEW YORK

THE BERKLEY PUBLISHING GROUP
Published by the Penguin Group
Penguin Group (USA) Inc.
375 Hudson Street, New York, New York 10014, USA

USA | Canada | UK | Ireland | Australia | New Zealand | India | South Africa | China

Penguin Books Ltd., Registered Offices: 80 Strand, London WC2R 0RL, England
For more information about the Penguin Group, visit penguin.com.

NIGHT VISION

A Berkley Book / published by arrangement with the author

BERKLEY® is a registered trademark of Penguin Group (USA) Inc.
The "B" design is a trademark of Penguin Group (USA) Inc.

For information, address: The Berkley Publishing Group,
a division of Penguin Group (USA) Inc.,
375 Hudson Street, New York, New York 10014.

ISBN: 978-0-425-25922-1

PUBLISHING HISTORY
Berkley mass-market edition / July 2013

PRINTED IN THE UNITED STATES OF AMERICA

10 9 8 7 6 5 4 3 2 1

Cover art by Tony Mauro.
Cover design by Rita Frangie.
Interior text design by Laura K. Corless.

ALWAYS LEARNING   **PEARSON**

ACKNOWLEDGMENTS

I want to thank my husband, Samwise, who supports my work with love and passion. Thank you to my agent, Meredith Bernstein; my editor, Kate Seaver; and my incredible cover artist, Tony Mauro. To my assistants, Andria Holley, Jenn Price, and Marc Mullinex—you guys help me keep on track. Thanks to my Street Team—for spreading the word!

A thank you to my Galenorn Gurlz, who make writing a lot more fun with their purrs and meows. Most reverent devotion to Ukko, who rules over the wind and sky; Rauni, queen of the harvest; Tapio, lord of the woodlands; and Mielikki, goddess of the Woodlands and Fae Queen in her own right, my spiritual guardians. And to the Fae—both dark and light—who walk this world beside us, may we see you in the shadows, and in the shimmer of ice. My spiritual grounding keeps me centered and focused.

And thank you to my Moon Stalkers, my fans and my readers, for your support and enthusiasm. You can find me on the net at Galenorn En/Visions: www.galenorn.com. If you write to me snail mail (see my website for the address or write via my publisher), please enclose a stamped, self-addressed envelope if you would like a reply. Lots of cool promo goodies are available—see my website.

The Painted Panther
Yasmine Galenorn

Lust is to the other passions what the nervous fluid is to life; it supports them all, lends strength to them all . . . ambition, cruelty, avarice, revenge, are all founded on lust.

—MARQUIS DE SADE

Revenge is an act of passion; vengeance of justice. Injuries are revenged; crimes are avenged.

—SAMUEL JOHNSON

The Beginning

So in time, the Court of Rivers and Rushes and the Court of Snow and Ice rose once again. Their beginning was bathed in blood . . . The blood of the innocent, the blood of the guilty. The blood of the holy and the blood of the damned. The old ways were passing, as new traditions and alliances emerged. Enemies became allies, and the Lost Ones came in out of the Wild to dance at the feet of the new Queen of Snow and Ice. It is thought that by joining with the civilized world, the Courts of Fae became more feral and primal than ever. But still, Myst, the Usurper, lingered, regrouping her forces, for the final battle yet to come . . .

—From *The Return of the Summer and Winter:*
A Historical Study of the New Courts of Fae

Chapter 1

As I stepped out from the forest, under the open stars, the dark silhouette of the Veil House warmed my heart, but it was a bittersweet moment. The house stood silent against the night sky, but signs abounded that it was slowly returning to life. The walls had been rebuilt, the roof repaired, and it was beginning to look like a house again rather than the bombed-out shelter that it had been. But it would never again be my home. After too many years on the road as a child, I'd returned to New Forest, Washington. I'd come home to my aunt Heather and the Veil House, only to lose both of them for good.

So much had changed over the past few weeks since I'd rolled into town. And so much was still in flux. Literally caught up by a whirlwind, I barely recognized myself now. Everything I'd ever thought about my childhood and heritage had been turned upside down.

A light flurry of snow fell softly, drifting flakes clinging to my shoulders like frozen butterflies. My breath hovered, a pale fog in front of me. Over the past weeks, I'd learned to hate the snow. Myst had destroyed my love for the icy months of the year.

"You'd better learn to love the cold," I whispered to myself. "Soon enough, winter will be your permanent home."

Standing on the precipice of a transformation, I would soon enter the realm of snow and ice forever. Today . . . today I was still Cicely Waters, Wind Witch and owl shifter. But soon, I'd be . . .

Who am I becoming, Ulean?

Are you afraid? Do not worry. The initiation will change you—make you stronger.

Again, I shivered. *That's what I'm afraid of. Will I still be me afterward?*

Ulean's laughter surrounded me, a gentle breeze that swept by, almost warm in its touch. The Wind Elemental had been with me since I was six years old. We were bound, and she guarded my back.

You will always be who you are. You'll just know more about yourself. You'll learn to control your emerging powers better. You'll be you, but you'll also be a queen. And I will always be with you. Lainule bound me to your service before you ever knew who or what you were to become. Her visions guided her. I will not leave you.

And then she fell silent, leaving me with my thoughts again.

I kicked a pile of snow, wishing for spring. Wishing for any season that involved green growing things. Myst, Queen of the Indigo Court—the Vampiric Fae, upstart winter queen—had brought the eternal twilight to town, determined to spread her ice and chill across the land. Her Shadow Hunters fed on bone and gristle and marrow and life force. Once we finally defeated Myst, the seasons would return to their normal ebb and flow. Until then, we were caught in her unwavering grasp, even though we'd driven her into hiding.

"Any sign of Shadow Hunters?" Rhiannon, my cousin, emerged from the wood to stand beside me. "I'm sorry I'm late—the Summer Court has been keeping me busy." She didn't sound exactly thrilled about the whole thing, but I knew that it was just her nerves.

I shook my head. "I don't see any. But they're out there. Somewhere. I doubt if they'll show themselves until Myst regroups her forces. Who knows how many of them managed to escape? And there were plenty of others scattered around the country. They'll come to her aid when she calls. She's just biding her time until she rebuilds her army."

"That's what I'm afraid of." Rhiannon glanced over her shoulders. "I wish I felt it was safe to go out alone. Do you think we should bring a couple of the guards?"

I glanced back at the trees. They were there, hidden in the woods, ready to join us if we required. But I'd managed to convince Lainule that—with Myst currently out of the picture—we really didn't need them. Especially since we were headed to the Emissary's mansion. Myst couldn't get through the vampires' defenses—not when she was at the peak of her power, and not now.

"I think we'll be fine. We're just going to Regina's . . ." I paused. "But soon enough, we won't be able to travel alone. Although, Lainule does. So maybe . . . maybe . . . they won't be on our tail every place we go." The thought of being watched everywhere we went didn't sit well with me.

As the dusk fell across the snowbound evening, Ulean whipped around me. She seemed agitated.

Trouble. There is trouble in the Veil House.

Fuck. Maybe we *did* need the guards. *Shadow Hunters?*

No, not Shadow Hunters. Vampires, and they have Luna with them. She's afraid—I can feel her fear.

I turned to Rhiannon. "Luna's in the house and Ulean says there are vampires in there with her." I rushed forward, wondering if the guards would follow. I had no idea if they could see us from where they were in the forest.

Rhiannon plunged through the snow after me. "Damn it. Lannan promised allegiance—"

I raced through the snow, slipping on the icy crust a couple of times. "I don't think it's Lannan."

A sense of dread seeped through me. We'd been cocky.

We'd driven Myst back and, even though we knew she was regrouping, the town had felt safe enough to wander around. We'd grown careless the past couple of days. So, when Luna had gone to the market alone, assuring us she would be fine, we let her go. Apparently, she was wrong, and so were we.

The back porch of the Veil House had been fully repaired and I bounded up the steps, glancing over my shoulder. No sign of the guards.

Ulean, can you warn Lainule we might need help?

I will. Be cautious, Cicely. I do not know what's going on in there. I cannot read the vampires' energies.

With Rhiannon on my heels, I slammed through the door and into the kitchen, skidding to a halt in case they were there. Nothing but a silent room.

The kitchen had been entirely rebuilt. The new color was chiffon yellow, pale as the cool morning light in early spring, and it spread across the room, a gradient of apricot blushing toward the ceiling. The trim had been replaced, and all the cabinets and cupboards. The workmanship was meticulous.

I glanced around, trying to decide whether to go up the back staircase to the bedrooms or—

A noise from the living room caught my attention and I slowed, motioning for Rhiannon to stay behind me. I felt for the sheath hanging off my belt, gripping the hilt of my new dagger. Lainule herself had given it to me, and it was fit for a queen—wickedly sharp, a magical silver alloy, and deadly. Behind me, Rhiannon drew her matching gilt-edged one. I wasn't sure how I felt about that. Rhia hadn't been trained in use of a blade, and I didn't want her stabbing me by accident. Or herself.

We peeked around the wall leading to the living room. Here, where the smoke had damaged furniture and wallpaper but not the actual structure, the walls had been stripped and now a pale green illuminated the room, and the antiques had been restored where they could be. New furniture replaced the pieces too broken to be fixed.

Standing in the middle of the room were two men—vampires by the looks of their eyes—wearing dark suits. Between them, they restrained Luna, each holding one of her arms. They were ignoring her as they talked in soft whispers over her head.

Luna was crying, softly, and I saw her shiver as one of the vamps reached down to tip her chin up so she was staring him in the face. He said something—I couldn't hear what—and she let out a whimper, then pressed her lips together.

"So, what the fuck do you plan on doing with my friend?" I stepped out from around the wall. I wanted more backup, but we had to do something.

The vamps glanced over at me, and then one snorted.

"Took you long enough, *witch*. We're here to deliver a message." He let go of Luna and shoved her forward with so much force that she went sprawling at my feet.

She landed hard on the floor, and I quickly bent to help her up. Struggling, she looked up at me, dazed. Her eyes were wide, and two ragged punctures marred her neck, dried blood from them coating her skin. I knew exactly what that meant.

"Fucking perverts, you fed from her." I whirled on them. "You'd better not be aligned with Lannan, or I swear, I'm—"

The first vamp sneered. "Shut up, cunt. Try being a little more respectful. You see, we don't give a fuck about your powers or your lineage or the fact that your oh-so-fragile neck is going to hold up a pretty little diadem."

"Quiet," his partner said. He pointed to Luna. "The *girl* is your message." They turned to leave, but he stopped and glanced back. "Next time we meet, the warning will be harsher. You might caution your friend about being so carefree. We could have broken her neck without blinking an eye and left her on the street. We could have turned her and taken her with us."

"Who sent you? Who are you working for?"

He laughed. "You'll find out soon enough. We're just

administering a gentle reminder that not all vampires in New Forest are as entranced with you as that sycophant Altos and his bitch whore sister."

I drew back my dagger, knowing it was a foolish move. But I had to do something. I couldn't take them down with it, but I could do my best to protect us—at least for a while. I moved in front of Luna.

"I don't care who hates me. Just don't take it out on my friends—" And then I paused. *Crap.* I knew who had sent them. At least, I was fairly certain. "Geoffrey and Leo sent you, didn't they?" Behind me, Rhiannon gasped. "Get back, don't let them near you." I glanced over my shoulder to make sure nobody was behind us.

The larger vampire snorted. He cocked his head to the side, his obsidian eyes gleaming. "Don't worry your scrawny neck about it. We're not out for the win. Yet. Just consider this visit a promise of things to come. Geoffrey loves the chase, and the hunt. But you'd better prepare yourselves, because when it's time to get real, little girl, you can be sure there won't be any place to hide."

And then, in a blur so fast I couldn't see them move, they were gone.

I stared at the front door. It was open, blowing in the wind.

"We're in deep shit, aren't we?" Rhiannon leaned close to me.

I nodded, staring at the snow that swirled in on the wind. "Yeah," I said softly. "And somehow, I don't think it's going to get any easier. Not for a long time."

⚶

Rhia and I managed to get Luna onto the sofa. I was attending to her wounds—the punctures were jagged and deep, and she'd lost a fair amount of blood—when Grieve burst through, followed by Kaylin and several guards.

Kaylin took one look at Luna, on whom he was crushing bad, and rushed over, sliding to the floor beside the couch. "Is she—" He glanced up at me.

"I'm not dead, if that's what you mean." Luna groaned and sat up, gently pressing her hand to the bandage on her neck. "But damn, I hurt, and I'm dizzy."

"There's no food in this place. We need to get you something to eat."

Kaylin pulled a candy bar out of his pocket and pressed it into her hands. "What happened? Did you cut yourself? Lainule said there were vampires up here . . ." He glanced around. The guards had already spread out through the house, making sure the coast was clear.

"The vamps are gone, for now." I let out a deep breath. "Geoffrey and Leo sent them. Luna . . . they . . ." My gaze went to the bandage on her neck.

Kaylin followed my look. "Those fuckers drank from her?"

His eyes grew dark. He was Chinese, and his long hair was pulled back in a ponytail. He looked our age—around his mid-to-late twenties—but in reality he was more than a hundred years old. With a night-veil demon wedded to his soul, Kaylin walked in shadows. He played in the dark.

"Yeah," I said slowly, standing so I could stop him if he tried to follow them. His eyes flashed dangerously, lighting with a fire I had seen only once or twice. "She'll be okay, Kaylin. They didn't feed enough to endanger her life."

Waiting for a moment till he calmed down and sat beside her, I turned to Luna. "Can you tell us what happened?"

She shuddered. "I was on my way to the market—I wanted to make apple pie, but they didn't have everything I needed at the Barrow. I thought I'd be fine. If anybody had to worry about going out alone during the day, I thought it would be you and Rhiannon. I argued with the guards until they let me go alone."

"Right. I heard." I'd vouched for her, told Lainule she'd be okay. I hung my head, sorry I'd ever opened my mouth. "You left around four, right?"

"Yes. I wanted to stop in at the bookstore to see if a book I ordered last week had come in. It felt so good to walk down the sidewalk without being afraid that the Shadow

Hunters would be hiding in the alleys." She grimaced and stretched her neck, wincing from the pain of the bite. Vampires could make you come by drinking from you, but the aftermath? Not so much fun. Kaylin and I helped her sit down again.

"I guess you should have taken a guard with you." I stopped, realizing I'd just spouted off the same advice Rhia and I had refused to take. With a sigh, I shrugged. "What happened?"

"I stopped at a coffee shop after that, then the market. When I came out, it was just after sunset. I was waiting at a bus stop to return here when they appeared, out from the alleyway. Before I knew what was happening, they grabbed me and dragged me into the shadows. My packages were on the ground, and they pressed me up against the wall. One of them turned to look at me, and that's when I realized they were vampires. I tried to look away, but . . ."

Vampires could mesmerize with their gazes, and Luna, as magical as she was, couldn't possibly hope to stand up against them.

"They both fed on me." Her voice was thick, and she blushed. "I *liked* it. They *made* me like it. I feel . . . dirty. Used."

"Yeah, they do that." I flashed a look at Kaylin that said, *Don't say a word*, and then knelt beside her. "Did they do anything . . . else to you?"

She shook her head. "They dragged me into a limo. And then . . . we were here. I thought they were going to kill me, but the one—the bigger one—just told me that I was lucky this time. Then he grinned and said that next time, he'd finish me himself. He said my blood was sweet." Another shudder, another look of horror. "That's right when you came in."

"Kaylin, take her back to the Barrow and make sure she's okay."

Kaylin said nothing but wrapped his arms around her shoulders and, once again, helped her stand. It was obvious she was weak. Luna was short, plump, and pretty. The demon within Kaylin's soul had given him extra strength and speed, though, and he picked her up as if she were light as a feather and carried her out the door, calling to one of the guards to accompany him.

As they left, I turned to Grieve and Rhiannon. "Want to make a bet this has something to do with our meeting with Regina?"

"You need to take guards with you, since I am specifically not invited." Grieve glowered. He hated it when I went into Lannan's territory without him, but there wasn't much we could do. Having them in the same room together was pretty much like holding a lit rag to a can of gasoline.

I bit my lip. "Twenty minutes ago, I would have said no. Now? Not so much. But they can't ride in the car. The iron would hurt them." I pulled out my cell phone and dialed Regina's private number.

Within seconds, the Emissary for the Crimson Court answered, her voice slick like honey and oil.

"Regina, Geoffrey and Leo just delivered a bloody message to us. I need to bring guards with us tonight. You will allow them through the gate, right?"

Silence for a count of one . . . two . . . three. Then she answered, in a voice that wavered only in the slightest. But that faint quiver told me there was cause for concern. "Of course. I'll tell my guards to be ready for them. How many are you bringing?"

"Five should do it. And Regina, thank you." Without waiting for an answer, I punched the End Talk button. I knew Regina well enough to know that she wasn't going to say anything more over the phone. I notified the guards of the sudden change in plans, and they took off, heading for Lannan and Regina's mansion.

As Rhiannon and I prepared to leave, I held out my arms. Grieve, my Fae Prince, slid willingly into my embrace. "I wish you could go with me, but so not a good idea." Softly, I kissed his lips, and he growled a little, causing the wolf tattoo on my stomach to respond. "I'll be careful, I promise."

"See that you are." His dark eyes were as black as those of the vampires, but their onyx cores were filled with gleaming stars. Platinum hair cascaded down his shoulders, and he reached up, solemnly, to stroke my face, smelling of cinnamon and apples. "You are my everything. You are my Queen. Do not let the darkness swallow you, my love."

Nodding, I turned to Rhiannon, who followed me out the door. The guards were already off and running toward Regina and Lannan's mansion. They would meet us there.

As we hurried to my beloved Pontiac GTO, several armed guards waited beside it, making sure we were safely tucked inside. I turned the ignition, dreading what the rest of the night held. Because I knew in my heart the news was only going to get worse.

⚓

"They're never going to give up until they get even, are they?" Rhia leaned her head against the window, watching as the evening dusk grew deeper.

I shook my head. "No. I don't think so. I wish I could say yes and mean it, but Leo and Geoffrey are dangerous. Not as dangerous as Myst, but we can't underestimate them. Regina sounded almost . . . afraid."

Rhia jerked around. "Afraid? *Regina?*"

"Yeah, I know—an oxymoron. But she sounded . . . cautious."

My stomach fluttered, a knot rising, but I pushed it away, focusing on the icy street as I navigated through the silent neighborhoods. So many people had fled New Forest, and though some were trickling back, the town seemed unnaturally quiet and subdued.

"We'll know what she knows soon enough." I turned onto the street that led toward Lannan's mansion. The estate had belonged to Geoffrey until he'd defied the Crimson Court and been ousted from his position of Regent. Now, Lannan Altos, the golden boy of the vampire nation, and my personal nemesis, had taken over the job.

The brilliant mansion lit up the night as we approached. Gleaming white with gold trim, the behemoth rose three stories high, with who knew how many stories below-ground. Columns lined the wraparound porch, and urns sported rosebushes now nestled beneath the snow. The tableau suggested a Grecian temple more than a mansion belonging to New Forest.

The entire estate sprawled across two acres, fully gated and surrounded by snow-covered gardens and security guards in dark suits. Vampires they might be, but they also carried guns and stakes and whatever else they might need to defend against enemies. With their obsidian eyes cloaked behind dark glasses, and dressed in black suits, the vamps had an old-time gangster look going on. But there was no mistake—they were *vampires*, far deadlier than the yummanii mobsters.

As we eased into the driveway, one of the guards hurried up to open my door. They knew my car by now and gave us only a cursory pat-down. I politely turned over my silver dagger—which they were cautious to avoid touching. I slipped it into the weapons case one of them carried. I'd pick it up on the way back.

Beside them stood *our* guards. I saluted to them and they bowed, which felt weird as hell, but considering I was in line to become the Queen of Winter, and Rhiannon the Queen of Summer, we'd have to get used to it.

I handed my keys to the valet. As we started up the steps, he carefully eased Favonis out of the way.

Rhia and I glanced at each other.

"After what happened to Luna, I hate going in without backup," she said.

"I know, but Regina will keep us safe. Even though she's the Emissary to the Crimson Court, I trust her. She *has* to be diplomatic, and she knows that the Cambyra nation would come stake her royal ass if either of us were hurt."

As soon as I rang the bell, the door swung open. The maid who answered was a bloodwhore, but with perfect makeup, her hair in a chignon, and a stiffly pressed uniform and heels, she had to belong to the Emissary's stable.

"We're here to see Regina."

The woman curtseyed, then led us through the spacious foyer, past the office that had once been Geoffrey's. But we didn't stop there. Instead, she led us to the next door down the hallway, where she tapped discreetly. After a moment, she opened the door, peeked inside, and whispered something. Then, standing back, she ushered us in.

As we entered the room, I was surprised to see that it was yet another office, but this was oh-so-official, with what I assumed was a print of the royal seal hanging over the cherrywood desk. The polished desk was a monster, filling a good one-third of the room. The top was clear except for an appointment book, a pen on a blotter, and a bronze statue that at first looked to be a woman kissing a man. As I drew closer, I saw that it was actually a vampire holding her victim.

Regina, behind the desk, stood as we entered. Blond, like her brother, she wore her hair in an intricate updo that must have taken an hour to fix. A black linen pencil skirt hugged her hips, and a red corset boosted her cleavage in an impressive display.

A large ruby teardrop flanked by two diamond baguettes hung around her neck from a gold chain. I knew they were ruby and diamond because Regina would never stoop to wearing costume jewelry. Matching earrings dangled from her ears, and her face was flawlessly made up.

Regina's eyes glowed with the soft, unbroken obsidian of all true vampires. She wore a neutral eye shadow, with thin, precise liner and heavy mascara that glittered with gold flecks. Her lips were crimson, moist and alluring, and her alabaster skin was like fine porcelain. When she smiled, the tips of her fangs showing, and motioned for us to sit, I felt a brief rush of hunger.

"Cicely, Rhiannon . . . please make yourselves comfortable." She waited until we were seated on the dusky mauve divan opposite her desk, then motioned for the maid to leave and close the door behind her. Sitting back, she studied us carefully, as if she were gauging what to say. Or, perhaps, *how* to say it.

I leaned back against the velvet of the divan. I'd learned never to rush a vampire. The more you pushed, the more they pushed back. So, we waited. Rhiannon nervously knotted her sweater sleeve in her hand, but after a moment, she let out a long breath and finally leaned back beside me.

Regina stepped from behind her desk, crossing to the front, where she leaned her butt against the edge, her long legs stretched out in front, ending in five-inch stilettos. She glanced at the door.

"Lannan will be joining us shortly." She held up her hand as I shifted uncomfortably. "I know you'd prefer to deal with just me, but the fact is that Lannan's input on this is vital. Trust me, the news isn't pleasant."

"I have a feeling your news is going to be just about as good as what just happened to us."

On that cheery note, we went back to staring at each other. Even though she didn't try to pull glamour on me, her gaze unnerved me. I licked my lips and yawned, quickly trying to cover my mouth. Were Queens even supposed to yawn in public? Flustered, I glanced up at the gorgeous vampire, and to my surprise, Regina flashed me a little smile—probably as genuine as she could manage.

"There are so many things changing. The old ways no longer serve your people, nor mine. We must learn to adapt. I think that our two nations have much to explore over the coming decades, don't you agree? Hmm?" Her voice was smooth, silk against skin, and I ducked my head, feeling oddly shy.

Before I could think of an answer, she straightened up. "I'm being remiss in my duties as hostess. Would you care for something to drink? Some wine, or sparkling water, or a café au lait?"

I was about to say no when Rhiannon surprised me. "Some sparkling water would be nice, with ice if you have it." She cleared her throat and straightened her shoulders.

"And the girl of light and summer can actually *speak*." Regina's laugh was throaty and rich. I could never tell if she was making fun of us or truly found us amusing. Either way, she rang a small bell and a different maid immediately entered the room.

"Sparkling water for the Queen of Summer. Cicely— what will you have?" Regina expected an answer, and so I blurted out the first thing that came to mind.

"Mocha, please, with extra chocolate." A jolt of caffeine would do me some good.

"Mocha, for the Queen of Winter. Extra chocolate and—I think—an extra shot of espresso would be in order for what we have to discuss this night." Regina dismissed her with the flick of a finger, and the woman scurried out of the room.

It was still hard for me to sit by and watch the vampires treat their servants like chattel, but even more disturbing was the realization that I was growing used to it.

After another awkward silence, the woman returned with our drinks. Directly on her heels was Lannan Altos, who swept over to Regina and kissed her hand and then her lips, his tongue playing over them. After the maid had given us our drinks, Lannan turned to face us.

Lannan Altos, Regina's brother and her lover. Originally from Sumer, they were two of the older vampires around. Lannan Altos, my bane.

Lannan of the golden hair that flowed down his back and the sleek, tight build. Lannan, the hedonist, whose obsession for me had become a dangerous game. Lannan, who had taken me down and made me grovel willingly at his feet. Lannan, who enjoyed games of humiliation at others' expense.

But Lannan—pervert though he was—had helped us when we needed it, though whether it was due to his own twisted agenda or not, I wasn't sure. And that meant I had to walk softly and try to keep out of his clutches and stay on his good side. He could do far more damage to me and our cause against Myst than I could do against him. *Yet.*

Rhiannon and I stood, giving him a cursory bow. As Regent, his position demanded it.

He moved in close, looming over me, and I was keenly aware of his presence. My body responded to him, remembering him in a way I didn't want it to.

"This matter was brought to our attention just this evening, so I apologize for my tardiness. You will forgive me, won't you? *Cicely*?" And he fastened his gaze on me, holding me entranced with those eternally black eyes.

I cleared my throat, mulling over the best response. After our last interaction—the day I'd left the mansion—I wanted nothing more than to kick him in the balls, but diplomacy won out.

"Of course." I turned to Regina. "But first, let me tell you what happened tonight." I told them about Luna and the vamps, and the message from Geoffrey. "We have to find them. We *have* to stop them."

Regina pressed her lips together before answering. Her voice was tight and brusque. "I have been in communication with the Crimson Queen. The situation is far more dire than you think."

Uh-oh. That couldn't be good. I glanced at Rhiannon. We waited for Regina to continue.

"When one of our esteemed Vein Lords went to visit the Blood Oracle yesterday, he discovered that . . . well . . . Crawl has gone missing."

"Missing?" At first I thought I'd heard her wrong, but one look at her face and I knew she was telling us the truth. Her four little words were enough to crumble the world.

Lannan stared at me, unblinking. "Make no mistake. It's true. Crawl is missing, and no one knows how he escaped from his prison." His voice echoed through the room, no longer smooth and elegant, but instead harsh. He was on his feet the next moment, pacing back and forth.

"Prison? Crawl's chamber is a *prison*?" That was the first I'd heard anything to that effect.

The Blood Oracle was esteemed, a seer among his people, revered as almost a god. I had no idea he was a prisoner,

though it made sense. I knew they'd kept him tucked away
between the worlds with good reason. The freakshow was
deadly, with no conscience whatsoever, and he'd had his
fangs in me once already.

Lannan glanced at me. "Crawl was imprisoned by the
Crimson Queen eons ago, when she first anointed him as
the Blood Oracle. He's far too powerful and dangerous to be
allowed among the populace, especially around breathers."

He paused by me, lifting my chin to stare into my face
with those gleaming black eyes of his. "You, of all people,
should know what he can be like, my sweet Cicely." And
the Golden Boy was back.

Shivering—from both his touch and the memory of
Crawl tearing into my neck with wanton thirst—I swallowed the lump rising in my throat and forced myself to
remain steady.

Rhiannon looked ready to faint. "How did he get loose?"

Regina grimaced. "Not without help, I can tell you that."

The idea of someone helping Crawl escape was ludi-
crous. "Who the fuck would help him get free? Who would
even think of something that stupid?"

She gave me a long look. "Consider the situation, Cicely. Who has everything to gain by causing mayhem? By
aligning himself with one as powerful as the Oracle?"

And then I knew. "Geoffrey . . ."

"Yes, Geoffrey and Leo. Word on the street is that
Geoffrey is planning a major coup against Lannan, while
Leo's out to kidnap Rhiannon. And both of them are out
for revenge against you, Cicely."

"But why *Crawl*?" Rhia was so pale she looked as
bloodless as the vamps.

Lannan answered. "Crawl can wield dark magic. Ever
since he tasted Cicely's blood, he's been obsessed with how
sweet and rich and tender she was. The Oracle does not
forget lightly. And . . . the Oracle's sanity long ago turned
to dust."

"Leo means to turn me into a vampire," Rhia said. "He
wants to turn me and keep me locked up with him."

Lannan nodded. "No doubt."

Regina regarded him somberly. "We believe that Geoffrey plans on turning Cicely over to Crawl . . ." She paused, shuddering. "I wouldn't wish my worst enemy to be at the mercy of the Blood Oracle."

The room fell silent. I could barely think, let alone speak.

Lannan cleared his throat after a moment and turned to his sister. "What are the Crimson Queen's orders?"

Regina held up what looked like an official decree. "Direct from the Queen: Our first order is to secure the safety of the newly arisen Fae Queens and the populace of New Forest. With Crawl free among the townspeople, the Vampire Nation could suffer irreversible damage to our reputation. Second: We return him to his prison. And third: We terminate Geoffrey and Leo."

"Do you know where they are?" I asked.

She let out a soft whisper. "No. We have no idea. I sent in guards to raid their last known hideaway earlier this evening. There was no trace of them or where they went. The owner of the club died without revealing their whereabouts. My men used every form of *persuasion* possible. The club owner died in the process."

I crossed to the big bay windows. Every morning, they were covered with steel shutters. Now, I stared outside, into the dim night. The snow was piling up again. Myst was still out there, gunning for us. And Leo and Geoffrey had freed a monster from his dark and fiery hell to claim the streets of the town for his own.

Myst was a holy terror, but at least, she was somewhat predictable. Whereas Crawl . . . Crawl was as alien as an insect, and as dangerous as any predator who ruled the top of the food chain. Crawl wanted my blood, and Leo and Geoffrey were only too happy to serve me up on a platter.

Lannan was suddenly behind me, making no noise with his approach. He placed his hands on my shoulders and leaned down to whisper in my ear. "Are you afraid, Cicely?"

I turned to stare at him over my shoulder. He wasn't

being sarcastic this time. His question seemed oddly genuine. "Yes, I'm afraid."

"My offer stands, you know. Let me turn you. Renounce
the world of Fae and join me. It would be easy for you to
fight back, then. With your powers, combined with me as
your sire, you could defeat Leo and Geoffrey."

His words entwined around me, and the wolf tattoo on
my stomach growled a low warning note. Grieve could tell
I was all too close to his rival.

I shook my head. "No. I refused to let Geoffrey turn
me—I would become a bigger monster than Myst. But thank
you. I think you really mean it—you really want to help."

"Don't be so quick to think you know my mind, girl."
Lannan let out a low laugh. "I just don't want to lose you."
But the look on his face told me that Rhiannon and I
weren't the only ones who were afraid. I turned to look at
Regina. She, too, wore a look of concern on her face.

As I stared back into the night, too aware of Lannan's
hands still on my shoulders, I thought I saw something dart
past the window. As I wiped my eyes, whatever it was
seemed to disappear.

It was all too much. Too many enemies. Too much
stress. I just wanted to go home and crawl under the covers,
but even home now had a new meaning, and was still an
alien and strange place. Rhiannon joined me at the window
and I took her hand in mine. We stood there, linked, twin-
cousins, fire and ice against the shadows outside, as they
grew dark and long, and looming.

Chapter 2

The first thing we did when we got back to the Barrow was check on Luna. She was resting, but still shaky. Peyton confided to me that Kaylin hadn't left her side since they'd returned.

"What happened? What did they say about the attack on Luna?" Peyton leaned against the counter—the marble tops gleamed against the dark oak cabinets that were hand carved and as old as time.

"Tell you in a minute." I wanted to breathe first, to sit down and relax. As I glanced around the Marbury Barrow, it hit me that this place was starting to become familiar. I still didn't think of it as home, but it was a safe haven, and there had been precious few of those lately.

"Let's have tea." Peyton put the kettle on and played with the knobs. I still had no clue as to how to work the Cambyra gadgets. The stove was fueled by both wood and magic, and I hadn't had a moment to pay attention to anything like that, with the rush of training we had been undergoing.

We were gathered in the common room that served as a combination dining-living-office space for our little group.

This room, and our private chamber of suites, made up our temporary home. Eventually, Peyton, Luna, and Kaylin would move back to the Veil House, while Grieve and I would take our place in the realm of Winter, and Rhiannon and Chatter would remain here, ruling over the Court of Rivers and Rushes.

There were no windows here in the Barrow, but a continual illumination from the golden lanterns hanging every few feet. The lights were magical—soft glowing amorphous orbs caught in the glass and metal lamps. Lainule said they were energy creatures, young Fire Elementals indentured by the Fae, before being turned loose on the world to grow.

Do they mind being forced into service? I had asked Ulean when I first found out how the Barrow halls were lit.

Mind? Ulean sounded slightly perplexed. *Do I mind being bound to you?*

I hope not. I would never knowingly harm you.

Do not worry on that account. You cannot harm me. Neither can the Fae harm the Fire Elementals. We are far stronger than any of the mortal races, even the full-born Fae. We can be destroyed, but there are few in the world powerful enough. Myst, in her glory days, could neither destroy nor harm her Ice Elementals. Even these bonds . . . we can break if we choose. Life is often illusion, Cicely. Illusion that is very real, very strong, but still—place the right amount of force in the right spot and it breaks.

As the lights flickered around us, I moved to help Peyton, reaching for the tea bags. "Let's have tea first, before we tell you what went down. It's a cold night out there, and there are monsters roving the town."

Shadow, a young Cambyra girl who was hovering behind me, snatched them out of my hands. "Allow me, Your Highness. A queen should never make her own tea."

I wanted to remind her that I wasn't Queen yet, but the Fae in the Barrow had already begun to refer to Rhiannon and me as such, and there was no going back.

"Thank you." Feeling conspicuous, I let go of the tea, standing back as she scurried over to a beautiful ceramic pot, hand-thrown, with delicate, hand-painted holly leaves and berries wrapping around the sides. She shooed Peyton out of the way and took over preparing the tea and scones.

We gathered in the seating area. I leaned forward, elbows resting on my knees. I was sitting on an ottoman, thick and comfortable, with a covering made of hand-woven linen, and for just a moment, I closed my eyes and let the warmth seep into my bones.

"What's wrong, Cicely? Is there something more going on than just Geoffrey and Leo's attack?"

With a glance over my shoulder, I sighed and stared into the fire.

"Yeah, a lot more. It seems that the Fang Brothers managed to free Crawl from his prison. He's loose now, somewhere out there on the streets of New Forest, looking for somebody to drink his dinner from. Apparently, Geoffrey is looking to turn me over to him, and Leo's out to kidnap Rhiannon."

There was a sudden hush, then Peyton slapped the table by her chair. "Fuck and fuck again. What are Regina and Lannan doing about this?"

"They have teams canvassing the town, but the truth is . . . Geoffrey and Leo could be hiding anywhere. Regina's offered to put a guard on the house. Since you guys move in a couple of days down the line, I told them yes— and I want no arguments. At least you'll be safe while you're at home."

"Not necessarily." Kaylin stretched out on an oak bench. It was polished to a sheen, and the workmanship was so detailed that I couldn't imagine how long it had taken to create. "Remember the day-runners? They might still have yummanii helping them."

"True. Which means we'll also station Cambyra guards outside the house during the day. The vamps can take over night duty." I frowned. "Before we left, Regina asked us to watch the morning news on television tomorrow. Apparently Lannan's going to give an announcement that they'll be reading on air."

"We'll have to go out. We can't watch TV here, that's for sure, and the cable hasn't been hooked up at the Veil House yet." Luna stood up, still looking weak, but her cheeks were beginning to glow rosy again. She was a yummanii bard; her magic was in her song. She'd come to us for advice and ended up staying.

I glanced at her. "You okay? You can stand without help?"

She nodded. "So where do we go? And yes, I'm doing better. The food and wine helped a lot. But . . . I never want to go through that again."

Peyton spoke up. "We can go over to Rex's apartment. He'll be fine with that." Her father had rented an apartment in town not far from the Veil House. Anadey, her mother, was still lurking in the shadows, running her diner, but she hadn't made another attempt to contact Peyton after she'd betrayed us.

"Good, I can charge up my cell phone while I'm there without worrying that somebody up at the house is going to steal it." Even though they were working for Regina, I didn't trust the vamps fixing up the house. Regina had paid for the restorations, though we could have gotten a loan from the Consortium—the magical guild we now rather forcibly belonged to—but for some reason, the Emissary had insisted on footing the bill.

"Soon enough, you must leave your toys and gadgets behind." Lainule's voice tripped lightly over the words and, at her melodic tongue, we turned. All of us rose, and Grieve and Chatter bowed, as Rhia and I dropped into deep curtseys.

"Your Highness . . ." I hadn't expected to see her. Lainule had been keeping to herself the past few days, except when she had called us in to instruct us in what would be expected.

She looked tired. Regaining her heartstone had saved

her life, but it also deposed her as Queen. However, Lainule seemed content to accept her destiny gracefully. The foliage around the Barrow was halfheartedly returning to its former glory. Once we crossed through the portals that cloaked the Marbury Barrow, though, Myst's snows and ice came rampaging back with a fury. But here . . . here the trees were green again, though with a faint orange glow, like we were at the end of a long summer.

And it truly was the end of summer. At least the end of the summer that had ruled here for who knew how many centuries. Lainule would preside over the initiation and coronation of Rhiannon and me, and then she and my father would leave, forever, back to the Golden Isle. Rhia and I would then be responsible for routing Myst and bringing the balance back to the world.

But for now, she was still here, with us.

She swept into the room and accepted a chair. "Regina contacted me. She warned me of what's going on with Geoffrey and Leo, and the Blood Oracle. You must *all* be cautious until they are caught and Crawl is back under lock and key. Nothing can go amiss. You *must* undergo the initiation and coronation without delay."

As she sat there, it almost felt like she was one of us. Regal though she might be, the aura of her rule was fading. It made me want to cry.

"We'll watch out. I promise. I'm also asking the guards to keep an eye on the Veil House during the day to protect Peyton and the others. Regina promised guards at night."

"It heartens me to know you are taking this seriously. Myst must be destroyed. The balance must return. And you, Cicely, must finally visit the Court over which you will be ruling. It's time to see your new home."

The Barrow here would become Rhiannon's new home. When she married Chatter—Grieve's best friend and now soon-to-be King of Summer—they would live here, in the warmth of eternal summer. My own home was destined to be colder, caught in the grips of the eternal winter.

I sucked in a deep breath. The thought of living in

perpetual snow and ice frightened me. "I wish . . ." But I stopped. There was no turning back, no walking away. Wishing for something that wasn't meant to be wouldn't make it happen.

"Yes, my child?" The Queen's gaze rested on me, glorious and yet like fading flowers.

"I can't wait to see my new home." I forced a smile to my face. She knew how I felt, but I wouldn't let her, or my father, down. I picked up the cell phone. "But I will admit, this is one thing I'm going to miss."

"Once you take the throne, you must relinquish some of the trappings that keep you tied to the mortal world. The changes in lifestyle will take some getting used to, but there are wonders, Cicely. There are wonders you haven't even dreamed of yet."

With that, she smiled, rose, and passed to the door. "Your father will escort you to your new home tomorrow at noon. Be here, ready to go. Your cousin may attend. And so may your friends." And, the hem of her dress whispering against the floor, she left the room.

⚜

I suppose this is the time for introductions.

My name is Cicely Waters. I'm twenty-six years old, and I'm one of the magic-born. Or at least, I always thought I was. I never knew my father, but had assumed he was the same lineage as Krystal, my mother. But a few weeks ago, I discovered that I'm also half Cambyra Fae—the Shifting Ones—and it threw my whole worldview into a tailspin.

So yes, I was born a witch, and I can control the wind. Or I'm learning to, at any rate. Until I was six years old, Krystal and I lived at the Veil House with aunt Heather and cousin Rhiannon.

When we were around five, Rhia and I met Grieve and Chatter out in the woods, and they secretly taught us how to increase our magic. They watched out for us, and we felt safe with them. Rhiannon and I made a pact never to tell anyone about them because my mother hated the fact that she was born to the magic and didn't want me meddling in it either. And so they remained our secret, and everything was fine, or so we thought. That was a wonderful summer— as good as it could get, in my opinion. Heather acted as mother to both of us, while Krystal boozed her powers into oblivion.

Then, a few weeks after I turned six, my world crumbled. Fed up with her life, Krystal dragged me kicking and screaming down the front steps and away from everything I'd ever known. I spent the next twenty years on the road— eighteen of them with her. We moved from town to town, scamming, stealing, and doing whatever we needed to survive. Krystal sold herself into the booze and drugs so deep that, by the end, there was no reaching her. She drowned herself in a haze, to get away from the clamor of voices and visions in her head. Even at six years old, I realized that the only way we'd survive was if I took over, and so I bucked up, stepped in, and—with Ulean's help—got us through.

Ulean warned me when the cops were on our tracks. She kept me from getting raped half a dozen times by telling me to get the fuck out of wherever I was. And she guarded me in the only ways she could.

Along the way, I also had help from the odd person here or there—they just seemed to fall into my life. The most important one was Uncle Brody, an old black yummanii man who, for the first few months when we were staying in Portland, Oregon, took me under his wing and taught me as many street smarts as he could. Maybe he could tell that Krystal was going batshit crazy. Maybe he just had a premonition that I needed his help. Whatever the case, he taught me the rules of the road. He also taught me to gamble so I could make money from penny-ante street games. And he taught me how to fight dirty.

"Cicely, girl, you have to learn how to hurt people," he told me once, when I flinched at learning how to jab someone in the nuts. "Because there are plenty of people out there just waiting to hurt you. And trust me, if you give them an opening, they'll take it. So don't let them in."

I paid attention; I learned to fight. And I used my wits and prescience to steer clear of potential situations.

And then, I'd also had my wolf . . .

When I was fourteen, Krystal met a man named Dane. I liked him and secretly hoped that he'd marry her and take us away from the streets. I think he would have, too, if my mother hadn't been so skittish about committing herself to anyone or anything. But at any rate, he took care of us for a few months, until Krystal stormed out in a tantrum, and Dane got his brains blown out.

Dane was a tattooist and he inked all of my tattoos. First, came the faerie on my left breast, a little feral girl peeking out from a patch of belladonna. Second, the black-work owls that encircled each of my upper arms. A pair on each side, over a moon with a dagger sticking through it. Matched sets, they heralded a part of my lineage I wouldn't know about until I returned to New Forest. And third . . . third was my wolf.

My beloved wolf stared out from just above my navel, a vine of green leaves, silver roses, and purple skulls sprawling behind him, starting down on my left thigh, crossing my abdomen in a diagonal line, ending under my right ribs. From the beginning, I knew my wolf was a guardian. What I didn't realize when I got the tattoo was that my wolf was a direct link to Grieve, who was a wolf shape-shifter.

The Cambyra Fae shift. All of us, half-breed or full-blood. Some of us shift into the form of an animal, but others—like Chatter—can turn into Elementals. Hence: the Shifting Fae. I'm part Uwilahsidhe, of the Owl Shifters.

My father, Wrath, is King of the Court of Rivers and Rushes—and I've known about him only for the past couple weeks. I'm the daughter of a king.

Wrath is Lainule's husband, and we recently discovered that Lainule's brother was Rhiannon's father. It seems our very existence was planned out from the beginning. Rhiannon and I were born for this moment, born to be Queens, born to fulfill a destiny that wasn't even clear at the time of our conception.

Add to that a past-life connection with Myst and with Grieve, and I feel pulled in so many directions sometimes it feels like I am coming apart at the seams. Myst is a monster, and I hate the fact that I was her daughter so many thousands of years ago. But she nurtures a grudge against me that was born back in the distant past and is determined to make me pay. She wants revenge for what I did to her then, and what I'm doing to her now.

Caught between worlds, caught between powers, I'm transforming so fast that sometimes I look in the mirror and don't even recognize myself. Oh, yes, I'm still five four, 140 pounds of muscle, and I still have long, straight, shiny black hair and emerald eyes . . . but on the inside, I'm changing. And I'm not sure what I'm becoming.

And that scares me. Just a little.

✦

By the time we finished hashing out matters, it was too late to do much, but I wasn't tired. Grieve took my hand and led me outside. Here, behind the barriers of the portals, at least Winter wasn't gripping us in her icy claws.

Grieve's skin had an olive undertone, and his features were alien and yet exotic. But his eyes . . . his eyes had always captured me. When I was young, they'd been cornflower blue. That had changed when Myst conquered Lainule's land, bloodied the Barrow, and killed and enslaved hundreds of the Cambyra Fae. She'd turned my beloved Grieve into one of the Vampiric Fae. She had drunk him down.

Like all Fae turned by either the vampires or the Indigo Court, Grieve had not died. Instead, he recovered, stronger than the vampires, stronger than the Fae. He'd become part of the Indigo Court, and his eyes had turned deep black, like the true vampires, but scattered with the sparkling stars marking the Indigo Court.

Only we'd managed to reverse some of the hold that

Myst had on him. Although still a dangerous predator, at least he was no longer at the mercy of the constant bloodlust that drove the Shadow Hunters. He was my Wounded King. But his eyes would never be blue again.

Most of the birds were silent by midnight, but the animals of the Summer realm were out and about, and we could hear them slipping through the woods around us. A snake slithered past and it suddenly occurred to me that, once we took our place in the realm of Winter, we wouldn't see snakes again. Or the giant banana slugs that inhabited the forests of the Pacific Northwest from spring to fall. Or robins, returning for the spring. A deep sense of loss began to sink through me, and I lowered myself onto a fallen snag covered with moss and mushrooms.

Grieve sat beside me, picking up my mood. I leaned my head against his shoulder, breathing in the scent of bonfires and rainstorms and chill autumn nights. He wrapped his arm around me and kissed the top of my head.

"How are you holding up? I know the training is coming fast, and it's not easy. But soon we'll be married and you'll be my Queen. We're going to make it this time around, Cicely." He nuzzled my neck, and I caught my breath.

Grieve held my heart hostage with love, and he knew how to make me respond in a way no one had ever been able to before. He freed me to soar.

I caught his hand and brought it to my lips, kissing his fingers. "I hope you're right. This lifetime hasn't been much easier than the last." Grieve and I were bound by a love that spanned lifetimes, soul-bound by a potion taken long ago when I was Myst's daughter and he was crown prince of the Summer realm. We'd been Cherish and Shy then, and in the end, our love had gotten us killed.

"I felt Lannan, yesterday, sliming on you." Grieve kicked a rock near the stump. "Someday . . . I will kill him."

"But not today. And not tomorrow. We need him, still. And remember, he no longer holds my contract. Now that

I'm Queen-Elect, I don't have to submit to him. Let it go, for now. Let it be." I didn't want to think about Lannan. "Tell me about the Golden Isle—where Lainule and Wrath are going."

Grieve let out a long sigh and stroked my hair back away from my face. "The Golden Isle lies long distant, in the mists. It is the homeland of the Cambyra Fae. Where we began. Where *all* of the Sidhe come from. We are born in body to this world now . . . though millennia ago, we were born in the Golden Isle first and then emigrated here. And when we die, when we begin to fade, we return to the Golden Isle. The islands are not paradise, but rather secluded, away from all other realms."

I pressed my lips together, thinking. After a moment, I gave him a sideways glance. "Lainule is dying, isn't she? Even though we found her heartstone. Tell me the truth. I need to know."

Grieve slowly nodded. "Yes. Once you reunite a queen with her heartstone, she begins to age in this world. Only by returning to the Golden Isle will she live out her natural life span." He looked like he wanted to say something but then shook his head.

"What is it?" I poked him gently in the side. "Tell me. No secrets!"

His dark eyes, with the swirling stars, turned toward me. "You do realize that as long as your heartstone stands and you are not murdered, you will not die. Becoming Queen, going through the initiation, will make you effectively immortal."

The forest echoed with silence. I closed my eyes, trying to wrap my head around what he was saying, but it seemed so huge, so immense, that there was no way of comprehending the full extent of what I'd gotten myself into.

I hung my head. "On a logical level, yes, I think I knew that. But it still hasn't hit me, yet—what this all means. Not in my gut. So much has happened in such a short time that I'm reeling with the changes. Sometimes I take a breath

and wonder if this is all a dream. A prolonged nightmare . . ."
I touched his hand. "Most of it, that is. Not you. You're the
dream come true."

He entwined his fingers through mine. "When Myst
took over the Barrow and routed our people . . . when she
turned me . . . the only thing that kept me going was the
hope you would return. That something would end the eternal winter. I know now that I can never return to who I was.
I was born to rule the land of Summer, I know it in my
heart. And now, I must take to Winter's throne. But it's all
right, because you will be there with me. And thanks to
Luna, and her sister—Zoey—I can control the Shadow
Hunter in my soul."

Bringing my hand to his lips, he grazed my wrists, nip-
ping gently and tasting the blood that flowed. His tongue
played gently over my skin and I closed my eyes, reveling
in his touch.

"Do you really believe that this time, we'll get our happy
ending?"

When he brought his gaze up to meet mine, his dark
smile widened. "I hope so, my love. Finally, after all the
years . . . I hope so."

※

Long ago, there was a vampire named Geoffrey. Only his
name wasn't Geoffrey at the time. But he had a yen for
power, and he was determined to take over the Vampire
Nation. His reasoning went thus: Turn the Dark Fae, and
the result—the Vampiric Fae—would be under his control,
with both their own powers and those of the vampires. And
it would make him stronger and more powerful and he
could throw down the Crimson Queen and take the throne
for himself.

Only it didn't work the way he thought it would.

First mistake: He picked the wrong person to turn. He
sought out Myst, who wasn't the Unseelie Queen, who
wasn't even the Winter Queen of the area, but who thought
herself a likely candidate. She had a thirst for power of her

own and wasn't one to knuckle under someone else's rule. She agreed to the bargain, and—being the brilliant leader she was—she let Geoffrey think she would go willingly into his control.

Second mistake: When Geoffrey turned her, he didn't count on the fact that turning the Cambyra doesn't result in the same end as turning a yummanii. He fed on her to the point of death, and then she fed on him. So far, so good, as far as the vampires were concerned.

But Myst didn't die. Myst didn't die, and she didn't respond to Geoffrey as her sire, as one of the yummanii would.

Instead, she began to heal. And her healing was fast and furious. As she returned to life, she changed. She rose from her deathbed, dark and terrible with black eyes filled with stars. Her skin took on a cerulean glow. And her powers were greater than the sum of both her heritage and Geoffrey's.

Myst rose from her deathbed and fed on the vampires keeping watch over her—draining them dry of both blood and energy. And then she turned those of her own kind, and so the Indigo Court was born, and the war between the vampires and the Indigo Court took hold.

But the Vampiric Fae had one up on the true vampires: They could breed. And the first child born to Myst was a daughter named Cherish.

And Cherish . . . was me.

Fast-forward to centuries later. A new land—one uninhabited except by a tribal culture who could not fight those of us belonging to the Indigo Court.

I was out for a morning walk when I smelled fresh prey on the wind. Summer grass and apples, oak moss and sunlight . . . and so I pounced. But my prey—a gorgeous young Cambyra prince named Shy—caught hold of me by the heart. A bond formed almost immediately, one we could neither explain nor deny. And so we ran away together, but our people followed, both sides furious. They hunted us down, and at the end, before they could kill us, we drank a potion to bind our souls and reunite us in a future life. We died in each other's arms.

And so, here we are. Brought together by a love forged long, long ago.

But Myst is rising to power. And behind her swarm the Shadow Hunters—the Vampiric Fae of the Indigo Court. We've slaughtered hundreds of them, but they are regrouping. They flock to their mistress, monstrous creatures who turn into ravaging beasts, who bite to the bone, chewing muscle and gristle, reveling in the blood of the fallen, siphoning the life force away from all they capture.

Maybe this time around, Grieve and I can put an end to it. Maybe we *can* have our happy ending, and help out the world, too. At least, that's the plan.

❧

"We need to sleep, love." Grieve stroked my face. "You promised to help Luna and Peyton up at the house tomorrow."

I nodded. "Give me a few minutes, would you? I want to take a moment by myself."

"Be careful, then. I will wait for you by the Barrow." Grieve kissed the top of my hand, then took off. I waited till he rounded the curve in the path before turning toward the Twin Oaks that formed the portal leading to the outer world.

A noise behind me made me stop, and I quickly spun around to find myself facing Check, one of the guards assigned to keeping an eye on me. I recognized him from when we routed the Shadow Hunters from the Barrow.

"Your Highness, please, don't go out there alone." He moved to my side and gazed down at me, a soft smile playing on his lips. All the men in Lainule's service were gorgeous—and his eyes were the same cornflower blue that Grieve's had once been. He was wearing leather armor, and a long sword by his side glistened with silver trim.

I paused, not wanting to cause him distress. "Check, you know that I'm not full-blooded Cambyra. Does that bother you? Do you mind that I'll be taking the throne?"

He frowned, then cocked his head. "No, Your Ladyship. I think . . . the days are over when the Cambyra can hide from the world. And someone who is born to both worlds might just be the way to forge that merger."

"Then, as you state, since I am not entirely from the Cambyra world, things will change. And one thing that has to change is that I won't live my life locked away in a tower. I'll take on the robes, I'll move to the Barrow, I'll lead the people in the best way that I can, but I won't be a prisoner. I'll be cautious." I stopped and smiled at him. "I'll be good. I won't try to ditch the guards. But I come from the world out there. And I need to come and go as I please. Do you understand?"

He cracked another smile. "I think I do, my Lady. But understand my sacred duty—I cannot let you go alone, not and mind my conscience. Please forgive me, but I plan on escorting you, and Fearless as well."

His companion stepped from behind a nearby tree. Fearless was as good as his name. Grieve had told me that he was paired with Check because Check always kept him in balance. They were both brave, and true to the Court of Rivers and Rushes. If anybody was going to protect me, I knew they would.

"The former Regent still walks abroad, and it is the night, when he will be waking," Check whispered, leaning closer.

That decided me. This was as far as I could sanely push the matter. Either they went with me, or I went back to the Barrow, because even though I chafed at the restraints, the truth was—Geoffrey and Leo were out to wreak havoc on us. And Myst was out to kill us. And I couldn't count on any place being truly safe at this point.

"Thanks, Check. I'd . . . appreciate the company." I led the way to the portal, although when we got there, Check slipped in front of me and insisted on going through first. I gratefully stepped back and let him.

The energy of the portal was like a brilliant, sparkling vortex, and I was slowly getting used to it. As I emerged from the net of magic between the Twin Oaks, I saw that Check was kneeling on the ground about ten yards ahead, examining the snow. The look on his face was one of worry.

Shivering, I realized that in my hurry, I'd forgotten to bring my coat. Once out of the realm of Summer, Myst's fury and vengeance had returned.

As I breathed in a lungful of cold air, Check stood, his face blank and stern. "We *must* return to the Barrow, Your Highness. Now."

"What's going on? What is it?" I hurried over to his side and leaned down. There, against the pale snow, was a patch of blood and bone, staining it pink. The size of my fist, the bone was fresh, and the blood on it still fluid and red.

Quickly, I pulled out my dagger.

Ulean, what do you sense? What's out there?"

She swept around me, agitated. *Cicely, get back into the realm of Summer. Now. There are dangers here.*

Before I could move, the bushes parted and a doglike creature broke through, jaw unhinging as it lunged for me. As I screamed, startled, Check pushed me out of the way. The Shadow Hunter snapped air, his jaws clenching on nothing, and then I saw behind him a great creature, pale white and looming like a mountain of flesh, with glaring eyes the color of dawn and features that were bulbous and fat.

"What the fuck is that?" I stared up at the creature as it lumbered toward us. I stumbled away, trying to get out of its path.

"Ice troll!" Fearless jumped forward, his sword out.

"Where did Myst find an ice troll?" Check grabbed him by the arm. "We can't engage. Our first duty—ensure the safety of the Queen. Walk away and live to fight another day, brother."

A look of frustration washed over Fearless's expression, but he immediately turned and grabbed me up, unceremoniously holding me by the waist. As we raced toward the portal, Check guarded our back.

I wanted to go fight—wanted to send them running. I

could do it, too. I could summon up a hurricane if I wanted
to, but the guards weren't giving me a chance. When we
were at the portal, though, Fearless had to put me down.

Whirling, I saw the troll and the Shadow Hunter hot on
our heels. I closed my eyes and summoned the winds.

No, Cicely—let it be, just go through the portal!

But I wasn't listening to Ulean. A swell of fury welled
up. I was sick of the whole fucking war. Sick of Myst and
her army. Of Geoffrey and Leo. I was stick-a-fork-in-me
done with everybody who was trying to kill us.

"*Gale Force . . .*" My whisper echoed through the air,
and the next moment, the wind caught me up. The whirl of
air grew within me, raising me tall against the night sky,
and I was no longer myself, but now queen of the winds,
queen of the air—the heart of the storm.

I grabbed control of the swirl of wind and snow and set
it to spin, driving the falling flakes that whitened the sky
into a frenzied dance. The vortex caught me up and I rode
the crest of the energy, the ripples and currents widening to
form a train in my wake, as I pushed the growing storm
before me. The fog and mist rose at my feet to buoy me up,
and I towered over the forest, my arms wide, gathering the
winds.

In case she was listening, I whispered, sending my voice
spiraling into the slipstream. "You want to play with the cold,
Myst? I'll show you what it means to truly be the *Queen of
Winter.*"

The ice troll and the Shadow Hunter stopped, staring up
at me as I loomed over them, dark and beautiful and feeling my power.

*Rein it in, Cicely. Rein it in—you know the storm can
take over. Bring the winds back.* Ulean was frantic, and her
voice finally penetrated my thoughts, which were a swirl of
power and energy.

But I couldn't. Not yet. I had vengeance to pay. I swept
down, bent at the waist from my place in the treetops, as a
whirling twister sprang up between my fingers. I set it on
the ground, in front of the ice troll and the Shadow Hunter,

and watched impassively as it thundered toward them, a terrifying tornado filled with ice shards and biting snow.

The Shadow Hunter screamed and the troll just looked confused as the icy twister rolled over them, ripping them up and into the center of the maelstrom. A shout of glee echoed from my lips as I watched the vortex rip them from limb to limb.

As Ulean pleaded with me, I thought—for just a moment—how easy it would be to give in to the power and allow it to carry me away. To become the heart of the storm and forget everything else.

But then Grieve's face flashed before my eyes. My wolf howled with worry. Placing my hand against my tattoo, I remembered why I had to remain Cicely Waters—magic-born, and Uwilahsidhe. Tentatively, and then with a firm hand, I reined in the storm, pulled the winds back inside me, and returned to my body.

I turned to find Fearless and Check staring at me. They said nothing as we returned to the Barrow, but I had the sense that they'd never look at me the same way again. They seemed almost . . . afraid. And I didn't much care for that feeling.

Chapter 3

Grieve was right inside the portal. Lainule stood directly behind him. Her eyes flashed as she gave me a look that made me feel two inches tall. She was pissed. She'd been concerned enough when the power over the winds had first transferred from a magical fan into my soul. And she'd already warned me against using the storms.

"Every time you use the power of the winds like that, you come closer to permanently shifting yourself into the Elemental plane of Air. And there, you would go mad. Yes, you'd be Queen of the Winds, but Cicely . . . I am not joking when I tell you that should that happen, no longer would you control your own mind or your destiny. You would belong to the wind itself." Lainule's voice echoed like thunder and I dropped to my knees, cowering at my feet from the force of her words.

"I'm sorry—I was so angry . . ."

Lainule let out a deep sigh. "Get up, girl, and listen to me."

I stood, hanging my head, too embarrassed to look at Grieve or the guards.

Lainule crossed her arms, watching me intently. "Cicely . . . anger unchecked leads to the forces that created Myst. If she hadn't been so jealous, she wouldn't have ever agreed to Geoffrey's plans. But she was furious at the world. Furious at her lot in life. She wanted to be the Winter Queen so badly that she was willing to put her soul on the line for her desires."

I'd never heard this part of the story. Cautiously, I looked up at her impassive face. "I didn't know that."

"Myst would have changed, yes, had Geoffrey turned her unwillingly. She might have been driven to madness. But . . . I do not think she would have become so ruthless. There is no way of knowing for certain, of course, but look at Grieve—he has found a way to harness the Shadow Hunter within. He *wanted* to harness it. Myst's fury, her jealousy and her anger drove her to become the monster she is." Lainule was more agitated than I'd ever seen her.

Angry with myself that I was the cause, I slowly knelt in front of her. "Lady, please, forgive me. You warned me about the powers of the wind, but I didn't think. I acted on impulse." I bit my lip, feeling like a chastised child who'd been caught with her hand in the candy jar after she'd been told *No*.

Lainule paused, taking a deep breath. She let it out slowly. "Child, understand. I am not scolding you to be contrary. I am trying to save your life and your sanity. The last thing we need is a crazed queen of the winds on our hands. It's bad enough with one monster out there. We need you as the Queen of Winter. You have obligations and responsibilities now, and if you ignore them, you put *everyone* in danger. I'm fading. I'll be leaving soon, and then . . . only you and your cousin will remain to cope with Myst and her Shadow Hunters."

She placed a gentle hand under my chin and tipped it up. I gazed into her eyes, which were as old as time. She was beautiful, and ageless, but the tips of her golden hair were now fading into an auburn red, and the faintest of lines marred the flawless skin on her face. Summer was fading into the autumn of her years.

A tear squeezed out of the corner of my eye. I hated disappointing people. "I really am sorry." I tried to look away, to look down at my feet, but she would not let me.

"And another lesson to learn. A queen, even should she be required to apologize, must never lower her gaze. Never again, Cicely Waters, will you lower your gaze to me, although I expect your obedience until the day you take the throne." Without waiting for my reply, she dropped her hand, turned, and, without another word, swept back to the Barrow.

Left alone with Grieve, Fearless, and Check, I wasn't sure what to say. They were all waiting for my word, and I realized that this would always be the way. Although Grieve would be my King, the queen of the realm held the reins of power. From now on, even when I was speechless, I would have to speak. Even when I was uncertain, I would have to make decisions. Because an entire realm would look to me for leadership. And *that* meant showing some measure of wisdom. I'd always felt responsible for keeping my mother and me alive, and now—when I thought I was free of that—I was responsible for an entire kingdom.

"I apologize to you, Fearless, and to you, Check. I put you in needless danger." I gazed into their faces, as Lainule had told me, and smiled softly.

"We act upon your will, my Lady. As you order, so we shall obey. Whatever you need, we are there." Check bowed, but I caught his gaze and his eyes were smiling.

Fearless merely bowed and murmured, "As you will, Lady Cicely."

Grieve waved them back to their posts and held out his arm. I took it, resting my hands on his elbow, and we made our way back to the Barrow. I'd learned a valuable lesson, and I didn't plan on forgetting it. The fates of others rested on my shoulders. It was time I wrestled my impulsive self under control. Because if I didn't, my actions would eventually kill someone—and not just the enemy.

In that moment, as we walked under the fading summer night, I felt like I'd aged a lifetime.

❧

Grieve led me to our bedchamber. The bed was a giant four-poster affair, but the mattress wasn't from Macy's, that was for sure. It was handmade, and perhaps the most comfortable bed I'd ever slept on. The quilt was thick, heavy, and hand-stitched. In varying shades of blue, purple, silver, white and black, the pattern formed a winter silhouette of the forest and stars.

As the lanterns softly illuminated the room, I turned to Grieve. "Are you angry at me?"

"Angry, my love? Why?" In the blink of an eye, he was naked. The full Fae were able to adapt their clothes from the energy in the air. I couldn't do it, but I admired the ability.

"Because of what I did. I put the guards in danger." I slowly unzipped my jeans and slid out of them, along with my panties. As I pulled off my turtleneck and unfastened my bra, Grieve raked my body with his gaze, his dark eyes soaking in the sight of me.

"You did what you will forever and always do—act on your own mind. I have accepted that about you, Cicely. You're going to shake up the throne, and take the Winter to a place it's never been before."

With a laugh, he slid under the covers and reached for me.

I joined him, kneeling on the bed by his side. "Hasn't Myst already done that? Somehow, I think the Court of Ice and Snow might appreciate someone in charge who isn't quite so adventuresome as I am."

"The Court of Ice and Snow has been dead since Myst murdered Tabera. I think the people of Winter just look forward to having someone sane in control." He slid up to a sitting position and reached out to take my hand in his. "Enough about politics. Come here. I need you."

And with that, I straddled his lap. Gazing into his face, I stroked the side of his cheek and brushed his hair back out of his face. A warmth began to steal through me, a heat sparking in my core.

Leaning in, I pressed my lips gently against his, at first only the lightest of pressures, but then my tongue stole between his lips, playing over his teeth, as love turned to lust and the sparks between my thighs blazed to life.

I ached for him, hungered for his touch, his passion, his kiss. All I could think about was how much I needed him inside me, how much I wanted to be at the mercy of his long, silken strokes. Moaning softly, I squirmed on his lap, the blanket between us an annoying impediment.

Grieve slid his hands around my waist, then cupped my butt, his fingers firm against my ass. He reached up with his left hand to brush his fingers against my breast, tracing light strokes across my nipple.

Gasping, I dropped my head back, exposing my throat— the most vulnerable thing I could do around one of the Vampiric Fae. But Grieve kept control. He squeezed my breast, then pinched the nipple so hard I had to bite my lip to keep from screaming. The pain awakened my passion. Letting go, he leaned forward and tongued my breast, curling around the nipple as he sucked softly.

His erection pressed against the cover, and as I shifted, he pushed the comforter back to expose himself, hard and rigid beneath me. I squirmed, trying to aim so that he would slide inside me, but he took hold of my wrists and rolled me over, forcing me back on the bed as he knelt between my legs.

I let out a sharp cry as he kneed my legs apart. Grieve and I were not gentle together. Our passion filled both need and fury.

"Don't move," he said, hoarsely. And I obeyed, arms over my head against the pillows.

He backed up enough to fasten his mouth over my clit, and his tongue began to dance, rasping along the ripples and folds of my cunt. I grew slick and wet.

I wanted to hold his head, but when Grieve said, "Obey," I had learned to listen. "Please, may I move my arms?"

He looked up at me, his eyes sparkling in the dim light, and nodded.

I clutched his platinum hair as it fell between my fingers, the long strands like silk in my hands. Grieve moaned, his breath tickling me even as I came, sharp and quick, hard like ice. I was still pulsing from the rush as he slid up between my legs, but now it was my turn and I pushed him back, rising as he sprawled on his back. He was firm and erect, and the hungry look on his face made me want to tease him, to drive him to that point where there was no more question, where he had to take me down.

Leaning forward, my hair draping over my shoulders, I lowered myself to rest my mouth on the head of his cock. Slowly, one teasing inch after another, I slid down the length, letting its girth force my lips apart as I took him into my mouth.

Grieve let out a gasp as I stroked him with my tongue. He tasted like salted caramel and I closed my lips around him, increasing the suction as I took him in long strokes. He reached for my hair, sweeping it out of the way. I looked up at him, wanting him to see my lips fastened around his girth, and his eyes grew wide and luminous. Knowing he was watching sent me spiraling into another orgasm, and I let out a choked moan, lightly scraping my teeth along the ridges of his cock.

Grieve grunted, deep and throaty, then leaned forward, slid his hands beneath my arms, and dragged me up to face him. He cupped my chin in his hands, saying nothing, but then, slowly, the mood changed, became darker.

I knelt on the bed, resting back on my knees, as his gaze fastened on my face. His dark eyes were unblinking and he began to breathe harder. In the dim light, his razor teeth—needle sharp—gleamed. Never shifting his gaze from my face, he raised my wrist, staring at me through those heavily lidded eyes. I caught my breath as he lowered his lips to my skin, brushing his teeth along the inside of my wrist, just avoiding the artery. A thin red line welted up as he broke through the skin. He slowly licked the blood off, one long stroke after another as more of my life welled up through the wound.

The venom of his bite rushed through me like a white-hot flame of hunger. While I was now immune to the charm it cast, the feel of him feeding on me sent me reeling, and I came hard and quick yet again, letting out a sharp cry as Grieve smiled triumphantly.

And then he stopped and brought his lips to my own, and I tasted my own blood on his tongue as he quietly laid me back and finally slid inside me, filling me full with his cock, stretching me wide and making me ache with hunger. He began to move, slowly at first, then driving into me with long, steady strokes. The world seemed to hang in stasis. Time stopped as he fucked me.

I drifted, rising higher with each thrust, and then, suddenly, we were flying, together. All I could feel was his skin, his hunger, the pulse of his breath matching the beating of my heart as I gave him everything, losing myself as I fell into the dark stars of his eyes.

Grieve stiffened, moaning softly, and then, slowly, came to rest with his head on my breast. "I am your King," he whispered. "And you . . . you are my Queen."

I couldn't say a word, I was so exhausted and so satiated, but he snuggled me under the covers as I slipped into his embrace, resting on his outstretched arm.

"Sleep, my love. Tomorrow, we have so much to do."

And—too tired and relaxed for words—I kissed his lips, and fell into a deep, undreaming slumber.

I managed to wake up before my lady's maid showed up. Having a stranger insist on helping me dress made me uncomfortable, but it was just another aspect to being a queen that I was going to have to compromise on. I slipped out from beneath the quilt, taking care not to wake Grieve as I did so. I needed a little time by myself, and as long as I stayed within the realm of Summer, I should be safe.

I missed being high up—missed opening the window

and being on the second story. Hell, I missed even having windows *to* open. Shrugging into a cloak, and not much else, I quickly padded through the Barrow. Most of the people who were up were servants and tradesmen and whoever it was that kept the palace running smoothly. I had pulled my hood over my head so no one would pay much attention to me, and before long, I stood at the edge of the Barrow, staring out into the early hours of Summer.

Inhaling a long, slow, deep breath, I shook off the feeling of claustrophobia. I honestly didn't like living underground and hoped to hell that the realm of Winter wouldn't have the same makeup. I needed windows. I needed the ability to look out and see trees. I needed the open sky.

As I raced toward the tree line, I heard someone behind me and whirled around. There, a sheepish grin on his face, was Check.

Ducking my head, I gave him a rueful smile. "I promise, I wasn't trying to leave the realm. I just need to . . . to . . . fly."

He cocked his head, then somberly nodded. "I understand. At times my nature calls me to go running through the woods."

"What are you? What do you shift into?" I hadn't yet figured that out, but, being Cambyra, he would be a shifter, too.

He shrugged, breaking into a smile. "A fox, my lady. I am a fox-shifter. Which is why I camouflage so easily in the woods. It is my nature." He glanced around. There was no one else near us. "You take your flight and I will stand guard by the tree. This is the tree that His Highness—your father—often comes to. I find it interesting that you should single it out."

I gazed up at the oak. It was gnarled and ancient and had been struck by lightning several times but rose dizzyingly into the sky. I glanced back at Check, then slipped out of my robe, naked except for my pendant. As I swung up to the lowest branch of the oak, I tried to avoid bark burn. I crouched, getting my bearings as I gazed up at the network of branches and limbs above me.

Standing, I balanced with my hand against the trunk, and then, in what was becoming familiar and easier moves, stretched up on my toes, grasping the branch above me. I used my feet to walk myself up to where I could swing onto it and then repeated the move, working my way up the thick trunk until I stood some thirty feet from the ground. I inched out along the limb, wincing as stray splinters caught hold of my pubic hair, but nothing seriously injured me, and then—I was overlooking the ground, with space enough to shift as I went into free fall.

I leaned my head back, staring at the sky, knowing that outside these protected walls, the long winter waited for me. And then, sucking in a deep breath, I spread my arms and legs wide, captured my courage, and toppled forward, into free fall.

There's something exhilarating about free fall, about watching the ground rush up to greet you. The rush of wind through the hair, the sudden plunge as you barrel toward the ground and then . . . and then . . . and then the shift . . .

My body began to morph, fingers to feathers, arms to wings, legs to taloned feet, shrinking in mass, transforming into a being so alien to myself and yet so familiar.

My Cambyra nature was that of a barred owl, and though I had yet to see myself in a mirror, at one point when we weren't on the run from Myst, Rhiannon had taken a picture of me in owl form so I could see what I looked like. As I had held the photograph, staring at the image, it struck me so odd that the creature in the picture was me. And yet so utterly familiar, even after such a short time.

In the picture, I was poised on a branch, my wings outstretched. My talons curved over the limb. My wings and tail feathers were a study in shades of grayish brown, striped with white, and my head and body, a blending of the two colors, interspersed almost as if I were a tortie cat. My yellow beak was the only pop of color on my body.

Now, those wings were standing me in good stead. I'd had to train them when I first began to shift . . . or perhaps, *adapt to using them* would be a better way to phrase it.

With a satisfied sigh, I caught the updraft and—Ulean laughing in glee beside me—swept up, buoyed on the currents in her wake. I spiraled, turning, twisting, rising to the top of the tree where I could survey the pale dawn.

The air swept past me as I glided, my wings riding steadily on the breeze. A rumble in my stomach told me I was hungry, but I reined in my desire to hunt. Mice didn't set well in my stomach, nor did rabbits, and as good as the warm blood and fur felt going down, it felt equally bad coming back up when I was back in my regular form.

I circled higher, almost dizzy with the joy of no longer being soil-bound. After making several laps over the tops of the trees, I straightened and headed toward the deeper part of the forest, intoxicated by the freedom. Ulean was beside me, catching my mood, shrieking with laughter as she slipped beneath me, causing me to rise even farther. I responded, going into a nosedive, pulling up as she rushed in front of me. She leapfrogged behind me, and I made another dive beneath her wake. I couldn't see Ulean, not unless I was dreamwalking with Kaylin, or when I was in the grips of the winds. But I could feel her, sense her presence, hear her on the slipstream.

We played tag, turning, wheeling through the air, caught up in the freedom that only flight can bring. In the past few weeks, the most precious thing in my life had gone from being my Pontiac GTO to discovering my ability to shift into an owl.

As much as I loved Grieve, as thrilled as I was to meet my father after all these years, nothing could quite compare with the rush and freedom of turning into an owl, of escaping the earth and leaving all my problems behind, even if it was for only a little while. I'd never before had anything remotely resembling the freedom that shifting shape brought to me. There were times when I enjoyed the change so much, when it felt so natural, that I wanted to just stay that way—fly off and never look back—but I couldn't do that.

As the sun rose, here in the realm of Summer, I regretfully turned back to the tree where I'd shifted. Another few moments and it came into view. There was Check, standing below, waiting at attention. I screeched loudly, then slowly circled lower, taking care not to buzz him, until I landed on a fallen trunk nearby. As I began to shift back, I slipped, nosediving for the ground. I still hadn't mastered a graceful return to myself—Check bounded forward and caught me, his arms lifting me before I could hit the ground.

Before I could say thank you, he draped the robe around my shoulders and then, with a flourish, said, "May I escort you back to the palace, Your Highness?"

He was so heartfelt, so gentle and yet so protective, that I couldn't help but give him a graceful smile. "You may." And so we returned to the Barrow, my need to fly assuaged for the moment.

✧

Grieve sat up, yawning, as I padded across the cobbled floor to where Druise, my maid, was waiting. She was trained to obey, and she would have stood there all day if I had told her to. As I stepped into the steaming bath she'd prepared, she quickly moved forward to wash my back. I started to wave her away, but the chagrined expression on her face stopped me. This was her job. This was what she did. If I refused her help, I negated her worth.

I wanted to linger in the bath, but we had to get over to Rex's place to watch the announcement that Regina had instructed us to. So after I'd lathered up and let Druise wash my back, I stepped into the towel she was holding and she wrapped me in the soft, warm fleece. I wasn't sure what material it actually was made from. The cloth felt like terry cloth, but I knew it wasn't.

As Grieve watched, she handed me clean underwear and black jeans. I slipped into them, then allowed her to help me into a cobalt blue corset top, leaning against the table as she laced it. Lainule had acknowledged that I didn't have to wear a dress if I wanted to, but she'd put her foot down at tank tops unless I was going out on a mission.

"You must wear something that sets you apart." Since nobody argued with Lainule, I had acquiesced.

And so, I agreed to the corset. Fashioned out of dyed leather, it was embellished with silver buckles and studs, giving me a badass but elegant look. The laces were black and silver. I wasn't sure quite what I thought of it, though I was leaning toward loving it. I had, however, put the skids on letting Druise lace it so tight that I'd have a hard time running in it. After a few days, I'd discovered that it actually did a good job of supporting not only my boobs but my back.

I sat down at the dressing table, and the girl began brushing my hair.

"What would Her Highness like me to do with her hair this morning?"

I frowned, wanting her to just call me Cicely, but that was another thing I was going to have to get used to: being addressed in a royal manner. I felt like Cinderella must have after the *happily-ever-after*: new to the Court, out of place, and hanging on for dear life.

"Just let it hang loose, thank you." I wasn't sure what I wanted, but that would be the simplest and get the morning routine over with. I had balked at letting her put my makeup on for me, and while she brushed away, I quickly smoothed on foundation, powder, eyeliner, and mascara, then rubbed a little light gloss over my lips. By the time I finished, Druise was done with my hair.

"Thank you, Druise. You may go now."

She curtseyed, turned, and left.

I pushed back from the vanity and turned to see that Grieve had emerged from the bed and was fully dressed. Of course, all he had to do was to focus on what he wanted to wear and, bingo, there it was. Today he was looking fine, in a pair of khaki cargo pants, with a royal blue V-neck shirt that showed off his biceps quite nicely.

I moved to him, and he held out his arm, slipping it around my waist and kissing me soundly. Glancing over my shoulder, I stared at the bed. It was so hard to believe that everything was happening so fast. Just a few weeks ago, I'd been in La-La Land, when Ulean had warned me that my aunt and cousin were in trouble. One phone call later and I was on the road, headed north, on a long drive up the I-5 freeway. And now . . . here I was in the palace of the Summer Queen, waiting for my new life to begin.

"What are you thinking?" Grieve asked.

I shook my head. "I don't know. Just . . . I'm watching things parade forward at a rate that boggles my mind. But no matter what, I'm with you, and that's all that counts."

And try as he might, that was all he could get me to say on the matter.

⚜

Everybody was waiting for us in the common room. We'd have brunch later on, so for now, we munched on a little fruit. As Peyton entered the room, I stopped short, staring at her. She looked so different.

Peyton was part Native American, on her father's side. She was also half-breed when it came to her powers. Her father, Rex, was a werepuma. He'd just reentered her life after being absent for most of her youth. Her mother had made sure that none of his letters ever reached her hands.

Anadey—her mother—was one of the magic-born. Peyton wasn't speaking to her right now. Anadey had tried to kill both Rex and me, and that didn't go down too well, with Peyton or with the rest of us.

Usually, Peyton was dressed in jeans and a sweatshirt, with a ponytail. But today her hair was long and gleaming, and she was wearing a pair of black trousers, with a peach tunic that set off the warm glow of her skin. Tall and statuesque, she looked radiant.

Kaylin let out a low whistle, grinning. "Pretty lady."

Peyton snorted. "If my business is going to open next week, then I need to start dressing the part."

Before the house had burned, we'd gone into business together—with me opening Wind Charms, a magic shop with spell components, and Peyton starting up the Mystical Eye—a magical investigations firm. Now, of course, it was out of the question for me to have a business, so I'd turned the reins over to Luna and she would take my place at the Veil House, together with Peyton.

"Well, the way you look would inspire me to hire you." I handed her a pear. "We're just grabbing a little something to tide us over till we get there. As soon as everybody's ready, we'll stop at Starbucks, then head over to your father's. If it's still okay with Rex, that is."

She slid into a chair and bit into the fruit. "Yeah, he's totally fine with us barging in on him. But it's cold out. If I didn't know better, I'd swear Myst and her Shadow Hunters are nearby."

I shivered, folding my arms across my chest. For a few minutes, I'd been able to push thoughts of Myst to the back burner, but now they came rushing back, and all of the warmth seemed to drain out of the room. Sure, Rhia and I were taking the thrones of Summer and Winter. And yes, our weddings were coming up. But nothing in the world could change the fact that we had enemies on all sides, and they were all out to see us dead. With a small sigh, I picked up a peach.

As I raised it to my lips, something made me pause and I glanced down at it. There, wriggling out through the skin, was a worm. And in that moment, I had my doubts as to whether any of us would survive through the winter to actually see spring come again.

Chapter 4

New Forest seemed like a different town in the daylight. Oh, the snow and ice were everywhere, and there was a bitter, frosty chill to the streets, but the downtown area was bustling with shoppers. But on closer inspection, they were hurrying, their expressions drawn and tense, like they were looking over their shoulders.

The same way we are. But at least Leo and Geoffrey were asleep for the day, and we had enough people with us that we could handle day-runners.

Grieve and Chatter didn't want to ride in the car. Along with a few guards, they would meet us at Rex's alone. So I drove, with Rhia riding shotgun. Kaylin, Peyton, and Luna sat in the back. As I navigated the streets, it occurred to me that in a few days, this—driving—might be a thing of the past. Lainule said that after the initiation, I'd be learning to travel like the Fae. Apparently, there were ways of allowing half-bloods to use some of the full-blood powers.

"Why so solemn?" Luna asked, looking over at me.

I shrugged. "Just thinking."

I *should* be happy. I should be *thrilled.* Didn't every

little girl want to be a princess? And didn't every little girl long for a happily-ever-after with her Prince Charming? Then why was I on the verge of tears? I blinked them away, and then, shrugging, I forced a smile.

"Peyton, what did Rex say when you told him we were going to converge on his house for brunch?"

She laughed. "He said as long as we chip in for the groceries, he'll cook."

"How's his leg doing?" Rhia asked.

Rex had been injured in a major skirmish with the Shadow Hunters. One of them had taken a chunk of flesh out of his leg, and without us he would have bled to death, if the Vampiric Fae hadn't finished him off first. He was on crutches but healing up fairly quickly. Luckily there was no infection—Weres weren't prone to them. But the wound had been bad, and he wouldn't be fully back in action for a while.

"He'll be off the crutches in a day or so—being a werepuma has its benefits, but he'll probably have a limp for months. At least he lives in a security building." She frowned, jabbing her thumb into her knee. After a moment, she let out a huff. "Mother called me yesterday."

The car fell silent.

"Why didn't you say anything?" Rhia cleared her throat and turned around to stare at her. I had to keep my eyes on the road, but I peeked in the rearview mirror. Peyton didn't look all that happy. I pressed my lips together, waiting. Anadey had tried to kill me. I didn't have much empathy for the woman.

"She apologized. She was in tears. I told her to fuck off. She begged me to call her when I've had a chance to cool down." Her throat sounded clogged, and I could hear the tears close to the surface, though Peyton prided herself on being the stoic type.

"*Cool down*? After what she did to me? What she tried to do to your father?" I shook my head. "That's a lot to push to the side."

Peyton glanced at me through the mirror, giving me a sharp nod. "That's what I told her."

We were outside Rex's apartment building, and the Cambyra guards were there on the street, waiting next to Grieve and Chatter. It seemed odd to see them in the middle of the town, on the sidewalk, during the day. They had changed their outfits to mirror more of a military getup—cargo pants, button-down shirts . . . but there was no mistaking them for the magic-born or for yummanii.

We tumbled out of the car. Silently, Peyton led us to the entrance, where she punched the intercom button, spoke to Rex, and opened the door when the buzzer sounded. Half of the guards followed us in.

Rex lived on the sixth floor and so we took the elevator, while three of the guards took the stairs, scoping them out. I wondered if this was how it was always going to be—always being on the lookout for enemies. When—*if*—we defeated Myst, would there be another force on the horizon looking to take over?

The building was relatively new, and nice. The walls were a muted sage green, with white ceilings and soft hunter green carpets. Rex must have been watching out the peephole, because as we stopped en masse in front of his door, it swung open, and a sturdy, tall man with a ponytail that reached his butt and a grizzled scruff of a beard stood back to let us in.

"Baby girl!" Rex propped his crutches against the wall, opened his arms and Peyton fell into them, hugging him tightly.

"Daddy." She smiled up at him—it had been only a couple of weeks since he had returned to her life. They had a lot of making up for lost time to do.

"You know where the remote is, Peyton." He gestured to the living room. "Let me get the food. Luna, would you help me?" He nodded for her to follow him into the kitchen. Luna's relationship with her family was more distant than strained; Rex seemed to sense her need to be included.

The apartment was still relatively unadorned. Rex had just moved in, and he had arrived with only a couple of suitcases and a backpack. Everything in the room had that *new* feeling, though it looked new from the thrift shops rather than from a department store. Utilitarian, the furniture was a mishmash of patterns, but it served its purpose and Rex seemed content.

We settled on the sofa and floor surrounding the TV, and Peyton tuned it to the local news channel. Grieve and Chatter stared at the screen, shaking their heads. Neither was comfortable around technology, and neither understood the appeal of TV. The guards had stationed themselves outside the door once they ascertained the apartment was safe.

Luna carried in the tray, followed by Rex, on his crutches. Cheese, lunch meats, bread, condiments, sliced tomatoes, and lettuce. And a big bag of cookies.

"If you want soda, there's some in the fridge," Rex said. We wouldn't find any alcohol in his house, since he was a recovering alcoholic.

The news came on and we settled down, quietly slapping together sandwiches as we waited for Marley Jonathon— the local news anchor—to finish wrapping up the headlines.

"In breaking news, we have a statement from the Regent of the Vampire Nation, Lord Lannan Altos. He is issuing a warning that all citizens of New Forest must obey."

Lannan's voice came on the screen, dubbed over a painting of the Regent. He was as gorgeous in the portrait as he was in life. A ticker tape under the news desk read, PREVIOUSLY RECORDED.

"Citizens of New Forest, we are facing yet another challenge. We are hunting three rogue vampires. They are to be considered extremely dangerous. They were responsible for five deaths last night. We are instituting yet another curfew, running from sunset to sunrise. We urge you to hang garlic braids at every window and door and keep alert. Report any unusual activity to the authorities, and also to our hotline—1-800-555-VAMP. I repeat, these vampires are rogue; they do not abide by the Treaty. They are dangerous and will kill."

I sighed, looking around. "Five more deaths. At least Lannan is being open with the citizenship of the town. That impresses me, as much as I hate to say it."

Grieve let out a grunt. "Don't give the creep too much credit."

Shaking my head, I mumbled. "Credit where credit is due. I didn't say I *liked* him. But Geoffrey, if he were in this situation, would have done his best to cover this up."

With an irritated shrug, Grieve let the matter drop.

The announcer was discussing the deaths. "All five are victims of a brutal massacre, perpetrated by the rogue vampires. The Crimson Court has put out a bounty on their heads, but it is only available to members of the Vampire Nation. All mortals are urged to *avoid* engaging them. I repeat: They are dangerous and will kill without provocation. The names of the dead are Robert Higgins, George Wendell, Mary Booth, Tregar Johnson, and Lida Lavine."

Peyton's head shot up. "Lida Lavine? Oh, that's going to go over well."

"Who is she?" I asked.

"The daughter of one of the most influential members of the Lupa Clan. She's a werewolf, and you know how the lycanthropes feel about the vampires." The look on her face said everything I was thinking.

Werewolves hated vampires, and they despised the magic-born. Come to think of it, they pretty much didn't like anybody but their own kind. They were the thugs of the Supe world, always in a gang, always banding together.

"Well, fuck. I wonder if Regina knows that. She has to, I would think. But it's going to mean an escalation in tensions that don't need any flaming." The Lupas were just waiting for trouble to set them off.

My phone rang, and I moved to the side to answer it. It was Ysandra Petros, the liaison between the Consortium and the Moon Spinners.

"Cicely, the Consortium has ordered you and Rhiannon to appear before the Elder Council." She didn't exactly sound worried, but I could hear an edge to her voice.

"Why?" My first thought was, *Too bad, get in line*, but I didn't say it. I liked Ysandra, and while I had a natural antagonism toward authority, the Consortium had been a big help to us when we were fighting off the Shadow Hunters during the last big skirmish.

"I don't know, but they've required your presence. I told them you can't possibly come before your initiation. I think . . . appearing as the Fae Queens . . . might better whatever position you have or need with them."

I pressed my lips together. She had a good point. "I think you're right. Did they accept your answer?"

"They don't have much of a choice. If you were just a regular society member, then it wouldn't fly, but seeing that you are both going to be leaders of your people, there's not much they can do to press the matter. I'll be in touch with you soon." And abruptly, she hung up. Ysandra wasn't rude, but she was brusque, and direct. I liked that.

As I hung up I caught sight of the time. We had to be back to the Barrow by noon, and while it wasn't that far to the Golden Wood, the walk back through the forest would take us a while—at least those of us not full-blooded Fae.

Peyton hugged Rex as we headed out, and he waved us on. As the door closed behind us, I heard the locks slide shut, and I realized that no matter how safe a person or place felt, in our world, safety was merely an illusion.

As we walked through the silent forest, the snow began to drift down again, hard. The sky was overcast, silver against the backdrop of the trees encased in white. The snow muffled the sounds of our passing, and nobody seemed to feel much like talking. Ever since we'd driven Myst back, it felt like we were dancing on the edge of a razor blade, waiting for that one slip to slice the illusion of our success into ribbons. She was still out there, the queen of the snow spiders, the Mistress of Mayhem, and she wove her deadly traps out of sight now. In some ways, it had been easier when we knew where she was, but for now, we could only speculate.

A movement to the right, behind a huckleberry bush, caught my eye. I stopped as a withered old crone shifted from behind the foliage. She was gaunt, with long, lean limbs, and a tooth that cunningly curled out from her upper jaw, over her bottom lip. Straggled, matted white hair cloaked her shoulders, and her clothing consisted of strips of gray rags that seemed to be sewn together in the semblance of a cloak and dress.

It was the Snow Hag, one of the Wilding Fae. She and her people had pledged themselves to my Court, and they'd come to our aid during the routing of Myst from the Barrows. They were cunning, the Wilding Fae, and old beyond time, but they could be reasoned with, *if* you were clearheaded and clever about how you phrased your words.

I inclined my head, acknowledging her presence—I'd recently found out she was considered one of the nobles among the loose-scrabble group.

"It would be a pleasure to speak with one of the Wilding Fae. One might wonder what she has to say." I had been taking lessons from Chatter in dealing with the group, because he was extremely good at diplomacy and had a knack for navigating the treacherous territory that came with interacting with them.

She grinned, snaggletooth and all. "One would think a Queen-to-be has been practicing her decorum. One might appreciate the effort, if one was a member of the Wilding Fae." She crept fully from behind the huckleberry bush. "This might be a time to discuss goings-on that are disturbing, should the Queens-to-be wish to further their knowledge."

I sucked in a deep breath. Whenever the Wilding Fae were disturbed about something, you knew it was bad. I licked my lips. "Such a discussion might be productive on all sides. What would it take, one might wonder, to engage in this conversation." I glanced back at Chatter and he nodded, encouragingly. It would seem I was holding my own.

The Snow Hag cocked her head to the side and caught a snowflake on her tongue. She touched her finger to her nose, then winked. "Some conversations have no price. Some discussions should be free of deals when events conspire that threaten the kingdom."

That couldn't be good. Whatever was going on had to be bad, if she was willing to give us information for free. The Wilding Fae loved to bargain, and when they were ready to forgo gaining something in return for their help . . .

I paused, then sucked in a lungful of the icy air. "It would seem that a Queen-to-be and one of the Wilding Fae might choose to discuss this matter, then."

Again, the twinkle in her eye, both threatening and yet contagious. And then she licked one gnarled finger and held it up to the wind, turning it until she found what she was looking for. She nodded.

"The Mistress of Mayhem, she comes in on the wind again, but not alone. She has regained a following. This is known, not conjecture. Her Shadow Hunters arrive from other lands. They gather, not in the Golden Wood, but farther out—in the mountains, on the craggy slopes where they can hide. She sends her scouts down to the edges of the forest, where they scurry through the shadows, blending, hiding, bleeding the deer for life force. They are reconnoitering, observing, lying in wait. It is hard for them to be patient; they thirst—the Wilding Fae can feel their hunger and their thirst. But the Mistress bids them feast lightly for now, so not to give themselves away."

I thought for a moment. We knew this would happen, but we didn't know it had already begun. Turning my thoughts over in my mind, I grimly looked at her.

"One might wonder where the Mistress of Mayhem hides herself now. Would it be a chance that someone near might know her location?"

The Snow Hag cackled. "If one hereabouts had that

information, a certain Queen-to-be would also have that information, but alas, there is no remedy. However, one might say that there are forces seeking her out, for just that reason. They sniff and seek and peek under branches, and root beneath the trees, hunting her down."

So the Wilding Fae were trying to find Myst's hideaway for us. That was some good news. I nodded. "One might wonder if there are still goblin dogs and tillynoks and ice spiders running free in the Golden Wood?"

Her eyes swirling, the Snow Hag cocked her head and smiled faintly. "When a certain Queen-to-be takes the throne, they will fall under her command, but for now, yes, they still run at Myst's command. One would caution to be careful on a journey back to the Barrow—there are dangers lurking, and even with guards, a certain party would be dangerously put to fight them."

And with that, she vanished into the snow as quickly as she had come. I stared after her, wondering at how strange my life had become.

Grieve rested a hand on my shoulder. "We should be off. There is a hike to go, since you cannot yet run as the full-blooded Fae do, and noontide approaches."

I nodded, and we set off again, and with every rustle along the way, I stiffened, wondering just what enemy lay behind what tree.

⚓

We had almost reached the Twin Oaks when a growl raced along the slipstream. I jerked around, looking in the direction from which it came. And then a high-pitched howl followed, echoing Grieve and Chatter dropped to the ground. I pressed my hands to my ears, the pain knifing through my head.

Be careful, Cicely—they're coming! Run, get back to the Barrow!

Ulean's warning broke through the pain, and I didn't wait to see what was happening but took off toward the Twin Oaks, slogging through the snow. A shadow swooped low behind me and, as Kaylin shouted, something caught me up beneath my armpits and carried me aloft. I screamed, kicking my feet against the air, not sure what the fuck was going on.

Cicely—you have to use your powers. Call on the winds!

What's happening? What's going on? Everything was a blur as I struggled against the tremendous force buoying me up. Everywhere, there was a haze—white and gray and blue. I blinked, trying to clear my sight, and realized that I was in the middle of . . .

Fuck.

Yes, a rogue Wind Elemental has you. I can't engage them without putting you in danger. You are on the plane of wind, and if it drops you, you will free-fall. I don't know if I have the strength to catch you and return you. If you engage the Winds, you can probably break away and I can lead you home. I think.

But Lainule . . . I promised . . .

There is no other way.

Frowning, I stopped struggling against the pull of the Wind Elemental and began to focus on summoning control of the winds. There it was, a little wisp . . . glowing, growing. I nurtured it, invoking the power of the air to rise within me, to swirl up and out, cloaking me with its strength. As it began to fill me with that rush, the sense of power grew and I leaned my head back, staring up, and at that moment, I could see what had hold of me.

The Wind Elemental was nothing like Ulean, who reminded me of sparkling lights and Faerie dreams. No, this was dark and cold and chaotic, with flashes of black and silver synapsing through the cloud that held me tight. There was a flare to the left as I struggled against its hold, and then, irritated, I whispered, "*Gale Force*," and the winds shot through my body, catching me up and away and blowing through the Elemental.

It grunted—I could hear it on the slipstream. I whirled around, staring. We both hovered there, in the midst of the clouds, and then I thrust my hands toward it and let the fury of the storm loose. It pummeled through the Elemental, punching a hole in its center. It began to reform but seemed more cautious.

Enough, now you can follow me out of here.

Ulean's voice was distant, and I paid it no mind. Caught in the thrall of the winds, out on the Elemental plane of Air, I wanted nothing more than to stay here, to race, to feel the freedom. The gale swelled within me, rippling out like concentric rings on a pond, and I let out a laugh— hearty and low and rich with the pure joy of the strength echoing through my body. I reared up, looming over the now-cowering Elemental, and took aim, turning myself into an arrow of wind and storm and raw force.

The Elemental turned, looking to flee, but I dove, ignoring the faint call as Ulean tried to rein me back. I was ready to fight, ready to spar, ready to prove my power, and I coiled and turned, spiraling down toward the wind spirit who had kidnapped me. Never again. Never again would I let myself be caught unawares. Never again would this freak of nature be allowed to harm anyone else.

As I penetrated its body, the Elemental let out a long shriek. I ravaged it, tore it to bits, split it asunder, using the fury of my twisting vortex of winds. A keen howl echoed through the slipstream as I played Cuisinart, like a propeller blade. The life force of the Elemental floated before me for a moment, and I found myself sucking it up, pulling it into myself, strengthening my storm as I absorbed its power.

Cicely! Cicely! Stop! Get off this plane, now. You are in grave danger!

Ulean's voice was urgent, but I refused to listen. And then, as I turned, looking for more prey, there was a brilliant flash—like lightning against thunderclouds—and I found myself falling, spiraling through the air, the power of the winds suddenly sucked away. Frantic, I twisted head over heels as I realized the ground would soon approach.

Shift into an owl, Cicely. Ulean was beside me, urging me to transform.

I'm still in my clothes—I can't get them off. I'll get tan-gled in them if I do.

And then, from somewhere in the distance, I heard a voice as beautiful as the night—as dark and rich and melodic as a rose garden on a summer's evening. I couldn't make out the words, but they were old, and vibrant, and coiled around me, and the next thing I knew, my clothes had drifted away—somehow I'd gotten them off. And I realized my free fall had slowed considerably and I was almost drifting on the breeze.

Now, shift! Don't question it, just shift.

Without wasting time, I shifted. Arms to wings, fingers to wing feathers, body shortening, feet to talons, and then, I was aloft, pulling up and out of the spell that had kept me from crashing to the snowy ground below. I circled the tree line. We were only a short ways from the portal.

Ulean, I will fly to it, because I have no idea where my clothes are. Can you tell Grieve and Chatter so they can tell the others?

Of course, Cicely. Go now.

And so, I flew directly to the Twin Oaks, never so happy to see two trees in my life. I lightly touched down on the ground, loosing my balance on the snow, and as I trans-formed back, I fell forward, into the icy banks of white. I scrambled to my feet and raced for the portals. Two of the guards had sped along, and they were there. One of them handed me his cloak, without a word, affixing it around my shoulders, and they took my hands and jumped through the portal with me, back to safety.

The others made it back with no problem. Shivering, I wondered what had happened to my clothing, when Luna approached and handed me my jeans, underwear, corset, jacket, and circlet.

"I have a spell that brings things to me. I just . . . brought your clothes to me when Ulean whispered that you couldn't transform because of them." She looked pleased as punch, and I grinned at her.

"Thanks for the strip job." I winked at her, then sobered. "Seriously, that's a handy spell. Keep in practice. If I ever need it again when we're out, don't hesitate."

She nodded. "I'm more than happy to help."

We had a few minutes before meeting my father, so I hurried to my room and dressed again. Druise once more tightened the corset laces for me.

"Can't we just do that and then use the busks to hook and unhook it?"

The look on her face spoke volumes. "We can, my Lady, if that's what you choose to do. But . . . this is . . . what I do for you. I'm not sure how to be your lady's maid, begging pardon. You don't seem to need me."

Feeling bad that I'd upset her, I flashed her a warm smile. "But I do, and I will more and more as time goes on. I don't think I'll need you quite in the ways a lot of the Queens would, but we'll work out our pattern." Motioning for her to sit down beside me, I waited until she uncomfortably complied. "Listen, Druise. I'm from a far different world than the life of the palace. And while I'll adapt on some things, the Barrow will have to adapt to me on others. We'll find a compromise that works for us both. Meanwhile, you keep doing what you do, and never fear—I like you. I'm not going to yank your job out from under you."

She frowned for a moment, and then a smile broke through her gloom. "Thank you, Your Highness . . . because this position means the world to my family. It's a step up for us—I'm the first one to stand this near to the Court."

Then it hit me. *This* was how it worked here. This job wasn't menial labor to her; it wasn't beneath her. It was actually a boost in status and—most likely—payment to her family. And she'd been worried that I'd turn her out. And *that* would have been a supreme disgrace.

I patted her hand. "Druise, take heart. You're my lady's

maid. Nobody else. As long as you are loyal to—" I started to say *Grieve* but stopped myself. It was time to think before I spoke. "As long as you are loyal to the King-Elect, and to me, then have no fear."

As she dropped to her knees by my side and pressed her forehead to my hand, a soft bell chimed in the chamber. I glanced around.

"That is the summons to Court, Your Highness." She quickly stood and stepped back, her cheeks flushed. "Are you dressed? Is there anything else you need?"

I glanced down. I was back in my jeans and corset, but my hair was a mess. "Would you mind brushing my hair again?" It would have been just as easy for me to pick up the brush, but I was starting to get it.

She beamed and motioned for me to sit at the vanity. The strokes of the brush felt good against my scalp, soothing me into a relaxed state.

Ulean swept up by my side.

Cicely, you did what you needed to in order to escape, but we have to find a way for you to control the winds. Lainule broke you out of the frenzy this time—

Lainule? You're kidding! I didn't know it was her.

Yes, she broke your concentration. She will tell you about it herself.

Wondering how Lainule had thrust herself into the plane of Air, I shook my head. Druise was finished with my hair, and so I thanked her, stood, and headed out to the Court, where Lainule was waiting with Wrath and the others.

She gave me a long look. "Ulean told me what happened. The Elemental wasn't aligned with Myst, I think. But there are powers in the wild now that are chaotic and running mad. This was not your fault. But we have to take you in hand and teach you how to direct these abilities that the fan transferred to you."

I gazed into her eyes. "How did . . . did you . . ."

"Remember, I told you that I owned the fan before you?"

I nodded, sensing that some sort of revelation was on the horizon.

"Cicely . . . the same thing that happened to you, happened to me. The fan's powers—became a part of me. But I learned to control them." She smiled then, tipping my chin up. "This is why I know how dangerous it can be to call them forth."

"There's more. The Snow Hag stopped us today." I told them about what she'd said. "Myst is nearer than we feared. And her Shadow Hunters are regrouping."

Lainule let out a sigh. "We'll send out scouts. That's all we can do for the moment, but at least we are forewarned."

"And now, wife, I must take my daughter and her fiancé to see their new home. Your friends may attend." Wrath motioned for me to follow. The others fell in behind Grieve and me, and we trailed after my father, out the door of the Court, while my mind whirled with thoughts.

Chapter 5

We exited the Barrow and I wondered just how we were to find our way into the realm of Winter. No one had yet told us how the realms were connected, and it wasn't something obvious to figure out.

Wrath paused and looked back at me. "The path to the realm of Winter is found outside Summer. Are we all here?"

I glanced around. Grieve, Chatter, Kaylin, Luna, Peyton, and Rhiannon . . . and me. All waiting. And behind them, Lainule waited, her robes shimmering gold and green. Her hair was turning fast now, the highlights auburn among the gold.

"We're here." I steeled myself.

"A moment." Wrath motioned to the side, and Druise ran up carrying a heavy cloak the color of twilight. She draped it around my shoulders and fastened it with a silver pin in the shape of a holly leaf. I rubbed my hand on the material. It was soft, almost like velvet, and warm.

I looked up at my father. He smiled and shrugged.

"You may be destined to become the Queen of Ice and Snow, my daughter, but even you will find the realm harsh and cold at first. That will change, of course, but for now, best you be protected. The rest of you, cloak up. Grieve and Chatter will be fine, but mortals and half-bloods must take care."

And out came another servant with a cloak for Rhiannon, matching mine but in a deep hunter green with a gold brooch, and slipped it over her shoulders, fastening it for her. Yet another servant carried cloaks for Luna, Peyton, and Kaylin. When we were all ready, we headed toward the portal, following my father.

As we emerged from the portal, I saw what my playing with the winds had wrought. The sky was shimmering with snow, the pale sun that had been trying to peek out through the clouds the past few days was gone, and a cutting wind was blowing the snow into high drifts. I'd taken Myst's handiwork and made it worse.

"Once we stop the Indigo Court, at least winter will fade normally," Luna said.

I bit my lip. "It will fade here, but . . ." I glanced at my father. "Where Grieve and I will be living, it will be perpetual winter, won't it?"

He nodded. "Yes, my dear. And Rhiannon will live in perpetual summer. I have a feeling you two are going to break tradition, though, and come out of your realms more often than Lainule did, or Tabera."

Grieve took my hand as we turned in a direction I had not yet been in—this was not the way to where we had found Lainule's heartstone, nor where we had journeyed to the realm of the Bat People. Instead, we were heading into the core of the forest, toward the Cascade foothills. There was no path here, but as Wrath moved forward, the bushes opened up for him, pulling back under their heavy weight of snow, as if they sensed his coming and acknowledged his presence.

"Who was the King of Winter? You said Tabera was murdered by Myst. But what about her King?"

He paused and turned. "Tabera was married to Shatter. As always happens when a queen dies and is not replaced, he died with her." The look on his face told me that his death had not gone easy.

"Did Myst kill him, too?"

"No." Wrath glanced up at the snow that fell softly, with a muffled hiss, around our shoulders. "When Myst came to this land, when you were her daughter, she didn't attempt a coup of the Winter Court. Not until this past year. She hid in the shadows for centuries, biding her time, and bred her court."

I had wondered about that—my memories of that time were nebulous, coming in snippets, and I had no clue of how things had gone down other than what I'd been shown.

"When did she kill Tabera?"

My father frowned. "Last year she came out of hiding, emerged and destroyed the Winter Court. Because we—and Tabera—kept to the traditions of having contact only during the Solstices when the reins of control change over, we did not know it had happened until Litha—the Summer Solstice."

"So you had no clue?"

He shrugged, a dark look clouding his face. "In some ways, we gave her the perfect setup. Tabera could have called for help, if we had kept closer contact. So Myst threw her down—she found Tabera's heartstone and destroyed it."

I shivered. Destroying a queen's heartstone was cold, deliberate execution. "And Shatter tried to avenge her?"

"Yes." Wrath started walking again. "From what the remnants of the Winter Court tell us—those who managed to escape and were not turned—Shatter planned out an assassination. But a few of his guards fell under Myst's spell, including his most loyal captain. Shatter's plan was exposed. Before Myst could kill him, Shatter destroyed himself, taking a number of Myst's new converts with him. He blew up part of the Winter palace. We've had a crew working on it nonstop since we routed her from the Barrow."

A thought crossed my mind. "Is Myst . . . will she still have Shadow Hunters there?"

"No," Grieve said. "When she routed Summer, she took up residence in the Court of Rivers and Rushes because it provided easier access to the town and their people."

Wrath nodded. "The guards and tradesmen have been working hard, and there are no signs of Myst or her Shadow Hunters. The Winter Court is ready and waiting for you."

I fell silent, thinking about everything he had told me, as we traversed the roughening terrain. Lainule, Grieve, Chatter, and Wrath had no problem, of course. They could walk on top of the snow if they wanted. Kaylin wasn't far behind them—he moved with an ease that belied the demon within him. But Luna, Rhiannon, Peyton, and I weren't faring quite as well. How the hell was I going to function once I actually moved into the realm of Winter if I couldn't even get around?

"I'm going to have to get snowshoes, I think, once we move in." I was grumbling and knew it, but the thought of a continual struggle to even get around in my own home was daunting.

Lainule glanced at Wrath. "I think we should tell her. I've hinted at it before, but I haven't come out and told her clearly."

"Tell me what?" *Please, oh, please, let it be something good for a change.*

Wrath gave her a nod. "When you and Rhiannon undergo official initiation, you will be able to move like full-blooded Fae. As we've said, the initiation will change both of you in ways you can only imagine. We can't tell you everything, but that much, I assure you."

I glanced at Rhiannon, a look of glee spreading across my face. She returned it with just as much enthusiasm. "That is awesome!"

Lainule laughed. "Oh, I wish I could stay to see what kind of courts you girls run. I know we can trust you, but in your hands—you and your cousin—Summer and Winter will never be the same."

Rhiannon's smile faded, as did mine. The reminder that Lainule and Wrath would be gone, forever, struck us yet once again. But then, Rhia hadn't gotten to meet her father, and he was dead.

We slogged along for another quarter mile until Wrath stopped and pointed ahead. There, in the center of a clearing, were two incredibly tall holly trees. Like the Twin Oaks, they radiated with a network of sparkling light stretching between them. I stopped, gazing up at their looming silhouettes.

"The Twin Hollies are the entrance to Winter. You think Myst's winter is cold—when we enter into this realm, you will understand the true nature of snow and ice." Wrath spoke in a hushed voice, almost reverent. "And when you take the crown, you will feel it to the core."

I took a deep breath and stepped forward, but the guards pushed in front of us.

Check held up his hand. "Your Highness, please, allow us to go first."

I stood back as he and his men went through, vanishing in a sudden crackle of sparkling lights. A moment passed, then another as we stood silent, waiting. Then Check peeked back through and motioned to us.

Wrath and Lainule took the forefront, followed by Grieve and me, and then by the others. Chatter and Rhiannon brought up the rear. As we crossed through the portal, it felt vastly different from the doorway to Summer. The basic impulse was the same, but a steady wind howled past, echoing as we shifted and flickered, and while I couldn't pinpoint exactly what made it so strange, there was a difference about it that felt colder, older, and harsh.

As we came out into the woodland, I gasped. I'd expected to just see the Golden Wood through winter, much like Myst had brought with her. But this . . . this was nowhere near anything I'd imagined.

The trees were coated with ice, and within the ice sparkled lights—radiant purple and blue and palest pink. They reminded me of Christmas trees, of ornaments that shimmered in the reflection of candlelight, and yet it was daylight here, like it was back in the Golden Wood.

The sky was overcast, a pale silver, and a faint dusting of snow lazily brushed our shoulders. The undergrowth peeked through mounds of snow, dark green against the stark white, and when I turned, the holly trees were also shrouded in show, their crimson berries brilliant against the blanket of endless winter.

A path stretched before us, but it was cloaked in a sheen of ice, shimmering with an internal light. Ahead, the trees thinned out, but the grove in which we found ourselves was silent, under a deep, unending layer of snow.

Up ahead, a barrow mound, similar to the Summer Palace, rose on stilts about fifteen feet above the ground. The support pillars barely showed beneath the cloak of snow, and the Barrow was swathed in white, and silent. Several of the guards were positioned around it, and a contingent of workers silently went about whatever they were doing: fixing doorways, patching holes that had been gouged into the side, all sorts of repair work.

As I stood there, it began to hit home that here, the snow never left. Here, it was always winter. Here, the trees never saw spring, summer, or fall.

"When you take up court here, Cicely and Grieve, the winter will truly return." Lainule smiled at me, her expression unreadable.

I must have gasped, for both she and Wrath turned.

"What is it?" Wrath inhaled deeply, then let out a loud cough.

The air was sharp, piercing my lungs with a clarity I'd never before felt, but it hurt like hell and I was grateful for the warm cloak that covered me from neck to toe. I'd need gloves, too, and a scarf and hat.

"The air is practically crackling with the cold. It feels like it could shatter my lungs if I breathed deep enough. And you say that winter will *return* here?" I turned around, looking in all directions. To the right, I saw a group of Ice

Elementals passing by, and they paused, looked directly at
me, and stopped. "Uh-oh . . . are they dangerous?"

Lainule shook her head. "No, they sense you are their
Queen-to-be. Even now, before the initiation, you reverberate with the energy of winter, Cicely. You are already
transforming, but you do not realize it.

Wrath let out a slow breath. "As to the winter, here it has
faded, just as summer is fading in Rhiannon's realm. Ever
since Tabera died, it has been so. Myst may claim the winter for her own, but she is not the Queen of Snow and Ice,
and so there has been no rule here for quite some time.
When you take the throne, the winter shall once again hold
sway here."

That scared me. If this was moderate weather for the
area, what the hell was it going to be like living here in *real*
winter? I moved closer to Grieve, who wrapped his arm
around my shoulders and kissed my forehead.

"It will be all right," he murmured. "We will adapt."

I glanced up at him, and the sparkling lights of his eyes
mirrored the flashing lights in the trees. My love, he was born
for the Summer but had been transformed and reborn a winter king. He leaned down, brushing my lips with his own, his
kiss so soft I could barely feel it in the numbing cold.

"As long as we are together, it will be okay," I whispered.

Wrath led us to the Barrow palace, and there stopped to
talk briefly with the guards. After they were finished, he
turned. "The palace has been restored. There was a lot of
damage, but everything is ready now. Come, Cicely, Grieve.
Enter your new home. As Summer's palace is called the
Marburry Barrow, so this is the Eldburry Barrow."

Silently, in a single line, we approached the entrance.
As each of us stepped through, a shimmering light flashed
pale blue.

I was prepared for a dark, musty place—it seemed that
the palace of Winter would be such. Summer was rustic but
elegant and warm, and even the air smelled like roses
there. What I encountered was nothing like I'd expected.

The central common court was spacious. I could barely see the ends, and the floor reminded me of polished marble, but yet, when I looked closer, I saw that it was a pattern of stones inlaid in the dirt. Lapis and creamy white quartz, clear quartz and sodalite and amethyst, all smooth pebbles inlaid into the floor, like cobblestones, but they were firmly rooted in the compacted dirt. Overhead, the ceiling shimmered like black onyx, with stars embedded in the tiles, in an overreaching arc that mirrored the night sky.

The furnishings were minimal but had clean lines. It seemed that as comfortable and cozy as the Marbury Barrow was, so the Eldburry Barrow was cool and minimalistic and clear.

I ran my hand along one of the nearby benches. They were carved from slate and highly polished, and several smaller tables looked to be the same. The chairs around them were made from some sort of hardwood.

My father saw me staring. "Yew. The wood in this barrow is yew, with accents of elder and holly. Back at Marburry, in the realm of Summer, it's mostly oak, with some willow and apple."

That made sense, when I thought about it. The trees of summer. The trees of winter. As I slowly walked through the room, my hand trailing along the smooth surface of one of the tables, I closed my eyes. The room emanated age and antiquity and history. The Marbury Barrow was bustling with life once again, now that Lainule had retaken control. I tried to imagine what it would be like here, with the Winter Court full. Images of the Shadow Hunters kept flashing through my mind and I kept pushing them away, fighting off the panic that rose when I thought of ruling this realm.

I whirled to face my father. "You promise, you absolutely promise that Myst is not a true Queen of Winter?"

He gave me a solemn nod. "I do. She has never held the throne, nor been through the initiation, and without the proper rites, the abilities that make the Queen *the Queen* . . . they are not there. She is not—and never will be—the

Queen of Winter. Her jealousy over that fact was what drove her in the beginning."

That meant that although the Shadow Hunters had lived here under her rule for a while, they had not been *of* this place. And that seemed to make all the difference in the world. Another thought crossed my mind.

"You mentioned that some of the Summer Court were originally from here and that they might wish to return home. What if . . . what if they were aligned with Myst? What if I get them back here and they attack?"

Lainule shook her head, and her golden hair shimmered under the cool and icy lights. "We have taken care of that. I did not tell you, but shortly before we routed Myst and retook the realm of Summer, we . . . cleansed . . . the ranks. We knew we might have a few traitors. We watched our backs, we listened to the wind, and weeded them out. They are no more."

Her voice was as cold as the room. I wondered what she had done to them. The look on my face must have read clear as crystal, because she gently placed one hand on my shoulder and her other hand on Rhiannon's shoulder.

"My girls, you must accept the reality that to be a queen often entails tasks that require you to be ruthless. I ordered the execution of the traitors and stood by to watch. A queen should never send someone to his death unless she is willing to stand by her order and witness it."

At the look on her face, Rhiannon and I simultaneously shuddered. Lainule's fingers gripped our shoulders tightly. She leaned in closer.

"You must get over your squeamishness. The world is a terrible and beautiful place, filled with life and filled with death. Those who take the helm must, at times, make unpopular and difficult decisions. It is the way of the world."

And then she let go and stepped back. "So, Cicely, what do you think of your home? Go exploring. There is nothing within these walls to fear."

As Grieve and I took the front, and Rhia and Chatter

swung in at the rear, we led our friends through the corridors. Lainule and Wrath stayed in the central chamber. Peyton seemed pensive. So did Luna, who was walking beside Kaylin. But he gave me a long look as I glanced back.

"She's right, you know." He slipped his arm around Luna as they strolled along behind us. "You have to be able to make these decisions without guilt. Remorse—that can be a good thing. But guilt?" He shrugged. "No."

I didn't say anything. Lainule was right, and so was Kaylin. I knew it, and by the look on her face, so did Rhiannon. That didn't mean it was going to be easy or comfortable, but sometimes, life just is what it is and there is nothing you can do about it.

The hallways reminded me of the hallways at the Marbury Barrow, except the lights were cooler here. "I wonder if they use Fire Elementals here for the lanterns, too? Or are they something different?"

Grieve smiled softly. "No, they're young Ice Elementals—they have their own glow. That's why the light here is of a bluish tint instead of the warm orange of the Summer realm. The Court of Rivers and Rushes is much cozier, in case you haven't noticed." He let out a soft chuckle and pulled me close to him. "But we'll make this place home, and we'll make it comfortable."

I leaned against him. "I think we have to. There's not much choice, is there? Can you tell me something?" I paused as we entered the section of the Barrow that held the bedrooms. The royal bedchamber was to our right, and as we entered, I stopped, gasping softly. The Eldburry Barrow might be cold and austere, but our bedroom-to-be was absolutely amazing.

It stretched out, almost as big as the throne room, and a thick, soft carpet covered the cobblestones. The tapestry was intricate, woven in swirls of blue and purple and silver, and the weave was thick and plush. I leaned down and brushed my hand against it—soft, it was soft as a kitten's back.

Dark, polished wardrobes lined the walls, along with a

vanity table and love seat. The wood gleamed, looking so smooth it almost might be glass.

The bed was a huge four-poster affair, the yew intricately carved with a labyrinthine design. Piled high with pillows, the thick comforters matched the pattern on the carpet, and overhead, the ceiling swirled with sparkling gems—iolite and sapphire, amethyst and clear quartz against a jet-black background. The jewels glowed from within, some inner luminescence that flickered through the dim light of the lanterns.

I turned to Grieve. "I . . . this is beautiful."

"You like it, then?" He leaned in, his feral teeth glistening in the light of the Ice Elementals.

I nodded. "I think . . . I think I will come to love it here. I think it will be hard at first, but this is a safe haven. I can live here. I can adjust." And right then, I knew I was telling the truth, not trying to bolster my courage. When I closed my eyes, I could see myself in a long fur-trimmed gown, wandering through the corridors, feeling the darkness of the long winter in the core of my bones and learning to embrace the shadow rather than fear it.

And at that moment, I opened my eyes again, and Grieve was kissing me deeply, his arms around me. "I can hardly wait to claim our marriage bed," he whispered. "Anywhere, loving you is a joy, but when we are married . . . when you are my Queen and I your King, all will be right with the world."

I didn't know about that—we still had Myst to deal with, and Geoffrey and Leo, but I decided to bite my tongue and leave the future to the future. I kissed him back, his arms strong around my waist, his heart beating against my own, and for one brief moment, I believed it was all possible.

"If you are done exploring, I have someone to introduce." My father's voice echoed through the chamber from the door.

The others had politely been ignoring Grieve and me, peeking into cupboards and testing out the thickness of the mattresses, but now we turned to see Wrath standing there. By his side was a short, dark-haired Fae whose gaze seemed to dart about, constantly observing everything going on. He was dressed in royal blue and purple, with silver epaulettes on his shoulder.

"Meet your Chief Advisor, Strict. He's trustworthy and will not lead you astray by either flattery or deception. Strict was Tabera's advisor, and he escaped the carnage when Myst invaded the Winter Court."

I watched him, closely, cocking my head as I tried to read his energy.

Is he truly safe?

But Ulean wasn't speaking.

He bowed, and when I held out my hand, he stared at it for a moment.

"Your Majesty should not shake hands with those beneath her," was his abrupt reply.

Taken aback and mildly annoyed, I frowned. Before I could help myself, I snapped, "That's how they do things where I come from."

The words didn't even faze him. Strict shrugged. "Your Majesty is no longer in the world outside. I'm here to advise you, and that is what I will do. You must act like a queen to inspire the respect for a queen. Incline your head gracefully if you wish to show favor upon meeting someone. Do not, or look away, if you wish to show disfavor."

Struck by how rude he was, I let out a little huff, but my father stepped in before I could say anything more.

"He speaks the truth, Cicely. You must learn to compromise, and in this case, it does not mean you win more than fifty percent of the argument. You have chosen to take the queenship on your shoulders. You must act the part."

Part of me wanted to rail—to say *I chose by default, without realizing*—but we were long past that point. Maybe I hadn't known, when I went to rescue Lainule's heartstone, what the result would be. But I knew that it would be life-changing and I'd agreed to follow through, without finding out what the consequences were. I had no one but myself to blame, and when thinking about the option—seeing Lainule fade and die or go out like a light when Myst found her heartstone—there was no question about it. I'd make the same choice again, if given a do-over.

Strict was waiting for my response. He wasn't afraid of me, and though he'd no doubt treat me with the respect accorded to the Queen, I had the feeling that he'd been matched to the job with a perfect fit. The advisor had to be someone who could point out the hard truths.

Slowly, I withdrew my hand and gave him a soft nod. "Pleasure to meet you. What do I call you? What's your title? I should know these things before we ever appear in public together."

"Call me Lord Strict. And for the Queen of Summer, my sister will be your advisor. We were born to a pair, much like you and your cousin, only we truly are twins. I came to the Winter Court to be fostered when I was barely off my mother's breast. The nature of this land suits me, and so I stayed."

Rhiannon, having watched the dressing down I'd gotten, inclined her head. "And your sister's name?"

"My sister's name is Lady Edge. She will be waiting for you back in the Marburry Barrow." And with that, Strict turned and left, not waiting for a dismissal.

I glanced at my father. "Intimidating."

"Good. You will need firm counsel. Both of you. There are so many things you do not know about our culture—your culture. And you must learn as much as you can in the next few weeks. But now, Lainule awaits. She insists you must return to the Marburry Barrow to rest."

He turned and slipped out of the room. I glanced at Rhiannon but she shook her head, and so we followed him, in silent formation, into the chill winter that waited outside the Barrow. Lainule had already gone ahead by the time we reached the portals, and so we slipped out of the realm of Winter into the hell of winter on earth. As we exited the Twin Hollies, I could smell blood on the horizon, and smoke, and an ill wind racing through. Old leather, black roses, and skeletons dancing on the graves of those who were long dead. Myst was out here, that she was—waiting. And Leo and Geoffrey, white snow-serpents hiding in the drifts.

We headed back to the Marburry Barrow, and I realized we were trapped in a frozen ocean of blood and pain. The austere beauty and coldness of the Eldburry Barrow beckoned to me. It had gone from being an unknown to being home. And I wanted to go home and hide my head under the covers.

Shivering, I pulled closer to Grieve as we began to slog our way through the drifts.

Chapter 6

There was no word the rest of the day from the Crimson Court about Crawl, but then, since most of the vampires were sleeping, we didn't expect any. Lainule had ordered steaming baths prepared for Rhiannon and me, and—mystified—we bathed in a large dressing chamber.

"I think there's something in the water," Rhia said. "Can you smell it?"

I inhaled deeply. "Yes . . . some herb or oil, but I can't place it. What do you think Lainule wants?"

"It could be anything, but I have a feeling . . . Cicely, will you be all right in the realm of Winter? It's cold there, and stark, and it frightened me." She shivered. "I could never live there. I don't think I have the stamina it takes."

I thought about what she said for a moment. "But the unending summer—it's going to be hard to adapt to that. No autumn, no spring or winter. Just summer forever. I think . . . I'll prefer the winter."

"As my mother said, fire and ice." Rhia gave me a rueful grin.

"Amber and jet." I grinned back at her. "Twin cousins . . . born to a day but to two seasons." Closing my eyes, I leaned back in the tub. "Eldburry Barrow is beautiful, if stark. I think I can make my home there."

"Do you feel like you're changing? Already, I mean?" Rhia's voice was soft, and when I peeked at her from beneath my lashes, I saw that she had relaxed into the heat of the water, too.

I inhaled a sharp lungful of air and then let it out in a slow stream. *Was I changing, already?* "The truth? I barely remember a month ago. I barely remember what it was like before I came back and found Grieve again, and Myst . . . so yes, I think I am."

And with that, I closed my eyes for real and let the warm sloshing of the water drag me under. I was dozing lightly when Druise and Mayja—Rhia's lady's maid—entered the room to dry us off.

"Her Majesty the Lady Lainule requests you come to the throne room," Druise said, to both of us.

"Can we have a bite to eat first? I'm hungry." My stomach was rumbling and I wanted nothing more than to gnaw on a chicken leg or something.

"I'm sorry, but she bade you come before you sup." Druise stared at the towel, and I could tell she was hoping I wouldn't put up a fuss. Sighing, with my stomach grumbling loudly, I let her dry me off.

The girls dressed us in long, loose robes—Rhia's was gold, mine was silver. They were shimmering and sheer, but as we moved the light reflected off them, glimmering brightly in the glow of the Fire Elementals. After pulling our hair back with a band, the maids led us through the hallway to the throne room.

There Lainule was seated on her throne, and she motioned for us to approach her. As we did, she gestured for us to kneel on matching pillows that sat at her feet. Lainule had never forced me to kneel in front of her before. Something was up.

I glanced around. Grieve and Chatter stood to the side, at attention, unmoving. Peyton, Luna, and Kaylin were sitting on a bench near one wall. They kept their gazes downward, and none of them looked at us.

Rhiannon and I knelt as Lainule waited. After a moment, she motioned to one of her maidens and the girl picked up a tray and knelt in front of us. On the tray were two chalices—ornate, one silver, one gold. They were foaming over with mist, and the faint scent of mint and chocolate rose from the silver goblet, while the scent of rose petals and honey rose from the gold.

"Tonight, you begin your journey. Tonight, you undergo your initiation."

Rhiannon gasped at the same time that I did. I knew it would be sometime soon, but Lainule hadn't given us a firm date. But now, it was here. It was time.

"I ask each of you, and your answer is binding. There will be no return from here out. No second chance either way." She stood, and—holding her scepter in her hand—said, "Cicely Tuuli Waters, do you accept the challenge to walk this path, to journey to the throne of Snow and Ice and take it firmly to heart until the day you so do die?"

Startled by the swiftness, wondering if this was the initiation itself, I stammered out an answer. "I accept the challenge."

"Rhiannon Lasair Roland, do you accept the challenge to walk this path, to journey to the throne of Rivers and Rushes and take it firmly to heart until the day you so do die?"

Rhiannon let out a long breath. "I accept."

"Then drink deep from the Chalices of Seelie and Unseelie."

As I slowly accepted the silver chalice, and Rhiannon the gold, Lainule spread her hands over our heads. "Drink now, slowly," she said. And then she began to chant.

From heart to tongue, from skin to bone,
From soul to soul, you now shall roam.

From night to day, from day to night,
From light to dark, from dark to light.
From wind and fire, the spell's begun,
From sun to moon, from moon to sun.
From fire and wind, we call the years
To wipe away all hope and fear.
To mark the deal as ever done,
To make the soul ever young.
To free the heart, to build the stone,
To mark the flesh, to brand the bone.
To sear the path forever more,
Destiny closes all other doors.

Her voice echoing in the background, I drank. The mist rose out of the chalice to surround me, and suddenly, I couldn't see Rhiannon anymore—or anyone. I was alone, and the sweet nectar slid down my throat like the strongest of liqueurs, flaming through with a frozen brand.

It sent me sweeping out of my body, into the mists, into the winds, into the cold of ice and snow, and I realized I was blind. I could not see, could only hear the howling of winds in the blackness. There were no words in my throat, no screams, no tears, no voice of any kind. Too startled to panic, I followed the ride as it coiled me round, swept me this way and that, and then, after a slow descent, I felt myself settle again back into my body. My vision began to clear. I let out a gasp but still could not speak. My tongue was frozen, my vocal cords unable to respond.

I wanted to glance at Rhiannon, but something inside said, *Don't*, and so I kept my gaze on Lainule, who was still standing there over us. I realized someone had taken the chalice from my hand.

"The initiation has begun." Lainule leaned down, looking first at Rhiannon, then at me. "You will meditate in silence until we come to get you."

And with that, two guards lifted us to our feet and led us out of the chamber before we could say a word or even look at each other. They separated us, keeping us at a distance, and Rhiannon was taken down a corridor to the right, while I was led down a passage to the left.

We stopped in front of a locked room, and the guard unlocked it, then escorted me in, glanced around, and left again.

The light was dim—emanating from the walls. I could see through the shadows enough to note that there was a bed, and a vanity, and a chamber pot.

As he shut the door softly behind me, I turned to find Druise waiting in the shadows. She curtseyed and pointed to a tray on the vanity, then quickly, silently, exited the room. I opened my lips, but nothing came out, so I crossed to the vanity. A sheet of paper—delicate and crackling—lay rolled in a scroll, tied with a blue ribbon. I picked it up, holding it for a moment before I pulled one end of the ribbon. The bow fell away, and I gently put the tie on the table, then unrolled the scroll.

A fine handwriting, delicate and yet at the same time strong, sloped across the page. As I began to read, the lights fluttered—the Fire Elementals flickering as if they were trying to escape.

> By the order of the Royal Court of Unseelie, the Supreme Court of Winter, it is decreed that upon the tide of Midwinter, at one hour before the striking of midnight, Cicely Waters, Cambyra Fae and Magic-Born Witch, shall ascend to the throne of the Court of Snow and Ice, in the northwest territory of the Northern Continent, where she shall reign until her death.
>
> By the order of the Royal Court of Seelie, the Supreme Court of Summer, it is decreed that upon the tide following Midwinter, at one hour after the striking of midnight, Rhiannon Roland, Cambyra Fae and Magic-Born Witch, shall ascend to the throne of the Court of Rivers and Rushes, in the northwest territory of the Northern Continent, where she shall reign until her death.

*Let nothing interfere with the fulfillment of this
decree, upon pain of death.*

Evanshide, Queen of Unseelie
Lyanshide, Queen of Seelie

The words blurred slightly as I stared at the scroll. Midwinter was . . . tomorrow. *Tomorrow.* The suddenness once
again struck home and I slid to the floor, leaning back against
the bed, shaking. What had seemed like a strangely distant
future had now become immediate. When we'd visited the
Eldburry Barrow, I'd logically understood it was going to be
my home, but I hadn't thought of myself as Queen. As . . .

Another image floating through my mind struck me
cold, putting a stop to my train of thought. *The heartstone.*
I'd rescued Lainule's heartstone.

I forced my lips to form a breath of air, barely enough to
send it on the slipstream.

Ulean, are you there?

*You are supposed to meditate in silence. But what is it?
Are you all right?*

I picked at the blanket hanging off the bed next to me.
*Lainule had a heartstone. Tabera had a heartstone.
Will . . . Rhiannon and I . . . how . . . will we . . .*

*Will you have heartstones? Yes. Every Fae Queen from
time immemorial has undergone the initiation.*

Is that what happens? Does it hurt? How do they . . . I
paused, realizing that of all the things I had feared, it was
the creation of the heartstone. I'd seen Lainule's heartstone
melt back into her, but how . . . how did they get it out of
her in the first place?

*I cannot tell you anything about the procedure, Cicely.
I'm sorry, but you'll have to wait. You'll have to walk
through the ice without my help. And now, I have to leave
you for the night.* And she was gone.

The night passed slowly. I thought about disrobing, but
they hadn't said we could and I didn't want to get into trouble, so I tried to sleep without ruining my gown. But my

mind kept returning to the message. There was no backing out now. The Great Courts of Seelie and Unseelie knew what was going on. They had ordered our ascension to the throne.

At around two in the morning, I tossed the blanket back and restlessly crawled out of bed. It was useless to sleep. I wanted to talk to someone, to verbalize everything that was going on inside, but there were no words. No sounds. Out of curiosity, I tried the chamber door and found it locked. Feeling a little claustrophobic, I retired to the bed again. I wanted to take another bath, but the maids had to fill the tubs with steaming water.

Frustrated, I returned to the bedroom and paced in my gown. I was hungry, but there was absolutely no food in the room. The bedroom was large, but with the door locked, it felt small and cramped. And there was nobody else around.

Feeling on the edge of panic, I slowed my breathing and tried to focus on calming down. Lainule had specifically said we should meditate, so I crawled back onto the bed and leaned against the headboard, pulling the covers up to my chin as I crossed my legs and let my head rest against the headboard. I closed my eyes and counted from twenty to one, feeling my breath come a little easier. With my eyes closed, it was easier.

A few minutes later, I started to relax, counting my breaths. *Inhale-two-three-four, hold-two-three-four, exhale-two-three-four, hold-two-three-four.* Several repetitions and the strain in my neck began to relax. Several more and I found myself starting to slip into that quiet state that precedes a trance, where my senses of smell and hearing and knowing heightened, even as the mask blocked the world away from my sight.

One more long, deep breath, and I tumbled down the rabbit hole.

⚜

The night sky spread above me in an expansive blanket of stars as cold as ice. The ice of the far north. The ice that never melted. The ice that existed at the top of the world, in a sheet, built layer upon layer, through the eons, from the beginning of time. Existing outside the world, and yet touching it, this realm breathed a snow-kissed whisper, a reminder of death and darkness and the sleeping hours of the night. To my left stretched a sheen of white, snowdrifts that rolled along like dunes on a desert. To my right, a dark ocean, covered by vast floes, glacial mountains calving their children into the churning water.

I turned, looking for some frame of reference, but nowhere could I find a clue as to where I was. As I strove for understanding, thunder rolled through the air as black silhouettes of blue spruce and towering firs thrust up from beneath the ice, like ancient standing stones. One by one, they rose, creaking, cracking the world apart in their birth throes, until they had created a forest encircling the ocean of ice. Snow clung to the boughs like moss, dripping down in frozen webs, a network of lace and frost.

Behind me, a low rumble shook the ground, and I reached out to balance myself but realized the quaking hadn't thrown me off balance. It was as if I were a frozen pillar, strong and steady in a world that was buckling around me.

I turned in time to see blocks of ice come flying in, landing in rows to create pillars. The pillars became columns and the columns became walls, crystal clear and unclouded. The walls soared into the heavens, with minarets and turrets, building a castle as I watched. When the last block flew into place, the drawbridge opened and I saw that the chains were silver, but the door, again, was ice.

And then all was quiet.

The silence echoed thick, suffocating, and heady. I opened my mouth to whisper into the slipstream but stopped. Lainule had cautioned me to keep silence. I pressed my lips shut, searching for some sign of what I was supposed to do or to learn.

And then, as I stood there, in the frozen wastes, a faint voice echoed within the recesses of my mind.

Go into the castle. You must enter the heart of Winter and ignite the fire that does not burn.

I steeled myself. I was doing my best to remain calm, but the truth was I was afraid. Terribly afraid. Wherever this place was, it was so dark and wild and inhuman that I felt if I stayed here long enough, I'd turn into a statue, a pillar of ice, unable to move, unable to feel anything except the bone-numbing cold. I'd become part of the living landscape, frozen forever.

One breath . . . hold . . . exhale . . . another deep breath and hold . . . and three . . .

As I exhaled for the third time, I forced myself to move forward. At first, something seemed off, and then I realized I wasn't sinking deep into the snow but instead walking on top of it. Maybe it had a frozen crust? But as I reached down to gather a handful of snow, I saw that it was powdery, icy cold, but not iced over.

Let it be. Let it go.

Nodding, I continued on toward the open gate. The ice drawbridge had lowered across a deep chasm, and I hesitated again, creeping to the edge to look over. The fracture splitting the surface ran on and on, with no end in sight, dividing the castle from the ocean and from me. I cautiously got down on my belly and scooted up, watching for any sign that the snow beneath me might break and slide into the chasm. When I neared the edge, I peeked over the side.

In the blackness of the abyss, twinkling lights shimmered. It was as if I were looking into the night sky, as if this bridge were the only thing connecting two worlds floating in space. Gazing long and hard at the reeling universe that existed in the chasm, I began to feel insignificant, the smallest dust mote in the world, and everything that had been worrying me dropped away as I stared into the mirror of eternity.

Cicely, you must cross the bridge. You must light up the castle.

The words weren't from Ulean—in fact, I wasn't sure where Ulean was. I almost called out for her on the slipstream, but stopped. Once again, Lainule's admonishment to keep silence rang in my memory and I stopped. How-

ever, the trick had been won. Whoever had sent me the message had managed to snap me out of the trance that had kept
me riveted, and I realized I could have quite easily frozen to
death, sprawled on the ice, staring at the panorama below.

I forced myself to my feet and set one foot on the bridge.
The entire span shuddered. Another step, another shudder.
As I slowly made my way forward, the sound of splintering
ice caught my attention and I glanced over my shoulder.
The span—the drawbridge—was fracturing, thin cracks
racing through it like delicate threads.

Panicking—I was directly over the abyss now—I shook
out of my fear and raced forward. There was no going
back. I bounded across the ice, with the fractures dogging
my heels. The sound of shattering followed my footsteps—
the bridge was vanishing behind me in a hail of shards,
falling into the abyss.

And then, one last leap, and I was on the other side. I
turned just in time to see the rest of the bridge shatter and
then go tumbling into the chasm. One second later, and I
would have gone with it.

My breath coming heavy from both the exertion and the
cold, I stared at the canyon of darkness. There was truly no
going back. I couldn't jump that far. And the abyss went on
forever. I was here, in the castle, and I could only move
ahead. With one last glance at the plain of snow on which
I'd first found myself, I shrugged, turned, and walked into
the castle.

⋆

From inside, the castle seemed to be faintly lit with a pale
luminescence, but there was an emptiness to it that was palpable. Statues of people stood there, frozen. They were in
motion, as if they had been walking the halls and suddenly
turned to ice and snow. Even the furniture was carved from
ice, and there was something terribly familiar to this place.
I looked for windows but could see none.

As I crossed the gleaming floor, my boots echoed
against the ice. Where was I? I knew this space—I *knew*

that I'd been here before, and yet I could not place it. Searching my thoughts, I wandered from room to room, seeking something to jog my memory. Once, I thought I heard whispering and whirled, but it was only the sifting fall of snow in a corner of the room, where one of the figurines suddenly lost form and crumbled into a soft pile of white.

Shivering now, more from nerves than the cold, I followed a long hallway that curved toward the heart of the castle. The hallway sloped down and the grade grew steeper. I cautiously followed it, wondering that I did not slip. My boots weren't that great on ice, but I seemed to be able to walk without problem here.

I descended, listening to the creaks and groans of the ice around me, but after a while I became aware of a faint singing. I couldn't understand the language, but overlaying a hypnotic drumbeat, a sinuous melody from a mandora and a flute beckoned me onward. A woman's voice rode the soft thunder of drums and the fluttering melody. She vocalized no words but matched meter with the music, becoming part of the melody itself. The melody and voice entwined so effortlessly that after a moment, I wasn't sure whether it was actually a woman singing or the instruments weaving the sound of the voice.

I followed the ribbon of sound, entranced, summoned by the chant. Rounding curve after curve, I spiraled down inside the castle, totally enchanted. Wherever the song was leading me, I had to go. And deep inside, I felt a quake of fear—was I being snared into a siren song? But no, instinct answered. This was a journey I must take. There was no going back, and whatever lay ahead, I had to face.

I don't know how long I walked, but I began to be aware of flutterings of spirits riding the wind beside me, following me as I passed. They collected behind me, ghostly formless wisps, in the shape of clouds and fog, of mist and dark shadows in the night. I wasn't afraid of them—they meant no harm, but for some reason they latched onto me, this train of spirits.

After what seemed like hours, I came to a wall that

blocked the hallway. I paused, not knowing what to do next, but the song continued; the ribbon of chant insisted I go forward. I reached out to the ice that barred my passage, and the moment my fingers touched the surface, it fractured, as the drawbridge had, and fell away, shards exploding to the ground.

I gingerly stepped over the pile of broken ice and continued on, my ghostly caravan following. The passage went only another ten feet and then it opened out into a chamber so large that I couldn't see the other side. The room was more like a cave, and great crystals thrust out from every direction of the walls and ceiling. The floor was rough and uneven here, and I cautiously skirted the treacherous spots, stopping by a crystal that was as large around as I was and easily fifteen feet long. Thinking it was quartz, I reached out to touch it, but my fingers slid over the icy surface and I realized that everything here was formed of the ice from this realm.

I picked my way through the jumble of icicles until I came to the center of the room, and there, on a dais, was an exquisitely carved box, formed from silver, with a cushion as white as a distant sun sitting inside it. The box was waiting for something, and I wasn't sure what.

Beside the dais, a block of ice lay waiting, covered with a silver blanket and, beneath that, a fur rug. I stepped forward, knowing what I needed to do, even though I had no clue as to why I was doing it. I slipped out of my clothes, dropping them on the ground beside the dais, until I stood nude, my nipples standing at attention from the chill. I shivered, so cold I couldn't feel my body, but then, the next moment, the spirits gathered around me and led me to the bed of ice, drawing back the blanket. I slipped beneath it onto the fur rug, and they gently tucked the blanket in around me.

As the song continued to play, I found myself drifting, deeper into trance, and the sound of laughter and clinking glasses echoed around me as I faded in and out of consciousness.

❧

Sometime later, I woke, thinking I was back in my bed, but realized I was still in the ice chamber, still beneath the silver blanket. Worried—I'd never stayed in trance this long or this deep—I started to sit up but the spirits swarmed around me, gently pushing me back. I waited, now aware that this was real, not a dream. This must be part of the initiation.

Then, a voice inside asked, *are you truly in this realm? Is this the heart of Winter?*

Another sound slithered through the chamber, one that didn't belong in the song. I craned my neck, trying to see what was going on, and sucked in a deep breath. Four Ice Elementals were headed my way. I struggled to sit up, but the spirits were stronger than I and they pushed me back onto the bed of ice. There was nothing I could do, nowhere I could run.

There will be no return from here out. No second chance either way.

The Elementals gathered at my bed, beings of ice, with no features on their chiseled faces. They were smooth, gleaming, beings carved from the very element that they embodied. What long thoughts hid behind their frozen visages? Did they feel? Did they love? Hate? Or did they simply exist on an alien plane? Somehow they seemed far more distant than Ulean, but then—perhaps, to others, she seemed just as aloof and cold.

They held out their hands over me—one at my feet, one at my head, one on each side, and a low vibration began to reverberate through the room. It echoed through the ice, echoed through the air, echoed through my body and set my teeth to chattering. I began to shiver and then to sweat. Afraid now, I tried to sort out what was happening. And then I noticed that the two Elementals on either side of me had their hands directly over my heart.

The heartstone. They're creating my heartstone.

As soon as the thought raced through my mind, I knew

it was true, and I tried to stay as still as the grave. As still as ice.

Mist rolled from their fingers like fog off dry ice and began to fill the chamber. I focused on the lone icicle I could see hanging above me. Point down, it was directly above my heart, and a sudden fear swept over me. It was huge, and if it broke off and fell, it would pierce my chest. The icicle glistened, shimmering in the mist and fog, and I found myself unable to take my eyes off it.

The Elementals joined hands around me, and a low, deep baritone filled the air, vibrating through the chamber, as they began to chant. Their vocalizations ricocheted off the walls, and the crashing of ice shattered in response. Their voices joined the siren song that had lured me in, and the drumming grew stronger, tattooing itself deep into my mind until all I could hear was the pulse of rhythm, the sharp edge of the voices, the rise of melody. The Elementals' chanting overlaid the sound, blending and weaving, until the entire world seemed to be made of ice and music and the chill blast of air that rolled in with the fog.

I realized that I was having trouble breathing—my chest felt tight, as if some invisible serpent were coiling around me, squeezing till I could barely think. My heart felt like it was expanding, with nowhere to go. I tried to calm myself, but now real fear took over, and I realized I could not move. The spirits and the mist were keeping me down, and the Elementals' singing was hitting me directly in my heart chakra. A shift . . . and another . . . something was happening to me. I struggled, still unable to speak.

Trying to gulp air, I thrashed, lungs burning as they worked to break free of the constriction. And then, as the world began to waver and I realized I was dying, a light began to glow over my chest, a bright, intense, bluish light that was white hot at its center. It was emanating out of me, rising up in a flowing stream from my chest, and it crystallized as I watched, forming into a fist-sized blue faceted gem. Breathing forgotten, I stared, mesmerized, as the gem took on a life of its own. And then I knew. This was my heart-stone. Whatever they were doing to me, it was creating the heartstone that would forever be a part of me.

As I relaxed, giving in to the sensation of death, a rush of wind blew through me and I began to spiral out of my body. In front of me was the shadow shape of a great owl. She was white, with black bands on her wings, and her eyes gleamed blue, like the ice of my heartstone. I gasped as she leaned forward and spread her wings. They were huge, and beautiful, and stretched out in a hush of whispers, waving a breeze before them. Every sweep of her feathers com-manded the wind.

The owl pressed her head to mine, and I caught my breath as she blended into me, merging, melding, folding her wings around me only to have them disappear as they entered my body.

I am you. You are me. This is what you are becoming.

The owl's thoughts became my own, as did her hunger and the dark pull to live under the moon rather than the sun. She was a predator, feral and fierce, but she was not evil—no, she was nature incarnate, the cycle of life in action. She let out a loud shriek as an agonizing pain hit me in the chest, stabbing so deep that I reeled back into my body. I opened my mouth and found my voice again as the owl's shriek became my own, soaring through the chamber as the searing pain sliced me into ribbons.

The icicle on the ceiling shivered and then came crashing down. As the point aimed directly toward me, I screamed *"No!"* and it shattered into a thousand pieces, showering the Elementals and me with tiny shards of ice.

And then, as quickly as the pain had descended, and as long as it had lasted, with a sudden rush, it rolled back through my body like the sea, receding in a wave, and van-ished in a single puff of mist. The Elementals stood back as I lay, spent and panting, on the bed. The spirits departed, and I was once again free to move.

As I slowly sat up, I glanced at my chest, expecting to see blood or a wound, but there was no sign of anything amiss. And then, as I glanced over, the silver box caught my attention. In the center was a glowing sapphire, as brilliant and vivid as any stone I'd ever seen. It pulsed with my breath, it shimmered with my thoughts. And I realized, there, in the silver chest, was the core of my existence. *My heartstone.* And as long as it stood, barring accident or deliberate attack, so would I stand.

Chapter 7

My heartstone. I slowly sat up. Reaching out, I passed my fingers over it. With a glance at the Elementals, I went to touch it, but one of the glacial giants gently grabbed my wrist, stopping me. And then I realized—I must never touch the heartstone again, unless I wanted it to reabsorb into me as Lainule's had reabsorbed into her. I withdrew my hand and nodded at the Elemental.

They stepped back, standing two to a side by my heartstone. I had the feeling I was supposed to do something now but wasn't sure what. I hesitated, not sure if I should stand up. What had the ritual done to me? How had it changed me?

As I was debating, a soft sound caught my attention and I turned to see Lainule standing there. She looked different— and then I realized her hair was almost entirely auburn now, with golden highlights peeking through. Faint lines criss-crossed under her eyes. She smiled at me softly, though, and her eyes were luminous and moist, as if she'd been crying.

"Rhiannon—" It hit me that if I'd been going through this, so must have my cousin. "Is she okay?"

"She passed through the transformation. She is alive

and her heartstone lives. Now the heartstones must be hidden, and then the two of you will undergo your coronations. Twice morningtide has come and gone in this realm since you ventured here."

"I thought our coronations were to take place on the Solstice?" Time in the Fae realms still confused me.

"And so they shall. In this realm, time passes at a different rate, just as it did when you entered my realm seeking my heartstone. Outside, in the Marburry and Eldburry Barrows, barely a moment has passed, and outside the portals, the same. Tomorrow night, you become the Queen of Snow and Ice, Cicely."

She held out her hand and I took it, rising to my feet, if a little unsteady. I felt odd, different. As I steadied myself on the side of the bed, she handed me the silver gown and I slipped back into it.

"What does it mean, having a heartstone created out of you? I mean, how will it affect me?" There was so much I still didn't understand or know, and I wondered if I'd ever fully comprehend what was going on.

But Lainule laughed, her voice rich and reverberating off the walls. "Trust. Trust that you can hold this post, wield this power, grow into your position. When I was first Queen, it was terrifying. I was petrified that I couldn't meet up to the expectations. The Queen of Rivers and Rushes who came before me, she was brilliant and gracious and everyone loved her. I can never be as genial as she was, but we each must mold our rule around the person we are."

"What was her name? And why . . . how did you become Queen?" I leaned on her arm as we walked along, still feeling weak and dizzy. Oddly enough, the cold of the cavern no longer fazed me.

Lainule let out a long breath. She ducked her head, then smiled again. "Her name was Iolie, and she was the morning sun. Everyone loved her. She ruled for . . . I have no idea how long. I came to the throne relatively young. She was old . . . old past counting. I know the names of the Fae Queens before her, but they are simply words against the mists of time, now. Iolie was . . . stretched thin. When a Fae Queen lives for thousands of years, she begins to wane, little by little. Iolie lived so long she grew weary of life. She chose to reclaim her heartstone and return to the Golden Isle. She outlived her immediate heirs, but I was her great-great-great-great-granddaughter. And so I became Queen."

We were progressing through the winding hall now, and every wall, every panel and tile of ice in the castle seemed to glow from within with a rich, blue luminescence.

"I don't remember the lights."

"You created them. Drawing forth the heartstone has given life to the realm again. This place is part of the realm of Snow and Ice—it is far from your Barrow, but it is still part of your realm. You have given your lifeblood, your essence, to this place, and it renews itself. You've brought rejuvenation and renewal to the realm."

She laughed again. "Oh, Cicely—there will be so many things for you to learn and to see, and to experience. Have you not noticed that you no longer feel the extreme cold?"

I nodded. "Is that part of . . . this transformation?"

"Yes. Just as Rhiannon no longer feels extreme heat. All full-blooded Fae can withstand the elements better than the yummanii or the magic-born, but you were not full-blooded. Now, though, that you have melded yourselves with the realms, you have the powers of the Queens. There will be more. But mark my words carefully."

Here she stopped and turned to me, holding me by the shoulders. "You are not invincible. Queens can die. Queens can be murdered. Accidents can happen, even with the heartstones in a protected place. Do not let down your guard and do not be careless."

I nodded, taking her words to heart. Seeing her almost fade and die had proved that point to me better than any warning could.

"What about hiding the heartstone?"

"That is your next task. The Ice Elementals will help you. They will be at your beck and call, and none can thwart their powers. If an enemy tries to turn them, if their magic is so strong that it might succeed, the Elemental Guardian will simply crumble to shards. You will always have four Elemental Guardians that will do your every bidding. Others of their kind will hearken to you, but there will always be four bound to you. If one is destroyed, another will take its place."

A thought struck me, and I almost panicked. "I'm a Wind Witch, not an Ice Witch. What about Ulean? She'll still be with me, won't she?" I loved Ulean and couldn't bear the thought that I might have to give her up.

Of course I will be. You merge wind and ice now. Fret not, I am with you, my friend. Ulean's whisper came racing through the slipstream, and I almost jumped for joy.

Ulean! You're here!

I served Lainule even though she was Queen of Summer. Elementals are not tied to strict rules unless they have been bound to one person, and we are bound. Although an Ice Elemental could not stand in the Court of Rivers and Rushes and survive. Just as a Fire Elemental would wisp away here and grow weak.

Relieved, I tried to stand on my own, but apparently I was still too shaky, and Lainule grabbed my elbow and wrapped her arm around my waist. It felt odd, the Queen herself being my support, but she simply smiled and I gratefully accepted her help.

As we entered the main hall of the castle, I gasped. The frozen tableau had come to life, and all the statues carved in ice were living, breathing members of the Court. Or at least, at first I thought they were, until I noticed they were translucent. But they bustled around in a silent hush of activity.

Not sure what to think, I glanced at Lainule. "Who are they?"

"Shades of the Court of Snow and Ice. They are the memories of those who grew so old they faded into time rather than retreat to the Golden Isle. Their memory still lives; they still go about their business but with no notice of what transpires today. They are the specters of your court."

"Specters . . . what about those whom Myst murdered? Do they still haunt these halls? Do they still haunt the Marburry Barrow?" I gazed at the specters as they trekked through the hall, stopping, speaking to invisible companions, hurrying by on errands long, long taken care of.

Lainule's expression darkened and her shoulders stiffened. "You may find, in the Barrow itself, that yes, there will be ghosts that walk the halls. If you do, then be wary. Hauntings—ghosts—are different than shades. Ghosts who walk because of violent deaths can be dangerous and, at times, envy the living to the point of attack. I will warn Rhiannon, too. So far, we have seen none since we moved back into Marburry, but that doesn't mean they aren't there, skulking in shadows. If you do find ghosts, there are those in the Court who know how to deal with them. Strict will know who to ask."

And then we were at the door.

Lainule turned to me. "Here I must leave you for the moment and go waken Rhiannon from her ordeal. The Elementals will help you hide your heartstone."

"I'm still feeling weak—"

She held out a small cake. "Eat this, and all will be well." And then she vanished—just disappeared from where we were standing.

The cake in my hand felt light, insubstantial, but I bit into it and a honey-rich flavor spread through my mouth, so delicate and sweet that I closed my eyes so nothing would distract me from the taste. As I swallowed, a warmth stole through my body, flushing me lightly, as it renewed and recharged me. A moment later, I felt like I'd eaten a full meal and was on the top of my game. Whatever those were, I needed the recipe!

Shaking my head to clear my thoughts, I turned to find the Ice Elementals standing near me. One held the silver box, now closed. But I could feel the beat of my heartstone within it, and as I gazed up into their impassive faces, it dawned on me that they were holding my life in their hands.

Two went ahead, motioning for me to walk behind

them. The other two—with the box—fell in at the rear. I wondered how we were to get over the bridge—it had shattered—but there, in a swath of brilliant gleaming ice, a walkway crossed the chasm. It was solid and this time, when I put my foot on it, it held fast, with no splintering.

We crossed the bridge and they turned to the left, leading me toward the horizon of trees. I expected to get tired, with all that had gone on, but my stamina stood steady, and whatever was in that little cake had given me plenty of energy. And—as I'd noticed when I first arrived—I was walking on top of the snow, not sinking in.

My thoughts were racing as we approached the tree line. I wondered what Rhiannon was doing. She was likely readying herself to hide her heartstone in the realm of Summer, and I imagined she was being led by Fire Elementals.

Ulean, are you here? I asked into the slipstream, but there was no answer.

She cannot hear you. One of the Ice Elementals turned his head to stare over his shoulder at me, startling me.

Why?

She is not bound to die for you should others attack. She cannot know the location of your heartstone and you must never tell her.

His words hit home. My heartstone . . . destroy it, you destroy me. And no one, not Grieve, not Luna or Kaylin or Peyton or Chatter . . . or Ulean . . . could know where it was hidden. My Ice Elementals and I would be the only ones who knew where it was, and they would die before giving up the information.

The ramifications of what we were doing were beginning to work their way into my brain. Even in the past day or two, I hadn't really understood the magnitude of the transformations we were going through, but now I was beginning to grasp how much was at stake and just how far this was going to take us from everything we ever knew.

We walked in silence for what seemed like hours, but the cold did not chill me, and I did not tire. I was, however, getting a little bored. But then we came to the tree line, and here the trees ceased being silhouettes and became tower-ing sentinels, dark in their boughs, covered with frozen ice and snow. I reached out to touch one of the limbs, and the tree shuddered gently as a dusting of powder fell to the ground, taking one of the icicles with it. A howl echoed in the dis-tance, and I whirled.

"Animals? There are animals here?"

Of course. They live in the frozen land. Elk and rein-deer, the bear and the wolf and the fox, the owl and winter rabbit.

They led me into the wood, deep into the heart of the forest, and more time passed under the silence of the wood-land. But as we progressed, here and there I heard the echoing call of a bird, the rustle of a bush with animals hiding behind it. Life began to make itself known, and I felt a deep unwinding inside, as if a knot had loosened that I hadn't even realized was there.

And then we stopped at the foot of a tall fir tree. A pale glow from the snow told me that there was an entrance to a portal here—I'd seen this before when we went after Lai-nule's heartstone. I stood back as one of the Elementals brushed away a layer of snow and opened a trapdoor. And then he turned to me, handing me the box.

You must go alone. When you have set the traps and wards, then follow the path out.

Traps? Wards? How am I supposed to do that?

You will understand when you are there. We cannot fol-low you in this part of the journey, but we will be waiting.

I took the box from him, cautiously so I didn't acciden-tally open it, and then I knelt and peeked into the portal. Just as I'd figured, there was a vortex. It was spinning like a funnel cloud, only I was looking in from the top. The colors here—unlike those of the portal I'd passed through on my journey for Lainule—were blue and pink and frozen purple and white so bright it shone almost silver.

I had to go through it. And I had to take the box with me and not lose hold of it. I thought for a moment, then hiked my robe up to just above my knees. I laid the box in the material, then folded it over and knotted it tightly, creating a pocket. Then, holding tight to the knot, I steeled my courage and leaped into the maelstrom.

⚜

Sudden chaos . . . then, a deluge of wind and hail racing past . . . I'm in the center of the tornado and the whirl of colors threatens to blind. A dizzying array, a magnificent specter of winter to come, of winter past, as I spin, caught in the vacuum sucking me down . . .

A waft of air . . . I've left my stomach behind in the rush of the fall, but now I whirl lazily, like leaves caught in autumn's grasp, but this is not autumn and the boreal wind is biting even in its softer moments.

Buoying up . . . caught on the currents, riding them down as the shadows flicker past, a cacophony of color blinds me as a phantasmagoria of whispers ride the slipstream, echoing in my head like shouts from a distant camp.

One last gasp . . . and the colors vanish as I hurtle through a layer of mist to land, crouching, on the floor of a long, narrow tunnel.

Slowly, I unfolded myself, standing as I tested whether I'd broken anything, but I was unharmed. I stood, barefoot, on the floor of the tunnel, looking for some sort of illumination besides the light coming from the flashing vortex above me.

Faint twinkles of light sparkled from within the smooth walls. They were ice. At least, I thought they were, but when I actually went over to touch them, I discovered they were glass—clear tiles with swirls of color dappling them. The colors of winter. The colors of my realm. Unlike Lainule's tunnel, the illumination was very faint from within them, but I was beginning to understand. The light must have faded when Tabera had been killed. Once my heartstone was in place, it would return to this shadowy realm, as would life.

I followed the corridor. There was nothing else here that

was living—that much was apparent. I hurried, wanting to be done with this, wanting contact with my friends again. It felt like I had been alone for a very long time, and even Lainule's presence hadn't done anything to dissuade that feeling.

There were passages off the main one, but I kept straight—something inside told me that I'd know when it was time to veer off, and true to my instinct, I finally came to a T in the path. I looked to the left, then the right. A spark of light caught my attention. As I stared at it, I knew that was the correct direction.

As I turned to the right, my feet urged me to go faster and I found myself running. It was as if there were a magnet on the other end, a force I couldn't ignore. I raced down the hallway and suddenly skidded into a chamber filled with ice and snow and giant crystals—this time they really were crystals. Snow serpents coiled around the clear spires, eyeing me with their eyes, as black as the vampires'.

I paused. There was something I needed to do here. Something I needed to say. As I waited, striving to find some kernel of understanding, one of the serpents uncoiled itself and slithered over to me.

"You would set a guardian here, young Queen?"

I paused, looking around. The path to Lainule's heartstone had been fraught with dangers and guardians. "Yes, but I'm not sure how."

"Ask, and it shall be done."

I gazed at the serpent and it flicked its tongue in and out, and then it rose, coiling up till it could look me in the eye. For a moment I feared it might strike me, and those great teeth would easily rip holes in my face, but then it tilted its head to the side and I reached out, not thinking, and lightly stroked its head.

"You are here to watch over my heartstone, aren't you?"

"I am, if you would have me."

"Please, guard the path, then. Do what you need to in order to keep my enemies from harming me."

And it was just that easy. A sense of watchfulness filled

the air, and every other serpent in the chamber rose to attention. I turned back to the guardian snake.

"What's your name?"

"Dark Fang. By this you shall know me. I stand for you, Cicely Waters. I shall stand for your queenship." And then he moved out of my way, slithering to the side, and I passed on.

Once beyond the crystal chamber, I entered a long hallway. There I found a brigade of skeletons, unmoving, carrying axes. I gazed at them carefully until I found the one that looked like the leader. All too aware that their blades looked deathly sharp, I approached him and looked him over. A ring lay at his feet. I picked it up and slid it on my finger. Immediately, the warrior snapped to full attention, as did his company.

"Guard these halls for me. Let none enter who seeks to harm me." It sounded as good as anything and was the only thing I could think of.

The skeleton bent down to one knee, his bones creaking as he did so. He bowed his head. "As you will." The wind whistled through his teeth, rattling like a stiff breeze through quaking aspen.

As I passed, they closed ranks behind me, guarding the way.

I continued on, curious to see what the third guardian would be. Somewhere, in the back of my brain, I had a premonition as to what might be waiting, and I prayed I was wrong. Myst used them, and they were deadly and cunning and magical, but I really, really didn't like them. But as I entered the next chamber, I saw that my intuition had been right.

A forest grew here. How it grew beneath the ground I did not know, but trees stood tall, swaying in the breeze, and dark bushes filled in the undergrowth. All were covered in snow. The sky was a pale silver, but I knew it was actually a ceiling. From that ceiling, an intricate web of lacework, spun from frost and snow and spidersilk, spanned the ceiling. And hanging from the center, ice spiders. Huge, white with golden accents, they were intelligent and fierce. I shivered, staring at them as they waited.

I can't show my fear. They may react, whether or not I'm to be the Queen. I have to show strength and control.

My heart was pounding, but I forced myself to walk up to the web of the nearest—and biggest—spider. She stared at me with glittering faceted eyes and let out a low hiss, moving one jointed leg ever so slightly.

I didn't flinch, just stood, waiting. This was a game of poker, and as of yet, she was the strongest guardian—and strongest foe—I'd faced.

Lowering herself to the ground, she scuttled to stop directly in front of me. I didn't step back, didn't look away. After another false run, she seemed to deflate a little. "You wish me to guard your chamber?"

"I do. Guard it against all enemies who would seek to destroy me."

A light flashed between us and she backed away, returning to her web. "Pass, Queen of the Realm. My sisters and I shall stand sentinel."

I crossed through the snowy underground forest, pressing on until I came to another opening. The chamber into which I stepped was empty, but behind an alcove lay yet another chamber and I knew this was my goal. I glanced at the seat by the doorway. No one was there. I had to trust that all was as it should be, and I passed by the empty chair and into the next chamber.

At the center of the chamber was a tower rising into the air. The chamber soared so high I could barely see the ceiling, and a rock quarry was off to the far right. The tower was circled by stairs made of ice, and I knew exactly what to do. I'd seen the result once before. I hurried to the pillar and began to climb the stairs. Below, a dizzying panorama spread out; the chamber was at least the size of a football stadium.

I hurried up the round staircase that encircled the tower, and when I reached the top, I found a dais. An indentation waited—just the size of the box with my heartstone. Untying the knot in my hem, I cautiously pulled out the box and opened it, one last time. I didn't touch the gem, merely watched the slow pulse of blue in the heart of the jewel. This was me. This was my essence. My life, and I held it all in my hands, in that one little box, encased in a gem that would—with luck—rest here until I was ready to walk into the mists.

Slowly, reverently, I placed the box on the dais. For a moment nothing happened, and then a dome of crystal covered the box, and the dais descended into the center of the tower. A rumbling caught my attention—the tower was shaking. Without thinking, I flung myself off the side and transformed into an owl, but instead of getting caught in my gown, as would normally happen if I forgot to undress, the gown shifted with me and I swung up and around the tower as it began to lower itself into the ground.

I flew down to the bottom and transformed back. As my clothing shifted back with me, I smiled faintly. Another perk of being the Queen.

The tower rumbled and grumbled its way into the floor, turning and twisting like some behemoth, and when it vanished, stones began to fly up from the quarry to the right. A structure built itself as I watched, each stone fitting in place until the top of the tower was hidden from view and the hole into which it had sunk could be seen no more. Lastly, a door sealed the front of the stone compartment. The door was silver, with a lock, and within that lock, a key. Lainule's heartstone had been locked away behind two keys—one for Summer, one for Winter. But I had the feeling that had been altered to be that way when the Queen of Winter had been murdered.

I reached out and slowly removed the key, holding it in my hand.

Now what? My heartstone was sealed away, but I couldn't keep the key with me. At that moment, a faint humming echoed from just outside the door and I followed it, the key firmly in hand. A woman sat on the chair that had been empty, and behind her a doorway was now visible.

She regarded me carefully, then handed me a velvet box. The box had a velvet cushion within, and an impression the size of the key. I set the key within the box and then closed it, looking up at the woman. She did not speak, but I knew what she was and I didn't want that deafening voice echoing in my head.

"You are an Air Maiden, are you not?"

She inclined her head.

"You will guard this chamber."

Again, she nodded. And then she curtseyed and I curtseyed to her—the Air Maidens were terribly powerful and their voices could rack the brain.

Satisfied, I turned back to the recess behind her and turned the doorknob. The door opened with a start, and I stumbled into yet another chamber. As I'd expected, there was a large pond, but the pond was iced over, and a dark shadowy woman knelt by the side of it. She watched me, saying nothing, as I walked to the edge.

There was no boat, no way to the center, but I knew where I had to go. I struck out on the ice, praying it would hold my weight. Once again, I found that I could glide across it with no problem. I crossed to the center of the pond and looked down. A hole, some twelve inches wide, marked the center, and I knelt down and breathed onto the water churning below.

"I have come. Reveal yourself to me." It sounded good, and it was what my instinct told me to say.

At first nothing happened, but then I glanced up to see the dark woman crawling along the ice. She reached the other side and spoke in some guttural language that had its roots in a culture so primal I doubted anyone could understand her. A moment later, a dais rose up from the center of the ice, and on that dais rested a silver bowl with cover. I quietly placed the box with the key into it, then replaced the cover and stepped back. With a low rumble, the dais withdrew back into the water, and the ice covered over as if it had never been anything but one solid sheet.

The woman pointed to me, then to the other side of the

lake, and I nodded, following her direction. As I came to the shore, I turned back. She was watching, waiting, and the entire chamber felt like it had gone on high alert. I stepped onto the shore, and there my Ice Elementals waited. I was about to say something when one of them blew on me with an icy breath, and I went tumbling into the darkness.

Chapter 8

When I opened my eyes, I was back in my room—the one I shared with Grieve—in bed. I sat up, wondering if this had all been just a weird dream, but one look at his face told me that it hadn't. Grieve was sitting on the edge of the bed, holding my hand, watching me.

As I struggled to shake myself awake, he pulled me into his arms. "You're all right." He let me lean back against the headboard but pressed my hands to his lips, and I realized how frightened he'd been.

I blinked. "What time is it?"

"Morning, my love." He shrugged. "Tonight is your coronation. But for all intents and purposes, you are the Queen of Winter now. You've created your heartstone and the guardians accepted their posts." He paused, then leaned down. "May I kiss you, Cicely?"

"Why do you ask?" I murmured softly, wondering at the look on his face.

He smiled softly. "You are the Queen. You will choose your consort. It's only proper for me to ask."

"Don't be ridiculous." I draped my arms around his

neck and pulled him against me. "You are the only man I'd choose for my Consort. Grieve, when will you understand how much I love you?" I kissed him once, twice, then spread my legs. I was still naked under the covers.

"I want to—oh, how I want to, but I can't." He kissed me again, then pushed himself back away from me. "I cannot touch you again until after you've taken the throne." He groaned as I let out a sigh. "Don't make this harder than it already is, woman."

I giggled and ran my hand over his crotch. "Oh, it's hard, all right."

"Pity, woman. Pity!" His expression melted my desire to torment him, and I pulled my hand away.

"When I have that crown on my head, I expect you to fuck me so hard, so long that I can't even remember my name." Wrapping my arms around my knees, I yawned. "I can't believe I'm still tired."

"You should be exhausted. The creation of the heart-stone, it's a harsh process and you'll feel odd for a while." He glanced at the clock. "Lannan wanted to see you last night. Lainule sent word that you won't be available to anyone until after the coronation. He was *not* amused." Grieve didn't look very happy either.

I grumbled. "Lannan . . . what the hell does he want? Don't answer that. It's bound to be bad news, no matter what. So, since I'm Barrow-bound until coronation, and sex is a banned activity, what should I do?"

At that, Grieve laughed. "Get up and get dressed. Your advisor, Strict, is waiting for you. It's time for a conference. I shall be sitting in, as King-Elect."

Oh great. Homework already?

"Is there a chance for me to see Rhiannon? I want to make sure . . ." I wanted to make sure she was okay, that they hadn't been telling me just what I wanted to hear.

"I think I can make that happen." He kissed me again, this time on the forehead. "You get dressed and I'll go talk to Lainule." As he headed toward the door, my gaze was fastened on his butt. He was wearing tight jeans, dark black, and a pale silver long-sleeved satin shirt. He'd switched his style, I realized. Instead of summer colors, he was now wearing darker ones—the shades of winter.

As Grieve closed the door behind him, I slipped out from beneath the covers and padded over to the long mirror. As I stared at my reflection, searching for any sign of where the heartstone had been extracted, I noticed that my skin had paled even further . . . and . . . what? I leaned closer.

What the fuck? My eyes, which had been a warm emerald, were now icy blue. The look was striking against my stark black hair and pale skin. I was still me, but a heightened me.

The door opened and Druise entered. She smiled at me shyly and dropped into a deep curtsey. "Your Highness, may I help you dress? The Lady Lainule has asked that you come down to breakfast directly, so there's no time for a bath. I'll make sure to prepare one for after your meetings." Her voice shook.

I winked at her. "Of course."

She crossed to the wardrobe and opened it, pulling out a long black skirt embroidered with sparkling stars, and a silver corset. "Will this be acceptable?"

Nodding, I turned to her. "Are you nervous, Druise?"

Blushing, she ducked her head. "Yes, Your Highness."

"Why? What's going on?"

Her cheeks grew even redder. "You . . . you're . . . the heartstone. Everyone knows you and your cousin have passed through the journey to create your heartstones. You are about to take the throne. Then . . . you really will be the Queens and everything will change. And I will be . . ." She paused, pressing her lips together.

"You'll be the Queen's personal maid. And this will impact your family and you in ways that you've never expected?"

At her look of relief, I knew I'd hit the nail on the head. She teared up, and dashed the tears away before they fell.

"Yes. I'm ever so happy. Please don't mistake me, Your Highness. But it's overwhelming. I'm not sure . . . am I

grand enough for the job? My family, they depend on me."
At that, she sank down, covering her face.

I leaned down and tipped her chin up so she was looking
at me. "Druise, listen to me. This is overwhelming for me,
too. I wasn't born to this—I never expected any of this, and
it's all happened in the past few weeks. We'll learn together,
okay? And speaking about grand . . . I'm not grand enough
for the job, but it's mine and I'll do it. So we'll muddle
through together, okay?"

She flashed me a grateful look and hurried to her feet.
"I'm sorry, Your Highness. I should never trouble you with
my worries."

"Nonsense. If something's wrong, I want to know. You
understand me?"

She nodded.

I smiled. "That's better. Let's get me dressed."

As Druise scurried to gather my underwear and bra, I
forced myself to wait for her. I wanted to pick up my brush
and just run it through my hair, but I was learning. No
more meltdowns.

She hooked my bra after I slid into my panties, and then
I slid on my skirt. She laced me into the corset and I pulled
my leather jacket over the top. As she brushed my hair, pulling it back into a sleek ponytail at my request, I dabbed on
some mascara and lip gloss. Lastly, I pulled on my favorite
boots and zipped them up.

The door opened and Grieve peeked around the corner.
"If you hurry, you can talk to Rhiannon before heading into
your meeting with Strict. She'll be at breakfast with you."
He motioned for me to hurry and I gave Druise a thumbs-up,
then followed him out the door.

Breakfast was held in our main gathering spot. We
weren't allowed out much to interact with the population
yet. Rhiannon was there, standing with her back to me. She
was dressed in forest green and gold, and when she turned,
I gasped because her eyes had shifted color, too. They were
gold, no longer hazel, and they glimmered with an unnatu-
ral light, just like mine.

She seemed different, taller and more regal. As she gazed at me, her face lighting up, I knew that she was seeing me in a different light, too. I grabbed her and hugged her, and she wrapped her arms around my waist and rested her forehead against mine.

"Was it terribly painful for you, too?" The look in her eyes told me that it had probably been harder on her than me.

"It wasn't a walk in the park, that's for sure. Are you okay?"

She gazed into my eyes, and it felt like we were testing each other, to see where we were. "Yes, but I feel so odd, and I miss talking to you. It feels like they're keeping us apart as much as they can."

"I think they might be." I glanced around. Lainule wasn't here yet, so I pulled Rhia aside. "You know they don't want us mixing now that we're moving to separate Courts. I know Wrath doesn't mind so much, but we're bucking tradition and it's going to be a struggle to make certain we don't just knuckle under because that's the way it's always been done."

Rhia shook her head. "We won't. Lainule and Wrath will be leaving soon, and we'll be the ones in charge. And you know Chatter and Grieve will do whatever they can to make us happy."

I studied her face. She meant what she said. I just hoped that we'd both have the courage to fly in the face of tradition and create something new out of the two Courts—because it was time, like it or not, for the world of the Fae to face the present and move forward.

"We'll talk. I have to eat—I'm starved—and then my advisor, Strict, wants to meet with me. I have a feeling this morning's going to be crammed with facts and figures and lists of things to remember." I frowned. "He lives up to his name."

"I'm meeting with my advisor, too. Edge. She's very nice, but I have the feeling that she'll live up to her name too, if I do something she doesn't like." Rhia laughed then, and I giggled with her.

"I'm glad you've had a chance to catch up, but we must

hurry. Cicely, Rhiannon, your advisors await. I will sit in with Rhiannon. Wrath, my husband, you tend to Cicely." Lainule was standing in the door, a faint smile on her face. Her hair had turned entirely auburn, a blazing bush.

I stared at her. "Your Highness . . ." It was impossible to ignore the changes in her coloring, on her face.

"Don't be surprised, Cicely. I warned you this would happen. And it's all right, truly. When I return to the Golden Isle, I will stop aging until the end of my natural life span. Until then, I continue to change." The Queen of Summer was now autumn's matron, and she looked tired, but happy.

"Rhiannon, Cicely, tonight you will undergo your coronations. Then you may plan your weddings. I am afraid that Wrath and I shall not be able to stay until then. But our hearts will be with you." And she turned, motioning to Rhia, and glided down the hallway.

Wrath nodded for me to follow him. I caught up to him, Grieve on my heels. For a moment, Wrath didn't say anything. Then he glanced back at us.

"Daughter, I am . . . there are no words to express how glad I am you came through the trial. I know what it entails, but we are never allowed to warn the prospective Queens what they will face." He looked tired, and when I looked closer, I saw that he, too, was changing. His face was lined, like Lainule's, and his jet-black hair was peppered with white.

"Will you truly be all right when you go back to the Golden Isle?" I didn't want to lose him. I'd only just found my father, and I couldn't imagine losing him again. "I wish you could stay here."

"I wish we could, too, my dear. But we can't. You, Cicely, and Grieve, you must take up the crowns without us to guide you. As well as your cousin Rhiannon, and Chatter. But you will have help where you least expect it. Do us proud. Defeat Myst and lead your people well."

He turned in at one of the doors to the side of the passage, and we followed. Inside was what appeared to be as close to a conference room as I'd seen in the Barrow. Strict was there, along with a woman whom I hadn't yet chanced to meet. She reminded me vaguely of Regina with her shimmering black form-fitting dress and upswept golden hair.

"Cicely, meet the keeper of the Treasury, Silverweb. She keeps the accounts. Not that money is all that much of an issue among the Courts of Fae, but still . . . we must keep tabs of what we accrue."

Silverweb gave me a quick curtsey, then immediately pulled out a thick ledger and hoisted it on the table. She was all business, and before I could sit down, she was flipping through the pages.

"Since the Court of Snow and Ice was overrun by Myst, we would think that the coffers were depleted, but the Indigo Court appears to have had no need of money. Most of the gold and silver was intact, as were a good share of the Eldburry Barrow's nonephemeral treasures. The vast majority of art, along with a great deal of our glassware, was destroyed in the battle for the Barrow, which is a tragic loss, but most of the precious metals were left intact, although a few pieces were dented. Restoring the Barrow cost a pretty penny, even with our artisans' volunteering. But the treasury is at sixty percent of its former reserves, we estimate." She pointed to some figures, but I realized I had no clue what the words beside them said.

"I can't read that. Just the numbers."

Wrath rubbed his forehead. "A stumbling block we did not think of—and it will be the same for your cousin. You were not brought up here, so of course you cannot read our language. I see we shall have to arrange for a tutor to start working with you the day after tomorrow. You must learn the tongue as quickly as possible."

I hadn't even thought of that little matter. Everyone around me had spoken to me in English. But now that I thought of it, it made perfect sense—the Fae would have their own language, their own dialects, their own lexicon.

Sobering, I stared at Strict, Silverweb, and Wrath. "I'll have to trust my advisors until I become proficient in the language."

"You have me, my love." Grieve took my hand. "I will translate for you when it is needed, and work with you when we are alone to help you master the language."

Strict leaned back. "This will be a learning experience for all of us. Meanwhile, I can instruct you in the laws of the land—take notes in your own language so you don't forget. You will be administering justice, Your Highness. You must know what boundaries are set and, if you so choose, change them."

I jerked my head up. "Change them? You mean if I don't like something, I can change it? Without questioning?"

He cocked his head to one side, smiling faintly. "If your changes are too disparate, the Greater Unseelie Court may call you to question, but for minor things? Yes."

And so we got to work—me with a notebook, Strict teaching me the legal system of the Court of Snow and Ice. I immediately understood that it was darker than Lainule's court. There was a greater leeway on suspect behavior, and harsher punishments for those things proscribed. The sorting out would take months, but as we progressed, I began to see that I was going to be Queen over a feral and wild populace.

Three hours later, I sat back, limp, with pages of notes I'd jotted down.

Strict leaned across the table. "It is much to take in, but that is what I and your other advisors are here for. We're to help you make this transition, and it will take some time. We all expect that. It was bad enough when I helped Tabera take the throne, and she was born for it. But you . . . you may have been born with the destiny, but you were not born into Court, so you are still unfamiliar with all of the ways of our people. *Your* people, too, you know," he added softly. "You are half Cambyra on your father's side. You have our blood running through your veins."

I'd been suspecting something for some time, and now I looked directly at Wrath. "You were born to the Court of Snow and Ice, weren't you?"

He paused a beat, then nodded. "Yes. I moved to the

Court of Rushes and Rivers when I met your mother. I fell in love with her, before she was Queen. I switched sides for her. But yes, the Winter . . . it is my true home."

I met his gaze. "You and Lainule, you crossed courts like Grieve and I did in our life long ago. Perhaps not quite the same—Summer and Winter do not battle, generally. But you defied tradition."

He winked at me then, his smile broadening. "That we did."

And then Strict dismissed me for the day. "You must prepare for your coronation tonight."

"Will Rhiannon and I take the thrones together?" I was hoping for a yes, but I already knew the answer.

"No. You will ascend to the throne in the Court of Snow and Ice at one hour before midnight. She will take the throne in the Court of Rivers and Rushes at one hour after midnight—when the year has begun to wax again. You will be moving to the Eldburry Barrow today."

"Today . . ." And then it hit me—this was it. Today was my last day as just Cicely Waters. Tonight, by midnight, I would be Queen of a strange land. And a strange people. I sucked in a deep breath, feeling overwhelmed. "I can't do this . . ."

"You can, and you will. You've passed through the hardest part. If you were not meant to take the throne, you and Rhiannon, you would have died when your heartstones were being extracted from you. There is no turning back, my daughter. You're just afraid. Go now . . . spend some time outside the Barrow, but do not stray far. Get a breath of fresh air and take your cousin with you." Wrath motioned to Grieve. "Attend them, and keep them safe."

Grieve bowed to my father, then took my arm, and we headed back toward the common room. Rhia was just sitting down to lunch with Chatter. Peyton, Luna, and Kaylin were nowhere in sight.

"Cicely!" Rhia jumped up and grabbed me. She had a look of panic on her face, one I recognized only too well. "I'm . . ."

"I know. Me, too. Let's eat lunch and then go for a walk. Grieve and Chatter can come with us, but we need to talk." I glanced around. "Where are the others?"

"Today's moving day. They're up at the house, putting things to rights."

"I want to go there. To help them. It will take our minds off tonight." I turned to Grieve. "You will go with us?"

He shrugged, and—with a sideways smile at Chatter—said, "Do we have a choice?"

"No." Feeling a little better, I sat down and dug into my beef and mashed potatoes.

❧

As we emerged from the portal, with Check and Fearless behind the four of us, I shaded my eyes. The winter was still raging, and it felt like it had when Myst had controlled the Golden Wood. She must be near.

As we started along the path, I gasped. "Rhia—look at you. And me!"

Instead of sinking deep, we were walking on top of the snow, like Grieve and the others. Marveling at the ease with which we were able to travel, I danced around, jumping up and down. My leaps made little mark on the surface, and—to my delight—barely scuffed the top layer of snow and ice.

"I can't believe this!" Rhia laughed. "But . . . can we run as fast as you guys?"

"I don't know, my love. Why don't you find out?" Chatter's eyes were glimmering as he teased her.

She took off, with me on her heels. Our speeds had increased, though we still weren't nearly as quick as the full-blooded Fae, but we'd definitely picked up steam. Grieve and Chatter were laughing at us, but we didn't care. We were like kids in a candy shop. We jogged through the woods, eager to try out our changing abilities. We reached the house in less than a quarter of the time that it would have taken before the change and ran laughing up the steps.

As we burst through the doors, giddy, an odd smell

caught my attention—one I was all too familiar with. I looked around, nervous now, motioning for Rhia to wait behind me. Grieve and Chatter came through the door, and I turned to them.

"Get the guards in here, now. Something's wrong. I can smell it." What I smelled was blood. And I'd smelled too much blood lately to be wrong.

Rhia's eyes narrowed. "I can smell it, too," she whispered.

Praying that we were wrong, that whatever it was we were smelling was throwing us off the mark, I moved toward the door leading into the dining room. Grieve grabbed my arm, shaking his head. Chatter had already darted out back, and now he returned with Check and Fearless.

The guards took the lead, motioning for us to stay behind until they'd checked things out. I didn't bother arguing. I knew it would be futile.

A moment later, Check shouted for us and I rushed through the half-open door, followed by the others. There, in the middle of the room, Peyton and Luna were huddled near Kaylin. The girls were tied up but conscious, and duct tape was strapped across their mouths. Kaylin, unbound, was sprawled on the floor, covered with blood, and he wasn't moving.

"Kaylin!" I pushed past Grieve, dropping to his side.

"I found a body over here!" Check called from the living room.

Grieve motioned for Chatter to go help him, while Fearless scouted the room and then ducked out. I could hear him going up the stairs—faintly but enough to tell me he was making sure we weren't going to be ambushed.

Rhiannon knelt beside me as I frantically ripped open Kaylin's blood-soaked shirt. His chest was unharmed, but he'd been stabbed several times in the side, and he'd lost a lot of blood by the looks of the pool of it drying around him.

"Kaylin!" I screamed at him, trying to jog his demon awake. His night-veil demon was strong, and maybe it could help me revive him. I began compressions on his chest, counting to thirty before I cupped his face and gave him mouth-to-mouth. Then back to compressions.

"He's still bleeding out!" Rhiannon turned to Grieve. "Give me your shirt! Now!"

As Grieve stripped off his shirt and handed it to her, I thanked whatever power it was that manifested his clothing as real and not *just* illusion.

Rhiannon rolled it into a ball and, maneuvering around me, pressed it against Kaylin's side, trying to stanch the blood. Grieve began to remove the duct tape around Luna's and Peyton's wrists. He gently tried to remove it from their mouths, but it was stuck firm, and finally, frustrated, Peyton shoved his hand away and yanked it off her face. Luna did the same. Both of them gave little screams as the adhesive ripped, leaving abrasions on their skin.

I was still trying to revive Kaylin. He wasn't coming around.

Luna crawled over to my side. "I can help."

I shifted to allow her room, and she took his head and placed it in her lap. Tears streamed down her cheeks, but somehow she found her voice and began to hum. The melody was haunting and made the hairs on my arms stand up. As she grew louder, the weaving sounds became words and she was suddenly singing.

"*Heal . . .*" Her voice stretched out into one long, sonorous note.

Hear me, dark-souled demon of mine,
Hearken to my song.
Come back from the night-bound shrine,
Come back into your body, strong.
I search you out, seeking across time,
I call you back with song and rhyme.
I call your soul, I call your breath,
I call you back from the door to death.
Obey me now, walker of the dreams,
It is not the time for you to leave.

Kaylin jerked under my hands—I'd been continuing the compressions. A moment later, he shook his head and weakly opened his eyes. Rhiannon removed the cloth—the bleeding had stopped.

"Kaylin, can you hear me?" I leaned down, looking into his face. His eyes were dark, flashing with red, and I could feel his demon close to the surface. We'd had words when his demon first awoke in his soul. In fact, we'd had a knock-down, drag-out fight.

"We hear you, woman."

So it was the demon. "Is Kaylin . . . is he with you?"

"Yes, but he's too weak to speak. His body has lost a lot of blood and needs attention. I cannot bring him back further from the veil until he's attended to. Even then, he will need a great deal of recuperation." The demon closed his eyes and Kaylin fell into a deep sleep, his breathing shallow.

"We need to take him back to the Barrow." I looked up at Luna. "What happened? Are you and Peyton all right?" I'd been so focused on keeping Kaylin alive that I'd forgotten to ask how they were.

"We weren't hurt. Kaylin tried to protect us, but . . . they were too strong."

"Shadow Hunters?" But I didn't think so. If it had been the Vampiric Fae, they wouldn't have stopped until all three of them were dead.

"No. I think . . . day-runners."

Leo. Or Geoffrey. It had to be one of them or both. "Did they say anything?"

"They were threatening to kill us if we didn't take them to you. Then Kaylin came in and started to fight them. He hurt both of them—bad."

"He killed both of them, actually." Check returned from the other room, Chatter behind him. "Two of the yumma-nii. Dead in the other room. Looks like Kaylin released his demon on them—they're ravaged worse than he is."

"They had tied us up by the time Kaylin stumbled in on us. He chased them into the other room and we heard a horrible noise—shouts and screams. Then Kaylin staggered back in, and he was trying to undo the tape when he passed out. Luna and I couldn't do anything." Peyton stared darkly at Kaylin. "I haven't felt so helpless since Myst captured me and had me in her lair."

Luna ducked her head. "I can do nothing magically without my voice. The duct tape . . . prevented it."

"It's obvious that we can't do anything until we catch Geoffrey and Leo. Come on; we have to get him back to the Barrow, and you two are coming with us. We should also take the bodies back. Maybe we can figure out some way of getting information out of their spirits." I stood back as Fearless hoisted Kaylin over his shoulder.

"I'll head back as fast as I can go. The rest of you follow, and be careful." He took off, a blur against the snow as we watched him race across the yard from the window.

I pulled out my cell phone and sat down at the desk to check my messages. Kaylin was in good hands, and he should make it. Fearless wouldn't let anything happen to him on the way there.

As I punched in Lannan's number, I knew he wouldn't pick up—he'd be sleeping—but I got his voice mail. "Geoffrey and Leo's sidekicks just about killed Kaylin, and they were threatening to do the same to Peyton and Luna. We have to find them, and we have to find them soon. I'm going through my coronation tonight, but tomorrow night I want to meet with you and Regina."

After leaving the message, I checked the news on my phone's browser. The headlines made me cringe. "Fuck. Another three deaths. Crawl—it has to be Crawl. He's always hungry, and he'll be gorging himself. I wonder if he's staying with Leo and Geoffrey, or if they just turned him loose to his own pursuits."

My messages showed that Ysandra had called me. I tapped in my voice mail password and listened. The news was just as bleak. The Consortium was demanding our appearance, and she had only been able to put them off for another two days. So day after tomorrow, we had to show up in front of them.

I told Rhiannon this, and she shook her head. "This is bad."

"Things are chaotic. I'm glad we're taking the thrones tonight. We've been spending so much time focused on this whole mess that we haven't had time to really pay attention to what's pushing our buttons."

Grieve cleared his throat. "The problem isn't that you've had to focus on the coronations. The problem is that there aren't any aspects to your life right now that aren't a priority. The Fae Courts, the situation with the rogue vampires, the Consortium, and Myst—they are all major concerns in their own right, and they are all competing for your attention."

I pushed myself to my feet and texted Ysandra that we'd be there. After I finished, I turned off my phone and asked Check to lock the front door.

Turning to Grieve, I shook my head. "I try to make up to-do lists, but they keep getting blown away by the other stuff coming in. Strict will just have to postpone the tutor for a while until we catch Geoffrey and Leo. You can work on teaching me until then, and you can keep an eye on anything that needs a translator to understand. I think, my sweet, that you and Chatter are going to have to do more than the former Kings had to do. Share-the-wealth kind of thing."

We headed out the back, Luna and Peyton in tow. The snow kicked in again and was beginning to fall in great, thick flakes. I realized that I wasn't shivering like the others. As we entered the Golden Wood, the afternoon was beginning to wear away. Even though I was about to become Queen of Winter, the chill mist and ice scared the hell out of me, because I knew Myst was out there, waiting. A lone owl began to hoot softly from a nearby tree, and I glanced up. Not my father, that much I could tell, but it was another Cambyra Fae—another one of the Uwilahsidhe. As we passed by, it flew down, dipping in front of me in an almost aerial bow. I raised my hand in salute as the pale glow of blue and white glimmered through the woods.

Chapter 9

When we made it back to the Barrow, the healers had swept Kaylin away and he was being worked on. Seeing that he was not one of the Fae, but instead one of the magic-born with a night-veil demon attached to his soul, they were having to feel their way around, but they'd bound up his wounds and prevented them from getting infected. Luna sat beside him, holding his hand, but he was still unconscious. I sat down beside her and took her other hand.

"How are you holding up?"

She shrugged. "I don't know. Everything has been so topsy-turvy the past few weeks that I'm not sure whether I'm coming or going. I never expected . . ." She gazed down at Kaylin's sleeping form. "I never expected to walk into this."

"You and Kaylin . . . are you . . ." I wasn't sure how to ask it—I knew he had it bad for her, and I knew she cared about him, but I wasn't sure how far it had gone between the two of them.

She quietly replaced his hand, making sure the blankets were tucked around him. The healer—who was standing in the corner—nodded to her.

"Can we talk outside the room?"

I slipped my arm around her waist and we strolled out. She was tense; I could feel the stiffness in her shoulders. Once we were in the hall, we found a bench and sat down. I kept my mouth shut, sensing that she was gathering her thoughts. After a moment, she sat back, leaning her head against the wall.

"I could love him. I really could. Maybe I'm on my way to doing so. But . . . life . . . so much is up in the air. Where are we going to be tomorrow? Next week? You and Rhiannon have your lives mapped out for you now, but *we* don't. Peyton and I want to get our businesses started, but now it seems we can't, not until Geoffrey and Leo are caught." She grimaced.

I hung my head. "And they're on the prowl because of Rhia and me. We're the cause of this."

She shrugged. "True. You are. But if you weren't here, if all this hadn't happened, I'd probably be dead or in the hands of Myst, if what you read for me in the cards that first day is correct. In fact, the whole town would still be in her grasp. So a little uncertainty? Not a bad price to pay."

"What about Kaylin?"

"We'll take things slow. One day at a time. See where it goes."

Her practicality startled me. I'd pegged Luna for a very talented, sensitive woman, and here she was thinking logically. I smiled softly, realizing my own preconceptions were showing.

"But you need to go. You have your coronation tonight."

"Will you be there? You and Peyton? I doubt if Kaylin will be in any shape to make it."

Luna laughed then. "He'll live, but no, he won't be there. I will, though. And Peyton, too—at both your ceremonies." She stood, then leaned down and planted a quick kiss on my cheek. "Thank you, truly. For everything. New Forest would be lost without you."

"Without you, too," I whispered back, hugging her tightly.

❧

It was nearly four in the afternoon and I was starving. I hurried back to the common area, where I found Druise, frantic, looking for me.

"Oh, Your Highness. We have to begin preparing you for tonight. Where were you? I looked everywhere." She seemed to be at loose ends.

"I was checking on Kaylin. The ceremony doesn't start until eleven P.M.—do we really need all this time?" I glanced through the cupboards. "I'm hungry."

"Then, please, my Lady, get something and let us retire. We have to bathe you and dress you and then you have to meet privately with Lainule." And with that she pressed a jar of peanut butter into one of my hands, and two pieces of bread into the other.

"Don't forget the jelly," I said as she hustled me toward my room. She ran back and grabbed a jar of grape jelly and a knife. I grinned. The Fae were getting used to our odd eating habits. When I'd asked for peanut butter just a week ago, they acted like I was insane. And they knew that they should never offer me fish of any kind. I was EpiPen allergic to the stuff and not long ago had accidentally ingested some. That had been a laugh and a half—not.

While Druise checked the temperature of the steaming bathtub filled with water, I hurriedly slapped together a sandwich as I shrugged out of my clothes. She untied my lacing and I shimmied out of my skirt, then my panties.

Next step: I handed Druise my sandwich as I stepped into the bathtub and sank into the steaming bubbles. The fragrance of cool mint and bayberry overwhelmed me, and I leaned my head back. She handed me a towel to wipe my hands on, then my sandwich, and I sat in the tub, letting the heat soak into my muscles, as I swallowed the food in eight bites.

"So," I said, licking my fingers clean, then plunging them into the water, "what am I wearing tonight?"

I expected there to be a fancy dress—after all, this was my coronation, but I hadn't been expecting anything like what Druise carried in from the other room. I sat there in the tub, slack-jawed at the sight of the garment she bundled into the bedroom. Unable to speak for a moment, I scrubbed myself with the washcloth, then reluctantly stood as she motioned for me to hurry.

"*That's* my dress?" I stood up, cautiously stepping out of the tub, and pulled the towel around me.

She nodded, a soft smile playing on her lips. "It's ever so beautiful, Your Highness."

And beautiful it was. The strapless gown was long, with a corset bodice that had a sweetheart neckline, and it billowed out at the waist into princess style. In shades of silver and ice blue, the bodice was embellished with dozens of tiny shimmering black snowflakes that glistened in the soft light of the room. The skirt draped into long folds, iridescent, hovering someplace between silver and twilight. The dress had no arms, but a pale gray fur cloak with a silver brooch would keep me warm. Druise laid it out on the bed, then added a pair of silver ankle boots, with a delicate heel and buckles that jingled softly as she set them on the floor.

I slowly crossed the room and stopped, running my hand over the material. It was incredibly soft and light, but warm. My stomach flipped, ever so softly, and I wasn't sure just what I felt. Pride? Not exactly. But anticipation, yes. And hope—oddly enough, a flicker of hope for the future was beginning to build in my heart.

As I stood there, I realized this was really it. I'd been running all my life, running from the nightmares that had chased my mother. I'd spent twenty years on the move, struggling to keep us alive and, after she died, trying to find my own way. And now, at twenty-six years old, I was about to enter a new world. Instead of running *from* things, I'd be running them. *That* thought scared the hell out of me, but I pushed the fear away.

I dropped the towel. "I guess . . . should I dress now? What time is it?"

She glanced at the clock. We kept them around because, even though time in the realms of Fae ran odd, we had to keep tabs on the outside world as well. "Four thirty. First, let me prepare you."

That sounded odd.

"I'm clean. Apparently that's not enough?" But I didn't want her to think I was grumpy, so I grinned as I said it.

She motioned for me to lie down on what amounted to a massage table. Druise wasn't all that skilled as a masseuse, so I wondered how this would go. But she waited till I lay down, then covered me with a light blanket. After that, she opened the door and whispered to someone.

In came a member of Lainule's court whom I had seen several times but never been introduced to. I had the feeling she was high in rank, and when she glided over to me, I felt all too nervous and vulnerable, lying there naked.

But Druise clapped her hands. "Your Majesty, please allow me to introduce Gera. She is Her Majesty Lainule's healing therapist. She's here to give you a massage."

Gera wasn't wasting any time, either. She pulled down the blanket, oiled up her hands, and dug in. I grimaced as she began to work her way into the knots in my back. As she adroitly manipulated my muscles, the immediate discomfort lessened and I began to relax. As I closed my eyes, I began to feel something beyond the massage—there was magic in her fingers. Magic permeated my skin, seeping from her fingers, loosening the strain in my body, eating away at the stress. As she worked along my spine, I began to breathe deeper, my lungs opened up, and I sank into the warmth of the blanket.

Within minutes, I was dozing, drifting in a sea of comfort. I'm not sure how long the massage lasted, but at some point I felt her oiling my legs with a lotion that smelled like freshly fallen snow and cinnamon, and I opened my eyes. She finished, then helped me slowly sit up.

I yawned and stretched. My muscles were loose and I felt like I'd had a week's sleep. My skin was also smooth and silky from the oils, and I inhaled deeply, filling my lungs with the fragrance.

"Thank you."

Gera dipped into a curtsey, then silently exited the room. I glanced over at the clock. It was almost seven. My stomach flipped a little and I wished I could jump ahead in time and get it over with. I was looking forward to the coronation, yes, but waiting for things always set me on edge.

"What next?" I looked over at Druise. She seemed to have the schedule down.

She motioned for me to sit at the table near the bed. "I bring you dinner, Your Highness. And if you're wondering, you are to see no one but me and those who attend you before the coronation. You will see His Lordship there."

Assuming she was talking about Grieve, I followed her orders and sat down at the table, while she brought in my meal. Hot bread, venison, a round of cheese, and a goblet of deep red wine, which went straight to my head. As I stabbed at the meat with my fork, I glanced over at Druise, who stood at attention near the table.

"Are you hungry?"

She shook her head, dipping into a quick curtsey. "No, Your Ladyship. Thank you for asking, though."

"Why can't I see anybody before the coronation?" I wasn't complaining, but it did seem odd.

"They . . . it's . . . there are always fears of assassination."

That got my attention.

I put down my fork. "Have there been threats? Tell me the truth now."

She blushed. "I'm not privy to that information. But there are always dangers for royalty, Your Highness. And there are some who might think since you weren't born in the Barrow, perhaps . . ."

"Perhaps I don't deserve to wear the crown." I finished the thought for her. She blushed again but nodded. "So Lainule wants to make certain Rhiannon and I actually make it to the throne."

Druise nodded. "And they only trust those of us who've undergone loyalty tests."

"Loyalty tests? What does that entail?" I was beginning to think that maybe, just maybe, this would be a rough gig for the next few years while I tried to immerse myself in the culture and learn everything there was to learn. I also was beginning to see how vast the culture gap was.

She bowed her head, just enough to tell me it hadn't been pleasant. "They search your mind. They search your heart. I'm not certain what they're looking for, but they found me true to the throne, and that's when I became your lady's maid."

Having had Kaylin thrust himself into my mind once before, I knew how invasive that was. I gave Druise a faint smile. "I think I understand. I'm sorry you had to go through that."

She cocked her head and shrugged. "I was glad to. This position . . . as I've mentioned before, it means a great deal to me and my family. It . . . the testing hurt, and it felt like they were inside my mind, able to see everything in my thoughts, but then I don't have much to hide, Your Highness. I'm not very complicated." Lowering her gaze, she fiddled with her skirt.

"That's not a bad thing, Druise. Not at all." I went back to my dinner, mulling over the thought that not only were there those out there not entirely happy about me taking the throne, but it was perhaps to the extent that Lainule was worried about someone trying to off me. And Rhiannon, too.

After I'd eaten, Druise removed the dishes, and I brushed my teeth and washed my face. I decided to put on my makeup, but when she returned to see me sitting down at the vanity, she stopped me.

"Please, let me. I've been given instructions."

I wasn't sure I liked the sound of that, but I allowed her to work her magic on my face and hair. When I finally looked in the mirror, I scarcely recognized myself. She had made my face up in an intricate pattern of scrollwork, in shades of shimmering blue and silver, that wrapped around my eyes like a tribal tattoo, coiling down to my cheeks. My lips were the palest pink I'd ever seen, barely more than a hint of color in the gloss—almost white.

She had pulled my hair back from my face into a pattern of braids and curls that hung down my back. For the first time in my life, I felt absolutely stunning, exotic. Perhaps . . . even beautiful.

"Oh, Druise, this is so beautiful. Thank you." I was afraid to touch my face, afraid I'd mar the makeup. "But what if I start crying?"

"You won't hurt it. It's waterproof." When she smiled, her eyes crinkled, giving her a cheerful, fresh look that made me want to take her in hand and polish her up a little and marry her off to some good-natured man who would treat her right and give her a lovely home.

"Now we dress you, Your Highness. It's past nine, and the ceremony goes on for a long time before the coronation." She motioned for me to join her by the bed, where the dress was spread out. I dropped my towel that I was still wrapped in from after the massage and crossed the room.

As I stepped into my underwear, she fastened the hooks of my strapless bra. I saw that the dress was two pieces— the skirt and the corset bodice—which made it much easier to get into.

She fastened the buttons of the skirt around my waist, and I immediately saw that I'd need to practice walking in it; the train trailed out behind me for a good ten feet. I raised my arms as she wrapped the bodice top around me, and then I held it snug while she began to lace it up. After she tugged and pulled it into proper alignment, she sorted out the skirt, draping it just right.

"Now if you'll sit on the bed, I'll put your boots on for you." She held up the silver boots and I saw that they, too, worked on a lacing system.

"You people need to start using zippers."

"I agree." She flashed me a smile. "I have a feeling we'll be moving more into sync with the rest of the world once you and your cousin take the thrones, and that isn't a bad thing at all. There are so many ways we could help the outer world, and they could help us. Although the Weres do not like us at all, and the vampires fear us."

That was the first time I'd ever heard one of the Fae say anything of that nature. Oh, I knew the Weres didn't like the Fae, but the vamps—afraid of them?

"Really, now?"

She nodded as she tugged the boot onto my foot and began lacing it up. "Oh yes, my Lady. The vampires have long feared the Fae. After all, look at what happened with Myst when they tried to turn her. They can kill us, but our magic is strong. At least it is among a number of our warriors and nobles—and we know how to use illusion."

Another thing I hadn't thought about. "Druise, do you have special powers? I'm only now learning about my own heritage as one descended from the Uwilahsidhe. What . . . are you one of the Shifting Fae?"

She nodded. "All of us are—all in the Court of Rivers and Rushes, and those who were of the Court of Snow and Ice. This land, it lends itself to the Cambyra. The Great Seelie and Unseelie Courts—the majority of them are not Cambyra. We're an offshoot. A variation. Did you not know that?"

I shook my head. "No, I didn't. As I said, there is so much about your world—my world, now, I guess—that I'm ignorant on. My background . . . Druise, I had a very harsh childhood and seldom managed to stay in school. I learned on my own. I had to. I didn't go to any academy like the New Forest Conservatory. I didn't learn magic from my mother, even though she was magic-born and I am a half-breed. Rhiannon is probably better schooled than I am, but . . . I'm not sure how much she knew of the Fae either."

"We keep to ourselves, Your Majesty. We always have. I doubt that many of your books teach much about us, though I may be wrong. As I said, I'm not very complicated. And while I can read and write, I had to work from the time I was fairly young."

That could have been centuries, given the life spans of the Fae. I chose to leave that question for later, but did ask, "What do you shift into?"

She smiled again, beaming. "I am one of the Avonsidhe. I shift into a deer." And with that, she finished lacing my boots and stood back, eyeing me up and down. "You are almost ready."

"What about my circlet?"

"Ah, but you take the true crown tonight, so you go with bare head. Here, Let me fix your cloak for you." She lifted the silver fur cloak and draped it around my shoulders.

"What is this fur?" I hoped it wasn't wolf; that wouldn't set well with Grieve. But she put my fears to rest.

"Rabbit. They were eaten, so the meat was not wasted, if that is worrying you."

As she adjusted the cloak, I saw that it had been lined with ice blue silk and had a deep hood. I stroked along the nap of the fur. It was so soft my hand sank into the pile, and I wanted to rub my face against it.

"This is so . . . I would say *beautiful*, but that doesn't do it justice. Is Rhiannon's outfit like this?"

She chuckled. "Oh, Her Ladyship Rhiannon's dress is as golden as yours is silver, with shades of green. But her cloak is not made of fur, but instead of delicate leaves and ivy vines and deep, red roses. And now . . ." She stood back. "I think we're ready."

Druise crossed to the door and peeked out, saying something I couldn't quite catch. Then she opened the door wide, and a contingent of guards came in. I was positioned in the middle—with four guards in front of me, Druise right behind me, and four more behind her. Another guard stood to my left, and one to my right. We were completely blocked in by the warriors.

As we stood, waiting, Grieve appeared from the hallway. He was dressed much in the same colors as I was. He blew me a kiss, then sobered and stepped to the front of the guard. With a loud "*Attention!*" he started out of the room, and we followed.

❧

The Barrow had been cleared, it seemed. Not a soul was stirring, and at first I thought they'd been told to keep to their rooms, but I couldn't hear any movement at all—the Barrow was still.

When we exited, however, a ring of guards stood around the Marburry Barrow, guarding it from intruders. I wondered where the coronation would take place—would it be in the Court of Rivers and Rushes, just outside? But my question was answered as we headed through the portal in the Twin Oaks, back into the winter world. A horse, as black as the night sky, waited for me, its sidesaddle giving me pause. Black leather, with silver embellishments, it loomed as the hardest challenge I'd been through yet.

Grieve stood back as the guards broke rank. Check and Fearless approached me. "With your leave, Your Highness . . ."

I wasn't sure what they intended to do but nodded and suddenly found myself hoisted up—very gently—into the saddle. Relieved to see a sturdy belt attached to it, I quickly fastened myself in as Druise gathered up my train and arranged it so it would trail in a fashion that wouldn't trip up the horse's hooves. She then made sure my cloak draped down in back and that it was snugly fastened in the front.

After she finished, the guards gathered to the sides of the horse. Grieve mounted a matching horse and took the lead, as the guards followed with me in tow. Druise swung aboard a horse behind me, this one gray dappled with white, and followed us, with one of my guards at her side.

Silver bells on the bridles jingled as we headed through the winter forest, the horses silently making their way through the falling snow. We wove through the woodland, through the towering firs, and I caught my breath when animals started to appear, standing at attention as we filed along the path.

Snow hares with their twitching noses, and winter white foxes, looking to camouflage in the snow. And there, a wolf, and to the left, a white stag watched us from the shelter of the trees, as if they gathered to send me off.

Or perhaps, they gather to greet the new Queen of Winter?

Ulean! I've missed you! Where have you been? I was delighted to hear her voice on the slipstream. I didn't feel fully myself without her near me.

Lainule had something for me to do, but I'm here now, and I'll be with you during the coronation and ever after.

I whispered into the slipstream. *I feel like I'm walking through a surreal dream, Ulean. My life—what is it becoming?*

What it was destined to become, Cicely. You will feel more like yourself tomorrow, this I promise you. All of the past few days—it has been so alien to what your life has been. And the initiation and coronation . . . they are journeys in their own right. You have passed through the former, and are nearly through the latter. So take heart. All will be as it should be, and tomorrow life will seem more akin to what you are familiar with. Enjoy today. Not every woman gets to become a queen. This is a day you will never forget. Even when you are at the long-distant end of your life, you will remember tonight.

Feeling less alone, I tried to relax. The rocking of the horse sent me into a light trance, and the snowflakes kissing my skin seemed to freeze against me, as if I were colder than they. I reached up to brush them off but then stopped, not wanting to disturb the makeup. The snow was falling thickly now, gathering in my hair, on my eyelashes, and while it was cool against my skin, I wasn't cold. The rabbit fur cloak kept me toasty, but I knew there was more to it than that.

I could run atop the snow now, like Grieve, although still not as fast. And the winter winds didn't bite through me.

Ulean, as time goes on, will I become immune to the cold and ice?

Not immune, no, but it will buoy you up; it is your realm now, Cicely. The chill winds of winter are your melodies, and the calving of glaciers your strength. You feared the darkness, but now . . . even after such a short time, how do you feel?

As I turned the question over, mulling it, deep in my heart I heard the answer. *I no longer fear living in winter. What changed?*

You changed. Your heartstone—it is bound to the Court of Snow and Ice, and so a part of your soul, your heart, is bound to the realm of Winter. When you are connected to something at such a deep, internal level, you can no longer fear it. You will grow to understand the winter, to become part of it. Are you beginning to understand now? You won't just rule the throne; you will be an integral part of the season.

And then it all clicked. I let out my breath in a slow stream, watching it fog into the air before me. Now I understood. I wasn't losing myself. I was becoming more than I ever thought possible.

And Rhiannon, she is going through this, too, isn't she? Only with the summer? She is becoming the heart of Summer.

You do understand.

We were approaching the twin hollies, and I stared at the portal. It crackled with energy and called to me like a siren, luring me in. But it wasn't setting a bait. No, I could feel it in my core—a resonance that I had only ever felt with Grieve. He looked back at me, his dark eyes flashing. And then, without a word, he rode through the trees, and a flash lit up the forest as he vanished into the swirling vortex of energy.

The guards led my horse toward the opening and I sucked in a deep breath, as I realized that I was going home.

A crackle of blue and white light then, a whirl of energy, the smell of ozone in the air, and the sprinkle of snow turned into a flurry as I crossed through the barrier. The night was dark here, lit by the clouds covering the sky, and in the distance I could see the lights of the Barrow within the grove. The castle in which my heartstone had been created was some distance from here—I had no clue in what direction, but I could feel the steady beat as my heartstone awakened the land. I resonated with this realm now, this world was part of me, and my fate was forever entwined with it.

We crossed through the clearing toward the grove where the Eldburry Barrow awaited, and as the jingle of the horses sounded through the night, I glanced up at the trees. They were sparkling with lights, the snowflakes illuminating them like fireflies. And standing between the trees, next to the animals, I caught sight of the Snow Hag and her kin—the Wilding Fae. They bowed low as we swept by.

I raised my hand, waving quietly, and the Snow Hag caught my gaze, and her snaggletooth smile spread into a wide grin. Her eyes twinkled in the darkness of the forest, and then we were past and they fell in behind us as we approached the Barrow.

There at the entrance stood a double line of guards, at least thirty of them, and they bowed as we came into sight. Grieve lightly jumped off his horse, and then he walked back to stand by my horse's side. Check reached up and took hold of my waist as Fearless and Druise untangled the train of my gown and held it until I was safely on the ground.

Check and Fearless stepped back, bowing, and as I turned, Grieve dropped to one knee, his head bowed.

"Your Highness," he murmured. "Allow me to lead you to the Court where the Lady Lainule awaits?"

"You may stand," I whispered, realizing that he would stay on his knee until I gave him permission. He rose, and my wolf tattoo let out an excited yip. He extended his arm, his palm facedown toward the snow.

Overwhelmed by the beauty of the night, by the sparkling lights that illuminated the air and the Barrow, and by the attention that was focused on me, I could only reach out and place my hand lightly over his. Our arms outstretched, my hand lightly resting on his, we approached the entrance. As we passed each pair of guards, they stood and fell in behind Check, Fearless, and Druise.

The horses whinnied softly, and the jingling of their bells echoed the soft chiming of the bells on Druise's shoes. I started to glance back, to smile at her, but something stopped me, and so I took another long breath as we passed through the shimmering arches. The great doors of the Barrow were standing wide, guarded by another troop of warriors, and I began to realize just how large of a contingent of guards rested under my command.

We entered Eldburry Barrow and crossed the common court, where Fae were milling—throngs of them. I wasn't sure if they were all from the Court of Snow and Ice, or if they were visitors from Marburry, come to see my coronation. But there wasn't time to ask.

The great doors to the inner court were open again, guarded by a line of warriors on each side, and they bowed as Grieve led me into the large chamber. It was beautiful, it was home. In the brief time that had passed from yesterday when I'd first laid eyes on it until tonight, I'd gone from fearing this land to loving it.

Ahead, at the back of the room, were two hand-hewn yew thrones, embellished with silver designs. Over them, against the wall, hung a huge tapestry of the snow and ice, of the moon and of owls and of wolves. It looked new, and I realized it was to represent my rule, and the rule of Grieve.

I glanced at him and quickly whispered, "Do you take the throne with me tonight?"

He shook his head ever so slightly. "I cannot, not until we are wed. But fear not, I will be with you, as your consort, until then."

Glancing to the side, I saw that seated near the throne were Luna and Peyton, Chatter and Rhiannon. Rhiannon wore a dress like mine, only as Druise had told me, it was of gold and green, and her cloak was woven of leaves and roses. Her hair had shifted, and I realized that it was no longer red but had changed to a honey gold, shimmering in the lanterns holding the Ice Elementals. And Lainule, her hair was deep red, almost mahogany.

As we approached the throne, my guards fell to the side, as did Grieve, and then Wrath swept in to stand by Lainule's side, his jet hair sparkling with frost now. I gazed up at my father, willing him to be young again, willing him to stay and guide me, but even as I wished, I knew it was simply that—a wish, a dream, and not a possibility.

Drummers beat out a tattoo as Lainule motioned for me to come forward. I approached, alone and feeling like the weight of the world was hovering over my head, a silver sword held by a thread of ice and snow.

And then it was a blur . . .

"Do you, Cicely Tuuli Waters, accept the burden of this crown . . ."

"Do you accept responsibility for the lives of your people . . ."

"Do you bind yourself to the Court of Snow and Ice . . ."

"Do you give pledge by your life, your soul, your heart-stone, to protect and defend the realm of Winter . . ."

"Do you leave past allegiances behind and cleave only to your responsibility as Queen of Winter . . ."

"Do you pledge to lead the Court of Snow and Ice in honor, courage, in both light and in darkness . . ."

The questions went on and on, and to each I murmured an affirmation, losing myself in the cadence of the ceremony. The lights flickered their cool light, and I had only eyes for Lainule and Wrath. I had been born for this moment, been led back to New Forest, been thrown into the fray against Myst, and she was still out there, waiting for me, hating me for taking the throne she could not have for her own.

And then . . . the last question came.

"Will you wear the crown, in joy? And will you wear this crown even when it weighs so very heavy upon your brow that you wish you were no more of this world?" Lainule lifted up a silver circlet like the one I'd been wearing, only more elaborate. Entwining silver vines coiled around each other, creating a delicate yet sturdy diadem. They met at a point in the center to wrap around a glowing black onyx cabochon. Below the gem, a clear, single diamond sparkled.

"I do so swear." I gazed into her eyes, my stomach flipping as she raised the circlet and lowered it around my head. The hairstyle Druise had given me allowed her to slip the ends behind my ears, and the crown settled onto my head with a shudder.

"Then, all who witness, hear and know this: Cicely Waters has taken the burden of this Court upon her shoulders and will now and forever be the Queen of Winter, the Queen of Ice and Snow. Let all who behold her fear and tremble. Let no one question her authority. Hail the Queen of Winter! Hail the new Faerie Queen of the Eldburry Barrow!"

And I stood there, amid the cheering and bowing that came from the crowds, wearing my beautiful dress and my sparkling crown, and my heart soaked up the frost that laid waste to the land, and my soul reveled under the rule of the longest night of the year.

Chapter 10

When the ceremony was finished, Lainule whispered to me that it would be a good idea if, for my first announcement, I declared Grieve to be my Consort and King-Elect. It was expected that I make some sort of speech, and so I stepped up to the throne. Hesitating, I turned to my father, and he nodded for me to sit.

Inhaling sharply, I looked around the Court. Everyone fell silent, waiting for me. Slowly, deliberately, I lowered myself to the throne, and a soft rustle of air rolled through the throne room as everyone exhaled.

"My first order of business is to declare Grieve my Consort and King-Elect. We are to be married, and he will rule at my side." I wasn't sure of how to phrase it, but by the appreciative murmurs, I apparently did just fine.

Wrath and Lainule knelt before me and I stared at them, feeling entirely disconcerted. After a moment's fluster, I hurriedly motioned to them.

"Please, stand."

They stood, again, silent, and I realized they were waiting for me to give them permission to speak.

"What do you want? I mean . . . what is it?" As I stammered over the words, my face began to flush and I tried to hide my embarrassment. I was *so* not ready for this.

But Lainule gave me a gentle smile and whispered something, and I could hear her on the slipstream telling me to be calm, to take it slow and everything would be all right. I inhaled a long, deep breath and let it out slowly, calming myself.

"Your Highness, we must return to the Marburry Barrow to see to Summer's coronation. If you wish to attend, your guard and advisor shall escort you. If you would give us leave to go . . ." Again, a gentle prompting.

This time I got it. "Of course, you may go. And trust me, I'll be there with bells on."

She laughed, lightly, and the rest of the Court laughed with her. I decided right then and there that they'd have to get used to a less-than-regal approach to the crown.

As they began to leave the room, I realized I had to dismiss everyone else. In a moderate panic, I looked around for guidance. Grieve was too far away to be of any help, but Strict was standing there, right by my side. He must have seen the indecision running rampant on my face because he leaned close to me.

"Your Highness, just tell me to dismiss the Court. We've had so little time to prepare that everyone will forgive you a few breaches of formality." He looked about ready to pat my hand but then pulled away.

I cleared my throat, grateful to him. "Strict, you may dismiss the Court."

"As you desire, Your Highness." He bowed, then turned to the man standing next to him. "Announce the dismissal."

His companion picked up what looked like a trumpet. I steeled myself for some raucous sound, but the notes that floated out of it were sublime, like a series of wind chimes that reverberated through the room.

A moment later, when the talking had died down, he called out in a loud voice that ricocheted through the room, "Court is dismissed. You may go."

And the crowd began to disperse, though some of them gave me a backward glance, as if they wanted to stay and meet me or hear me say something. I turned to Strict.

"If these were normal times, there would be a celebration, wouldn't there?"

He nodded. "Yes, Your Highness, but these are not normal times, and as long as Myst is looming out there, we have to be cautious. We've given leave for small parties but have promised the people that when Myst is overthrown, both the Summer and Winter Courts will celebrate for a week."

"Myst . . . yes." As I looked around, I realized that this had been where Tabera had died. She'd died here, her blood soaking into the floors. I wondered if she was watching, from wherever the Cambyra spirits went when they died. Or had she gone on, long past caring?

Sobered, a little giddy, and oddly feeling anticlimactic, I motioned to Grieve. "We need to go to Marburry Barrow. I have to see Rhiannon take the throne."

"Yes, but you cannot wear your coronation dress, now that you are Queen. It wouldn't be proper. The only reason she wore hers is that the coronations are happening so close together. She did not intend to upstage you."

"She didn't upstage me, and frankly, as lovely as this dress is, I'd rather be in something easier to move in." I reached up to take off the crown, but Grieve stayed my hand.

"From now on, at all times when you are out of your chambers, you must wear the crown, just as you did the Queen-Elect circlet. Even when you go into New Forest, and yes—I know you will still be doing so. I've given up expecting you to fully conform to our ways. I don't think that's even possible." His eyes glimmered, though, and he laughed.

"I miss us-time. We haven't had much time together the past few days. I miss spending time with the gang. Honestly, I'm scared, my love."

"Save that talk for our private chamber," he cautioned.

"Come, let's get you into something more comfortable, and then we will go watch Rhiannon take her place at the helm of Summer."

❧

Half an hour later, thanks to Druise and Grieve, I was in yet another dress, this one easy and comfortable to move in. It swept the floor, yes, but it was deep indigo blue and sparkled with beaded crystals. It had long sleeves and a deep V-neck, and it snugged in at the waist with a silver belt, then flowed easily down around my feet. I kept the silver boots—they were cute, and when would I have a chance to wear something that impractical again? And of course, I didn't touch the makeup or crown. I gave Druise leave to head out for the Marburry Barrow ahead of time.

❧

Grieve was dressed in black trousers and a shirt matching the color of my dress. It set off the platinum of his hair, and I leaned into his arms as he pulled me to him.

"Are you happy, my love?" His voice shook, just a little, and I realized he was terribly afraid I'd regret my choice.

I wasn't sure how to answer. "The learning curve scares the hell out of me. And so does Myst. I'm dreading the next few months—except for our wedding. But . . . I'll get used to it, and I'll learn to love it. I just . . . so many changes in such a short time. It's overwhelming."

"Then be overwhelmed in my arms, my love." And he kissed me, long and deep, and I noticed his scent had shifted. The bonfires and apples had vanished, and now he smelled like frost and crisp, northern nights. Like spruce and pine, and bayberry and cinnamon.

I snuggled into his embrace, not wanting to go any-where, see anyone. But Rhiannon was waiting and I would be there, supporting her all the way.

Check and Fearless were waiting for us, and they bun-dled us into a sledge pulled by a team of white horses with silver bridles. We went sailing across the snow toward the portal. Once there, another ten guards were waiting to escort us through. On the other side, we began to run, although they held themselves back to keep pace with me, and we danced over the snow, feet barely touching the drifts. I reveled in the feel, though I had a sudden urge to turn into my owl-self and fly there, but I knew that would throw the guards into a tailspin and so decided to restrain myself.

Now that I could change form even in my clothing, I envisioned a lot more trips *up yonder*. Especially on days when the Court got to me, and I had the feeling there would be plenty of those.

Ulean, are you with us?

Yes, I am with you. It was a beautiful coronation. Congratulations, Cicely. I'm glad that you made it through.

You were with Lainule when she took the throne, weren't you?

Yes, I was. And I will be with you as long as you need me. When you have a daughter, if she takes the throne, I will eventually guide and help her.

A daughter. Children. The concept had entered my mind, especially when Grieve and I were together, but now it hit me that I would be expected to have an heir to the throne. And if I didn't give birth to a daughter, perhaps Grieve would have to do what my father had done. That thought hit me in the gut. I pushed it away, not wanting to think about it right now.

I'd better think about that some other time.

As you wish. Be cautious in these woods—there are dangers about, Cicely. You would do well to tell your guards.

I started to turn to Check, but as I did, a low growling filled the air as shadows moved out of the forest to attack us. What the hell? I couldn't see who our attackers were at first, but then the snow cleared for a moment. We were facing a group of Shadow Hunters.

Damn! I'd left my dagger at home. I looked around wildly for a weapon, but Grieve shoved me behind him, where Check and three of the other guards surrounded me, dragging me away from the fray. Frantic to help, I tried to make them let me go, but they held firm as the remaining six guards and Grieve moved to attack.

"I can call the winds—I can summon—" I'd barely managed to get the words out when one of our guards went down.

"We're closer to Marburry than Eldburry! Get the Queen and King-Elect out of danger!" Fearless glanced over his shoulder at us. The Vampiric Fae attacking him began to loosen his jaw and was quickly shifting form.

"Watch out! Behind you!" My scream cut through the air as the Shadow Hunter launched himself at the guard. They went down in a scuffle, blood flying.

I managed to break away from the guards and through the haze of swirling snow, I whispered, "*Gale Force.*"

As the wind swirled around me, catching me up, I reveled in the power, but when I felt myself slipping, I forced myself to focus solely on the Shadow Hunters, aiming directly for them. I fought the seductive siren song of the wind, and when Ulean blew around me, I reached out to her for help.

I need to control this thing. I need to use it rather than be used. What do I do, Ulean? How do I rein it in?

She whistled by, buoyed up by the swirl of air. *Focus on the core of the storm. Can you see it? Look for it, it will be a sparkling note—a brilliant chord in the middle of the symphony.*

I looked. When I was caught up by the thrall of the winds, I could see into their realm, and now I looked this way and that, and then—I saw it. A white-hot core, a light so bright I could barely look away once I'd seen it. The heart of the storm. The heart of the wind.

I see it! What now?

Do not dive into it—no matter how much it calls to you, resist. Instead, reach out, touch it, and demand it obey you. Tell it what you want it to do.

I hesitantly obeyed, and when my fingers met the light, a shiver raced through me, like a lover's seduction, and I wanted nothing more than to give myself over to it. But I remembered what Ulean had said, and instead I steeled myself against the call.

Obey me. Follow my command.

The wind did not respond. I tried again, forcing as much strength and control as I could into my words as they filtered through the slipstream. After a moment, the wind began to bend, and the light responded.

I pointed to the Shadow Hunters. *Attack them and only them.*

And the storm responded, barreling down on the group, driving them back. The Shadow Hunter attacking Fearless let go and began to back up, but the storm still caught him in its grasp, tossing him into the air like a light breeze might catch up an autumn leaf. The Vampiric Fae retreated into the woods, and I retracted the winds, willing them to calm, and ran over to Fearless, dropping to my knees by his side. He was limp and bleeding against the snow.

Two of the guards pushed past me to gather him up. Grieve, Check, and the other guards bundled me up and we were off, as fast as they could run, to the Marburry Barrow.

We reached there before the Vampiric Fae could gather themselves for another attack, and we were through the portal without further incident. The guards of Summer took one look at us and called out a group of warriors to go hunt down the Shadow Hunters, while we were escorted into the Barrow.

There they wanted to bustle me off to the coronation room, but I refused.

"Not until I know what shape Fearless is in."

"Your Highness, are you sure? We will let you know later." Check held my gaze, his expression unreadable, but his voice was soft.

"Yes, I'm sure. He was fighting to save us out there." I held my ground, and he took me to the infirmary, where the healers were already at work on the guard. Fearless looked a frightful mess. He was bleeding so profusely it was hard to tell where all of the blood was coming from. I watched, silent, as they pulled away his clothing. Because he was unconscious, he couldn't dispel it.

As the wounds on his leg and arm came into sight, I felt faint. Huge gashes and punctures from the jaws of the Shadow Hunter were pouring blood. The flesh had been mangled, looking like so much chewed raw meat. I shuddered, nausea rising, as Grieve joined me.

He stood behind me, holding my shoulders. "Lainule's guards are out there now, hunting them down. There will be blood in the forest tonight. How is he doing?"

"I don't know," I said quietly. "I didn't want to interrupt them while they're looking him over."

One of the healers looked up then, and she dropped into a curtsey. "Your Highness, I'm sorry, we didn't notice you before. We're trying—"

I held up my hand. "Don't apologize. You're trying to save him, I know. I'd rather have you do that than curtsey any day. How is he, do you think?"

She bit her lip and glanced back at Fearless's prone figure. "He's sustained severe damage to his leg and arm. I think we can save him, but I don't know . . . I don't know what will happen to his leg. The arm, we can probably salvage. We can make no guarantees. There is an element to the venom of the Shadow Hunters that encourages bleeding and discourages healing. He won't be able to go back to your Barrow for some time, however. We don't dare move him until he's stabilized."

I stared at Fearless. "Do what you can. Keep me updated." And then, feeling all too abrupt, I turned and exited the chamber.

"You need to change your dress, my love." Grieve pointed to a large bloodstain that marked one side. *Fearless's life force.* I must have gotten splashed with Fearless's blood when I'd tried to help him out in the woods.

"I guess I do." I turned to Druise, who had appeared at the door.

"I heard what happened. Are you quite all right, Your Highness?"

I nodded. "I'm fine, but I need you to find me a dress, quickly. I'll be in . . . my old bedroom." To Grieve, I said, "Love, go ahead and tell them I'll be there as soon as I change. I think we still have a little time."

"But hasten. Don't tarry." He bowed and then hurried out of the room.

I rushed back to the common room, where I found Peyton lingering over a cup of tea. She looked tired, and surprised when she saw me.

"Peyton, what are you still doing here?"

"I needed a break and some tea, and I checked on Kaylin. He's still worse for wear, but he'll be all right."

"Our enemies are out in full force. I'll tell you more later, but right now, I need a dress. This one . . . oh, no time to explain. Just help me find something to wear." All of my things had been moved to the Eldburry Barrow, it appeared, but Druise came bustling in, carrying a pale silver dress. It was an ankle-length sheath, very Grecian, with ties at the shoulders to keep the straps together, and a draped bodice.

I scrubbed the blood off my leg where it had soaked through the other dress. The silver gown fit, although a little loose, but I didn't care. My hair was still in fairly good shape, and my makeup was slightly smudged, but we didn't have time to worry. In the dim lights, it wouldn't show much. I adjusted my circlet so that it was setting evenly, and the three of us headed for the central hall.

We managed to get there shortly before the ceremony was to begin and, as unobtrusively as possible, we made our way to the front, where I slipped into my seat next to Grieve, and Druise sat behind me. Peyton took her place by Luna.

The music started minutes after we sat down, and as the ceremony progressed, I realized that it was a mirror of my own. Only this time, I could see just how extensive and taxing it had been. Rhiannon looked spectacular, shimmering like summer in her dress, with the train billowing out from behind her. As Lainule put her through the same question-and-answer ritual she had me, I could almost see a transfer of energy going on between them.

Lainule placed the crown on Rhiannon's head, and I found myself tearing up. My cousin had been through so much in the past weeks, and this—while incredible and wonderful—had to be stress beyond the limit. But she withstood it well, and Chatter's gaze followed her with absolute love and devotion. He would never hurt her; he would never abandon her.

The ceremony ended, and as we all watched, Lainule stepped up to the throne one last time and looked over her people.

"You have served me well, my friends. You have stood by me; you have survived the scourge of Myst. But thanks to that dread Queen, I must return to the Golden Isle. I leave you in capable hands. Winter and Summer will balance again now, and with Queens who are also cousins, they will be friends rather than enemies. Bear with our new Queens—they have a steep curve ahead of them, and we must all make this transition easier for them. They will lead you into new territory; they will change some of the old traditions."

At the murmur from the crowd, she added, "Do not argue this. Our tradition of isolating allowed Myst to come through and nearly destroy us. Our refusal to allow Summer and Winter to meet led to Tabera's death and . . . nearly to my own death. So do what you can to help. Do not fight the changes coming. They are necessary to our survival. Again, thank you, and for the last time, as your Queen, I bid you good night."

And with that, Lainule removed her crown from her head, and Wrath removed his, and they turned and walked away.

My lower lip began to tremble and tears ran down my cheeks. I turned to Grieve, stricken, and saw that he, too, was crying. And then Rhiannon stepped up to her throne, looking dazed, and—with the guidance of her advisor—did as I had and dismissed the Court.

The trial was over. We were the new Fae Queens. A new journey had begun . . . and yet . . . old enemies were just outside the gate.

⚜

We met in the common room again, after the hall had cleared. Luna and Peyton were quiet. Kaylin was stretched out on the chaise. Grieve, Chatter, Rhiannon, and I gathered around the table. As we sat there, quietly eating a simple dinner of cheese and bread and meat, the door opened and Lainule and Wrath entered. They looked tired, and my heart went out to them. I silently stood and ran over to my father, throwing my arms around his waist. He embraced me silently, kissing the top of my forehead.

"I don't want to lose you, now that I've just found you."

"I know, my daughter. I know." He rocked me back and forth. "But the tide waits for us with eager hands. If my Lady does not return to the Golden Isle now, she will fade and die within days. And I would go with her wherever she journeys, so great is my love for her."

Biting my lip to keep from crying, I nodded, squeezing my eyes shut. I knew there was no option, but this was so much harder than I'd thought it would be. In the short time that I'd known him, I'd come to love him, like the father he was.

"The Golden Wood is in your hands, my dear niece. And in Cicely's. It is the home of both Courts, though the rule shifts through the seasons." Lainule gratefully accepted the chair Grieve drew out for her. "Our prophets knew this day might come; hence the preparations and birthing of you two girls. We didn't know exactly when, but we knew . . . it was possible."

"Is there anything we should know? Who are the prophets? Can we talk to them? Is there anything we should be on the lookout for?" If there were any more prophecies that involved us, it seemed that we should find out more about them.

Wrath laid his hand on my shoulder. "Strict will help you

with all of that. And his sister, Edge, for Rhiannon. The two of them will meet with the two of you jointly to go over the million details we didn't have time to address. They are to be trusted, girls. They are bound to both thrones, bound to their courts. They will die before they betray you. Of all the advisors you will meet, they alone you can trust with your lives and the lives of your people."

Rhiannon leaned over and took Lainule's hand. "You are my aunt. I will miss you—I didn't get a chance to meet my father."

"There is no help for that, child. He gave his life defending the Barrow against Myst." She patted Rhia's hand. "Your fiancé will help you master the craft of your Fire. Your advisor will help you understand how to shift into your alter-form. And Cicely, Ulean tells me she was helping you with the wind. She will teach you how to control the power, now that I have no time left."

Her words sounded so very final.

"When do you have to leave?"

"At the latest, before the cock crows, but we will go after we leave this room. Now that I am no longer Queen, I will age at a great rate and that, I do not wish to do. We have packed our things and they have been sent on ahead. Tomorrow night, Rhiannon, you will sleep in the Queen's chamber." She stood, wearily. "Do you know, when Tabera and I took the thrones, we never again saw one another? Only on the changeover days—midwinter and midsummer—and then we barely spoke. We had no great love for one another, but we were isolated, each to our realm."

"So you never saw her again?" Luna asked.

Lainule shook her head. "Only on the Solstices. She kept to her realm, isolated from the world. As for me, I only began venturing out when the prophets said there might be a need to know the outer world in the coming decades. I sent her word, asked her to join me, but she would not. Since Tabera would not answer my messages, Wrath and I took it upon ourselves to carry through the directions the seers gave us—which led to your births.

Now the world of the Fae is expanding and will never again be the same. But that is a good thing."

She stood, after a silence. "It is time, my husband. It's time to go home."

Wrath gave me another hug, so tight I could barely breathe. "I will not see you again, not for centuries. If ever. Be strong, Cicely. Remember what little I had time to teach you. Be strong and compassionate in your rule, but do not flinch when duty calls. And forever remember, I'm proud of you. You know that, don't you? I'm so very proud of you."

I began to cry in earnest. We were all crying. My father. Lainule. Rhia, Grieve, Chatter. Luna and Peyton were nose deep in tissues, and even Kaylin was tearing up.

"Safe passage home." I clung to Wrath, burying my head in his chest. Then, slowly, I let go and turned to Lainule. "Thank you, for everything. I have no words . . ."

She reached out and kissed my cheek. "I am the one who should be thanking you. You saved my life, Cicely. In a saner world, I would be proud to rule over Summer with you as my opposite. But the world has gone mad. Never forget that Myst is still on the prowl. She will seek you down, try to destroy you. Never let down your guard until she is dead."

I nodded. "I promise."

And then, after a long hug for Rhiannon, Lainule turned to Wrath. "Come, my husband. One last journey, and then we can rest on the shores of the lake, under the silver moonlight. Our homeland awaits. It has been so terribly long since I came to these woods."

We followed them out, down the hall to a locked chamber. Strict was there, and Edge, and they opened the door and we all went in. In the center of the chamber, a cloaked figure knelt, a woman, and in front of her was a glowing orb, hovering about four feet above the floor. She murmured something I couldn't catch, and the orb grew brighter, lengthening and widening until it formed a glimmering rip in the fabric of space. Colors shifted and spun, and emanating out from that rip were the scents of honey and sweet wine and snow and rain and summer grass and the soft whispers of twilight.

I longed to go through, to follow the call, but Ulean kept me steady.

Eventually, Cicely, you will journey through this portal, but not for a long, long time. It is not in your destiny . . . not now.

Feeling for Grieve's hand, I held tight, and he squeezed my fingers. We all kept silent, not wanting to disturb the spell. Lainule and Wrath looked at each other, then at us. Together, they walked down the line, giving each of us a kiss, even Peyton. When she came to Luna, before she pressed her lips softly against the bard's head, Lainule whispered, "Pass this to Kaylin, if you would."

And then I was hugging and kissing my father yet one last time. I drank in the feeling, bound it tight. He slowly let go, then without another word turned to Lainule and took her hand. He kissed her softly.

"My Queen. I will follow you anywhere. To the Golden Isle, and when it is time, into the embrace of death."

Her lips crinkled. "Let us hope the latter is still a ways off, my love."

They walked to the portal, and—without a backward glance—plunged through. The light brightened, so white and hot that I had to shield my eyes, and then it faded. The orb was gone. Lainule and Wrath had returned to their homeland, forever.

I said nothing but rose to exit the room. A page was waiting. He knelt at my feet as I tried to keep my composure.

"Your Highness, I have news of your guard. Fearless? They were able to save the leg, but he will be incapacitated for a long while."

I nodded, not trusting myself to speak.

Grieve thanked him and then stopped him as the boy started to run off. "What time is it?"

"Time? Nearly dawn. The sun breaks in the Court of Rivers and Rushes."

I looked up at my love. "The longest night is over. But the journey . . . just begun."

And since there was little left to say, I told Rhiannon I'd meet her in the common room come noon, and then, slowly, quietly, and with a full guard accompaniment, Grieve, Druise, and I headed back to the realm of Winter to get a few hours of sleep.

Chapter 11

Four hours of sleep later, I opened my eyes, groaning as I realized I had to get up in time to get bathed and dressed and over to meet Rhia by noon. And then I remembered: Wrath and Lainule were gone, and the depression of the night hit me all over again.

As I sat up, I saw that Grieve was already awake and gone. Wondering what the procedure for the day would be now that I was officially in charge, I also saw the silver bell sitting on my nightstand. I rang it and within less than two minutes, Druise entered the room.

She dropped into a deep curtsey as I pushed back the covers and slid out of the bed. "I need to dress for the outer world today. I'm meeting my cousin and we're going shopping. I need to be able to take my clothes off and on easily, so jeans and a sweater, please."

Druise nodded. "Yes, Your Highness. What would you like for breakfast?"

"Bacon and eggs. Toast." I yawned and padded into the bathroom while she popped out to give my order to whomever it was that would be bringing my breakfast. That was another thing I'd have to get used to—I wouldn't be doing much cooking from now on. Not that I liked to play around in the kitchen much, but raiding the refrigerator at night wasn't going to be quite as simple now.

I finished in the bathroom—somehow they managed toilets and running cold water, though I had a feeling they didn't quite work like the ones back home. After washing my hands and then brushing my teeth, I sauntered back into the bedroom. Druise had returned, and she had set up a steaming bowl of water.

"I'm going to need a bath every morning, Druise. We're going to have to rig up a better way to get hot running water for me, because I'm used to showering twice a day and that's one thing I don't want to compromise on."

She nodded. "I'll take care of it. We may need a couple of days to set it up, but your wish is our command, Your Highness." She soaped up a soft cloth and began washing the leftover makeup off my face. "Breakfast will be here in a few moments. His Lordship is with Advisor Strict and bids you to rest today. He said, 'There will be time enough tomorrow for the running of the realm.'"

I smiled. "His Lordship is a sweetheart. But yes, I do need the day to recuperate. The past few weeks have been hard." I must have sounded defeated because Druise slipped behind me and began rubbing my shoulders as I dried my face and applied moisturizer.

"I'm sorry, Your Highness." She sounded so sad that I forced a smile to my face.

"I've lived through worse. I'm just . . ." I stopped. At one point, Wrath had told me, *"Don't show your vulnerability. Not to those who depend on you."* And I knew that I couldn't talk about my fears to my lady's maid. Another wall went up, another invisible boundary line. But then, when I thought about it, I'd erected plenty of boundaries when I was on the road with Krystal. I'd hoped, when I returned home, that I could tear down some of my barriers, but apparently my destiny in life wasn't geared toward allowing many people in my inner circle.

The servant with breakfast appeared and I ate up, suddenly aware of how hungry I was. Meanwhile, Druise got my jeans ready, along with a warm black V-neck sweater and a silver jacket. I dressed quickly, then quickly applied day makeup—dark shadow that made my newly blue eyes pop, and a sheen of barely there gloss.

Standing back, I observed myself in the mirror. Not bad. I was looking far more pulled together than I used to, and my 140 pounds of muscle was taut and strong. As I allowed Druise to affix my circlet on my head, I realized that I'd promised to meet with Lannan tonight. *Joy o' joys.*

When I was done, I headed for the door. "Druise, you stay here. I don't want to subject you to the outer world just yet. It's going to be a big surprise, if you've never been out there."

She dipped into another curtsey. "Thank you. But you will take the guards?"

I grinned at her. "I doubt if I could get out of here without them. Yes, I'll take Check and . . . well, Fearless is out of commission for now, but I'll take guards with me." Actually, after the attack the night before, I really didn't want to go out without an escort.

Check was waiting for me outside the door, with another guard. "Your Highness, may I introduce Teral? He will be filling in for Fearless."

I nodded at the new man, who looked big and burly enough to take on just about anybody. They fell in behind me.

Those who returned to the Court of Snow and Ice—and there were quite a number of them who had made the move—had been calling me "Your Highness" since Lainule had first made the announcement that Rhia and I were to become the new Queens. But today, as I walked through the halls, each person near me dropped into a curtsey or bow until I had passed by. I stood a little straighter, suddenly more mindful of my appearance.

"Check, can I ask you something?" He'd served with Lainule, and before that, with Tabera, I'd found out, always as one of their personal guards.

"What do you wish to know, Your Highness?"

"Should I . . . do I say anything when they bow like that?" I wanted to add, *I'm clueless*, but decided that could be left unsaid.

A little smile crept out. He shook his head. "It's not necessary. If you greet everyone who bows to you, you'll never have any time for anything. It's . . . it goes hand in hand with being the Queen, Your Highness. You'll get used to it, and you'll come to expect it. Her Highness Lainule may have been born to her post, but she was just as uncertain when she took the throne."

I jerked around to face him. "You were with her when she was young? When she took over the Court of Rivers and Rushes?"

He nodded. "I was born to the year she was. We were . . . I was thought to become King-Elect, and then she met His Lordship Wrath."

The long stretch of history of this realm, of the people who made it what it was, flashed before my eyes.

"You were from the Court of Snow and Ice even then?"

"As was my brother, Lord Wrath."

Brothers. That meant . . .

"You're my uncle?" I stared at him, searching for the resemblance, but could find none.

He shook his head, again, the flicker of a smile gracing his face. "Not by blood, no. Wrath and I were oath-brothers, much like His Lordship Grieve, and His Lordship Chatter. We were in training together, and we were assigned to be . . . what you would call exchange students in your world . . . at the Court of Rivers and Rushes. There I met Lainule, and she and I fell in love. It wasn't passionate, but the kind of love that feels like it could be a steady glow. And then I introduced her to His Lordship Wrath. At that moment, when their eyes met, when they looked at one another, in that moment I knew I'd lost her. I stepped aside."

"And so my father became the King and you . . ."

"I pledged my honor to them and changed courts. When

you have fallen in love with the sun, you can't just walk away. I swore to protect the both of them—she whom I'd loved, and he whom she loved."

"Did you hate my father?" I had to know. It might affect how he looked at me.

"Hate him? How could I hate the man who was my brother, even if he did sweep away the woman I loved?" He sounded so sincere that there was no way I could believe otherwise.

"Thank you for telling me. There's so much about my father I don't know . . . I barely knew he *was* my father before he had to leave." As we approached the exit to the outside, a thought struck me. "Some of you—Grieve, Chatter, you, Fearless . . . you have names that, in English, describe . . . qualities. Others like Lainule and you, Teral, don't. What's the difference?"

Teral glanced at me, a quizzical look on his face. "How are children named in your world?"

"By their parents," I said, confused.

He cocked his head, and I had the feeling that hadn't been the answer he had expected.

Check laughed. "When women are pregnant, they visit the seers. The seer tells them whether their child will be what are known as Will-Begots. The children have extremely strong abilities and life forces, and their destinies are specifically focused. While the stars do not speak of exactly what these destinies are to be, the children who are Will-Begots always end up having a lasting effect. Will-Begots are named after those attributes that speak strongly in their soul to the seers."

"So you are Check . . ."

"Because I keep others in check. Grieve, because his soul sang of grief to the seer when he was young. And so forth. Those who are not Will-Begots are named whatever their parents choose to name them." He opened the door and escorted me out, with Teral behind us.

The blast of winter startled me, but only for a moment. The sled awaited and I settled myself in, allowing Check to spread a thick fur blanket over me as we headed to the twin hollies. I had a dozen more questions, but I decided a few at a time were enough.

Are you with me, Ulean?

As you need me, always.

Then let's go.

As we approached the portal, I wondered how the town would look now. And if Rhia and I could be just cousins, out shopping, ever again.

❈

Rhiannon was waiting for me just outside the portal by the Twin Oaks. She was wearing a pretty dress, but it looked a lot like the ones in her closet—a sage green sheath dress, and she'd added a golden belt. Her boots were brown and knee-high, and she wore a brown velvet coat over the top of her dress. A golden circlet with a yellow topaz centered in it mirrored my own silver crown. Two guards stood watch beside her, and Check and Teral joined them.

"Where are Peyton and Luna?"

"They're waiting up at the house for us. I made sure they took guards with them. Rex has promised to act as our chauffeur for the afternoon." She stretched, and the crown around her head gleamed.

"It seems odd." I glanced around at the woodland. "For the past few weeks, their lives have been integrally connected with our own and now . . . now it feels like we're splitting off into different directions. I feel kind of isolated."

"I know what you mean. In a way, I think you've got it easier. Tabera has been dead for some time. You don't have to follow directly in the footsteps of someone who was beloved by her people. I feel like I'm going to be compared every time I turn around. *Lainule did it this way . . . Lainule said that . . . Lainule would have made a different decision.* Chatter says that I'm overthinking the matter, but . . ."

"But it's true." I reached out, took her hand. "You're

right, it is going to be harder for you. But you'll do fine. I'll do fine. We have to believe that."

"We'd better go—they'll be expecting us soon." Rhia turned to the guards. "We're ready." And so, with two in front of us and two to the rear, we took off, running at top speed until we spotted the edge of the Golden Wood.

As we slowly exited the forest, slowing to a normal pace, the Veil House was lit up and looked warm and cozy from the outside. Luna was standing on the back porch, and she waved to us and said something over her shoulder.

"Are they safe? What if the day-runners come back?"

"Chatter and I ordered a dozen guards to keep watch. They're hidden around the property. Luna and Peyton should be safe. Kaylin can't join them yet; it's going to take him a while to recuperate." Rhia waved to Luna, then stopped, turning to me. She moved me off to the side, out of the way of the guards. "I miss this. I miss hanging out with the others, even though we were fighting Myst. I even miss the warehouse. I don't know how to be a Queen, Cicely. I'm scared."

I took her hands in mine. She had lost the regal look and now just was my cousin, afraid and looking too tired. "I know, I feel the same, but there's no going back. Our heartstones belong to the realms. We're due to marry soon. We'll adjust, somehow. I just wish Lainule and Wrath hadn't had to go."

I took a deep breath and leaned over to kiss her cheek. She hugged me and then, after a moment, we turned, hand in hand, and ran up to the porch, where Luna and Peyton were waiting.

✴

By two thirty, we were walking down the streets of New Forest, like four normal young women on a shopping spree. The guards walked discreetly in back of us, with Rex by their side. The shoppers who passed us whispered, and I had the feeling we were known entities.

Ulean swept against me. *If you don't need me right now,*

I would like to explore the area, see if I can find any sign of Shadow Hunters.

Go. We're just going to be shopping. Everything will be fine.

The streets were coated with ice, and the cars that went by drove slowly, cautiously as they navigated through the ever-building snow. The sidewalks were dangerous and slippery, and twice Luna almost fell. Rhiannon wasn't doing so bad—apparently our transformation had helped her on the snow and ice, the same way Grieve and Chatter and the other Cambyra managed it. Peyton wore thick-soled hiking boots, and they gripped the ice with a surety that I'd never felt. But I—I could practically dance across it now, and I did a couple of delighted spins around the others, giggling as I glided over the thick chunky ice.

At first, Peyton and Luna seemed a little awkward, but after I'd skated around them on my tiptoes, they began to laugh and we were off and chatting again, like nothing had changed. Behind us, the guards whispered softly among themselves, and I decided *not* to listen in on their conversation.

We arrived at our first destination—a bridal shop. Since our weddings were coming up so quickly, we'd convinced Lainule, before she left, that we could buy our gowns and not worry the seamstresses with making them. She reluctantly had agreed.

Desiree's Bridal specialized in unique wedding gowns. It stood across the street from the old Abby Theater. Like most of downtown New Forest, the building was redbrick and had a vintage, Old World feel to it. The Abby Theater had been built more than sixty years earlier, and I wasn't even sure it was still in business—there was no placard out front announcing any show, and the marquee at the top of the box office was dark.

A three-story clock tower—also brick—ran up one side, housing an ornate clock face. I'd read somewhere that the clock had never once lost time. The same person—a man who was now in his early eighties—had been given the job of making sure that it ran consistently and evenly. Every hour, on the hour, chimes rang out, echoing through the streets.

"After the coronation dresses, I'm grateful we're picking out our own wedding dresses," I said. "I've never worn anything so beautiful yet so cumbersome. It will be a relief to have something elegant and yet easy to move around in."

"You know we won't get away with simple, but we can push it as far as possible." Rhia turned to Luna. "You will be my maid of honor?"

Luna sputtered. "I . . . I . . . up there in front of everyone?"

"You'll have company, because Peyton's going to be my maid of honor, and since we're having a double wedding, we'll all be up there together." I grinned at her.

Peyton gave me a sharp look. "That's the first time I've heard about this."

"That's because I haven't had a chance to tell you yet."

"*Tell me*, is it? Not ask?" But the twinkle in her eye told me that she was joking. "So, what are we to wear? Hopefully not godawful satin dresses with big bows and poufy sleeves?"

Rhia snorted. "I wouldn't wish those on my worst enemy. No, we'll figure that out when Cicely and I find our dresses."

And, laughing, we entered the shop. The guards waited outside, though Rex followed us in to keep an eye on us. I squirmed, feeling all too watched. For the umpteenth time I wondered how I'd ever get used to this gig.

But the uncomfortable sensation vanished as we entered a world of tulle and satin and silk and lace. While the theme was definitely bridal, the designs and colors were far from traditional. Elegant, intricate dresses, some sweeping to the floor, lined the walls. Princess gowns and draped Grecian dresses and mermaid hems and tea-length frocks— all in vivid jewel tones and delicate pastels—exploded in a maelstrom of colors and textures.

On the center tables, accessories abounded: tiaras and

clutches, rosettes and handkerchiefs and everything a bride could want to finish making her wedding ensemble shine.

As Rhiannon and Luna started down one side, Peyton and I started down the other. I immediately nixed the idea of a mermaid gown. I didn't like the lines on them. And I wasn't Cinderella—my coronation dress was the closest I'd ever get to a princess gown. Fit-and-flare gowns were just about the same as mermaid dresses in my book, so those were out.

Peyton pointed to a horrendous bubble affair. It looked like it was pieced together from bubbles made of netting. The sleeves were so huge around the shoulders that they could have held watermelons, and there were so many ruffles and tiers of lace that all I could see was a mound of fabric pieced together.

I snorted. "You aren't getting me anywhere near that monstrosity. Why don't *you* try it on?" But then, as I turned, I caught sight of it. *The dress.* And I knew, right then, right there, it was mine.

At first glance, it was a drape of silver lace over pale gray chiffon, with royal blue lace straps that led to a key-hole back. Form-fitting but not tight, it had a low-cut bodice and a beautiful beaded sash that matched the straps. The sash tied in a bow in back, with the ribbons draping down to calf length.

"That one," I said. "What's the train like? I don't want to trip over it."

Peyton peeked around back, motioning me over. The train of the gown was delicate tulle. "This looks like it drapes out in back. I think they call it a chapel train."

"Yes, it's a chapel train." One of the saleswomen hustled over. "But if you tuck it here and here, you can see that it folds neatly into a bustle for dancing." With a few minor adjustments, the sparkling silver train was transformed into a bustle that looked like it had been made that way.

"I love the color. I love that it isn't stark white or ivory." I turned to the saleswoman, whose name tag read RHONDA, and, my hand still fingering the hem of the dress, said, "I want to try this on."

"Of course, Your Highness." At my startled look, she smiled. "We were told you and your cousin would be coming in today, looking for your wedding dresses. While we're not used to the Fae frequenting our shop, let alone royalty, we're here to serve."

Speechless, I watched as she lifted the dress down from the display rack.

The dresses weren't on mannequins, but instead they hung separately on individual racks on the raised dais that circled the room. The boutique probably had a hundred dresses total, and by the looks of them, the store was geared toward women with unusual tastes.

As I followed Rhonda to the dressing room, I glanced over at Rhiannon. She was still sorting through dresses, but she looked happy rather than frustrated, and the clerk who followed her was carrying two dresses already.

I slipped off my jeans and sweater and let Rhonda slide the dress over my head. It was a sample size, and didn't fit right, but she was able to adjust it so that I could tell how it would look. As she wrapped the sash around my waist, I began to smile, and when she led me to a mirror, I caught my breath.

The dress might have been made just for me. It was simple, elegant, but it matched my style, and my circlet glimmered softly in the light, echoing the silver of the dress. The splash of royal blue on the straps and sash set off my eyes in an arresting way. I still wasn't used to the change in color, but now they shimmered with an icy frost.

As Rhonda spread out the train so that it trailed behind me, I couldn't tear my gaze away from the mirror. "I cannot believe . . . this is me." It was more beautiful than my coronation dress, and so much more *me*.

Peyton let out an uncharacteristic squeak. "You're so beautiful, Cicely. I love it." She shivered, grinning. "You look like the Snow Queen."

I laughed then. "I *am* the Snow Queen, remember?" Turning to Rhonda, I smiled softly. "This is it. Can I get it in a week? I'll pay for a rush."

She inclined her head gracefully. "Of course. We will make it happen. What about a veil?"

I glanced at Peyton. "I suppose it needs to be fitted to my crown." She nodded, and I turned back to Rhonda. "Something swept back from my face. I'm not a shrinking violet. Maybe . . . in silver lace to match my dress? Midback length? I don't need to go tripping over extra material."

"I think we can create the right one."

"Wonderful. I also need a maid of honor dress for Peyton here. In the same royal blue as the sash on this dress. Something tea length, satin, sleeveless. Maybe a simple retro-fifties frock?"

"Let's get you out of this so I can measure you; then we'll search for Peyton's dress." Rhonda, in a flurry of movement, had me out of the dress and was measuring me every which way. She wrote down my measurements, then was out of the room, off in search of a maid of honor's dress. One vintage tea frock in royal blue later, we had our outfits. Rhiannon had found her gown—a sheath of pale gold with green beading, elegant and vintage—and we decided Luna would have a dress matching Peyton's, but hers would be forest green. By the time we'd finished and paid the deposits, it was nearly four thirty. Rex was sitting in the corner, a cup of coffee in hand, reading a book.

"We need coffee. There's a shop right around the corner." Rhia pointed toward the corner of Broadmore and Williams.

I glanced up at the Abby Theater clock. Four thirty, and sunset had already fallen. "Coffee sounds good. Actually, a steaming hot mocha with whipped cream sounds fantastic. I have to visit Lannan tonight. Anybody want to come with me?" I didn't expect them to say yes, and they didn't fail my expectations.

"No thanks, but we'll take you up on that mocha." Peyton snorted. "The less I have to do with Lannan Altos, the better."

Behind her back, Luna nodded vigorously.

As we started toward the corner, the streetlamps came on. They were wound with garland and sparkling lights, and against the snow-shrouded dusk, they made for a picturesque sight. The Winter Solstice celebration in the Barrows had been postponed until our double wedding, given that the coronation had taken place on the Solstice. And Christmas, for those yummanii who celebrated, wasn't for another few days.

Luna slipped a little and I steadied her, cupping her elbow. She was bundled up in an ankle-length tan coat with fur trim, and her boots were lace-up granny boots with thick chunky heels. But the sidewalk was rough, the ice kept melting and freezing over the new snow, and it was obvious the city hadn't been out to clean roads for a day or two.

As she righted herself, a long black car pulled up to the sidewalk near us. A sudden stab of fear hit me. I knew who owned those cars—vampires. My gut instinct took over and I whirled around, frantic. The guards, who were flanking us closely, saw my expression, and Check leaped forward as the car doors nearest the sidewalk opened.

Out jumped Geoffrey and Leo, along with a couple of other vampires.

Rhiannon screamed, stumbling back, as Peyton tried to shove herself in front of Rhia. I frantically reached for my dagger and then realized I'd left it back in the Barrow. *Clumsy, careless fool!*

The vampires were on us, and Check led the guards to the front. Rex yanked his daughter out of the way, sending Peyton spinning into the snowdrift behind him. I heard a scream, and as I fought my way toward the front, one of Rhiannon's guards went soaring over my head, limp and bloody.

"No!" Luna's scream cut through the evening. I struggled to push past Check and Teral, but they wouldn't let me by. Check shoved me back, a black look on his face, but I managed to dodge around him, just in time to see Peyton scrambling to get out of the way of one of the vampires, who was looming over her, fangs bared. Rex let out a shout and dove in between them, a stake in his hand. Where he'd gotten it, I didn't know, but as he met the vampire's chest with the tip, the vamp roared and then, as the wood penetrated his heart, he turned to dust.

Rex staggered back, a look of horror on his face. I followed his gaze and saw Leo, holding Rhiannon by the arms. He was shoving her into the backseat of the car.

"No!" Screaming at the top of my lungs, I started forward, but again, Check grabbed me by the shoulders and dragged me back.

Rex was closest to them, and he grabbed Leo's arm, trying to break his grip. Geoffrey suddenly appeared behind him, and before we could make a move, before the shout could fall from my lips, he had plunged his fangs deep into Rex's neck, the blood fountaining out from the wound. He bit again, viciously, and ripped a long strip of flesh as he did so.

Rex went down, and Geoffrey yanked him up like a rag doll, grinning at Peyton with bloody lips as he administered one last bite. Rex's head lolled to the side. Peyton shrieked and started forward, but Teral grabbed her back.

I broke free from my paralysis, realizing that Leo had managed to drag Rhia into the car. As I started to race forward, Geoffrey jumped to block my way but pulled back when the remaining guards pushed me between us.

"No!" *Ulean, help us!*

"Your time will come, Cicely. You owe me. You owe me everything, and I will have my payment." Then, before Check could reach him, Geoffrey jumped into the car and they roared away, taking Rhiannon with them.

Peyton sank to Rex's side, her moans filling the air. The snow was drenched with blood, stained pink, and around us, people were staring, milling around but not coming near.

"They have the Queen of Summer," Rhiannon's remaining guard whispered.

"They have my *cousin*." I was angry, furious that we had been so concerned about clothes that we'd let ourselves get careless; I wanted to grab a car and chase after them. But they were gone, and we had no clue as to where.

Ulean swept by. *I will see if I can find them. I'm sorry, Cicely. I should have stayed with you.*

Go, please. See if you can track them down.

"Rex is dead." Peyton looked up at me, tears streaming down her face. Her hands were stained with his blood, and she leaned to the side, vomiting.

I was so worried about Rhia that I'd almost forgotten about Rex. Now I knelt by Peyton and softly took her by the shoulders, lifting her away from Rex's body. She started to cover her face with her hands but then stopped as she saw the blood. Trembling, she gave me a look that told me she was one step away from a breakdown.

"Check, Peyton needs help. We have to get to Lannan Altos's mansion." Lannan, freak though he might be, would help us. He would do everything he could to help us find Geoffrey.

Before we could move, another shriek rang out, this time across the street near the theater. We all turned, just in time to see a figure creep out from the shadows, face bloody and eyes blackly luminous. He was tall and thin beyond thin, stretched like an insect, his long limbs resembling a walking stick as he crept forward. His glittering gaze turned my way, and he scuttled toward the road.

Crawl. Crawl, the Blood Oracle of the vampires. Crawl, the seer who had long ago left any humanity he had in the dust. Crawl, who had tried to rip out my throat, who had escaped from a prison he should never have left. Crawl, who had no more compunction about ripping open a baby's throat as I did about eating a piece of chicken. And he wanted *me*.

"Check, I have to get out of here. That's Crawl."

Check murmured some curse under his breath, but it

was Luna who sprang to action. Rex's car was three spots down. She dove for Rex's body, rifling his pockets, and came up with the keys. Grabbing Peyton by the arm, Luna dragged her toward the car. I followed, leaving the guards to deal with Crawl.

"Meet us at Altos's mansion!" I called out, jumping into the backseat next to Peyton. We slammed the doors just as Crawl crossed the street. He was strong, too strong, and Check knew it. He and the other two guards withdrew, waving for us to get a move on.

I cannot go, Cicely. The vampires won't let me in. The vampires hated the Elementals—they couldn't read them, and the Elementals could sense things about the vampires that the vampires preferred to keep as secrets.

Then wait outside the gates there for us.

Luna gunned the car, and with Peyton still crying, she floored the gas and we screeched away from the curb. She took the turn at breakneck speed and pointed us in the direction of Lannan's manor.

"Watch out!" I grimaced as we almost hit the curb.

"I'll try," Luna said over her shoulder. "It would help if I could drive." And with that statement, we went weaving down the street.

Chapter 12

Lannan's mansion was lit up like a firecracker. As we swerved into the drive, I leaped out, not waiting for the valet to open the door. The guards had arrived, Check was standing by the on-duty security chief, and they looked like they'd been having a talk. I hurried over, with Luna leading Peyton behind me. The car had managed to survive Luna's haphazard driving and we'd arrived in one piece.

"We need to see Lannan. Now." I stared at the security chief, whom I recognized from previous visits. "And Regina, if she's around. And I do mean *now*."

After a moment's silence, he inclined his head and from behind those dark glasses said, "Go in, Your Highness. I'll call ahead."

As we hustled up to the mansion, Peyton still a wreck and moving only because she was on autopilot, it hit me that for the first time, we were entering the mansion with at least some power on our side. We—or at least I—was royalty. And that counted for something among the vampires.

Peyton was still covered with Rex's blood, a fact that struck me as several vamps turned our way. But Regina met us at the door, and she took one look at Peyton and motioned for the maid to take her into the bathroom.

"Clean her up, put her in clean clothes, and then bring her in."

"I'll go with her," Luna said. "She's had a horrible shock tonight."

"Very well. Bring them both when they're ready," Regina motioned for the maid to take them off, then turned to me. "Come. Lannan is in the study."

I wanted to burst out with what had happened but decided it was better to wait until we were behind closed doors. As we quick-stepped along the corridor, Regina glanced at me.

"Nice crown."

I wasn't sure what to say, and I wasn't up for small talk. I just nodded at her, catching her gaze. It didn't do to look vampires eye-to-eye, but right now, I wanted her to *see*. I wanted her to see my anger and fear and worry. After a moment, she nodded.

"Come. We'll do what we can," was all she said as we reached the study and passed through the doors.

Lannan was leaning back in one of the recliners, playing with some sort of puzzle. He was wearing a pair of black leather pants, an open crimson shirt, and a thin gold chain around his neck. The black and red set off his golden hair, and when I entered, he slowly put the puzzle down on the table and crossed one leg over the other knee, lounging back.

"Cicely, how nice of you to drop by. Or rather . . . Your Highness, the Great and Wondrous Queen of Snow and Ice." He hadn't lost the patronizing tone to his voice, but he slid honey over his words, making them simultaneously a compliment and an insult.

"Gee, thanks." Now that I *was* Queen, I felt a little less intimidated. It would be harder for him to hurt me and get away with it.

He patted the seat beside him. "Come. Come sit next to me."

I stared at him for a moment, wanting nothing more

than to smack him one, but there wasn't time. Silently, I
took the seat next to him. He started to reach out one hand
toward my knee, but Regina cleared her throat.

In a falsetto, she said, "*Royalty*, dear brother. Remember."

With a disgusted sigh, he hesitated, hovering over my
leg, then withdrew his hand and instead placed it right next
to his crotch.

I let out an exasperated breath and turned to Regina.
"Leo and Geoffrey kidnapped my cousin. They killed Rex,
Peyton's father, and dragged off Rhiannon. And Crawl is
out there, on the prowl. He came after me, but we managed
to get away before he could reach us."

"Dear Geoffrey let you escape through his fingers?
Crawl, I can understand. He is old and wily, but distrac-
tions plague him and it's not necessarily difficult to get
away from him if you see him coming first. But *Geoffrey . . .*" Lannan gave a shrug. "So he finds out he's not
exactly the god he sets himself up to be."

I ignored Lannan's comments and once again addressed
Regina. "*Did you hear me?* Leo kidnapped my *cousin*. Rex
is *dead*. And Crawl is killing people."

"I heard you. Yes." Golden Boy gave me a shrouded look,
and for a moment, I wondered what ran through his head
after all these years straddling the world of the living and
the dead.

"I want your promise. If Leo hurts her, *I* get to kill him.
Slowly. But think for a moment. If he tries to turn her—and
we know he will—who's to say what happened with Myst
won't happen again? Rhiannon is part Cambyra."

Regina crossed to the door. "Wait here. And Lannan—
watch yourself." She gave him a dark look as she left the
room. He merely arched his eyebrows.

Great, just what I wanted. To be alone with Lannan.

"So, how does being a queen suit you? I think it doesn't.
Suit you. Not by the look in your eyes." Lannan leaned
toward me. I'd have to push him away in order to stand up,
and that wasn't my idea of the wisest move.

"I'll grow into it." I stared at him for a moment. Lannan

had his faults, but he was blunt and direct. I'd give him that much. "There's a lot to learn."

"You're smart. You'll pick it up." He regarded me quietly for a moment. "I suppose, if I should touch you now, you'd sic your guards on me."

Annnndddddd . . . he just wouldn't let up.

"Lannan, can't you just give it up? Give me up? I don't know why I interest you, anyway. I'm not a vampire, I'm not your type." I was too tired and worried to resort to subterfuge.

"You might think that, Cicely, and you'd be right in one way. But I always get what I want. As for not being my type . . . there . . . you are mistaken." His voice was back to being smooth, seductive, and he ran his fingers up my leg, pressing hard through the material of my jeans. "I'll never sweet-talk you, never woo you. But give me the chance and I'll fuck you so hard that you'll forget Grieve, forget that crown you're wearing, forget anything but me."

Instead of cringing away from him, I just stared at him. "My cousin is in the hands of a psychotic, abusive vampire. You really think I'm going to focus on you at the moment? Lannan, you are smarter than that." Apparently, the changes in my life had given me more courage.

Lannan let go of my leg, gazing into my eyes with those dark orbs of his. "Regina should be back and then we'll tackle finding Geoffrey. But if you think I care all that much about your cousin, make no mistake: Rhiannon does not interest me. Preventing her death will prevent a host of problems, so I will do everything I can to further that end. But, Cicely, never underestimate the power of desire. *What I want, I get.* It may take some time, it may take some planning, but I always get what I want."

"You no longer hold a contract over me. If you want the money back you paid me, I'll give it to you. But Lannan, I'm no longer in your service. No matter what you think about it—or even what *I* think about it—I'm now the Queen of Snow and Ice. I've been through the rituals and coronation. I've changed." I wasn't sure whether I was try-

ing to convince him or myself. Lannan set me whirling, whether or not I liked the fact. But right now, Rhiannon
needed me, and Lannan's pressure wasn't helping matters.

Lannan stared at me for another moment, then seemed
to relent. "You are worried about your cousin. I do understand." He crossed the room, then turned back to me.
"Geoffrey is single-focused, a trait I also understand. He is
set on overthrowing the Crimson Court and in taking down
you at the same time. Which means he will probably leave
Leo to his own devices. And that, my sweet, places your
cousin's fate at the whim of that upstart whelp."

Three weeks ago, I would have never believed Geoffrey
capable of the betrayal that he'd shown the Crimson Court,
nor the insanity that had created Myst's people. But deception in my world seemed to be at all corners.

Except Lannan and Regina. The thought was disturbing. I stared at the vampire, realizing that—from the
beginning—the two had been more open and aboveboard
with me than just about anyone. Even Lainule had tried to
sell me out to Geoffrey, in her fear over Myst finding her
heartstone.

As Lannan and I continued our stare-down, Regina
opened the door. She glanced at Lannan, then at me.

"Everything all right here?"

I nodded, slowly. "Yeah, everything's fine. At least
here. Where are Peyton and Luna?" A sudden fear swelled
up that perhaps they'd been swept away, too. There were so
many monsters on so many sides.

But Regina calmed my fear. "They've cleaned up and
are in the parlor, having some tea. Do not fear, they are
guests and will not be touched or bothered. I thought it best
to let the girl relax for a moment, considering her loss."

She settled herself behind her desk. "I've assigned extra
guards to the town. They're hunting Crawl now. As for
Geoffrey and Leo, I've doubled our efforts to find the trail
that will lead us to them. But I'm thinking we could use
magic in the attempt. Cicely, do you know any seers?"

I frowned. "I'm not sure, but perhaps . . . the Consortium.

They'll have to help us since I'm a member. I'm supposed to meet with them tomorrow, Rhiannon and I. I'll call Ysandra and see if we can up that meeting to tonight." But that still meant Leo had the entire night to torment Rhiannon, because by the time we met, even if they could help me, it would be near morning.

My resolve faltering, I sank back into the chair, covering my face.

"Cicely, are you . . ." Regina stopped, then crossed to my side. She sat beside me, smoothing my hair back. "There's nothing I can say to make this easier. I can't—and won't—make false promises that everything will be all right. But I do promise we are doing everything we can to find them. To save your cousin."

I looked into her face and, for the first time, felt like Regina was seriously trying to extend an olive branch. True vampires usually didn't concern themselves with *breathers*. They were near the top of the food chain, and they left no doubt about that fact. But tonight, Regina's expression was almost friendly.

"Thanks." I told myself I wouldn't cry, but a tear slipped down my cheek. Regina reached out, gently wiped it away. I swallowed the lump in my throat and looked at her. "First Myst captures my aunt and turns her into a monster. Now Peyton's father is dead, and Leo's kidnapped my cousin. And we all know what *he* intends to do. And I'm sitting here, doing *nothing*. I want to be out there, finding her. I want to canvass the streets, to hunt her down, to pound on doors."

Lannan moved over to the chair opposite us and sat down. "I'll go out. I know several vampires who will talk to me where they won't talk to anybody else. If anybody's hiding Geoffrey and his protégé, I'll find out who." He hesitated, then reached out and placed a hand on mine. "Cicely, we'll find her. But don't do anything stupid. Crawl is still out there, and until he's found, you're in danger. Take your guards with you wherever you go. Even . . . take that idiot prince of yours. I'll give him this: He'd die to protect you."

I started to bristle, but Regina gave me a soft shake of the head. She motioned toward her desk. "Call the Petros woman. See if she can meet you tonight, and if she can, my driver will take you."

I pulled out my cell phone and flipped it open. It still had a few bars of charge left. A quick tap to my contacts, and then another to Ysandra. *One ring. Two rings. Three rings.* On the fourth she picked up.

"Cicely? What can I do for you?"

I glanced at the clock. Six thirty. Two hours since Rex had died. "We need your help and we need it now, Ysandra. Geoffrey and Leo captured Rhiannon, they killed Rex, and now we have no clue where to find them. We need the Consortium's help."

A quiet hush followed, and then the next moment, Ysandra simply said, "Where can I pick you up?"

"I'm at the Regent's mansion. Luna and Peyton are with me. I'm worried about Peyton; she watched her father get killed. Geoffrey did it." I paused. "Rhiannon and I underwent our coronations last night. Leo has a Fae Queen in his possession."

Another soft pause, then, "I'll pick you up in fifteen minutes. Be waiting for me, the three of you. And, Cicely, I need not tell you this is dangerous news, not only for your cousin's health but for New Forest, for the Golden Wood, and for you." She hung up without another word.

I turned to Regina. "Ysandra's picking us up. Will you walk us out?" I didn't want to be alone, even though I knew my guards would be there. I didn't want to stand out there in the night, without someone watching over us.

Regina nodded. Lannan said nothing, but he threw on a trench coat and then turned to stare at me before sweeping out of the room, his hair golden against the black of the material.

⚓

Regina waited with us until Ysandra's car pulled up. Luna was somber; Peyton was shell-shocked. Nobody said much of anything. As the silent snow swirled down to our feet, I wanted nothing more than for my father to show up. Even in the short time I'd known him, he had come to represent security to me, and now, once again, all of that had been stripped away.

Check took a step closer to me, leaning down. "Your Highness, is there anything I can do?"

"Learn how to ride in a car," I said, a little churlish. Then, biting my tongue when he looked crestfallen, I let out a sigh. "I'm sorry. It would help, but I didn't mean it to come out so . . . nasty. I'm just . . ."

"Never explain yourself, Your Highness," was his reply.

I smiled at him then, but the smile didn't last. I couldn't sustain it. When we'd routed Myst, everything seemed like it was on the right track. Now everything was shot to hell again and sliding downhill fast.

Ysandra pulled up, and as Check bustled Peyton and Luna into the backseat, I leaned into the front. "Where are we going? My guards need to know."

With a glance beyond my shoulder, she handed me a piece of paper. I glanced at it. The address was written down, but the writing was glittering and I had the feeling that it was magical, to be invisible to prying eyes not approved for such communication. I handed it over to Check, who read it, then gave a quick nod to Ysandra. The moment I was in the passenger seat, buckled up, the guards took off in a blur to meet us at our destination.

Ysandra eased out of the parking loop, stopping for a moment outside the gates for me to contact Ulean. Then we headed onto the snowy streets. She looked like she wanted to say something, but with a glance in the rearview mirror at Peyton, she shut her mouth and kept silent.

The rumbling of the engine against the muffled night was the only sound as we eased along the ice-slicked roads. I watched the street signs go by, one by one, wondering where we were going. The address hadn't been familiar to me, but Check seemed to have recognized it.

After a time and a maze of turns, Ysandra edged into a parking lot next to a small building on the outskirts of town. A single light illuminated the front door, and there seemed to be no guards—in fact, no sign of any life around it.

"Where are we? Is Ulean here?" I was reluctant to get out of the car till Check showed up, but Ysandra removed the keys from the ignition and opened her door.

I am here, Cicely. The barriers did not stop me.

"At an area far safer than just about any you've ever been to. Don't fuss. Your Elemental is here, your guards are here, and so are guards from the Consortium."

"Where?" But she'd already gotten out of the car and was busy helping Peyton out. I decided that if Ysandra felt safe, we probably were, and cautiously opened the door. The moment I set foot into the empty parking lot and stepped out of the car, the entire landscape shifted and changed. I could see more than a dozen cars now, near ours, and not only my own guards but at least eight members of the Consortium's elite task force, as they were called. They were really units of magical warriors, specially trained for combat situations. Highly skilled magicians, witches and sorcerers, they could stand up to the strongest of enemies.

Breathing easier, I looked around and the barriers of the illusion became clear. The lot and building were surrounded by a force field.

"From the street, this looked empty. Can anyone see us here?"

"Only if they are magically trained." Ysandra gave me a little shrug. "You think I would allow you to walk out into a deserted lot? Come, Cicely, you know better than that." The prim taskmistress was back. Ysandra was a pretty woman, but she looked like a librarian, behind her glasses and long skirts and stiffly pressed button-down blouses, and a chignon that hid the length of her voluminous hair. She also happened to be an incredibly strong witch, and I'd seen her strike down a group of werewolves once with no more than a single incantation.

We followed her into the building, leaving the guards behind.

The building itself was also an illusion, covering up something far grander than I'd expected. On the outside, it was a simple three-story office building, its paint fading and its brick weathered.

On the inside, however, the building belied the non-descript exterior. White marble floors, veined with green and red, gleamed, polished to a high shine. The walls were the same color as the morning sky. Benches of the same marble lined the walls, and a center counter of the same material overshadowed the entrance, with an illuminated sign that read, INFORMATION.

Beyond the information desk, a staircase wound up to the second floor, and there was an elevator to the side. Ysandra motioned for us to follow her, and we passed the information counter, stopping for Ysandra to show the woman a badge. She waved us on to the right, down a hall behind the bank of elevators.

Ysandra led us through the hushed corridors. Even though they were bustling with activity—I'd never felt so much magic congregated in one place before—the sound of footsteps was muffled, and people talked in low tones. It almost felt like we were in a hospital, except there wasn't that sterile, sick smell or the sense of worry that permeated the corridors.

I nodded. *Ulean, wait for me.*

Always, Cicely.

Standing back, Ysandra ushered us into what turned out to be an auditorium. There were rows of seats—much like in a large study hall—all facing the stage. But there, the resemblance to a university ended.

On the stage, a long raised table stretched out, covered by a pleated cobalt cloth that draped to the floor. Behind the table, sitting in five of the thirteen chairs, were three women and two men, all in black robes, with some sort of cobalt insignia that I couldn't read.

Ysandra paused, then leaned down to whisper to me, "Good. All the Council Members present are favorable to you. There are three who do not approve of you and your cousin, but none seem to be here today."

"Well, thank heavens for small favors." I didn't mean it to come out so snarky, but the way things had been going, I wasn't inclined to be so favorable to anybody who didn't like me.

We edged our way down the sloping aisle, till we reached the front. There, Ysandra motioned for us to sit in the front seats while she climbed the steps leading to the lectern facing the Council.

"Your Eminences, I have brought Her Majesty, Queen Cicely, the Queen of Snow and Ice from the Cambyra nation, before you. She is also a member of the Consortium, leader of the Moon Spinners."

I stood, not sure if I was supposed to bow or curtsey or say a word. But as I opened my mouth, Ysandra motioned for me to sit down again.

"We have a grave situation. All other questions as to the legitimacy of having royalty among our ranks must wait. For the present, the Moon Spinners are part of our organization and they need our help."

The woman who appeared to be the head honcho gazed down at us. "We've heard." When I jerked, startled, she stayed any response I might make. "Do you know who I am, Your Highness?"

I shook my head. "No."

"I am the Mother of the Consortium, you might say. I am the eldest member of the Council. I have the final say, although the Council has a right to vote their opinion, and a majority tends to rule." She paused. "You seem surprised that we know about the attack, but by oath, word travels, Your Highness, and the Consortium has ears and eyes every which way. We know that the former Regent of the Vampire Nation kidnapped the Summer Queen. We also know that the Blood Oracle is on the loose."

"Your Reverence." Ysandra motioned for Peyton to stand. "Peyton Moon Runner, a member of the Moon Spinners. Her father was killed by Geoffrey today."

The Reverend Mother of the Consortium—that was all I could think of to call her—let out a soft murmur. She looked at Peyton. "Your father sought to protect you." To Ysandra, she said, "What do they need?"

Ysandra looked back at me, then at the Reverend Mother. "I think . . . besides protection, a seer. We need to find out where Geoffrey and Leo are. We have to find Rhiannon before Leo turns her. If he tries . . . she is part Cambyra and we know what that can do."

The Reverend Mother looked at us, then at Ysandra. "We shall withdraw and consider the matter. Wait here." The five members of the Council silently stood and, making no sound other than the soft swishing of their robes, disappeared behind the stage.

As we watched them go, I turned to Ysandra. "They know far more than they let on, don't they?"

She gave me a wry smile. "My dear, the Council of Elders probably knows what the head of the Akazzani eats for breakfast, and what color underwear he wears. The vampires think they rule this world, and we let them think that— it's safer that way. But the real power . . . the real power was just in this room. The Council . . . they may not be as old as the vampires, or shape-shifters like the Cambyra, but the magic that flows through their veins is strong and powerful and has its roots in the very bones of this world."

Peyton leaned forward, staring at her hands. "I barely knew him. You'd think that I'd get a chance to know him better, but no. They wouldn't let me have even that. I've lost my mother and now my father." She looked exhausted, but her tears were gone.

"Are you . . ." I'd started to ask if she was okay, but that was stupid. Of course she wasn't okay. Feeling helpless, I looked over at Luna.

Luna rubbed Peyton's shoulder. "What do you need from us?"

Peyton gave her a sideways glance. "A good bed without the fear that somebody's trying to kill me or my friends. A stiff drink. Maybe someone to sing me to sleep." She shrugged.

Taking her hand, Luna squeezed it tightly. "I can at least sing you to sleep. I'll stay in your room tonight. I'm sure we'll have enough guards posted around the house to stave off an army. Anyway . . . they got what they wanted." With a quick look at me, she murmured, "Almost."

"You don't have to walk softly around my feelings, Luna. I know that Geoffrey wants me as much as Leo wanted Rhiannon, though for different reasons. And he's not going to give up yet. Nor will Crawl." Standing up, I started to pace, folding my arms across my chest. "Oh, why won't they hurry? I have to find Rhia . . . I need to find her *tonight*."

Ysandra cleared her throat. "They will take as long as they take. There is nothing to do that will hurry the Council." She sat down beside Peyton and pressed a small bottle into her hand. "Take four drops of this on the tongue. It will help, but it will not dull your senses."

As she proceeded to try to persuade Peyton to take whatever was in the bottle, Luna motioned me off to one side.

When we were away from the area, she turned to me and, in low whispers, said, "If they won't help us, I might be able to do the job. You need a seer. While I'm not a natural-born clairvoyant, I do have a spell that might work. It requires a great deal of energy and runs to shadow magic, but I'd be willing to do it. We have to get Rhiannon back."

I gazed at her, gauging her expression. "You're afraid," I finally said. "Whatever this spell is, it will work, but you're afraid of it. Why?"

Luna rubbed the back of her neck, but all she would say was, "The price is high. But it's a price I would be willing to pay."

I tried to get more information out of her, but she clammed up. A noise at the back of the stage signaled the Council's return.

They motioned for us to reconvene, and we took our seats again. After a moment, Ysandra stood and we followed suit, remaining on our feet.

The Reverend Mother cleared her throat. "In the matter of the Petros appeal for help, the Council has deemed this: We will lay the spell of Greater Protection on the house and woodland in which the members of the Moon Spinners reside. In the matter of providing a seer, we decline."

I started to say something, but Ysandra grabbed my arm, warning me with a shake of her head to shut my mouth. She turned back to the Council.

"In the matter of the Moon Spinners' eligibility for membership now that two of the members are royalty of a sovereign nation, we will address that after this situation is resolved. This meeting is adjourned."

As the Reverend Mother stood and headed back the way she'd come, followed by the others, I wanted to jump on the stage, to drag her back and hammer home why we needed the seer. But Ysandra held me back, her nails digging through my turtleneck, into my arm.

After the auditorium was empty, she let out a long breath.

"Never, ever contradict the Council. They can be deadly foes, and they have long memories." She frowned. "I'll do what I can to find a seer on the side, someone who can divine the whereabouts of Rhiannon and Geoffrey and Leo."

I waited for a moment but was surprised when Luna didn't speak up about her spell. After a moment's hesitation, I simply gave Ysandra a gracious smile.

"Thank you. We need rest. We're exhausted. Grieve must be worried sick about me. I have to let Chatter know what's happened." The weight of so much pressing on my shoulders was almost more than I could bear. I dropped to the nearest chair. "I'm so tired. Even getting back to the Barrow's going to be a chore tonight."

"The guards will help," Luna said, softly taking me by the arm. "Ysandra, Rex's car is still at the Regent's mansion. We have no way home tonight. Can you drive us back to the Veil House?"

She held up her keys. "I was planning on it. I'll talk to the guards, tell them to meet us there. Meanwhile, let's get you something to keep you on your feet until you get home."

On the way out, she stopped at the information counter and talked to the girl behind the desk. After a moment, the girl handed her a small paper bag and Ysandra gave each one of us a cookie. It smelled heavenly, but when I bit into the ginger-molasses round, a warmth flooded through me, lifting my energy until I could manage my way to the car. Peyton was still quiet but seemed a little calmer, and Luna—whom I'd seen surreptitiously sliding her cookie into her pocket—tucked her in the back of the car.

Two other cars pulled out with us. Ysandra told us they contained members of the Consortium's Elite Force— guards to make certain we found our way home. All the way home, I rested my head against the back of the seat, staring out into the darkened night. All I could think of was that Rhiannon was out there somewhere, in the hands of an abusive, vicious vampire, who wanted to turn her, use her, and make her his slave.

Chapter 13

By the time we reached the Veil House, the guards were there, with extra sentries stationed around the perimeter of the land—both from the Summer Court and from Regina's camp. The vampires and Fae kept a close watch on each other but seemed to be coexisting without a problem, at least for now.

Chatter was there, too, waiting for us, as we entered the house. The look on his face told me he knew what had gone down. Heartbroken, I opened my arms and he slowly embraced me, tears flickering on his lashes.

Grieve was in the corner, and after a moment, he came forward and took Chatter by the shoulders, leading him to the sofa. Luna steered Peyton into one of the rocking chairs and tucked an afghan over her, then went in the kitchen to make a pot of tea.

Bleakly, I sat down at the desk and ran my hand over the restored surface. Heather had loved this desk, and Rhiannon, too. And Heather had been turned by Myst. We had staked her when we found her in the woods. Now . . .

would I be forced to take the same measures to my cousin? Would I be forced to drive a stake through her heart, too?

"Damn Leo. Damn him to fucking hell." I slammed my fist down on the desk. "I'll stake the motherfucker and cut off his head and fill it with garlic."

Everybody stared at me. At that point, Luna returned from the kitchen, a tray of tea and cookies in hand. She pressed a cup into Peyton's hand, waiting until she had taken a sip before moving on.

I winced. Peyton had lost her father—right before her eyes. Geoffrey had ripped him to shreds and she'd been forced to witness the murder. She was hurting as much as I was. I crossed to her chair and knelt by her side, taking her hands in mine.

"What can we do? Is there *anything* we can do to help?"

She leaned her head against the back of the chair, weary. "No. Thanks, but . . . there's nothing anybody can do now except to find Geoffrey and kill him." After a pause, she added, "I suppose I need to find out where the police took Rex's body and go about claiming it. And then, I guess . . . I bury my father."

I waited for the tears but they didn't come. "Peyton . . ."

As if she knew what I was thinking, she set her teacup aside and pressed one hand over mine. "I'm all cried out, Cicely. I guess . . . I'll cry again later . . . when I've had time to sleep. But for now . . . I'm just numb."

I brought her hand to my lips and kissed it softly, then reached out and stroked the bangs out of her eyes, brushing her hair back. "Drink your tea. Close your eyes. Rest. That's probably the best thing you can do right now. Tomorrow, we'll help you with the . . . arrangements."

"Tomorrow, you'll need my help. Leo has Rhiannon. Geoffrey killed my father. I'll be damned if I let those bloodsuckers take her, too." She closed her eyes and within a few moments was breathing softly, asleep.

I glanced at Luna, questioning.

She shrugged. "I spiked her drink with a strong herbal

sedative. She'll sleep through the rest of the night, so we might want to carry her up to her room when we're done."

"You're sure it's safe?"

"Yes, positive." She handed the rest of the teacups around and passed the cookies. I took one, realizing I was starving even though it was hard to think about food right now.

Turning to Grieve, I slumped down by his side and leaned my head on his shoulder, rubbing his sleeve with my fingers. "What are you doing here? Should we all be away from the Barrows right now?" The thought that Myst might choose this time to attack again, when we were at our most vulnerable, wasn't all that far from my mind, but I didn't want to voice it.

Grieve shook his head. "No, they'll be fine. The guards are thick as honey there, and Strict and Edge are watching over the Courts. Now . . . tell us everything that happened."

And so, with Luna's help, I did. As we came to the part where Leo snatched away Rhiannon, Chatter paled, and anger flashed in his usually agreeable gaze. The room grew warm, and a light breeze swept around him.

Ulean, what's going on with Chatter?

Can you feel the heat? His fire is up. He's repressing the instinct to summon the flames, but you can still feel them rising in his fury. But he has experience and even in his grief and anger, he can control them, I think.

Unlike a number of the Cambyra Fae, Chatter didn't shift into an animal or bird, but instead a pillar of fire. He was unusual in that way, but the ability wasn't unknown.

Grieve was watching him, and I felt the wolf tattoo on my stomach pacing uneasily. "Hold yourself steady. You can't do anything to help her if you lose control."

Chatter gave him an abrupt nod, and within the blink of an eye ceased to be Grieve's buddy and became the fiancé of my cousin. The easygoing nature was gone, replaced by a man who loved his sweetheart and would kill to get her back. He leaned back in his chair, crossing one leg across the other knee, silent and brooding.

"So what do we do?" Grieve looked at me. "I can send

men out to search for them, but the vampires are difficult to find when they want to hide."

I glanced at Luna. "You said . . . if we didn't get the seer, you could help?"

She hung her head. After a moment, she let out a short sigh and toyed with the edge of the throw that hung over the back of the sofa.

"Yes, I can do it. And I will. But . . . I'll need sleep first. I'm exhausted, and if I hope to control the energy, I have to be at the top of my game." She glanced at the clock. It was now close to midnight. "Tomorrow morning, we'll do the ritual. I know it's a long time to wait—I know it puts Rhiannon in danger—but I can't make certain the spell doesn't backfire if I'm not alert."

I didn't want to wait, but I knew how exhausted I was, and Luna had to be close on my heels. The last thing we needed was magic gone wrong. I wanted to pace, to move, to do something, but my body refused to respond.

"We're all exhausted. It's been a horrid day." Any excitement or joy of shopping for our wedding gowns was swept away by the reality of the dangers we were facing. Bleakly, I stood. "We all need sleep. Grieve, should we return to the Barrow? Or can we crash here? There are plenty of guards outside, both Fae and vampire."

He nodded. "We'll stay here. I'll send word to Strict and to Edge." He slipped out the back as I glanced, once again, at Chatter.

"Chatter . . ." But I stopped when he looked at me. His shrouded gaze was dark and brooding. His long dark hair was pulled back in a ponytail, and while I'd always liked Chatter, I was beginning to see him in a different light. I was beginning to see the man that my cousin had fallen in love with.

"You can't help me. And I can't say anything to make *you* feel better. Except that when we find them, we'll tear them apart. But, Cicely—" He leaned across the table and took my hand, staring intently into my eyes. "Leo's mine. Rhiannon may be your cousin, but she's my fiancée, and she's my love. And if he touches her, he'll find out just how ruthless the Fae can be, and why the outer world fears us. Vampires are dangerous, yes, but they flaunt their power. While we nurse our powers, and nurture them, and then use them like a strike of lightning."

Wearily, I patted his hand and stood. "Yeah . . . that's something I'm learning how to do, still."

Grieve returned, and Luna asked him and Chatter to help her carry Peyton to her bedroom. I followed, trudging up the stairs. After the guys left, Luna and I undressed her and bundled her into her nightgown. The sedative kept her out like a light, and we tucked the blanket around her. Luna sat on the other side of the bed.

In a whisper, she said, "I'm going to sleep here, in case she wakes up with nightmares. The bed's big enough."

"Grieve and I will take Kaylin's room, and Chatter can sleep downstairs on the sofa."

She nodded, yawning. "I wish I could do the magic for you tonight—"

I stopped her. "Don't sweat it. You're right, we all need sleep. We're on last gasp here." With a quick hug, I softly closed the door and met Grieve in the hall. Chatter had already gone downstairs.

Kaylin was supposed to sleep in Heather's old room, and as we entered, memories flooded back. I pressed my lips together, trying not to think about all the bloodshed and carnage that had gone on over the past few weeks. Grieve shed his clothes, as he always did, and I stripped off my own. Climbing under the comforter, I turned out the light and lay on my side, staring at the silent fall of snow outside the window. We didn't say anything. There wasn't anything left to say. When I finally fell asleep, my dreams were filled with the mist and snow and ice, and the screams of Rhiannon, begging me to come rescue her.

❧

Morning light didn't make anything better. The guards were waiting to fill us in on the state of the Barrows—which were, for once, doing fine. Peyton, on the other hand, was quiet and withdrawn. Over breakfast, she toyed with her phone, until I finally asked her what she was thinking about.

"I'm debating on whether to call Mother. She probably doesn't know Rex is dead. She'd probably be glad for the news." A gloom had settled over her face, and a cloud seemed to surround her.

I kept my mouth shut. The fact was, Anadey probably *would* be glad to hear Rex was dead. She'd betrayed our trust, tried to kill me, tried to have Rex killed, and now I wondered if she was in league with Geoffrey and Leo, but I didn't want to come out and say so.

But Peyton beat me to the punch. "You think she might be acting with them, don't you? That she might be cozying up to them."

I shrugged. "I don't know, but considering what she did, I wouldn't put it past her."

Luna handed me a plate of eggs and bacon and set a stack of toast in the center of the table. Grieve took a piece, and so did Chatter, but neither of them was saying much. They seemed to give way to me, and I realized that—even to my love and his friend—the fact that I was now Queen took precedence over just about everything.

As we ate, one of the guards knocked on the kitchen door, then let himself in. He knelt by my side, bowing his head. "Your Majesty, a package was delivered for you. We took the liberty of opening it to make certain there wasn't anything dangerous inside." He held out a DVD case, but it was one that you burn yourself, not a preformatted movie.

I gingerly took it, staring at the disk. "Where's the wrapping?"

He handed it to me. Whoever had opened it had done a good job of keeping it fairly intact, because it was easy to see the postmark—New Forest—but also easy to see there was no return address. Just *Her Highness Cicely Waters, Veil House, New Forest, WA.* There was no postmark, so whoever had sent it, had to have paid the messenger to deliver it.

A fluttering in my stomach told me this wasn't good. It wasn't good at all. I pushed myself back from the table and stood, heading into the living room, where there was a DVD player, the others following.

As I slid the disk into the machine and turned it on, Luna flipped on the television. I didn't want to sit down. For some reason, I was sweating cold, and it felt like I might be better able to handle whatever was on the disk if I was standing up. Chatter joined us, and I suddenly turned to Grieve.

"Take him out. Just do it. Both of you go outside."

"No," Chatter said. "If this has anything to do with Rhiannon, I need to see it. And you can't stop me, Queen or not, Cicely." There was a finality to his words that made me shiver, and so I just shrugged and hit the Play button.

The screen flickered, and then a room came into view. It was dimly lit, with a red ambiance. Several people were in the room, but they were on their knees, staring at the floor. By the furnishings, I knew they were in a dungeon somewhere. I'd spent enough time hanging around the scene with my mother to recognize a fetish setup when I saw one, though most were run by perfectly respectable and sane people, not sadistic vampires. To the left sat a spanking bench; to the right, stocks and a bondage table. There was what looked like a metal web or netting that covered a red-brick wall.

And in the center of the film, dangling from wrist cuffs from the ceiling, was Rhiannon. I caught my breath, stiffening. This was no fetish bar. She was hurting, that much was obvious. And in most fetish clubs, actual damage didn't play into the scene, except for some of the underground clubs and vampire setups.

Behind me, Chatter let out a low moan. Rhia was wearing a sheer red gown, with no underwear or bra beneath it. Her hair hung loose, and she was staring at the camera with a terrified expression. But then I realized it wasn't the camera she was staring at, but something in front of the camera that was invisible to us. Or . . . *someone*.

She struggled, trying to back up. "Please, please don't. Leo, please, stop!"

The next moment, her head snapped back and the imprint of a hand showed red against her cheek. She cried out, twisting, but she couldn't get away from her attacker. The others in the room stayed where they were, kneeling, although I saw a couple of them look up when they seemed to think they weren't being watched.

"I like it when you say my name, Rio. You remember your nickname, don't you? The one you used to love me to say." Leo's voice echoed out from the television, and it took everything I had not to jump up, to run crazed searching for her. Chatter let out a growl and I sensed, rather than heard, Grieve, trying to calm him down.

Rhiannon said nothing, but the next moment her head went back as Leo—or one of his cronies—grabbed her hair and yanked. Her throat was exposed, and I jumped up. But he didn't bite her. Instead, a thin red weal began under her chin and ran down to between her breasts. She tried to turn her head, but the blood trickled down her chest.

"That hurt, babe? Good. Bitch. Whore of my dreams. You're going to hurt a lot more before I get done with you, Rio, because, my sweet, you ran away from me. Your cunt of a cousin turned you against me. Wait till Geoffrey gets hold of her—we're going to serve her up to Crawl, watch him take her apart, inch by inch. He knows tortures I can only dream about. The great Queens of Summer and Winter will be on their knees, begging for every breath."

My stomach lurched. Chatter cried out and I heard something crackle. Turning around, I saw flames flickering off his hands. I paused the DVD. "Don't! You *cannot* destroy this house—it will do no good. As horrific as this is, we have to know if she . . ."

"If he kills her." Chatter's look terrified me. I'd thought Grieve was dangerous, but the King-Elect of Summer was about to turn into a flaming pillar and go burning the house down around our shoulders.

I turned to Grieve. "If he can't control himself, get him outside."

"No, I told you before." Chatter glared at me but then slowly withdrew the flames into himself. "Leo dies. He dies a thousand deaths."

"And every one of them will hurt. Let's finish this so Luna can use her scrying spell to find out where the fuck they are. Then we rescue Rhiannon and take the freakshow down."

A moment later, reassured he wasn't going to explode, I pressed Play and the DVD started up again.

Rhia struggled as someone ripped her robe away. Tears running down my face, I forced myself to stand still, watching. We couldn't see Leo, but what he was doing was obvious by her movements and soft whimpers.

"Like it, bitch. Love it. Beg me. Come on, beg me."

The sound of his voice echoed in my memory. Lannan . . . forcing me to his feet, forcing me to say and do things I never would have done . . . all through the control of his voice.

"Please, Leo, please . . . *fuck me*." The words sounded forced, and I knew—we all knew—they were. Rhiannon choked as the manacles around her wrist opened and she was forced down on her knees. I knew what was going on, it was obvious. After a few seconds, I closed my eyes, my stomach churning. The thought of what he was doing to her was horrifying, but the fact that we couldn't see him but could hear his grunts made it worse, somehow.

After a few moments, she choked and spit out a long string of fluid. The next moment, she went flying across the room, where she landed with a hard thud on the pillows. Her wrists went back, over her head, as an invisible force pinned her down and another shoved her knees apart.

"You'll never forget me." Leo's voice was ragged, and Rhiannon stiffened. She began to whimper again, but I could tell he was forcing her to enjoy it, controlling her will, and she let out a shriek. I winced, not wanting to see Chatter's face. I knew from experience that she couldn't help it. He had control of her body, though I knew she was fighting against him.

And then, finally, it was over. I held my breath as she was manhandled to face the camera. We could hear whispering, and then Rhiannon, beyond tears, stammered out a message.

"Cicely . . . Leo . . . he says that if you don't turn yourself over to Geoffrey, they'll turn me."

And then Leo's arrogant voice broke in. "My little whore here, my little Fae-fucker, is right. Cicely, you mistress of demons, get your ass to the town square by tonight or I'll unleash a foe worse than you've ever dreamed. You think Myst is bad? I know how to drive this little beauty of mine insane. I know how to *break her*, and then after I break her, I'll drink her down and turn her. And *you* will have been responsible for creating a monster. Now aren't you sorry you poked your fucking nose into our business?"

Rhia let out a cry. "No, don't do it. Don't do what he—" She stopped as the crack of a blow echoed through the room.

"Tonight. Eight P.M. If you aren't there by midnight, your cousin will have vanished forever and a new queen of fire will rampage across the land. And won't that be a *delight* with two demented Queens on the loose. We know Myst still lives. Oh, and Chatter? She's *mine*, so suck my dick."

And then the DVD ended.

As the screen went blank, the house grew deadly silent. My breath came in shallow pants and I was doing my best not to go stark fucking mad. Not trusting myself to speak, I slowly stood up and turned off the TV.

Peyton roused herself out of her gloom. She stood, straightened the hem of her sweater, and was the first to break the silence. "*Whatever* you need me to do, I'm here."

Joining her, Luna pointed to the sofa. "Please, move this and bring in a small table. I'll get ready to cast the spell and we'll find out where they are."

I turned to Grieve and Chatter. Grieve looked somber; Chatter looked ready to kill. He had changed in the past ten minutes. We all had. Without a word, he and Grieve grabbed the ends of the sofa and shoved it out of the way. Then they went out to talk to the guards. I moved off to the side while Peyton helped Luna get things ready and put in a call to Ysandra Petros.

When she answered the phone, I told her what had happened.

"I'll be right over," she said. She was not a woman for small talk.

"You may not like what you see us doing."

"I'm not worried about that. The Council needed to do more, and they didn't. They aren't even getting around to casting the spell of protection till later this week. I'm tired of the bureaucracy." And with that, she hung up.

"Ysandra's coming over. I think she's going to help us." I wanted to run to Lainule, to tell her what was going on, but she wasn't here anymore. And Regina and Lannan were asleep for the day. But that meant that so were Geoffrey and Leo. If we could pinpoint where they were before dark, we could take them out more easily, even though I didn't want it to be easy on them. I wanted them to suffer. I wanted them to realize their lives were ending and know that I was responsible. I wanted to torture them like they were torturing Rhiannon.

As Luna set a black candle and a crystal ball on the small circular table now in the center of the room, I stared at the DVD player. I couldn't bear to think that my last vision of my cousin might be . . .

"Cicely?"

I turned. Luna was standing behind me, her hand on my arm. "What do you want to do with that DVD?"

"What I want . . . is to destroy it. But I think . . . first Regina needs to see it. And the Consortium. Then, perhaps, they'll realize just what we're up against. I keep thinking they don't realize how ruthless Geoffrey and Leo are." I stared into her eyes. "But maybe I'm fooling myself? Maybe they realize and just don't care? Or maybe they care, but not nearly as much as I want them to."

I wasn't sure what to do. Luna decided for me, reaching around to pop the DVD out of the player and put it back in the case. She paused, then slid it into her purse. I started to protest, putting my hand on her purse, but she caught hold of my wrist and shook her head.

"No. Leave it. I don't want you staring at this. I don't want you haunting yourself with it. I'll keep it until we show it to the Consortium and Regina. After that, we can destroy it." She slowly untangled my fingers from the strap of her purse and ran her hand over my cheek. "I wish I could help more. I hate seeing you worry. I hate seeing everybody upset. Come, we'll get ready and I'll cast that spell and do what I can to find where they're keeping her."

There was a sound in the kitchen and I whirled around, but it was just Grieve and Chatter returning, with Ysandra behind them. She was wearing a fur-trimmed trench coat and she slipped it off, revealing a white starched shirt with a ruffled front over a long quilted skirt. Her hair was, as usual, in its chignon, and her rectangular wire-frame glasses gave her a studious look, but she really was a beautiful woman when you looked beyond the stern exterior.

I gazed into her eyes, and my resolve gave way. The older woman opened her arms and I fell into them, sobbing against her shoulder as she patted my back.

"We will take care of this, Cicely. We'll find her and go after her." After a moment, she pushed me back by the shoulders, and the prim magical adept was back. "Dry your tears. Crying has to wait. We don't have time for tears."

I struggled to catch my breath and, as Luna pressed a couple of tissues into my hand, dried my eyes and blew my nose.

Ysandra looked around. "What are you doing?"

Luna faced her squarely. "I'm going to cast a Locate spell."

Ysandra cocked her head. "What tradition are you using?"

"Family. My family has several innate abilities, and one is to find lost people. We go through our ancestors for the

energy." There was something about the way she said it . . .
I couldn't catch the meaning, but Ysandra seemed to understand, because the Consortium member blanched, pulling
back.

"Ancestor magic . . . you realize how much those spells
can cost you?" Ysandra almost sounded afraid.

Luna let out a slow breath. "I know. Trust me, I know. But
this is the only way. We can't afford to let another night pass
without finding Rhiannon. They want Cicely to show up
tonight in the town square by eight o'clock or they'll turn
Rhiannon. You know they'll do it, too." Luna shrugged. "I'm
not going to let that happen. Since the Consortium won't
engage a seer for us, it's up to me."

Ysandra pressed her lips together, a thoughtful look in
her eyes. After a moment, she gave one short nod. "As you
wish. What backup do you need? This isn't one of the
spells in my repertoire, but I can provide energy to help.
Just let me know what you want me to do."

Luna laughed softly. "Be prepared in case anybody
comes through whom we don't want in here. You know
what these spells can conjure up."

"Are you in danger if you do this?" I broke in. No matter
how much I wanted my cousin back, I couldn't let Luna put
herself in danger in order to rescue Rhiannon and I was
getting the distinct impression this spell was far more powerful than I had first thought.

Luna shook her head. "Don't sweat it. There's always
danger when you run family magic and you're yummanii.
Magic for our people works different than for the Fae or
the magic-born. It's more unpredictable, and we are more
easily possessed and entranced."

I had heard this but had never had the opportunity to
really sit down with any magic-using yummanii to discuss
it. And since I'd met Luna, our lives had been focused on
fighting Myst and not much of anything else.

"I didn't know that. Then how do you get up the courage
to use your magic, if it's so chaotic?" But even as I asked, I

realized my question was moot. My mother had run away from her heritage, but most of the magic-born embraced their gifts. There was no reason why the yummanii wouldn't do the same. "Never mind. What do we do next?"

Luna motioned to Ysandra. "I don't usually work in a magical circle unless it's a powerful ritual, like the one my sister did for Grieve. But for this spell, I think we should call the veils of protection. Can you do that without interfering with the resonance of my magic?"

Ysandra nodded. "Yes, protection grids and veils are pretty standard across most magical systems. Especially since my magic is of the pure form, as in purest sense— while I can call the lightning, my energy tends to be that of magical force, untouched by any specific elemental nature."

"Then set up a veil that allows spirits from my past to come through but no others. I'm a good medium, although I don't often talk about it, but I don't want to fight off all the ghosts looking for someone to give them a voice." Luna turned toward the stairs. "I'm going up to take a quick ritual shower. If you would ring the table with salt, then cast the veil of protection, that's all I need." With that, she was off.

Grieve and Chatter had moved to one corner of the room and were talking in low, soft tones. Ysandra motioned me toward the kitchen.

"Show me where the salt is. I don't care for poking around through others' drawers. You never know what you might find."

At first I thought she was joking, but as we entered the kitchen, I glanced at her and realized she meant every word.

"We had twenty-pound bags of salt until the Veil House burned, but I believe it was ruined in the fire." I began rifling through the cupboard, coming up with a box of sea salt. "Will this work?"

"Yes, that will be fine." She paused before turning back to the living room. "Cicely . . . did Luna explain what the spell might do to her? The way payments work in the yummanii magical world?"

I shook my head. "No, but she seemed pretty solemn when she first told me about it."

"When did she bring it up?"

"When we were at the Consortium, while we were waiting for the Council to come back with their decision." I frowned. "Ysandra, just how dangerous is this for Luna?"

Ysandra paused, the box of salt in hand. She let out a low breath, then gave me a little shrug. "The danger with this type of magic is that every time one of the yummanii seeks the help of their ancestors, they run the danger of being possessed by the spirits who come to their summons. If the spirit is determined, they can take over the body—walk in and set up shop."

"Is that the only danger?"

She headed back into the living room. Over her shoulder, she said, "No. If the spirits don't possess them, there's a chance the magic will. And there are no guarantees what that will do to them. Kaylin's night-veil demon? That demon can be tame compared to what the magic can do to the yummanii if it claims them. Luna's a powerful bard, far stronger than she realizes. But I don't think she's done this sort of spell before. I suppose," she added, "we'll just have to see what happens."

As she began to pour the salt in a circle on the hardwood floor, I backed away, letting her focus. We needed all the protection we could get, but now my worry was for Luna. I wondered . . . did Luna have any inner demons that would leave her prey to the magic coming through her? And even if she couldn't withstand it, did we really have a choice at this point?

Chapter 14

When Luna returned, she was wearing a long black dress, belted with a silver belt. It was off the shoulder, velvet, and hugged her curves. With her hair trailing down her back in black ringlets and her dark eyes ringed with silver, she looked positively magical. Luna was around thirty-five, and for once she didn't look vulnerable but experienced and softly aware.

She motioned to the table, where two chairs were waiting. Ysandra took her place in a third seat, in the northern quarter of the Circle. Peyton, Grieve, and Chatter sat outside the Circle, where they wouldn't interfere with the flow of energy. I sat opposite Luna, my back to the east, while she sat in the west, facing me. The crystal ball rested in front of her, and as she lit the black candle, the flame sputtered and caught fire.

I waited for her instructions.

After a moment, she began to hum . . . a long tone, haunting and distant, and then it became a melody, weaving in and around the room, encircling and braiding its way through the air.

Ulean, what is she doing?

She is calling on the spirits. Her voice is the lure, bait-ing them to come to her aid. The ancestor spirits, they do not give help freely. They must be wooed, persuaded. Sometimes cajoled. And then they exact a price—there is always a price to pay when sourcing the spirits.

That frightens me. Will she be all right?

Time will tell, but there is no stopping the ritual now. She has cracked the portal; she cannot close it at this point.

I focused my attention on Luna again, watching for any sign that she might be in trouble. I still didn't know what I was supposed to do, but she would tell me when it was time.

Outside, the sky had clouded over, dark and thick, and now, with a crack of thunder, snow lightning lit up the air, and then huge flakes of snow began to swirl down in a fren-zied dance. The lightning flashed again, the low rumble of thunder making me want to jump. My nerves were on edge; I felt raw as flesh stripped from muscle, like a swarm of bees were grazing my skin with their stingers. Shivering now, I struggled to remain still, to not disturb Luna's trance.

And then a soft whoosh swept though the room and something was there, with us, in the Circle. A presence, weighing down on my shoulders, thickening the air till it was so dense that I couldn't catch my breath.

But Luna didn't seem to notice. She was bent over the table, her gaze focused on the crystal ball. Her hands barely cupped its sides as a thin mist began to swirl inside the crys-tal, and then it rose out of the ball to filter into the room.

It was viscous now, and my lungs worked at a ragged pace. I'd never experienced asthma before, except for the anaphylaxis when I got hold of fish, but this was all too reminiscent of the latter. I gasped, unable to force enough air into my lungs. I couldn't tell if the others were suffer-ing, but then Luna brought her head up, her gaze locking mine, and I realized that it wasn't Luna looking at me, but someone else, from behind her eyes.

"Whom do you seek?" The voice that echoed out of her cut to the bone, vibrating far too deep to be her own. It was masculine, smooth but forceful, and as each word reverberated into existence, it echoed for a moment, then was gone as if someone had snatched it away.

As the question hung there, I realized it had been aimed at me. I tried to calm myself so I wouldn't stumble over my words.

"I need to find my cousin Rhiannon, the Summer Queen." I wasn't sure whether to go on and explain what had happened, but my lips pressed shut, and it occurred to me that whoever I was talking to, he might just have a broader vista of knowledge than I did. If he needed me to elaborate, he would ask.

Apparently, the spirit did not. After a moment, the voice boomed out through the room again. "Look where time strikes in the heart of the village. Look for the dungeons deep within the ground."

We had a poet on our hands, apparently. I waited, again unsure about whether I should say anything else. And then there was an uneasy laugh, and Luna stiffened, her eyes glowing with a pale blue fire.

"There are secret ways in, through the alleys and down into the streets. Be cautious, for the creatures from the heart of the world walk there, emerging from their lairs, and even the blood-drinkers fear them and steer toward the light."

And then, with another sigh, Luna's mouth opened and the spirit spoke once more. "Daughter of the son of the son of my daughter . . . this one is talented and can speak for the dead . . . and so she shall."

With another whoosh, the presence rose out of Luna in a visible cloud and vanished from sight. Luna collapsed on the table, almost knocking over the candle. I grabbed it before it fell, managing to keep it alight. Ysandra hurried to Luna's side. She felt for Luna's pulse, then motioned for me to blow out the candle.

"Lights—one of you outside the Circle turn on the lights, and bring us some water and brandy if you have any in the house." Ysandra leaned Luna back.

Luna was unconscious, but she was murmuring something, and Ysandra slapped her gently across the cheeks. Luna began to open her eyes. "Here, you stand beside her, make sure she doesn't fall out of her chair while I open the Circle and bring her the brandy."

As I quickly obeyed, my mind flew to the spirit's words. *Look where time strikes in the heart of the village . . .* What did that mean?

As Peyton stepped into the now-opened Circle and handed Ysandra the bottle of brandy and a glass, she caught my attention.

"I know where he's keeping her," she said. "I know what the riddle is referring to. The clock tower—the one across from where they killed Rex. They're hiding beneath the Abby Theater."

"Crap! You're right—you have to be!" I wanted to run off, to head out and rescue my cousin right this instant, but first we had to take care of Luna.

At that moment, she began to come around as Ysandra held the brandy to her lips, dribbling a few drops into her mouth. A moment later, she blinked and Ysandra motioned for her to hush, to say nothing, but to finish the drink.

After a few minutes, in which we all waited, tensely, Luna cleared her throat, and when she spoke, it sounded almost as if she had laryngitis.

"What . . . I don't remember anything about what happened. Did we get an answer? Did anyone come through?"

Ysandra stared at her, a grave look on her face. "Yes, one of your ancestors most definitely managed to speak through you, and we have our answer as to where to look. But Luna . . ."

Luna paled. "What is the price? Did they say what the price will be?"

Ysandra nodded. "Yes . . . although it was only hinted at, I know what they are talking about. The dead will start hounding you—you are to be one of their speakers. You have a natural talent for it, and now they know that. This is heavy magic, indeed, and not one that is borne lightly. I'm afraid we're going to have to do some focus work teaching you how to strengthen your warding and personal barriers of protection."

Closing her eyes, Luna let out a slow breath. "I said I was willing to pay the price. I guess . . . they are taking advantage of that."

I wasn't sure what was going on—both Ysandra and Luna seemed to understand something I didn't. But thoughts of Rhiannon crowded in, pushing away my worry over the bard.

"We have to get down there before dark. Before the vampires rise."

Luna jerked her head up, sharply. "So we know where to look?"

"They gave us a riddle, but Peyton has figured it out. The Abby Theater, below the streets. There's a dungeon down there. And they have Rhia locked away." I jumped up. "What are we waiting for? Let's gather the guards and go."

"Patience, winged one." Ysandra held up her hand and motioned to Grieve. "Get a dustpan and whisk broom, please, and sweep up the salt. I've opened the Circle, so it will be safe now." To Chatter, she said, "Bring some cheese and meat and bread. Luna needs her strength back. Channeling the dead is a serious undertaking, not to be taken lightly or shrugged off."

As both Grieve and Chatter hurried to her command, Ysandra motioned for Peyton to enter the Circle with us. "How are you feeling? Can you go with us, or do you need to stay here? Your father . . ."

"My father died protecting me. I'm not going to cower away. His death will have meaning." She paced back and forth. "I still haven't told my mother. I suppose I should find out what her reaction is."

Ysandra frowned. "I'm not sure that's the wisest move at this moment."

"I won't tell her anything else. But I need . . . I need to make her realize this hurt me. I need her to know that someone is mourning my father. If she knows, if she's in

league with them, that's all she'll know. If she's not, then
maybe it will jog her into being the person she was, before
all this shit came down."

She stood there, defiant.

Ysandra finally nodded. "Very well, but if I motion for
you to stop, you stop. Grief can make us say the stupidest
things without realizing what we're doing."

"Fine. We have a deal."

As Grieve was sweeping up the salt and Chatter placed
a plate of carefully sliced meats and cheeses in front of
Luna, along with a dinner roll and butter and honey, Peyton
punched in a number on her cell phone.

A moment later, she cleared her throat. "Anadey . . .
yes, it's Peyton . . . Why? Because you tried to kill one of
my friends and my father—isn't that enough reason for me
to stop calling you Mother?"

A pause. We were all listening, blatantly, but Peyton
didn't try to lower her voice. She rolled her eyes at me, then
gave her head a tight shake.

"Too fucking bad. You brought it on yourself. I just
wanted you to know that part of your plan worked. Rex is
dead . . . Yeah, that's what I said." Another pause, then,
"Vampires. Just the way you planned it out." After yet
another pause, she let out a sigh. "I don't know whether to
believe you or not, but fine. You're sorry. And so am I. Rex
was a good father, Anadey. And you kept him from me all
of those years. I don't know if I can ever forgive you."

I winced. The pain in Peyton's voice was palpable, and
the anger right below the surface. I gave Ysandra a long
look, and she nodded back. We needed to get Peyton into
some counseling when this was all over.

If it ever is . . .

We'll do our best to make it happen, Cicely. Ulean's
soothing breeze wrapped around me like a cloak. I let out
a soft murmur of contentment.

Thank you, my friend. I wish you could help Peyton.

*I wish so, too, but she cannot feel me, not very well, not
even when I try to contact her.*

Peyton was struggling now. Tears were welling up in her eyes and her voice sounded raspy, as if she had a cold. "Fine, I believe you're sorry. Sure you are. But your jealousy and your anger kept me from having a father most of my life. You can never make that up to me . . . *I realize that.* No, I said . . . Stop. Just stop. I've got to go." She paused one last time, then whispered, "No . . . not right now. Maybe sometime. Maybe . . . but now, I can't come over. I just can't. Bye . . . Anadey."

As she flipped her phone shut, she slumped into one of the chairs. "She wants to see me. But I can't. Not now. Not till I know things are taken care of with Myst. Not until . . . I believe she means it when she says she's sorry." She glanced at me. "Mother wants to see you, too. She wants to apologize."

I recoiled. "I don't think I can do that. At least not now." Being at the mercy of her spell, feeling her drain away my feelings and energy . . . No, I couldn't forget that. Not ever. And I couldn't forgive it.

Ysandra leaned down to peer into Luna's eyes. "Are you feeling better?"

Luna nodded. "Yes. So let's get our asses in gear and go save Rhiannon."

※

Check and Teral joined us. We explained to them where Rhiannon was and what we thought we might be facing.

"Vampires, at least, but they'll be sleeping. But the other warning, I'm not so sure about. They mentioned the *creatures from the heart of the world*. They said the vampires were afraid of them so much that they sought out the light. Does anybody have any clue what the spirit was talking about?"

The very sound of it made my blood run cold. The Shadow Hunters were bad, but whatever the warning was, it wasn't about them. I knew that in my heart. No, this was something older, colder, from deep in the earth. And whatever could scare a vampire had to be fucking badass.

"I wish Kaylin were here," Luna said. "He's really good at knowing all sorts of things like that. How is he? Is there any chance he can join us?" She turned to Check. "Can you find out?"

Check nodded. "As you wish, miss. I will send Run to the Barrow and he'll talk to the healers." He excused himself and headed back through the kitchen.

Chatter pointed to the clock. "Time's ticking down, people. I know it's not even noon yet, but we need to get our plans together. Sunset comes early these days, and once the sun goes down, Geoffrey and Leo will rise. And they expect to see Cicely in the town square at eight."

I snorted. "They'll see me all right, but a lot sooner than that, and on the other end of a stake." I had a headache, and as I tried to rub my temples, the circlet interfered. I reached to remove it, but Ysandra stayed my hand.

"The Queen must never remove her crown save for in her bedchamber." She smiled at me, almost sympathetically.

"You sound like Lainule now," I grumbled, but in secret, it felt good to have her order me around. Ysandra might not be the Queen of Summer, but she was stronger and wiser than me, and I had a feeling I'd be coming to rely on her more and more as time went on. And I was learning all too quickly what it meant to be the one in charge, and I wasn't sure I liked it.

"Lainule and I had a talk before they left for the Golden Isle." She hesitated, then rested a hand on my shoulder. "You are not alone, Cicely. You aren't alone."

"All right, if there are dungeons below the Abby Theater, how do we get to them? Where could the entrance be? I haven't been in there since . . . well . . . since I was five, I think. I can't even remember what Heather took Rhiannon and me to see." I searched my memory—not because the show mattered, but because it was one more link to a past I'd never see again. And then a vision of dancing toys came to mind and I clapped. "Oh! It was *Babes in Toyland*! Anyway, is it even open anymore?"

Ysandra shook her head. "The Abby Theater shut down over ten years ago. Lack of funding, I think. Or perhaps lack of interest. We don't have the time to ask City Hall to give us blueprints, and even then, we'd have to present a special request as to why, so we're out of luck there. We may just have to break in. If Lannan or Regina were awake, they could probably get us in there without a problem since they effectively run the town government."

"Yeah, but by the time they wake up, it will be too late, since Geoffrey and Leo will also be awake. Okay, so we leave a message for them, letting them know what we're doing in case we get waylaid. They might be able to help us if that happens. Then we go in through the alley, which means making sure nobody spots us and reports us. Again, Lannan could get us out of trouble, but by that time . . . too late." I frowned. "The spirit said that there are ways in through the alleys and down in the streets. I'm guessing back entrance and sewer system."

Peyton made a face. "I'd really rather not go down in the sewer system."

"Well, it would be easy enough to get lost in there, that's for certain. But if we have to, we have to. So wear old clothes." I leaned forward, resting my elbow on my knees. "So what do we take with us? What weapons do we have? I can stir up a tornado, but inside, that could do more damage than it might help. I've got my queen's dagger, but I'm not all that adept with it."

Grieve spoke up, arching one eyebrow. "Do not forget. We have the entire armories of the Marburry and Eldburry Barrows at our fingertips. The guards will be going with us, and frankly, they're not going to want you going in at all."

"Too fucking bad. That's my cousin in there." As I spoke, Check entered the room again, dropping to one knee by my side.

A ghost of a smile flickered across his face at my statement, but he said nothing of it. Instead, he brought news about Kaylin. "The night-veil heals quickly, but he is not going to be allowed out of the ward. The healers say he took far too much damage from the vampires and must build his blood supply back. We could not give him a transfusion because of the changed nature of his body from the demon who is bound to him."

Kaylin couldn't have blood transfusions?

"You're serious? We can't ever give him a transfusion if he needs it?"

Check rose to his feet, standing at attention. "Correct. Normal blood could kill him. The demon changed his DNA, which changed the structure of his blood. It bleeds as freely and as red as yours or mine, but it is not yummanii, nor is it magic-born, nor fully that of the night-veil. He's a hybrid, as are all of the Children of the Bat People."

Well, that was that. No way would I allow Kaylin to go with us if he wasn't at his full game. "He's out, then."

"Your Highness . . ." Check hesitated, shifting from one foot to the other.

"What is it?"

"Please reconsider going. The guards and I can take care of this matter." But even as he said it, the expression on his face told me he knew I was going to brush him off.

"You know my answer to that. But you and the guards . . . gather weapons. We go in at a force. We're also going to have to deal with Geoffrey's stable who are loyal to him. The day-runners, the ones who fight back, we'll have to dispatch. But his stable . . . they are probably under thrall and not necessarily there of their own free will, knowing the former Regent, and Leo. I don't want them hurt if we can help it."

"That will put your cousin in danger, Your Highness. Bloodwhores work to the will of their masters." A sense of gloom filled his voice.

I wasn't sure what to do. I looked over at Ysandra, but she shrugged, indicating this was my decision. Turning to my love, I said, "Grieve . . . what . . ."

He stopped me before I even got the question out. "I would not give them quarter. But . . . this is your decision,

Cicely. You are the Queen. You're in charge, and it's up to you. We have to get Rhiannon back before they turn her."

It felt wrong, condemning a group to potential death just because they had fallen in thrall with Geoffrey and Leo, but they had made a free choice to do so. They'd chosen to go with the vampires when they were ousted from power. And now they might have to die for that choice.

"We do whatever we need to in order to rescue my cousin. But . . . if there are children there, and I sincerely hope there aren't . . . spare them." Having made the decision, I felt settled, at least. "We'll need stakes . . . what else? Silver weapons work against vampires. Sunlight, of course. Garlic!"

Luna jumped up. "We have plenty of garlic in the house. The minute Regina's crew cleared out, I brought several long garlic braids in here to discourage them returning. I can run a thread through the bulbs and we can wear them . . . or we can just keep them in our pockets. I'll go break apart one of the braids right now. There should be enough for most of the guards."

As she hustled into the kitchen, I glanced down at my clothes. "We need to wear fighting gear. I'm still dressed in what I was wearing last night. Check, please have one of your men run back to the Barrow and bring me a pair of dark jeans, a turtleneck, and my dagger. I left it there. Also . . . have Druise make certain I have clean underwear." It felt weird to talk to the guard about panties, but right now, I didn't care. I just wanted to get into that theater and get Rhia back.

He bowed and was off. Peyton and Ysandra took over on the garlic while Luna went upstairs to change. Grieve and Chatter were out organizing the guards. That left me alone. I wandered over to the wall, where a picture of Rhiannon and Heather hung. They looked happy, but even then, there was a cloud in Rhia's eyes. The incident that had happened when she was thirteen had changed her forever, just as my mother's dragging me away to live in the streets had changed me forever.

Another picture also graced the walls. Rhia must have dug it out of storage. It was the two of us when we were five. It had been taken shortly after we met Grieve and Chatter out in the forest. We were wide-eyed, happy and laughing in the photograph, with the wind playing with our hair, sweeping it across our faces. In the background, the Veil House sparkled on a rare summer day.

I lifted the photograph off the wall, thinking back to that time in our lives. Twenty-one years had passed . . . but it seemed like a lifetime ago. I gently pressed my lips to Rhia's image.

We're coming for you, cousin. We're coming . . . hang on.

She will. She's strong. Ulean's presence enveloped me, and I leaned into her cool strength that flowed around me.

I hope you're right, was all I whispered back.

❊

By the time we set out—a large force—it was one thirty. But we had twenty guards with us, and Grieve, Chatter, and I were at the helm. We couldn't go in en masse, or the cops might interfere, so we'd have to trickle in, to avoid surrounding the building.

We all had garlic on our persons, and backpacks with stakes, ropes, and anything else we thought we might need. My dagger was firmly strapped to my thigh, around my jeans, and my turtleneck was snug and warm beneath my leather jacket. I'd opted for a lighter leather, one that was easier to maneuver in, although it would still protect me against some attacks, a lot like armor.

Luna wore a pair of thermal leggings beneath a thigh-length tunic, with a light jacket and knee boots. Peyton was in her usual jeans and a polo shirt, and she also wore a leather jacket. But it was Ysandra that made me blink. This was the second time I'd seen her dressed for action, and both times it threw me.

She was wearing a catsuit—black this time instead of white, and it fit her like a glove, showing off a curvy but toned figure. The one-piece was banded around the hips

with a silver belt, off which hung several gadgets that I
didn't recognize. Her hair was in a braid instead of the
usual chignon, and she reminded me of a modern-day
Emma Peel from the old *Avengers* show that I'd seen on
late-night TV reruns. All she needed was a Mr. Steed to
make the image complete.

The weather was on our side. The snow, which had
tapered off for a few days after we routed Myst from the
Marburry Barrow, had returned with a vengeance, which
meant Myst was near. It wasn't a fit day out for man or beast.
I only hoped the Queen of the Indigo Court would hold off
until we were done with our mission. Once we had taken
care of Geoffrey and Leo, then we could turn our attention
to her again.

Don't forget Crawl is out there, too. Ulean's warning
sent a shiver down my spine.

Trust me, I won't.

As we approached the town, we broke into groups. The
Fae could run in a blur. Some might see them, or sense that
something had just passed by, but for the most part, they
could get in without being noticed. We, however—at least
Luna, Peyton, Ysandra, and I—had to be more cautious.
And since Grieve and Chatter refused to leave our sides,
they, too, had to slow their movements to our own. And I
sure didn't trust my ability to control my new speed enough
to make use of it under these circumstances. Too much
rode on our ability to remain unnoticed.

As we approached the Abby Theater, I glanced around
the sidewalks. There weren't many shoppers out. The
weather was atrocious.

"We're due for whiteout conditions," Luna said, holding
up her phone. "I just checked the weather report, and we
could have a blizzard on our hands."

"We don't get blizzards here," I said, but then shrugged.
"Although, with Myst, I guess we do now. At least we'll be
inside for this, but if we are out, and anybody gets separated from the group, try to find shelter."

I pulled my jacket tighter, making sure it was zipped all

the way up. Lights dotted the streets here and there, mostly from small businesses hoping someone would brave the weather to come buy their goods, but the cars were scarce and pedestrians even more so. Which was a good thing for us.

We slipped into the alley next to the theater and followed it around to the back. The old parking lot behind the building had been turned into a junkyard. A fence ran around most of it, and inside, junker cars filled the lot. But again, signs of life were scarce, and that ran in our favor.

The back of the building was a testament to the word *weathered*. It had fared worse than the front, though I wasn't sure why, but the brick was broken and cracked, and graffiti artists had done their best to cover the walls with everything from gang tags to actual art. I recognized a Lupa Clan tag and shook my head. The werewolves liked to mark their territory, all right.

There was an old set of double doors that looked welded shut, but when we examined them closer, I saw they were just covered with rust. But then something else caught my eye—a large grate in the middle of the alleyway behind the theater. I knelt by it, running my fingers around the edges. Unlike most of the other grates along the road, this one had no plant life growing up around it. It wasn't caked with dirt, debris, or ice. I wrapped my fingers around the grating and tugged. It shifted, just a little. I tugged again, and it shifted again.

"The grate—it's loose. I think it may be some sort of secret entrance." I stood up, wiping my gloves on my pants.

Grieve and Chatter leaned over to look at it. A moment later, Grieve let out an "Aha!" and a click sounded in the air, and the grate opened easily, like a trapdoor.

"There's a lever there." He pointed to one side. "Flip the lever, and it releases the locking mechanism."

I cautiously glanced down the dark hole. "What's down there? Is there any way to find out without dropping a light in there?"

Chatter shrugged. "Give me a moment." He lay down

on his stomach on the road and dangled one of his hands down through the entrance. A moment later, he pushed back to his knees. "A ladder, running down. I don't know how far it goes—it's impossible to tell from here, but there's only one way to find out."

"Where are Check and the other guards?" I glanced around, nervous that maybe they had gotten waylaid by Shadow Hunters. But I needn't have worried.

"We're here, Your Highness." He stepped out from a nearby car on the other side of the fence. Within moments, all twenty guards were visible. "We just take care not to touch the cars and we're fine. The fence is not iron."

"We found an entrance, Check. I guess . . . we'd better go find out where it leads to." I started for the grating, but within a blurry flash, Check was by my side, restraining me. He was gentle in his restraint, but it was definitely a *don't do that* pressure.

"Allow Teral and me to go first, Your Highness. There can be no compromise on this. You cannot go in that dank hole without us checking that it's safe enough for you. There could be anything down there." The look on his face was firm, and I realized there would be no give on this.

I stood back, both frustrated and relieved. This was the way it would be, for the rest of my life. Rule and regulations, always having to consider that putting myself in danger put the Barrow in danger.

With a soft smile, I motioned to the grate. "Then go. You two, then Grieve and Chatter, then the rest of us will follow. Leave ten guards out here to keep watch, though. We can't take a chance that somebody's going to notice the open grating and come after us."

"Now you are thinking like a queen." Check smiled, saluted, and then motioned to his men. "You heard her. Race, take nine of the men and hide, keeping watch. If we need you . . ." He paused.

I broke in. "If we need you, I will send my Wind Elemental to fetch you."

Ulean, you can do that, can't you? If I need you to, you

*can make yourself heard to at least somebody in that group,
can't you?*

*Yes, there are two who have the ability to hear me if I so
choose.*

Good. Thank you.

"Okay, it's decided then. Ulean will come warn you if
we need help. Check, let's get this show on the road. You've
briefed your men on what we need to do?"

He nodded, then swung himself over the edge of the
grating. "And it's into the pit," he said, as he disappeared
from sight.

As I watched Teral, Grieve, and then Chatter vanish into
the hole, I wondered what the hell we were going to find in
there. And there was only one way to know. I steeled
myself, then—with a deep breath—lowered myself onto
the ladder and descended into the darkness.

Chapter 15

The tunnel into which we were climbing was dark and dank, and cold. I didn't think it led to the sewers, even though it looked a lot like a sewer grating built for leaves and rainwater runoff. It wasn't sloped down to encourage drainage, so it might be a decoy.

I was glad for the gloves I was wearing—the rungs were so icy that bare skin would stick to them, I was sure of it, like a tongue to a frozen pole. A showering of snow drifted down on our backs, but immediately after I was down far enough on the ladder, Ysandra was coming after me, so she took the brunt of the swirling flakes, and then Peyton, then Luna, and then the rest of the guards.

The tunnel seemed to go on forever, through the darkness with no lights. We didn't dare use flashlights or any sort of illumination because of the chance we might warn those who were down below.

Sounds echoed through the passage, the sound of our climb soft against the clinks and distant clangs—all noises inherent to this place reverberated around us. I thought I heard the *whoosh* of heating units or air-conditioning, machines that were recognizable. But other noises, from farther below, struck me as odd. Soft squishes. A distant call that might be a scream, or a roar. Or maybe, maybe these echoes were in my imagination, spurred on by our surroundings.

One rung after another, I stared straight ahead at the wall behind the ladder. I could barely see anything and went on faith that the rungs below me would be there. They weren't iron—iron rusts, and whoever had built this place had made it secure and solid. Maybe . . . bronze, or steel, or some other metal. Whatever it was, the guards seemed to be having no problems with it. Of course, they were cloaked and wore gloves, so the essence of the metal wouldn't leach through, even if it was iron.

And then, from below, I heard Check whisper something into the slipstream. "I'm down," he said.

Another few moments, and I found myself at the bottom of the ladder, and I stepped to the side, ready to steady Peyton and the others as they came off the rungs. Within moments, we were all safely gathered at the bottom. Looking up, I couldn't see the top.

"How far did we come?" I turned to Check. "Do you know?"

His voice echoed in the darkness, even though he kept it low. The resonance down here was incredibly sensitive. "A distance. I'd say at least three stories down, if you want to use a house as a measurement. Maybe four."

So at least sixty feet. Probably more like one hundred, I thought, glancing around. It was dark. Too dark. We'd never be able to see where we were going or what might be coming toward us.

"We have to risk a light. There's no alternative." I debated on whether to pull out my flashlight—it would help, but it was very bright and might be overkill, considering the situation into which we were headed. We wanted to see enough to find our way, not advertise ourselves like a blue-light special at Kmart.

Chatter solved that problem. He held out his hand and whispered something, and a tennis ball–sized orb of fire appeared, hovering in the air next to him. It was bright but not blinding, and it softly illuminated our immediate surroundings.

"That fire thing you've got going on there is handy," Peyton said.

He gave her a faint smile. "It serves its purpose."

I glanced around. We were at a crossroads in the tunnel, with passages leading to both the left and right and straight ahead. I frowned, trying to figure out which one we should take. But Teral knelt by the juncture where the three passages met and pointed to something I couldn't quite make out.

"Here—there are signs of tread going in this direction." He gestured to the passage that led straight ahead. "I think there has been more traffic in this tunnel."

"That would be the logical choice, then." Once again, I realized they were waiting for me to make the decision. I cleared my throat. "Let's go. Check, Teral, lead on."

And so we moved forward, with Check and Teral at the front, and behind them, Grieve, Chatter, and me. Then came Ysandra, Peyton and Luna, and the other eight guards. I wondered how we were going to keep quiet, but except for the soft footfalls of Ysandra, Peyton, and Luna, there was no noise save for our breathing.

The going was slow because Check and Teral insisted on checking the passage for booby-traps every ten feet, but I knew better than to hurry them up. The place could easily be rigged, and I didn't want to be responsible for anybody blowing up or getting impaled by spikes, Indiana Jones style.

Chatter's light kept abreast with us, and he created another and sent it back to hover alongside the guards in the rear. We were able to see, and no doubt anybody getting close enough to us from either direction would see it, but the illumination wasn't so bright that it immediately called attention to itself.

Besides, Cicely, not everything that walks in the depths uses eyes to see.

Ulean's offhand comment gave me the chills, even though I knew she didn't mean to. But the thought of some creature who didn't need vision, snuffling and scuttling through the darkness, wasn't my idea of a good time.

"This certainly isn't as welcoming as the tunnel was where we went in search of Lainule's heartstone. Or even where . . ." I stopped. I'd been going to say where I'd hidden my own heartstone, but I knew, instinctively, that I should never talk about that moment, that experience. The only one I would ever talk about it to was Rhiannon. And even then . . . as much as I loved her . . . the inclination to protect myself fully rose up and, with sadness, I realized that there was now a barrier between us, whether or not we wanted it there. The Queens of Summer and Winter were natural opposites.

Grieve glanced back at me, then smiled softly. "No, this is not a friendly place. There are dangers here. I can feel them in the slipstream. If you stop and listen, you can hear the rumblings from the depths."

I nodded. So it hadn't just been my imagination. I let myself drop into the slipstream as we continued along the corridor. Grieve was right. The distant pounding of something dark and large, reverberating like a low hum, echoed up to surround me. It was so low that I doubted the others—those who weren't tuned in to the slipstream— could hear it.

"I can't hear it, but I can certainly feel it." Ysandra spoke up, breaking the silence. "There are ancient creatures who live in the earth, and most haven't shown themselves for eons, but that doesn't mean they aren't there. We would do well to walk softly, lest we waken anything that should be left sleeping."

"Creatures, or spirits?" Luna asked.

"Both," Ysandra answered.

And with that, we continued along. I was beginning to worry about the time—how long had we been at this? It felt like hours, but logic dictated it couldn't be more than an hour since we'd arrived at the Abby Theater. Finally, concern overrode reason and I turned to Ysandra.

"What time is it? Is it still daylight? Are the vampires still asleep?"

She stopped to pull out a pocket watch from the belt on the sleek black catsuit she was wearing. "It's two fifteen. We have time, but we shouldn't dawdle."

"I think we've found our way in," Check said, interrupting. He pointed ahead to where the passageway ended in a wall, against which a large metal door barred our way.

"Finally . . ." But now, fear began to creep in. The vampires were still asleep—they had to be—but that didn't mean their guards wouldn't be fierce. The amount of bloodshed I'd seen in the past few weeks was overwhelming, and we weren't done by any means.

Check examined the door. "I don't see any traps."

Ysandra pushed forward. "Let me look. I can tell whether there's magic set on it, although it doesn't necessarily mean there's a trap there." She knelt by the keyhole and whispered something low. A moment later, she stood, frowning. "Yes, there is some sort of magic here, but honestly, I don't recognize it. It isn't from the magic-born."

"Could be a trap, could be a warning system. Is there any way to defuse it?" I joined her, gazing at the door as if staring hard enough could reveal its secrets.

"Not unless I know what kind it is to begin with. I could try, but if it's a trap, I might set it off. Same if it's a warning system. I think . . . we're just going to have to brave this one and deal with the consequences." She frowned again, resting her chin on her hand.

"Let me ask Ulean to see if she can find out what's on the other side. She should be able to cross through it—"

"Not so fast. Remember, the vampires hate Elementals. The Elementals can read them too easily. So they might have it warded against them." Luna held out her hands and closed her eyes. "This *isn't* yummanii magic, that much I can tell you."

"If it's not yummanii and it's not from the magic-born . . . then what the hell is it? Weres don't use much magic. Fae? I think we'd recognize it." Confused and a little worried, I stepped back. "Let me ask Ulean what she thinks."

Ulean, can you pass through the door without setting off whatever that magic is linked to?

Ulean swished past me, then paused.

I think I can. This is not built to keep out my kind, Cicely. Whatever the magic is, it's ancient, meant to keep out far larger creatures than me . . . or you. I think it will sound, though, if the door is actually opened. It's meant to keep out creatures of the flesh more than those of spirit.

I told the others what she had said. "That means the vampires are afraid of physical threats, and big ones at that. What the fuck could be . . ." I paused. "The creatures from the depths. Suppose they know enough about them to be afraid?"

Any creature that made *vampires* afraid was something for us to be afraid of. That had proved only too true with the Shadow Hunters, and if my gut was right, whatever was down here was bigger and badder than Myst. I suddenly wanted to be on the other side of that door, if it could protect us.

Ulean, cross over and let me know if anybody is on the other side. And with a silent whoosh, she was gone. Within moments she was back.

Yes, there are armed guards over there. I don't think I set off the alarms. But there are three men over there, and they have big guns. There's also a woman, and she carries no weapon. She feels magical, though, but I can't tell whether she's yummanii, or what. They don't seem to be aware that you are on this side, so I'm thinking that the door is soundproof.

"Thanks." I quickly relayed the information. "Guns, not good. And big guns, so not good. We need to go in on the offensive. So what have we got?"

But at that moment, a noise behind us sounded and we

turned at the shout of the guards. It was murky, with Chatter's lights being our only illumination, but there, charging toward us, loped a creature at least twelve feet tall. He was truly a monster—bipedal, but with long, thin arms, and tentacles coming out from both sides of his torso.

His face was troll-like—lumpy and deformed. His mouth was circular, like a lamprey's, and razor-sharp teeth ringed the opening. But his eyes were what struck the most fear into my heart—they were cunning, and alien. Whatever this was, it was no Wilding Fae or Elemental, but something ancient and wicked, from the early days of the world.

I pulled out my dagger, but self-preservation prevailed and I let the guards push in front of me to meet it. Ysandra moved to the side of the passage, where she could get a clear shot at it, and she held up her hand and began reciting an incantation. I clapped my hands over my ears, remembering only too well how powerful her magic was.

The creature closed in on us, totally unfazed by our numbers, and as it neared the first line of guards, Ysandra let loose with her spell. Everyone within earshot went down on their knees as her command ricocheted through the room, sending shock waves reverberating through the tunnel.

The monster skidded to a halt, looking confused, but it didn't drop. I'd seen Ysandra stop an entire gang of werewolves with the same spell, but it barely slowed this thing. Less than ten seconds later, it picked up steam again and was headed our way. The guards waited, swords drawn, looking nervous but holding their ground.

Then, as it neared us, an alarm filled the air and a light suddenly flared from the sides of the walls, illuminating the corridor. The door in back of us swung open, and I knew immediately what was happening.

"Hit the deck! Dive!" I leaped to the side, and the others followed suit as a spray of gunfire spewed down the corridor. We went flying, out of the way. I landed on my knees, hard, slamming against the wall. My shoulder took a jolt that made me think at first I'd dislocated it, but self-preservation won out over pain, and I squeezed against the walls.

The bullets were aimed dead center down the hallway, at the troll-cum-fishman, and their ricochet was enough to knock down a small elephant, but it didn't seem to do any good. The thing kept right on coming, and now it was focused on the guards from behind the door and not on us. It staggered forward, not hurt but thrown off balance by the glancing blows of the bullets that ricocheted right and left.

We were all in duck-and-cover mode, but I managed a glance over my shoulder before Check came flying over to shield me. What I saw was the guards tossing their guns and getting ready to fight it hand-to-hand.

"It's a tredobyte!" one of them shouted.

As the creature barreled past me toward the door, a piercing siren lacerated the air, sending me reeling. I covered my ears as I pressed to the wall. Check leaned over me, acting like a human shield as we tried to avoid being trampled.

I leaned against the stone. Another noise sounded from behind us, and a massive jolt reverberated through the tunnel. I whirled to see the tredobyte go down and the day-runners swarm over it, pouring some sort of liquid on it. The liquid hissed against the creature's flesh. It let out a solitary shriek and was still.

We stood, slowly, eyeing the yummanii. They seemed as shell-shocked as we did, and before they could assess who we were and react, I charged, leading the others as we swarmed, knocking them to the ground and disarming them. We stood back, Peyton, Ysandra, and I holding their guns, while my guards held the men and woman by their arms. The woman opened her mouth and Luna lunged forward, slapping her hand over the woman's mouth.

"Gag her. She uses magic of some sort and we don't want to chance her unleashing a spell." She held the gun out of the woman's reach. "Fuck! She bit me; somebody hurry up!"

As another of the guards gagged the woman, Luna shook her head, looking at it carefully. A drop of blood welled up, but it didn't look too serious.

I turned to the tredobyte, examining the creature. It was huge, with reptilian scales like snakeskin covering its body. The tentacles were limp against the ground, and they looked like those of an octopus. I poked one with the butt of the gun and it flipped over, showing barbs that could so easily hook into the skin. I wasn't sure if they contained venom, and I wasn't about to find out. Bipedal, yes . . . but far from anything we'd seen before. Definitely not Wilding Fae, and not anything remotely like the Shadow Hunters.

"I have no clue what this thing is." I looked up at Check. "But it's all muscle . . . there's no fat on him. He could probably mow down a tank. I don't know what they used on him, but whatever it was, it worked and left a long gash in his side." Gingerly, I used the barrel of the gun to push back the flesh of the open wound. Beneath the scaly surface, the muscle and bone were apparent. Blood flowed in a thick ooze, but it was dark and muddy in color and had already clotted, even though the wound was still fresh. The edges of the gash were corroded, and I suspected the liquid had been some sort of acid.

After a moment, I figured we'd learned all we could about this thing and stood up, turning to the guards. The yummanii they held captive struggled, but their mouths were gagged and hands bound by now, and they looked both defiant and afraid. I gazed at them, wondering what the hell to do. If we killed them outright, it would make me feel like a murderer. But could we let them live?

You have no choice, Cicely. Ulean's voice was gentle around me, a gust of warm, embracing air.

Check stood there, looking at me. I knew what I had to do, even though I didn't want to. They worked for Geoffrey and Leo; they weren't about to switch sides. It meant death for a day-runner to sell out.

"Find out what you can and then . . ." I turned away. "Find out what you can, then do what you need to."

Check slowly made his way to my side and touched my shoulder. "Your Highness, I know this isn't easy for you, but you have to be the one to say the words." He gave me such a look of sadness and understanding that I wanted to hug him, to reassure him that everything would be all right.

Steeling myself, I looked into his eyes. "Find out what you can and then . . . execute them." The echo of what I'd just ordered rattled through me like bones rolling in a coffin.

He nodded, then motioned to his men, and they followed him to one side, dragging the day-runners with them. I didn't want to watch; I didn't want to be there, but since it had been me who had ordered the group to their death, I had no choice. I wasn't a coward and—as Queen—no doubt, I'd have to do this again, someday. And . . . I'd killed. In self-defense, yes, but I'd taken life before. How could I flinch from standing vigil?

As Check and his men held the day-runners against the wall, questioning them, trying to find out what we could about Geoffrey, Leo, and this complex, it was obvious the yummanii weren't going to cooperate. They kept silent, refusing to speak. The wounds on their necks were deeply scarred. All of them had been fed from at one point or another.

After a few minutes, Peyton looked at me. "We aren't going to have any luck, and with those Klaxons going off, surely they'll be waiting for a report upstairs. We have to get moving or they'll be fully armed and ready for us."

She made a good point. I motioned to Check. The look on the day-runners' faces told me they knew what was coming; the men's eyes went wide while the woman closed hers, steeling herself. My guards were quick and humane, and as their daggers expertly slashed their throats, the blood poured to the ground. Within ten seconds, they were all unconscious, and within another twenty, they'd bled out enough to die.

Somber, feeling my heart weigh heavy in a way it never before had, I turned back to the room in which they'd been hiding. Stepping over the creature on the floor, I led the way in, followed by Check, Grieve, Chatter, and the others.

The room was large enough to house our entire party, and we glanced around, keeping an eye on both the door to the passageway and the door leading to what was undoubtedly the hidden lair housing Geoffrey and Leo's operation.

What had been down here before? After all, the pair had only recently been on the run. Or did someone else control this lair, only allowing the two of them to make use of it? With these questions racing through my mind, I joined the others in poking around.

A logbook sat on the table, listing alerts. It looked like the last one had been three days ago, and all that was noted was *Enemy dispatched. Korbant.* Whether Korbant was the name of the creature they'd killed or the person logging the incident was impossible to tell. The rest of the entries for December were just initialed with the words *No threat.*

The room was filled with display cases, which in turn were filled with weapons. Big-assed guns that had been modified to blow away something with the hide of an elephant. A few flamethrowers. And a few other weapons that were hard to identify. I didn't want to muck with them just in case one backfired.

"What lies through that door?" I started to walk over to the inner door, but Check was in front of me in a flash. He gave me a look that stopped me cold. I backed away, letting him check it out. But at least there was something I could do.

Ulean, can you peek behind that door?

A moment, then another.

Cicely, I can only sense a maze of twisting passages, but I can go no farther. There are blocks against my kind. I can see just beyond the door, but then a magical barrier prevents me from moving forward. No doubt the vampires set it up—it has the feel of new magic. And Geoffrey knows you have me with you, so I imagine it's his doing. I have no idea how you're going to get through there before the vampires rise.

I looked over at Peyton. "What time is it? Do you know?"

She pulled out her phone, checking the time. "No cell service down here, but it's past three thirty now. We don't have a long time till the vamps wake up, do we?"

"Fuck, no. We have less than an hour. Come on; no matter what, we have to get through there." I motioned to Check. "You want to go first, fine, but we have to go. Ysandra, any chance you and Luna can see if there are any magical traps on this door?"

Ysandra and Luna pushed to the front. After a moment, they both shook their heads. Ysandra said, "I don't think so, but there's so much magic beyond this door I can't tell for certain."

"We should close the outer door," Grieve said. "And lock it again. If another one of those . . . tredobytes comes wandering in, we don't need to be dealing with it as well."

Two of the guards who were standing sentinel by the door moved to close and bar it. They turned back. "We're ready when you are, Your Highness."

"Then let's go." I braced myself, praying that whatever might be on the other side of that door wouldn't turn us into toast.

Check moved into position in front of me, along with Teral, and then motioned to the nearest guard, who yanked open the door. For one moment we were facing clear hallway, empty, but the next, a rolling mist poured out from nowhere, and in it were a host of forms. Shadows, they weren't physical and yet not illusion. As they swarmed us, something grappled my throat.

Choking, I reached out, trying to get ahold on the shade, but my hands plunged through the filmy mass. Gasping, I struggled, but my fingers kept slipping through the shadow.

Ysandra let out a long cry out in some ancient tongue, and a blast rocked us, knocking us all to our feet as a forked chain of lightning filled the area, leaping from one shadowy creature to the next. They lit up like luminescent fog, then quickly burst into ethereal flames and vanished.

As I sat up, rubbing my throat, Grieve hurried to my side. "Are you all right, my love?" He lifted me up, and I nodded, still sputtering a little from the chokehold.

"Is everyone okay? Luna—Peyton?" I turned to check on them, but the guards were already helping them up. Everybody seemed to be fine, if a little shaken. "We have to get moving; that set us back a few minutes. What the fuck were those things?"

"Some sort of magical trap," Ysandra said. "They weren't real spirits, but magical constructs, and once I realized that, I knew I could shatter them." She dusted her hands on the legs of her catsuit. "Whatever created them is dangerous, though. That's an advanced spell, and I have my fears about what may be on the other end of it. There must have been a way to deactivate it in the outer room, but without knowing what to expect, it would be hard to find the trigger."

And with that lovely thought, we entered the hallway. I only hoped that less than forty-five minutes would be enough time to find Geoffrey and Leo before they found us.

Chapter 16

Forty-five minutes isn't a long time, and it feels even less when you're facing a maze. As we entered the hallway, I stopped short. Instead of running just left and right, or even straight ahead, there were numerous passages opening along the horizontal wall, each leading into the darkness.

There weren't any signs, and the only light was diffused, from overhead recessed lamps. The shadows were deep and my stomach lurched again. How the hell were we going to find our way through to where Geoffrey and Leo were sleeping in the time we had left?

"What do you wish us to do, Your Majesty?" Check stood at attention, waiting along with the other guards.

I looked hopelessly over at Grieve, not knowing where to start. My love lowered his gaze, looking uncertain.

After a moment, Ysandra spoke up. "Cicely, I have a suggestion. We don't want to split up, obviously—that would be dangerous. But I think . . . if Peyton turns into her werepuma self and tries to sniff out Rhiannon . . ."

"That would work!" Peyton began shedding her clothes,

totally unabashed. "Do we have anything of hers with us I can use for a reference point?"

I started to shake my head, but Chatter spoke up.

"I do." He slowly pulled out a handkerchief from his pocket. "She gave me this to hold for her . . . she was crying over the fact that Leo and Geoffrey were out there. I took it to hold for her . . . and never had the chance to give it back."

The look on his face said everything that needed to be said. Ysandra took the lace cloth and waited for Peyton to stand back, then slowly begin to shimmer into her Were form. I'd seen her change before—when we rescued her from Myst—and it still mesmerized me. As her limbs lengthened and her skin took on fur, the cougar that emerged from the shifting bands of light was sleek, muscled, and glorious. She let out a huff and padded over to Ysandra.

Ysandra held out the handkerchief. Peyton took a long whiff of it, grumbled a bit, and then turned and began investigating the openings to each passageway. After a moment, she paused by one of the middle ones and looked back at us, then headed down the corridor. We followed, Check, Grieve, and Chatter at the front, along with four of the guards, and the rest at the back.

The hallway was brick—the entire building seemed to be brick—and it ran along smooth, with no sign of any openings until we'd gone a good seventy-five feet; then there were two doors at the end, one to either side, and a door in front. Peyton sniffed at the left door, then the right, then stopped in front of the center one, waiting.

Ysandra incanted a spell. After a moment, she shook her head. "I don't think there are any traps, but I can't be sure." She kept her voice low.

Check motioned to one of his men, who cautiously turned the handle. *Locked*, he mouthed.

I motioned for him to move. This was one area where my years on the streets would come in handy. Examining the lock, I realized it was older—probably from when the theater first opened. A warded one, which meant it would be easier to pick than some of the more modern types.

"Ysandra, give me one of your hairpins."

She pulled one out of the intricate braid and handed the stiff metal pin to me. I bent the end into a crook, then inserted it in the keyhole. Jiggling it counterclockwise, I eased it around, avoiding the ward, until I felt it catch, and then I eased it back as the latch slowly slid open. With a *click*, the door was ready. And so were we.

I stepped back, letting Check go first with a couple of his men. I really didn't like hanging back, as much as going ahead scared the crap out of me, but there wasn't much use fretting about it, because I knew Check and Grieve were right. I was Queen now, and I owed it to the Eldburry Burrow and the people of my court to stay as safe as I could.

They pushed through, with Peyton at the lead. She snuffled and sniffed, her nose against the floor as she searched for the scent. The sleekness of her haunches mesmerized me; she was beautiful, muscled and taut. Her eyes, the rich brown they were when she was in her two-legged form, were haunted. She might be young, as far as half-Weres go, but she had seen a lot of life, and I had the feeling there was more in Peyton's background than she had told anybody.

We moved in behind the guards as they began their trek down the hallway, following Peyton. This hall sloped up at a slight angle, like an aisle between theater rows, and the runner that lined the center of the floor was old and faded. I paused, kneeling down by a brownish spot. Though it was old, I knew immediately it was blood. Dried blood, long past its time. There had been violence here at one point, though of what nature we couldn't know.

We were more cautious now, moving as silently as we could, because there were doors along the side—widely spaced and not clustered together. The chance that there could be someone on the other side was too great to risk making noise.

We continued up, following the curving hallway. It reminded me of the theaters where a central cinema or stage was flanked on both sides by hallways, leading the patrons to the various sections of the gallery.

By my estimation, we were too far belowground still for the Abby Theater's main galleria. As far as I knew, there had never been any rumor of an underground performance area. And by the looks of the carpet runner and the flaking paint on the walls, this section had to be as old as the theater itself. Grieve and Chatter wouldn't know anything about it, but maybe Luna might.

"Luna, do you remember if the Abby Theater had an underground stage? Because there's no way we're near street level, yet look at the way the hall curves around the inner wall."

She followed my gesture. "I see what you mean. But no, I don't ever remember there being mention of an underground level. In fact, I don't . . . no, there was never any mention of it. I used to sing onstage here when I was with the Youth Symphony. All the changing rooms, the prop rooms—they're all at street level. And I don't remember any staircases going down, either."

I wanted to stop, to take a look behind some of the doors, but we didn't have time, and with Peyton hot on the trail, we couldn't afford to break pace. I steadied my nerves and tried to quiet my curiosity.

"Do you know what time it is?"

Luna pulled out her phone and checked. "Five minutes till four. We have twenty-five minutes. Cicely, we may be in trouble."

If we didn't find Geoffrey and Leo and stake them soon, we *were* going to be in trouble. Even if we only found Rhia and could get her out of here before they woke, that would be fine. But the feeling in the pit of my gut warned me we might not be so lucky.

As we rounded yet another bend in the ever-ascending hallway, we came to a door to the left side. Peyton stopped, suddenly, stiffening as she stared at it, her head bobbing uncertainly at first, and then she padded over to it, sniffed again, gave a huff, and began to transform back into her normal self. The beautiful, sleek animal vanished as the regal native woman returned.

She motioned to me and we stepped off to the side. I handed her clothing to her as she began to dress.

"She's in there. I can smell her there. There are others with her, yummanii by their scents. I have no clue if any vamps are there." She shimmied into her jeans and zipped them, then fastened her bra and pulled on her shirt. "We have to hurry—it's getting late, isn't it?"

"Yeah, it's later than you think." I motioned to the door. "Check, we don't have time to mess around anymore. Head on in."

Check burst open the door and we poured in, en masse, in hopes of overwhelming whoever was on the other side.

The room was wide and long, and now I realized where the dungeon was that Rhia had been filmed in. The red-brick wall with the net covering it was to our right, and the various play toys—the spanking bench, stocks, and bond-age table—were meticulously placed around the room. The walls were redbrick, and long curtains hung in panels—drapes of red and black velvet and satin. The ceiling was a good fifteen feet high, and the acrid odor of incense filled the air. I could have sworn there was a drug in it. The scent was intoxicating and heady, but I managed to keep a handle on my senses.

There were five men in the room, but they looked to be in a stupor, and at first I thought this was going to be easy. We could stun them, grab Rhia, and run. If we could find her. As I looked around, I first thought Peyton must have been mistaken, because she was nowhere in sight. But then I heard a noise and glanced up to see a cage hanging about eight feet off the ground, and in that cage, Rhiannon was hunched over, sobbing.

"Rhia!" I couldn't help it—I called out her name and she stiffened, then clutched the bars, staring out the side of the cage.

At my outburst, the men definitely noticed us, struggling to get to their feet. But Check and the guards wasted no time, wading right in. Within moments, all five of the yummanii had been stunned and were out cold. Check crouched, then leaped up, grabbing hold of the cage, as he climbed atop it.

There seemed to be no way to lower it to the ground. The switch to do so was probably hidden along the wall, behind one of the curtains. Check wasted no time in leaning over the side to work the padlock on the cage. He shouted, though, pulling back. The lock was iron.

"Get me up there!" I could pick it, and the iron wouldn't hurt me.

Teral and another of the guards took hold of me, boosting me up to stand on their shoulders as they braced my ankles and legs. I wavered, but managed to catch my balance, and as I grabbed hold of the cage for support, Rhia's fingers crept out, wrapping around mine. Her face looked haunted and her eyes were bleak, but she was smiling and weeping.

I pressed my lips to her hands, then gently shook her off. "Let me get this open. We have to get out of here now, because the vampires will be awake in less than fifteen minutes."

"Oh, Cicely . . ." She sucked in a deep breath. "Hurry! Leo said he'd be back to . . ."

I shushed her and went to work on the padlock. It was easy, and within a moment I had it sprung. The door swung open, and I reached in for Rhiannon and helped her scoot to the edge, hanging her legs over.

"Are you hurt?"

She shook her head. "Not . . . I don't know how to answer that. I can run."

"I understand." I kissed her on the cheek and then leaped down. She waited till I had cleared away from the guards, and then she swung down, hanging from the edge as the guards caught her and helped lower her to the ground. She steadied herself, and I noticed the bruises on her wrists and face.

Chatter slowly walked forward. Rhia shivered, looking

wide-eyed and afraid, but all he did was open his arms. She fell into his embrace, pressing her face against his shoulder, and he wrapped his arms around her, enfolding her in his love and safety while avoiding her back, where we'd seen her being caned on the DVD. He kissed her hair, pushing it aside lightly with one hand, and then kissed her forehead.

"I thought I'd lost you," he whispered. "I thought I was going to lose you forever, and I couldn't bear it."

She squeezed her eyes tight, and I hated to break up their reunion, but time was ticking down. I turned to Peyton, and she held up her clock. Four fifteen. We had less than ten minutes.

As I glanced around the dungeon, the feel of decay and pain set in, and all I could think about was getting out of here. I wanted to stake Geoffrey and Leo, but they'd be awake in minutes, and it was far easier to think about fighting a sleeping vamp than one on his feet.

"Let's get out of here. I don't know if we have time before the vamps wake up, but we have to try. I want Rhia out of here and safe before we attack. I left word for Lannan and Regina. The second the sun sets, he and his men will be on their way."

Check nodded. "Let's go . . ." He took the front and led us out of the room, but the minute we were in the hall, I knew something was wrong. The hallway seemed convoluted, and though I was sure we'd come from the right, which should be downhill, everything was reversed. The hall to the right sloped up. Not sure what to do, Check looked back to me.

I thought for a moment. If we went back the way we'd come, we'd be heading . . . up? But what if it was an illusion, meant to make us think we were going the wrong way, yet instead leading us into a trap?

"Ysandra—" I turned to ask her if she could sense an illusion around us, but she was staring toward the right, her eyes wide. "What is it?"

"Something is coming. We have to move, *now*." A look of absolute terror washed across her face. "Whatever it is, I don't want to be around when it gets here. And neither do you. To the left."

"But that's not the way we came!" I protested for a second but then stopped, because on the slipstream, from what seemed like a million miles away, I could hear the hushed whisperings of creaking coffins and falling earth, of graveyard dirt scattering as creatures rose through soil and rock.

He comes . . . he has awoken early and now he comes in on the wind. The master is free . . . the great seer is risen from his isolation and he walks among us now.

In that moment, I knew who they were whispering about, and my blood ran cold. I turned, horrified, and shot off to the left like a bat out of hell. Crawl was coming—Crawl, the Blood Oracle. Crawl, the seer of the Crimson Court, and next to Myst, he terrified me more than any creature walking this planet. Crawl, who wanted my blood, who wanted to drink me and turn me into a hollow husk, who had ripped my throat open with his deathly hunger and wanted more.

The others followed as I tried to navigate the passage, but it started to twist and turn, and I realized that up and down— left and right—none of it made any sense. Reality had bent, my perception was askew, and there was no guessing where we were going. I didn't care. I wanted to be anywhere but here because damn it, Crawl was on the move, and when he arrived, he'd mow through us like a herd of children after a packet of juice boxes.

As we raced along the hall, Chatter holding Rhiannon steady, I pulled out my cell and glanced at the clock. Not quite four eighteen. Three minutes and the vamps would rise, but as old as they were, there was a chance Regina or Lannan might be able to clear their coffins a little early. If they slept in coffins. I'd never bothered to ask, to be honest. Shaking the wayward thoughts from my mind, I glanced at the bars. We'd reached a point where there were two—not the greatest reception, but it might do. I punched the speed dial for Regina's number and pressed the phone to my ear as I hurried along the convoluted passage.

"Emissary's office, may I help you?"

I recognized the voice as belonging to Regina's day-runner secretary. "I left a message earlier for Regina. This is Cicely and we're running from Crawl. We need help." I didn't have time to be diplomatic, and the next moment, I found myself placed on hold. Another moment and Sasha was back.

"She's getting up now. I told her you need her; she'll be here as soon as . . . here she is." The phone changed hands and Regina came on the line.

I burst into a breathless explanation of what was going on. As soon as Crawl's name left my mouth, she reacted.

"We are on the way. Do your best to stay out of his reach, but, Cicely—be cautious; he is tricky and has many powers that you don't know about. He can bilocate, which few vampires can do, but he is one of the oldest Vein Lords and he bears the mark of the Crimson Queen. She sired him and nurtured him and he suckled at her breast, fangs plunged deep in her alabaster skin, as he was reborn."

I stopped for a second to tuck my cell phone away, but the image of Crawl's insectlike limbs and hideous grin stayed with me, and I was on the run again. I remembered his teeth on my shoulder, and my body burned with the memory. The rasp of his tongue against my wrist, the ripping as his fangs sank into my skin, the fetid smell emanating from his body . . . these images rose to my thoughts, clouding out my reason as my fear rose up again. I let out a strangled scream, stopping as Check turned to make sure I was all right.

We rounded the corner and stopped short in front of a pair of double doors. But behind us, I could feel Death coming, in an ancient body, long, long past any humanity Crawl had ever possessed, if he had ever *been* mortal. He marched on, and I knew he would be here far too soon—before Regina and Lannan could arrive. And our guards, strong as they might be, were no force against the powers of the Blood Oracle.

I pushed forward, beyond the guards, any sense of reason fleeing, and burst through the doors. There, staring at us from a large table in a very large room, sat Anadey—Peyton's mother. She was with Geoffrey and Leo. We were fucked. We were *so* fucked. Caught between two sadistic forces, with nowhere to run.

❦

Peyton stared at her mother and then let out an oath. "What the fuck? You are still with them? Even after they killed Rex? Even after they attacked *me*? You *bitch*!" She lunged forward, but one of Check's men caught her back and, kicking and struggling, she finally submitted, the look on her face murderous.

Geoffrey stood, very slowly, a steel-cold grin lighting his face. "Oh, isn't this lovely. We knew you were in the building, but waiting was definitely a torture. Leo and I had a bet going on whether you'd make it this far, Cicely, before Crawl caught you. I won."

And he moved—in a blur—stopping just out of reach of my guards, who drew their daggers of silver. Geoffrey took a cautious step back. Leo was brooding, staring at us with open hatred. The gangly look was gone—the vampiric glamour having taken hold of him—and I felt a thud in the pit of my stomach as he gazed at me, a malefic grin spreading across his face, then turned his attention to Rhiannon.

"My sweet little whoregirl. And her ever-so-soft boy toy, Chatter. You have a big fat cock for my sweetheart? For my *fiancée*? You stick that big old cock of yours up her cunt? Did she scream? Did she squirm and say, 'Oh, Chatter, fuck me, fuck me up the ass?' " The look on Leo's face turned from perverted to baleful, and Rhiannon paled, crying out as she stumbled back a step.

Chatter stood firm, holding her tightly, but he said nothing. I could tell he wanted to rise to the bait, but he was smart, and he held his tongue.

All too aware that Crawl was coming behind us, I wanted to shout for the guards to go after Geoffrey and Leo, but my fear that they'd all die before Lannan's reinforcements could arrive stayed my order.

But then the odds turned, and not in our favor. A door on the far side of the room opened and a group of vampires— no doubt Geoffrey's cronies—entered. We were outnumbered by a good fifty percent. We were going to have to fight. With a heavy heart, I motioned for Chatter to move Rhia out of the way.

"I think . . . I have no choice," I said softly, closing my eyes to summon the winds—my strongest ally. "Let her fly, and make it a good one, because folks, we are not going to get a second chance."

⋇

A brief pause, then three deep breaths as the ticking of the clock on the wall slowed to almost no movement. In that framework between making a decision and acting on it, a world of thoughts can run through, a river flowing wide and deep—so full, we cannot see the individual images. We cannot hear what our minds are saying, because the adrenaline is building as we prepare ourselves to die.

In every battle, there is a death. The loser may laugh it off if the war is short and sweet and without cost. Or the loser may bleed out, if the war is to the death. Either way, when the call to march comes, there's that one moment when we stop, reflect, and realize that yes, today we may die, today may be the end. And then—we move. And that pause, that breath, becomes forgotten in the heat of the battle.

And so it was here, as always. I pivoted on the fulcrum of my feelings, feeling the swing from fear to acceptance to readiness to . . . action.

As the guards moved forward, their silver blades flashing, the vampires cautiously spread out to form a half circle around us. They were leery, but truth was, unless the tip went center into their hearts, no harm would come to them. So they had fairly decent odds of surviving an attack by my men.

Check would not let me move to the front. He and two of his men pushed us back, but Grieve and Chatter joined the guards, and though I didn't want them to, so did Luna and

Peyton. Peyton looked fit to kill, and I was afraid she'd head directly toward her mother, but instead she quickly stripped off her clothes, tossing them to the side, and turned into her werepuma self. Then she launched herself onto the table, growling low and rumbling. Anadey screamed and backed away.

Luna began singing a low dirge, and Ysandra glanced at her, then joined in. Somehow they were amplifying their powers, joining together as they cooked up some sort of spell. Whatever it was, I let them be and focused on my own source of power—the wind.

I called up the winds, trying to keep control of them, not letting them entrance me like they usually did. And then, as they began gusting lightly around my fingers and through my hair, I closed my eyes, sinking into their siren song. Ulean was not here to help pull me out of it this time if I got lost, and neither was Lainule, so I'd have to manage on my own.

I lowered my chin to my chest and then, as the power settled within, raised my head, staring ahead at the vampires, and under my breath, in the lightest of tones, I whispered, "*Gale Force*," and a stiff breeze sprung to hand, quickly gusting into a howling wind that raced past me, carrying my spirit with it. I spun up and around, growing tall. Like Myst, I towered over the room, looming larger than life in my spirit. My body was still below, but I was rising out of it, trembling in the storm that raged around me.

The howl of the winds ripping past me tore anything light not rooted down off whatever surface it had been on and sent it flying through the air, spinning topsy-turvy into the maelstrom. Within moments, the room was in chaos, with both my guards and the vampires struggling to stay on their feet.

I moved forward, growing still stronger, my spirit rising still taller, laughing as the power began to take hold. I leaned back, letting loose my laughter, and it echoed, a shattering of crystal, over the roar of the storm.

But somewhere inside, I could feel the caution—the

warning signs as my delight in controlling the forces grew—
and I struggled to compose myself, standing on the edge of
the insanity that the power brought with it. As I wavered,
holding back just enough so that I didn't destroy the building as well as the town, my guards launched themselves at
the vampires.

Geoffrey had moved back, as had Leo, and their grunts
were fighting the battle for them, trying to wear down my
forces. The slash of the blades glinted in the light, though
the sound had been lost in the face of my storm, and I
watched in horror as the vampires attacked my men.

*This is war; this is what it means. This may be in your
future yet again, so you'd better get used to it.* The thought
ran through my head and I tried to shake it away, but the
conviction grew. After we took care of Geoffrey and Leo,
we still had Myst to battle, and she would not make it easy
on us.

I gathered my breath and went back to holding the storm
steady, preventing myself from sinking deep into thrall. I
couldn't see what was going on. If I tried to focus on the
fighting, then I lost track of the winds and they would either
fall away or catch me up, neither of which would help. As it
was, even though they also hindered my men, they were
throwing the vampires off track. My guards knew what to
expect from them, but the vamps—Geoffrey and Leo
included—had no clue of how to handle the whirlwind raging around them.

But then, a shriek raced through the room, and I lost my
concentration. It was Peyton, and she was screaming in
pain. As I let go of the storm, the energy suddenly wrested
away from me and spiraled out to fill the room. A great
groaning and creaking shattered the air as the sudden
twister—the remnants of my gale—spun out of control and
crashed through a nearby wall, the brick spraying pebbles
on anyone near the area. The building shook, moaning as
it took the direct hit, but all I could think of was that Peyton was being hurt.

Geoffrey had caught her in his arms, and he was biting

into her neck. I raced forward, but Check caught me before I could travel more than a few paces, motioning for his men to go in my stead. As I watched, helpless and terrified, they pushed through the fighting, but before they could get there, Anadey began to scream and beat on Geoffrey's back.

"My daughter—don't you hurt her! Let her go!" Mother Bear was out, it appeared. She clawed at him, and in that moment, Geoffrey dropped Peyton, who fell to the ground and immediately scrambled away. He turned to backhand Anadey against the wall so hard the room shook again.

She snapped against the brick, her head jerking forward, then back again in a whiplash motion. Then, slowly, she opened her mouth to speak, but slid down the wall to puddle the bottom, and her eyes closed as her head lolled to the side. A bloody streak covered the wall where she'd landed. As far as I could tell, Anadey was dead.

Peyton began to sob, but she had the presence of mind to get out of Geoffrey's reach. My men advanced on him, blades cautious and glittering, but then—in one of those moments where the ground shifts and the world changes— everything stopped as someone yanked me away from Check, out of his arms.

Gasping, I turned to gaze upward at my captor. And there, staring down, leering with uncontrolled desire and hunger, stood Crawl.

As my stomach flipped and I realized he was launching his fangs toward my throat, I began to scream, and scream, and I couldn't stop.

Chapter 17

Crawl stared at me, holding me tight by the neck, preventing me from moving without cutting off the breath flowing through my windpipe. His lurid face was a mask and mockery of what once had passed for human. But his birth had been so many thousands of years ago that there was no telling what race the Blood Oracle had been, or what he'd looked like, or even if he'd been old or young when turned.

With blackened skin that looked like it had been long ago burnt to a polished hue, he was limber and thin, like sticks held together by a taut, wired force. And he was hungry— ever hungry. I could see it in his eyes. I could feel it in his aura. I could hear it in the energy crackling around him. When he leaned down to sniff me, brushing his tongue over his fangs, I knew I was simply a snack to him, a plaything until I broke and couldn't be fixed.

Grieve moved to run forward, but I struggled, holding up my hand. Chances were, if anybody interfered, Crawl would squeeze and that would be it. He liked his blood fresh, but freshly dead was nearly as good, and chances were he wasn't going be too particular.

I struggled to breathe, trying to slow down my heart so I didn't go into a panic attack.

Crawl leaned in, looming over me, sniffing at me. His lidless eyes were black as night. "We have missed this one, we have. She is known to us, we remember the scent, we remember the taste. We remember how sweet the blood rolled onto our tongue, and how loud her screams were."

"L-let . . . m-me go." I managed to stammer out a few words. Begging would do no good. While I wanted to tell him, *I'm the Queen of Winter and you endanger your people by threatening me*, I couldn't get it out, and it would have been a waste of breath. The room started to spin, and all I could see was his hideous face staring down at me.

Grieve's voice rang out. "If you hurt her, you're staked. Put her down and we'll come to a calm end."

My wolf growled, shifting, and I knew that Grieve was one step away from attacking Crawl. I prayed he wouldn't. Crawl would break my neck, then mow down the entire party, and Regina had warned me that he had powers we knew nothing of.

"Her blood is sweet and hard to forget. Yes, it is." He pressed the remnants of blackened lips against my throat, and once again the scent of mothballs and decay filled my nose. I let out a cry, shifting slightly as he opened his mouth to strike.

"Put her down, Old Master." Regina's voice echoed from behind us.

Crawl snapped his head around, fire filling those glimmering black orbs that passed for eyes. He snarled. "This one is mine. She is my drink of life."

"Put her down, or I will summon the Crimson Queen. You are not to be out walking, ancient one. You know the rules—you must return to your lair. The Crimson Queen herself has decreed this. You *must* bow to the Mother." The sound of her heels on the floor clipped with precision, and I could tell she was making her way over to us.

"Cicely, hold still. Do nothing." Lannan must be trailing Regina, judging from the direction from which his voice came.

Crawl growled like a dog protecting his bone. He turned back to me, and the next thing I knew, we were being body-slammed.

Sprawling, taking me with him, Crawl lost his grasp. I tried to roll out of the way, but he landed on my legs and held me fast.

Lannan was shouting.

The weight of the Blood Oracle—far heavier than I would have imagined—kept me pinned. I turned, trying to claw my way out as he struggled with Lannan, who was attempting to pull him off me. The sounds of the two vampires fighting was like a horrible battle between two lions, kings of the hill waging war over the queen.

My hands on the floor, my fingertips pressed hard against the tile, I struggled to drag myself free. Check and Grieve were running toward me, and I held up one hand to them. Grieve reached down, his fingers clutching mine. He began a steady tug, trying to ease me out, as Check slid his arms beneath mine.

I groaned as something snapped in one of my legs. Not a loud snap, but enough for me to know that a muscle or a tendon or something had ripped. A few seconds later, the pain hit in my ankle.

I gritted my teeth, trying not to scream, but at that moment, Check managed to dislodge me and I pushed away the numbing ache.

As he pulled me from beneath Crawl's body, there was a momentary lull in the fight, and then something long and sharp with several blades ripped through my leg, tearing into the flesh.

I screamed as the blood began to fountain, the gashes burning their way into my leg. There were screams—I think from Luna—and a lot of shouting, and the next thing I knew, Crawl's hand was off my leg.

"She's bleeding out—look at those wounds!"

"Get her jeans off her."

I wanted to ask where Geoffrey and Leo were. I wanted

to see what was going on with Crawl. But all I could do was stare unfocused at the ceiling while someone tugged on my jeans. The pain of the material sliding over the wounds was exquisite agony, and I moaned, biting my tongue to keep from screaming again. I was fading in and out now and slowly began to feel myself sliding out of my body. I shifted. And then, as everything began to go black, I heard Lannan.

"You have no choice. She needs my blood—it will bring her back from the brink because, *Princeling*, if you don't let me do this, your fiancée will die and take the queenship down the drain with her. When Crawl wounds, be it his fangs or his talons, there must be a transfusion of vampire blood. Any magic-born or yummanii bitten by the Old Master is doomed to bleed out. She's not so far gone that it will turn her, but there's very little time. Do you want her to live, or will you let her die?"

As his words began to sink in, so did the realization that I was dying, and that once again, Crawl was responsible.

Grieve let out an anguished cry. "Go then, do it . . . I know what will happen, and I accept. *Just save her.*"

The next moment, somebody was forcing my lips open, and then a few drops of blood began to trickle into my mouth, and it was the sweetest ambrosia I'd ever tasted. Rich and thick and familiar. I licked my lips to catch the stray beads, sucking them in. Suddenly so thirsty I wanted to scream, I opened my mouth willingly as Lannan pressed his wrist to my lips, an open cut bleeding slowly, and I suckled, taking his force into my body, feeling it cascade down my throat.

As I eagerly drew his blood into me, the pain in my leg began to subside as a warm, sinuous energy unwound from the base of my tailbone, snaking its way up my body, flushing me deep like a blush to the core.

I let out a slow moan, this time from pleasure rather than pain, as the blood raced down my throat, freeing me from the ache of my torn flesh. But then it started—the heat racing around my cunt, waking me up as it traveled up through my breasts, through the road map of veins running

through my body. I sucked deeper still, the crimson river
flowing through me, infusing me with health and strength
and desire.

And then my eyes opened, and I was staring up into Lannan's face, that glorious mane of golden hair falling around
his shoulders as the jet black eyes watched me. No breath,
no rise and fall of the chest, and I tried to remind myself
that he was dead, that he was a vampire, but all I could
think about was having his hands on me, having him hold
me down and drive himself into me again and again until I
forgot everything except those ancient, glazed-over eyes.

The very air acted like an aphrodisiac on my skin, ruf-
fling past like a ribbon of silk, and I let out another moan
as every faint whisper of wind became a tease, as every
sound became amplified. My body was a live wire, sizzling
like hot oil, and I reached up, grabbed hold of Lannan, and
pulled him down to me, locking my lips with his.

A faint sound caught my notice, and my wolf howled,
but I pushed it away. The only thing that existed at the
moment was the Blood Fever, the drive to spread my legs
and beckon my dark angel inside. I kissed him, deep, prob-
ing his mouth with my tongue, running it over his fangs.

Lannan stared down at me, a triumphant smirk on his
face, but then he held me down, pausing, and looked up.
"I'm taking her out of here. The Blood Fever is so high that
she'll die if I don't quench it. Regina, you know what to do
with Crawl. The rest of you—my men will escort you to
safety. Geoffrey and Leo are still at large."

His words registered through a fog, and I let out a faint
whisper.

"Geoffrey—Leo—my cousin . . . Rhia?"

"Shush, my sweet Cicely. You are still weak, and you
burn with Blood Fever. Save your worries for later. Your
cousin is safe, and so are your friends."

In the haze of lust, my skin was so hot it felt like I was
going to burn into a crisp, burn into a cinder. I fell silent.
Vague images fluttered past—Grieve, my love, but even
my heart couldn't withstand the flame racing through my

veins. I thought I caught a glimpse of him, but then, in a flash, he was gone and I wasn't sure what was real and what wasn't.

The next thing I knew, we were traveling at blur-speed, and as I watched the walls rush by, I began to sweat. The Blood Fever was hitting, and hitting hard.

Blood Fever. Whenever one of the still-living drank from a vampire without being turned, the blood boiled in the system, churning through the veins like a river of passion, driving mortals into raving nutcases. The only release, the only way to calm the blood, was to fuck your brains out—to ride the drive into submission. Primal forces were unleashed with Blood Fever, filling the body, overriding logic, overriding love.

We passed into the night; somehow we were in a car—Lannan's limousine—and he laid me back against the seat, the leather creaking as he adjusted me beneath him. The smell was old, and moneyed, and I wondered how many times Lannan had fucked someone in this car.

He held me down, pinning my wrists over my head. "Move your hurt leg to the side," he whispered.

I slid my left leg to the side so it was off the seat, bending my knee so my foot was braced against the floor. I was sweating, the glistening beads slowly trickling down my face, dripping onto my chest. All I could think about was how close his lips were to mine, how cold his hands were against my skin, how there was no rising and falling of breath from him. He had conquered death, and I hated him. And yet . . . and yet . . . I craved the force of his body against mine.

Lannan licked my neck, trailing his tongue down toward my breasts. "Salty. You're salty. And your breath, it comes so hard. Panting, are we? Girl, you want me. I can feel it. And this time, I want to hear you say it. Beg me, Cicely. Beg me and I'll give you *everything*."

I shifted, my back sticking to the leather. My cunt ached so bad that I thought I'd never be satiated.

"I hate you," I whispered.

"I know. Say it anyway." His gaze fastened onto my own, and as he stared at me through those obsidian eyes, I fell into them, deep and dark, and tumbling down. I caught my breath, my pulse racing as the sweat continued to bathe us both, a baptism of passion.

"I want you. I want you . . . a part of me has always wanted you." Hating myself as I said it, but realizing it was the truth, that there was some hidden darkness within me that drove me to him, that secretly hungered for his touch. Grieve owned me, heart and soul, but chemistry was chemistry, and something in Lannan spoke to a part of me that was broken and twisted and would never be fixed.

"I wish I could drink from you tonight," he whispered, licking my neck. "I'm hungry for your blood. I want to taste you, but for now I don't dare. Crawl wounded you deeply, and his venom is still within your system. But I'll give you everything you want from me right now. And more."

And then his lips covered mine, and the world fell into a long, dark hole where there was only steam rising between us, and the feeling of his hands on my wrists, of his mouth against mine, grazing my lips with his fangs. The kiss went on and on, as I let myself flow into the abyss in which my dark vampire lived.

The lights of the city were a blur as we passed through the snowy night, and the flutter of snowflakes bathed the road in a muffled silence. And all the way to his mansion, Lannan spun me out of myself, out of my head, into the dark fire that radiated from deep within him.

As we pulled to a stop, the driver opened the car door, and without a word, Lannan lifted me in his arms. I barely sensed the maid who opened the door, the dim lights of the sparkling chandelier, the scent of opium and incense that wafted out from the party room where Lannan and Regina played with their bloodwhores.

And then we were in what I thought was Lannan's bedroom, the crimson walls reflecting the light from the Tiffany lamp in the corner. A sudden fear caught hold of me and I whimpered, but he shushed me and I fell silent, totally in thrall. My body was burning, and I began to phase in and out.

Flash . . . a glimpse of the Golden Boy, laying me out on the bed. *Flash* . . . the ceiling fan overhead spinning far too slowly, like slow thunder. *Flash* . . . the shedding of clothes, and I was naked and felt like I could finally breathe. *Flash* . . . I glanced down, a glimpse of the scars on the torn and rent flesh that Crawl had so lovingly given me. *Flash* . . . Lannan, standing there, tall against the silhouette of the light, and he was nude, his skin an unearthly alabaster. *Flash* . . . and he began walking toward me as I understood this was *real*. It was going to happen. And there was nothing in the world that would stop us this time.

He was on me, then, looming over me as I pressed against the burgundy velvet of the bedspread. I began to breathe heavily.

"How do you want it, baby? How do you want me?" Lannan's victorious grin made me angry, and yet . . . and yet . . .

"If this is going to happen, don't make it sweet. I won't take *sweet* from you. If you're going to fuck me, then make it rough, because it will never happen again, and I want to remember you for the bloodsucker you are." Unsure where my words had come from, I suddenly felt stronger. "I want more of your blood. Give it to me."

He blinked, for the first time looking unsure. But then he laughed and lifted his arm. With the precisely shaped nail of his index finger on his right hand, he sliced through the flesh, and as I watched, the blood burbled up, slow and thick, viscous like honey. I eyed it hungrily, the fever driving me on. And from somewhere deep inside, as I reached for his wrist, I flashed . . .

⚹

The man was pretty. He was pretty and he was alone and he was in the forest, gathering firewood. I stared from behind the huckleberry bush, my thirst rising. The pale blue of my skin mirrored the layer of ice on the lake nearby, and as long as I kept to the snow, I blended in fairly well. My eyes, dark and filled with stars, had adjusted to the light of day.

I preferred to hunt during the night, but the bloodlust had driven me out of the Barrow, and I needed a quarry. I needed blood and sinew and flesh. But first . . . Yes, the man was very tasty, with long dark hair and deeply tanned skin. He was clad in leather and he was kneeling, examining something near the base of a tree.

I slipped out from behind the bush . . . clad only in a gossamer gown like my mother, Myst, Queen of the Indigo Court. Walking barefoot atop the snow, I left no tracks, made no sound. The animals of the forest had backed away; they knew I was near and that I was on the prowl. But the pretty man had no idea who was coming for him, and that was as it should be.

I slowly sauntered up behind him, until I cast a shadow over his shoulder in the fading afternoon. He turned, the lovely man, and his startled look turned to fear as I smiled, my razor-sharp teeth gleaming in the dim light. I cocked my head, turning it this way, turning it that, examining him.

He stood, the wood he'd gathered scattering as he stumbled back. He said something—I didn't understand what, nor did I care—and then turned to run. I decided to give him a head start. It was more fun that way.

I waited a beat, then another. And then, just when he thought he'd escaped, I started to run. I ran in a blur. I ran in a flash. I ran on the wind and through snow and with a laughter that trailed two steps behind me.

It took him a moment to realize I was coming for him, and when he did, he screamed, falling by the side of the lake. He glanced at it, as though he might crash through the ice rather than face me.

"Can't have that, pretty boy. We haven't played our games yet." I knew he couldn't understand me, not my *words*, but he saw the razor's smile in my eyes and let out a strangled cry.

It was too late.

I caught him by the hair, yanking his head back. Instinct urged me to attack, to shed his blood, to gnaw his bones, to rip at the sinew and flesh, but I was hungry in more ways than one. I dragged him away from the lake and ripped off his clothes. He wasn't anywhere near my strength, and when he put up a fight, I grabbed one of his arms and squeezed it, breaking the bones. He screamed again, this time from pain rather than fear.

"Kiss, kiss," I said, leaning in to press my lips against his. *Nobody* resisted Cherish, the daughter of Myst. And truth being, the minute my lips were on his, he stopped fighting. The venom in my kiss had him snared, and I climbed atop him, riding him hard, riding him rough, riding him even as my teeth nipped holes in his flesh. I bloodied his lips and then his neck, and then, as I came—hard and hungry—I lunged for his throat, shifting into my creature as I did so. I fell into the bloodlust with a fury, until there was nothing left on the ground but a few bones and the stain of glorious, delicious blood.

As I transformed back into my normal shape, I pulled a shred of tendon out of my teeth. Leaning down at the edge of the lake, I rinsed my mouth and washed my face—and then stood to begin my next hunt.

I was nowhere near satiated, but the pretty man would hold me for a while. Laughing, I raised my arms to the sky, reveling in the fall of snow, and sauntered away, my belly full for the moment. But there was more blood out there, calling my name, and the thrill of the kill never grew weary.

⚜

Blinking, I found myself back in the moment, sucking on Lannan's wrist. The blood made me feel stronger, and I could feel my powers returning, my body healing. Once again, he'd saved my life, and now . . .

"You always thought you were the master," I whispered, rolling him over and climbing atop him. "You wanted me, you're going to *get* me, but on my rules, *do you understand*?"

He laughed, low and dangerously. "You think so, little girl?"

"I know so." I plunged down on his cock, driving him into me. The chill of his flesh penetrated me, spreading through my body like a lacework of frost spreading across the window. I leaned my head back, groaning as he filled me full, driving deep into my core. As I began to move against him, he grabbed my waist and rolled me over, grinding full into me.

"I'll show you who's your master, girl."

And with that, he thrust against me, impaling me on his icy, cold length. I closed my eyes, spiraling into the frenzy, wanting every inch to fill me up, to take me down, to throw me into the flames that were burning my body.

As he fucked me raw, my wolf began to howl. I reached out, stroked him, brought him into the fold as Lannan leaned down and bit my nipple, piercing it. The pain became pleasure and the pleasure became ecstasy as he licked up the thin trickle of blood dripping down my chest.

"I had to taste you," he whispered, pinning me down with his weight. "I can't drink much from you, but I had to taste a few drops. My sweet Cicely . . . I told you this would happen."

He pulled out, flipping me over. "I'm not done yet, and neither are you." He drove into me from behind, deep into my pussy as I rested on all fours. "I asked you once if your fair prince has ever fucked you in wolf form. Answer me, tell me . . ." His words were strained but the command was evident, and in my state, I was in no space to deny him.

"No, no . . . never . . . I wouldn't do that . . ." I let out a low moan as he reached around and began to stroke my clit. The energy was so thick I could barely breathe, and I began to spiral down into the abyss, falling deep, spiraling into the pit of flames as he continued to work me.

"My name. Scream my name. I want to hear you beg for release. I want to hear you beg me, on your knees like this, my cock shoved so far up your cunt that you'll never forget

I was in you. Every time you sleep with your Wounded King, you'll remember this, and you'll burn for me."

I was close, so close, the fever burned so brilliantly that I felt like the phoenix, consumed by her own flames as they danced around me. And then, as I neared the pinnacle, Lannan leaned down and bit my shoulder blade, viciously, and his fangs drove deep into me.

The pain mingled with orgasm as I came, so hard I wavered, almost passing out. And as the fever roared in my ears, I heard myself screaming.

"Lannan, fuck me, fuck me . . . never stop . . . don't stop . . ." And then, poised on the edge, I swan-dived into the darkness, and the flames crackled as I fell so deep and so far that I didn't know if I'd ever return.

Chapter 18

I opened my eyes, unsure where I was. Every inch of my body ached, and at first, I couldn't remember why, and then I looked around and realized where I was.

Oh motherfucking hell. No, no . . . it wasn't real . . .

But as I pushed back the covers and saw the healing scars on my leg, I knew that I hadn't imagined anything. The wounds were raked into my skin, scabbing over, and there didn't seem to be any infection. The muscles had knit quickly, but my leg was stiff and sore. I tried to focus on the mundane, tried to ignore what I knew I'd have to face sooner or later, because the longer I put it off, the longer I could avoid facing the ramifications of what had happened.

Images kept breaking through—Lannan's face, the feel of him holding me down, the feel of . . . I moaned, grabbing a pillow and hiding my face in it. What the hell was I going to do now? And now, would he ever leave me alone? And how would I face Grieve? In the cold light of day . . . Well—I wasn't sure if it was morning or not, but now that I was out of the grip of the Blood Fever, I could think clearly, but I wasn't sure I wanted to. Then another horrifying thought hit: While I was pretty sure they'd collected Crawl, Geoffrey and Leo were still on the loose. That much I was certain I remembered correctly.

And if they were loose, Rhiannon and I were still in danger.

I looked around, trying to find a clock. There were no windows here, but then again, neither was Lannan anywhere to be seen, and I wasn't sure whether he slept here. I doubted it—too vulnerable for a vampire to sleep where anybody could walk in on him. No, he had to have some secret lair. This was just where he brought his blood-whores . . . and his conquests.

Again, a shudder ran through me. My wolf whimpered with a mournful, lonely yip. I reached down, unsure whether to make contact, but I had no choice. I pressed my hand against the tattoo and gently whispered, "I'm so sorry, my love. I would have done anything to avoid what happened, but happen it did and there's nothing we can do about it."

My wolf paused, snarled a moment, then another whimper, and I felt a wave of sadness and love pour through. I hung my head, but then I paused, looking at my leg once more. Lannan had saved my life yet again. I would have bled out; I would have died without his blood. What had happened was infinitely better than the alternative, and Grieve had to understand that.

I examined my heart. How did I feel about Lannan? Searching deep, looking for honesty, I examined my feelings. What did I feel for him after our night together?

Vague images floated through my mind: our bodies moving in rhythm, my sweat covering both of us, the cold feel of his hands on my body . . . the passion was strong and undeniable, but my heart felt untouched. The Blood Fever had left me connected to Lannan but not tied like before. Something had shifted, and I had the feeling it had everything to do with my heartstone.

I slowly stood, testing my leg. The gashes were going to leave nasty scars; there was no help for that. At least they had closed, and Lannan's blood had saved my life. When they healed, I'd have tattoos inked over them. A rite of passage, acknowledging my ascension to the throne of Winter, perhaps.

My clothes weren't on the bed, so I crossed to the door and paused. I wasn't ashamed of my body, but the idea of stepping out of the room, buck naked, with still-healing scars? Not such a good idea, especially if it was still night and the vamps were out to play.

I looked around the room, hoping that Lannan might have stashed a spare robe. There was a closet over by the dresser—I hadn't noticed much in the way of furnishings the night before. But now I could see that the antiques here were well maintained, highly polished, and carefully oiled. No clock that I could see. But a dresser, dressing table, armoire, coatrack—and there I saw a hanger with a delicately embroidered robe on it.

The robe was blue, and an owl was emblazoned on the back. Lannan had left it for me. I slipped it off the hanger and put it on, tying it with the belt. A pair of silk panties were hanging next to it, but I had no intention of accepting underwear from Lannan. I left them hanging there and headed toward the door.

As I opened the door, the scurry of activity and the sight of housekeepers polishing the grand foyer told me that it was most likely daylight. Regina and Lannan chose not to be bothered with things like that when they were awake. I caught the eye of one of the maids, and she hurried over to me.

"Your Majesty—you're awake. The Master told me that when you are ready, I'm to offer you a bath, and the Emissary has left you new clothes. Your friends are waiting in the other chamber for you. What do you wish to do?" She flushed, as if she realized her words had come in a long spurt with no breath separating her sentences.

I thought for a moment. Though I wanted to see the others now, perhaps it wasn't the best plan to show up in a robe. A robe that Lannan had given me, no less. The clothes would probably have Regina's style all over them, but they'd be from the Emissary, not from my vampire nemesis-turned-lover.

"I'll take a shower and then dress. Would you let my friends know I'm all right and that I'm getting ready?" I glanced around the hall, finding the grandfather clock. It was ten A.M., and the clock let out a series of ten chimes. "It's morning, isn't it?"

"Yes, Your Majesty. You've been asleep most of the night. The Master ordered you left undisturbed till you woke. He said you needed your sleep. Please, wait in the room for a moment and I'll be back to draw your bath. I'll go speak to your friends."

"If Rhiannon—Her Majesty the Summer Queen—is there, please ask her to return with you. Luna and Peyton, too." I turned back to the room and, fidgety now, sat on the bed, waiting. There was a bookcase of old books against the wall, and I glanced through the titles, but they were mostly sex books, history books, and coffee table tomes, heavy and filled with pictures. I took one off the shelf, but after flipping through a few pages of pinup models and tattooed wenches, I realized that I couldn't focus.

Everything that had happened was still so fresh in my mind, and yet still a blur of sensation and passion and drive. My thighs ached and I slid the robe back, looking down to find bruises on them from where I'd straddled Lannan, from where he'd thrust between them, driving himself deeper and deeper into me. Closing my eyes, I realized that I couldn't let Grieve see them. He'd know they weren't from Crawl. He knew Lannan had fucked me—there was no getting past that one—but I didn't have to throw it in his face.

A moment later, the maid returned. She motioned for me to follow her through a door to the right, near the bed. As we crossed the threshold, I was surprised to find a massive bath, tiled in a pale white with splashes of black. The room was huge, with a built-in vanity, a linen closet, and a separately partitioned toilet—for human guests and bloodwhores, since vampires didn't need them. In the center of the room, on a platform, sat a huge spa tub. All thoughts of a shower went down the drain.

"Can I take a bubble bath?" I turned to the maid, wanting nothing more than to drown myself in hot water.

She nodded. "Of course, Your Highness. Your cousin, the Summer Queen, will be here in a moment. One of our female guards is accompanying her, leaving nothing to chance."

I sat on the bench as the maid began to fill the tub. She offered me a variety of scents with which to stir up the bubbles. I chose a lightly scented vanilla, and as the water frothed up a lather, I slipped out of the robe and draped it over a chair. There was a full-length mirror against one wall and, as the water burbled away, I examined myself.

The gashes on my legs, scabbed over though they might be, were hideous. They were long and thick, and there were five of them—one for each one of Crawl's talons on the hand that had managed to get ahold of me. The scabs would heal and fall off, but I had the feeling that I'd be marked forever.

The bruising on my thighs was fairly evident, but it was less disconcerting than the fang marks on my breast. Lannan hadn't drunk from me per se, but he'd bit me and nibbled, and the marks were there, a reminder of the fierceness of the night. While there were various other bumps and bruises from the fight in the underground passage, nothing else I could find marked me as Lannan's play toy.

Hell, who are you kidding? He was your play toy, too. Blood Fever or not, you remember the night, and you remember the hunger you felt.

Shaking the thought away, I stepped into the tub, wincing as the hot water welcomed me in. I settled into the mound of bubbles and leaned back, letting the warmth of the water wash into my sore muscles, over the scabs on my legs.

I was just closing my eyes when a soft knock at the door brought the maid to her feet from where she was sitting at the vanity table.

She answered the door and escorted Rhia in. Rhiannon was dressed in jeans, which was startling in itself, and a brown leather jacket. Her hair was pulled back in a long braid, and there was something about her expression that left me sad. There was something missing from her eyes—an innocence. The frightened, haunted look that had both been tragic and made her the woman she was had vanished, and now fire filled her eyes.

She rushed over to me, kneeling by the tub, and took my chin in her hand. I leveled my gaze with hers, holding nothing back. We were cousins; we had no secrets other than where our heartstones were hidden, and that secret was absolutely necessary.

"How . . . has your leg healed up?" I could hear the question behind the question as she leaned on the edge of the bath.

I reached out and covered her hand with my own. "I'm alive, and that's what counts. My leg is a mess, but it's healing, and it wouldn't have if it hadn't been for Lannan." I lifted it for her to see, and she grimaced.

"Lannan didn't hurt me. The Blood Fever had me in thrall, and I needed him. He didn't humiliate me. He just . . . gave me what I needed. And what he's wanted for weeks now." I could see the doubt waging war on her face. I entwined my fingers through hers. "I'm telling you the truth."

"If you say so." She looked like she wanted to say more.

I was about to ask what happened after Crawl had attacked me, where Geoffrey and Leo went, but first, I needed to know how she was. Leo had brutalized her, and Rhiannon wasn't as resilient as I was.

"What about you? We saw the DVD." I didn't want to embarrass her, but she had to know.

"The others told me." She bit her lip. "Leo . . . I can't just go along the same as I've always been and still expect to rule as the Summer Queen. My initiation led me through a dark journey. I almost didn't make it, Cicely, but I pulled through. After Leo caught me, the strength I drew on from that, the power that kept me going through the initiation, that's what helped me survive him. What you saw on that video wasn't the worst of what happened. I'll tell you about it all when I'm ready but not now. Not with him still out there. But I *will* tell you this: I'm ready to claim my power. Chatter is going to teach me, along with a few of the adepts from the Marburry Barrow, not just how to *control* my flame but how to increase it."

I paused, then let out a long sigh. While Lannan had humiliated me before, I could never truly say he'd raped me. Abused me? Yes, but not like Leo had assaulted my cousin. "How's Chatter?"

She hesitated for a moment, then dipped her finger in the bubbles and swirled them around. "He's different. Not in a bad way—not to me. But this changed him, too. He's no longer . . ."

"No longer Grieve's sidekick?" I smiled at her.

"Right. He's going to make one hell of a formidable Summer King. I guess this had to happen, but . . ."

"If it had only happened another way," I said softly, and she nodded.

I was as clean as I was going to get, and it was time to face the music. "Is Grieve out there, waiting?"

She bit her lip. "Yes. Cicely, last night was the hardest thing he's ever done. You should have seen his face when Lannan carried you off. He loves you more than life itself, and for him to let Lannan do what he did . . ."

I stepped out of the tub, and Rhia sighed. "Your leg looks so painful."

"That's why Grieve allowed it. I would have bled out. These aren't chicken scratches. I almost died."

I stared down at my legs. The bruises on my thighs were evident, but Rhia delicately avoided mentioning them. "He's a pain in the ass, but the fact is that Lannan saved my life. What happened last night, happened. I'm not caught up in thrall by him, nor am I in love with him. Grieve and I will move beyond this."

In that moment, I knew it was true. Rhia seemed to understand. She stood as the maid brought over an upholstered bag. Rhia took it and waved her away.

"I brought you some clothes. Druise picked them out."

As I toweled off, she withdrew a long indigo skirt, which wouldn't rub against my wounds; a pair of panties; and a gorgeous black and silver corset. I suddenly realized that my circlet was missing.

"My crown—"

The words had no more than escaped my lips when the maid jumped up. "I'll fetch it for you, Your Majesty." She vanished out the door and I began to dress, Rhiannon helping me into the corset.

"I swear, I know Druise likes to pull my laces, but I'm going to have her fix a few of these damned things so I can just slip into them and hook them up. If she's not around, I need to be able to get them on without her help."

Rhia laughed. "I know. My lady's maid is the same way. We're bringing change to the Barrows, you know. Things will never quite be the same as they were." She tied me off and then stood back. "You look good." Picking up a bag of makeup, she held it out to me.

I was about to wave it away but then realized—I was the face of the Court of Winter. When I walked out that door, that was how everybody was going to be looking at me. There was no more choice. I had to take more time, had to pay more attention to the formalities of the situation. I flipped on the lighted mirror at the vanity and settled myself on the bench, swiftly applying my game face.

"Things have changed. Our lives . . . once we find Geoffrey and Leo . . . and once we take care of Myst . . ." I looked over my shoulder at her. "Can you imagine what our lives will be like in twenty years . . . thirty . . . one hundred? We're going to live a long, long time, and right now it's hard to comprehend what all of this is going to mean. We're still so caught up in the adrenaline of what's happened—and the enemies we're facing . . ."

She laughed, coming over to hug me and give me a quick kiss on the cheek. "I *know* we don't realize all that's happened. It's all been like a dream—everything is so topsy-turvy. But we'll figure it out. After all, you and I are amber and jet."

"Fire and ice." I grinned. "Did you ever think that when we used to call ourselves that, it was actually true?"

Shaking her head, she turned somber again. "No, but maybe we had a premonition about it. Maybe my mother did when she nicknamed us that." She paused. "We have to find Leo and Geoffrey. None of us will rest with them still out there. Regina left us some information that might help."

"They got away in the mayhem." I frowned.

"Yeah. When Crawl had hold of you and all the guards were focused on you, they managed to slip away. So they're on the run again. But Regina had her men tear through that place."

"Do they know who originally built the underground structure?"

"No, though it looks like it was used by some group studying the creatures from the depths. She's going to station a group of her own vamps down there, and Ysandra is going to assign members of the Consortium there, too. They want to know what's going on—where those things are coming from. And to figure out just what they are. They'll be working in tandem."

That sounded like a solid plan. "When they find out, we need to know. We can ask Strict and Edge who our historians are at the Barrows and see if there are any records there, although who knows how much Myst destroyed when she rampaged through both? But if there is anything recorded about them, we'll find out and turn the information over to Regina and Ysandra. Whatever they are, those creatures could threaten the city."

I was dressed. Druise returned with my circlet and I put it on and stood back. "I'm ready. Let's go. We've got vampires to catch." And I had a fiancé to calm, and to remind how much I loved him, no matter what had happened.

❋

Grieve was waiting in the foyer, along with Peyton, Check, and several of the guards. He stood there, looking at me as I walked down the hall. I paused, unsure of what to do. I slowly raised my skirt so they could see the long scabs running along my leg. His face crumpled and he just held out his arms and I raced into them, the night fading like a bad dream.

"My love, my love . . ." His whispers enfolded me in a shroud of love and remorse as he kissed my hair, kissed my face. Then, holding me back by the shoulders, he looked into my eyes. "You're all right?"

I gazed at him, willing him to see how much I loved him. How much he meant to me. "I am, thanks to you. And . . . thanks to Lannan. He saved my life." I knew it hurt, but it had to be said.

A wash of pain crossed Grieve's face, but he quickly shook it off. "I know. And . . . I know." That was all he said, but I could read every nuance of what lurked behind those words. He would accept what happened because it *did* save my life. Because it was the only thing that meant I was here this morning instead of lying cold on a slab.

"I love you. You're my betrothed. We will rule Winter together." And with that, I kissed him once again, and his arms encircled my waist and we were all right. I knew there would come a time we'd have to talk about what happened, but that time was not now. We had work to do.

Grieve seemed to sense this, also. "We're meeting at the Veil House to discuss routing Geoffrey and Leo. We have leads on them, thanks to Regina's men. Ysandra and Luna are casting another locating spell to pinpoint the spot."

That worried me. "Should Luna do another so soon? The spirits already told her she would be paying a price for the one she cast earlier."

"There's no choice, and it matters not. She said now that they've claimed her, there's not much more they can require. She's created a compact by that first spell, so she might as well take advantage of the connection."

I nodded. It made sense. "Then let's book. I want to get out of here. I want to find those freaks and be done with this. I'm ready to close the chapter on Geoffrey and Leo's little reign of terror."

As we headed out into the snowy day, I glanced back at Lannan's mansion. I would have to deal with him in the future, yes. But somewhere, inside, I knew that—no matter if his obsession continued—we were done. Something had shifted, and though I couldn't pinpoint what it was, our relationship had changed forever.

Cicely! You're awake and all right! Ulean's voice blew past, a euphoric sweep of cool air swirling around me.

I've been better, but yes. I'm all right. Lannan . . . things have changed.

I know what happened. And you are right—your life, the lives of your loved ones and friends . . . the very nature of New Forest is shifting. And it must—it is the nature of life to change. Leo and Geoffrey stand in the path of that shift. As does Myst. But you . . . the wounds are healing? And you came through the Blood Fever . . . ?

I could sense her hesitation. Ulean could be discreet at times, diplomatic when she wished, but this felt different.

It's all right to talk about it. Lannan and I have reached a crossroads in our relationship. He saved my life and he pulled me through the Blood Fever. And while I know he enjoyed it . . . somehow I do not think he wanted it to happen that way. Only time will tell what comes from this. But Grieve and I are good. And my heart belongs firmly where it always has—in my Fae Prince's keeping.

Then all will be well. Come, they await you at the Veil House. There is hunting to be done.

And with that, Rhiannon and Peyton and I climbed into the waiting limousine, while Grieve and the guards took off at blur-speed. As we pulled out of the driveway, I turned my thoughts toward the future. There was no going back.

Chapter 19

The ride home was silent. Peyton was staring straight ahead, and then I remembered: Anadey was dead. Anadey had attacked Geoffrey to save Peyton, and she'd died for it. She'd turned on us, but in the end, her love for her daughter had brought her through. But that meant Geoffrey had killed both of Peyton's parents, and I could see the hatred simmering below the surface.

I reached out, touched her arm. "We'll get them. I promise you with all of my heart, we will destroy them."

"I want blood vengeance." She looked up at me, her face set. "My father was going to take me to his people. I will still go, when all of this—Geoffrey, Myst—is over. I will tell them Rex is dead, and see if they will still let me journey on a vision quest to become part of my tribe."

"What about the diner?" Rhia asked.

"I have no interest in it—I'll sell it, and then be able to fund the Mystical Eye fully. I've washed my last dish." And with that, she lapsed into silence. Rhiannon and I left her alone. We both had been through our own private hell. None of us was up to talking much.

The snow was swirling, and I realized that this would be my world from now on. Snow and ice, the unending winter. When spring came to New Forest, I would remain in my frozen realm, venturing out only here and there. I gazed up at the silvery sky, letting the steady fall of flakes mesmerize me.

By the time we reached the Veil House, it was nearing lunchtime. We silently slipped out of the limo and I waved to the driver, who nodded and pulled away. As we jogged up the steps, I stopped and held out my hand to gather a handful of flakes. They were beautiful, truly, lacework sculptures every one, and they were, in a sense, my children. I turned back to the house and followed Peyton and Rhia inside.

We gathered around the table, and I was surprised to see Kaylin there. He still looked rough, but he smiled at me, leaning back in his chair. I kissed him on the forehead as I passed.

"Good to see you, dude. How are you?"

"Not up to a fight, that's for sure, but I wanted to be here."

I nodded, looking around. Luna and Ysandra were there, looking grave. Check and his men were lining the walls. Grieve and Chatter took their places, as did Rhiannon, Peyton, and I. When we were all seated, Druise appeared from the kitchen. I was startled to see her, but she was carrying a plate of sandwiches and a bag of chips. She set them on the table, then curtseyed to me.

"Thank you, Druise." I paused, sensing her worry. "I'm all right. I was injured . . . but I'm healing." To prove the point, I stood up and backed away from the table, lifting my skirt just enough to show everyone the long gashes on my shin and calf. A collective gasp told me that I hadn't been imagining how bad they'd been.

"Now that we have that over . . . what about Crawl? What do we know about Geoffrey and Leo? Obviously, I was out of it after Crawl got hold of me." I left that thought hanging, not wanting to go any further with it.

Luna and Ysandra looked at each other, and then Ysandra spoke. "Last night, after Lannan took you away, we noticed that Geoffrey and Leo had disappeared. Regina sent her men to track them. Chatter sent a couple of the guards who have excellent tracking skills, as well. Grieve and Rhiannon took off for the mansion, to make sure you were going to live, while the rest of us stayed to help the vamps clear out the complex."

I hadn't realized that. I chanced a sideways look at Grieve. He'd been there, all night, while Lannan and I . . . He caught my gaze and smiled, slowly. The feral side of him looked hungry, but whatever his feelings, he kept them to himself. Oh yes, we'd be talking later. But for now, things were at rest.

"Were they able to track them?"

"To a point. They tracked them into the town but lost them. However, earlier this morning Luna did a location spell—she called on the spirits, and we think we have the answer." She pushed a pad of paper over to me, and I looked at the tidy and precise writing. Even in a crisis, Ysandra was composed.

I picked it up and read aloud.

> Look to the east, in the gloom and the shade.
> Deep in the cavern where water runs through.
> Near the sweet station, in honeyed glade.
> Where your quarry sleeps, waiting for you.

"I am pretty sure I know where it is," Luna said. She looked tired but focused. "I used to go out there with my folks because they put in time volunteering at the community gardens next to Sugarbee's Honey. The company owns over a thousand acres on which they grow wildflowers, for their honey. Obviously, they keep bees."

I stared at her. "Do you know of a cave near there?"

"There were several. I used to play around them, but I never went in. My mother would have trashed me if I had.

Zoey did, though. She was always getting in trouble." She shrugged. "But there is a creek out there, and I think it runs through at least one of the caves."

"Then we head out. Not going to be so easy since it's winter. We have a little over four hours till sunset. How long will it take to get there?" I stood up. "We don't want them to have any advantage that we can spare."

Kaylin struggled to lean forward. "I can't go, but I will tell you this. Remember: They're cornered. They're desperate. They won't hesitate to destroy anybody who gets in their way now. The game is over and they know it. They have nothing to lose."

And on those solemn words, we armed up. Two of the guards took Kaylin home while we checked our weapons and made sure we had everything. Check brought reinforcements from the Barrows. We were going in thirty guards strong. I put in a call to Regina's secretary and gave her the information of where we were headed. If we didn't find them by dark, it would be nice to know the cavalry was on the way.

We headed out. The guards followed Grieve and Chatter, on foot at their top speed. Peyton, Luna, Rhiannon, Ysandra, and I took Ysandra's car. I wondered how long we could go on like this. It had to end soon. There was no more wiggle room.

The afternoon was dark, and so we drove with our lights on, just to be cautious. The road to Sugarbee's led east, into the Cascade foothills. During summer, it was a beautiful drive, but now, with Myst's unending winter still claiming a full grip on the land, it was treacherous. We wound through the narrow two-lane highway, through snow-covered fields interspersed with ravines tangled thick with bramble and briar. The trees, tall firs and spruce, were blanketed with a heavy layer of snow, weighing down their limbs till they were touching the ground. And every sweep of the headlights caught the swirl of fresh flakes, muffling the road with an icy silence.

Grieve and the rest would meet us at Sugarbee's. They could move so fast that—given the traffic and roundabout way—it wouldn't take them much longer than our car.

Ysandra was driving, and a moody silence filled the car. The miles passed by until, twenty-five minutes later, we pulled off onto a side road. This would take us out toward the Snoqualmie National Forest. The snow was deeper here and coming down faster.

"You have snow tires on this thing, don't you?" I glanced uneasily out the window. The SUV was small—a CRV. We were making decent headway, given the afternoon traffic and how icy the road was. But SUVs tipped at the most inopportune times, and I was nervous as we went by some of the ravines. Tumbling down one did not appeal to me.

She gave me a humorless snort. "Yes, I do. Trust me, I don't want to go skidding off the road any more than you do." With a glance at her GPS, she pressed a button and the device started, giving her step-by-step instructions to reach Sugarbee's. The going was slower than normal, and traffic was starting to build. A number of techies lived out in the rural areas and commuted into the Bellevue-Redmond area for work.

Another thirty minutes and we reached the turnoff for the honey company. It was closed for the year, although a small store was open, selling holiday gifts. Ysandra pulled into the parking lot and turned to Luna, who was sitting in the backseat.

"Change places with Cicely. I'll need your guidance from here on out. GPS can't give us those cave locations."

Luna shivered in the icy air, but I barely noticed it. Being the Queen of Snow and Ice had its perks. I hurried into the back as soon as she scrambled into the front, and I saw that she'd locked the door. We waited there for another fifteen minutes until Grieve popped out from behind a tree and waved at us.

We gave him a thumbs-up and headed out, this time at a slower pace with Luna directing. Easing out of the parking lot, we followed the road for another half mile, then turned to the left, which led into a park opposite the wildflower fields belonging to Sugarbee's. The gates were still open; it wasn't dusk yet, so we eased in and Ysandra managed to find a parking space where she could plow through the snow. It was obvious that no other vehicles had come through here recently.

When she shut off the motor, Luna said, "Along that trail there, then through the woods a little, and the caverns aren't far off. If Geoffrey and Leo are in there, however, we'll play havoc finding them. The cave system is like a maze and, at least when I was a kid, they had warning signs up all over the front. They were afraid that somebody would go exploring and get lost. The entrance isn't on one of the main trails, but it was near a big sign that gave information on the area and the wildlife around here. I hope it's still up, though I'm pretty sure I remember the way."

"Well, there's Grieve and the others," I said, pointing to the trailhead. "Let's get this show on the road. It's already two ten. That gives us a little over two hours to find them and stake them. And as we saw yesterday, that isn't always enough time."

We hopped out of the car and met up with Grieve and the guards. Silent, we followed Luna as she took the lead between two of the burliest men. She needed to be up front, but we wanted her to be protected at all costs.

Luna, Peyton, and Ysandra couldn't walk atop the snow like the rest of us, so we had to go at their pace. One of the guards walked in front of Luna, breaking the trail for her, which did help speed us up a little, but it was still slow going, and I knew the three women and Rhiannon had to be cold.

The snow was coming down in thick flakes, sticking to our lashes, dusting our hair and clothes, but we moved through it unspeaking. While Geoffrey and Leo would still be asleep, they might have brought day-runners with them. Even though we hadn't seen any other vehicles out there, we didn't dare take a chance on alerting anybody. So we went on silently.

Finally, Luna stopped, looking frustrated. "I know it was off this trail somewhere, but I don't see that sign. Everything looks different in the winter."

I moved up beside her. "I have an idea. Everyone, wait here." And then, stepping back, I began to transform into my owl self. Thank heavens I didn't have to strip anymore. As my body began to shift, a freedom raced through me, although the gashes on my legs seemed to hurt worse during the transformation, and I wasn't sure why.

Arms became wings, fingers became feathers, and as I took flight, soaring over the others, I breathed easy for the first time in a while. But the freedom turned to high alert as I swooped, dipping a wing, and then headed off, following the trail, scanning the ground from above. I needed to find the sign Luna had been talking about.

The snow was trickier in owl form, and I picked up the pace, slowly beating my wings as I did my best to keep a straight path through the storm. From above, the world was a frozen wonderland, brilliant and white and covered in chill mist that swirled up from the falling snow.

I began to make sweeps, to the right, then the left, and then—I saw what looked to be a pile of wood under a mound of white. I slowly circled in, trying to discern what it was. As I approached closer, I saw that it was a sign, broken and falling apart. I remembered what Luna had said and flew off the main path, searching among the trees until I came to a clearing near the frozen stream. And there, beyond the stream, against the rock face of the fern and moss covered cliff, was the cave opening.

Bingo. Found it. Now to bring the others.

I will get them. I can speak to Grieve. Ulean took me by surprise, but in a good way.

Ulean! I didn't know you were here.

You truly thought I'd let you go off on your own without watching over you? I am bound to you, Cicely. And then she was gone and I settled in a tree near the cave.

While I was waiting for them, I glanced around, looking for any sign of day-runners, but there were no footprints in the snow, no sign that any mortal had walked these woods for as long as it had taken the snow to pile up. I did, however, see a deer meander by, stopping to eat a few leaves off one of the fern fronds peeking out from the white that blanketed the area. And a fox raced past, chasing a mouse. My instinct to hunt stirred in my belly—the mouse looked like good pickings, but I repressed the urge, letting the fox have his dinner.

Finally, after I was certain there were no dangers that I could sense, I flew to the ground and returned to my normal state. As I stood, shaking my hair back, a noise made me whirl. How the hell had anybody managed to sneak up on me? I had been keeping a close watch.

No person stood there, but an Ice Elemental. It bowed to me, stiffly, and tilted its head, as if it were waiting. And then I saw yet another join it, and I realized they were drawn to me because I was their Queen. I ruled their world. Wiping my eyes, I wondered how I might communicate with them. How could I talk to them? And could they help us?

As I was hesitating, unsure what to say, a rush of wind encircled me. Ulean had returned.

The others are on the way. What have we here?

How can I speak to them? Do they know I'm their Queen?

Yes, they do. I suggest you speak into the slipstream. Focus on the meaning, not the actual words. They may be able to understand you, because it is your nature to communicate with them. Ask them to guard the area against the Shadow Hunters—Myst is surely not that far away.

With that thought, I hesitated no longer. As I spoke into the slipstream, I tried to focus on the meaning behind what I was saying.

My friends . . . I would have you guard this wood. I would have you keep the Shadow Hunters at bay. Here I visualized Myst and tried to force the essence of her cruelty and the vicious nature of the Shadow Hunters into my thoughts. *Do not let them enter these woods. Destroy them if you see them. They bring death to our people.*

Stopping, I waited to see if they'd react. And react they

did. They gave me another short bow and turned, gliding off into the woods again, seeking, hunting the Hunters.

Will they tell the others of their kind?

Yes, I believe they will. But Strict can instruct you better in their ways than I can. You have much to learn, Cicely, but a lifetime in which to learn it.

At that moment, the others burst into the clearing. I pulled out my phone and glanced at the time. 3:05. "We have a little over an hour left. There are the caves; let's get a move on."

Ulean, can you go inside, see if you can find Geoffrey and Lannan?

I'm on my way.

I told the others what she was doing, and we cautiously navigated along the stream bed. The creek wasn't terribly deep, but it ran along as far as we could see, with boulders peeking out of the frozen water that covered its surface, curving and bending to fit the topography of the forest.

The last thing we needed was for someone to crash through the ice. Finally, finding no way over without crossing the surface, I instructed Check and his men to carry the other women across. Rhiannon and I could walk atop the ice, along with the rest of the Cambyra Fae.

Once over the ice, we hurried to the entrance of the cave. Ulean was waiting for me. Agitated, she blew this way and that, which told me there was trouble.

What's going on?

I found the way to their chamber, where they sleep in their coffins. They've been here before, Cicely, that much is obvious. But there is a problem. The way is barred and you will have to fight through.

We have thirty guards with us, what could withstand our force? Surely the day-runners can't fight us off.

Not day-runners. If only it were so easy.

Then who is in there guarding them?

Ulean howled. *Shadow Hunters. They have over a dozen of Myst's people in there—although I cannot find the Mistress of Mayhem herself. But the Shadow Hunters look starved, and they are scuffling for blood. The blood-lust runs thick and harsh, and I can feel them aching for the kill.*

I stared at the cave. Shadow Hunters! Had Geoffrey made some sort of alliance with Myst after all? But no, they were at war.

How . . . what the hell do you think is going on, then?

They are chained, with plenty of give to the chain. I think he captured them and is holding them like a pack of wild guard dogs.

As I reluctantly turned to the others and told them what we were facing, my heart sank. Shadow Hunters . . . we had come through so much already in the past couple of days, and while I knew we would soon be facing Myst again, I'd hoped not to have her people along for the ride this time.

"Then the guard goes in first. Your Majesty, you and the Summer Queen must stay out here. We will fight this battle." Check was doing his best to sound firm, but I shook my head.

"I know that's probably smartest, but I cannot allow my men—and they are my men since I am the Queen—to go into battle against the Indigo Court without me there. It's unthinkable." I held up my hand. "No arguments. But know this: We take no quarter from them. Kill every Shadow Hunter in the place that you can lay hands on. And do it quick and clean. I don't care if they might know where we can find Myst. We don't have much time. We need to mop this up."

And so we marched in, twenty of the guards in front, ten behind us.

※

The cavern was fairly empty, like many of Washington's caverns, and while it had its own form of cave debris, it obviously wasn't an old mining tunnel, but instead naturally formed. The walls were damp; around this area moisture crept in everywhere. Moss and mildew clung to the rock, and the smell of mold filled my nostrils. The walls were slick, and I wondered if there were bats here—immediately thinking of Kaylin as the image sprung to mind. I didn't know if bats hibernated for the winter, or whether they were hiding in the recesses of caves like this one.

Chatter immediately created several glowing balls of the Faerie fire he could summon in order for us to see. Even though the light would give us away, we couldn't function without it. They bobbed along beside us as we headed deeper into the cave.

Pulling my thoughts together, I focused on the mission at hand. The guards ahead of us were silent, walking like they might be in a dream, alert, but not tense as we navigated the labyrinthine maze.

Ulean was whispering to Check, who seemed to be able to hear her, leading them toward the Vampiric Fae. And then we curved yet around another bend and found ourselves face to face with the Shadow Hunters.

※

Shadow Hunters. Among the most vicious creatures that ever lived. Myst's army of the damned. Vampiric Fae, and at one time, so many eons ago, I'd been one of them—Myst's daughter. The flashback I'd had when I'd been with Lannan haunted me. I was always aware that part of me, lurking far below the surface, still yielded to their siren song. There was a predator inside me, even though I'd never allow her to surface. That was what Geoffrey had wanted to do—turn me like he turned Myst, into a creature of the dark and endless night, not true vampire, but stronger than both Fae and vamp. And I'd rejected him.

Shaking my head to clear my thoughts, I jerked up as the guards swarmed in. The Shadow Hunters were on chains, and they lurched against their bondage. At least they wouldn't be free to do more damage than they could while chained. But I stopped mid thought as one in the front row growled low and harsh and broke off his collar, racing forward.

"Trap—it's a trap! The chains are false!" Check turned, pushing his way through his men, aiming directly for me, even as another guard swept up Rhiannon in his arms. Check grabbed me and we were on the move, away from the sudden fray. But I forced him to set me down—gave him a direct order.

"Your Majesty—it's a trap. They're off their tethers— Geoffrey knew we would find him and he set this up." Check kept glancing over his shoulder as the sounds of battle grew loud, including the screams of some of my men.

"I don't care. You get your ass back there and help. I won't get in the front lines, I promise. Just go. The men need you. Luna, Peyton, and Ysandra need your protection more than I do. I'm giving you a direct order, mister!" I shoved him back toward the fight.

Reluctantly, he turned and obeyed. I watched him go, then stepped back.

Ulean, I must raise a storm so terrible and swift that it will kill these Shadow Hunters in their tracks. Can I do it and still retain control over the wind?

That is problematic. To fight this many, you will have to use close to the full measure of your connection to the winds. It will be touch and go, because you need to raise a twister, and the energy of the vortex—it takes on a life of its own.

I'd done so before, but not as large, and for this, I needed fast and furious and deadly. A scream echoed from in front of us, and I could hear my men as the Shadow Hunters broke into the front lines, ripping and shredding flesh and bone.

I have no choice. Guide me, Ulean, if you can. Help me stay steady.

I have your back, Cicely. I am here.

And so I screamed out, "Clear a path. Now!"

As they gave way, I summoned up the winds, drawing them into myself, at first coasting on their power, but then embracing them, feeling them begin to flow through my

veins like blood pulsing thick. They buoyed me up, raising
me high into the cavern, as I rose up against our enemies. I
gathered the churning winds, twisting them into a swirling
mass, spinning them round and about. And then, I whispered, "Twister," and the world went crazy.

❧

The tornado sprang out of my hands, the swirling winds
rising quick and swift, forcing their way out from me. The
vortex roared, howling as it lurched forward, picking up
speed. In the enclosed chamber, it became a vehicle of
death, picking up anything that wasn't fastened to the walls
or floor and using them like arrows, shooting them from
out of the vortex to impale the rock walls.

My people scurried away, crouching, trying to avoid the
rising winds that threatened to pull them in. I worried, trying to control the storm's path, but it was like trying to herd
a bunch of cats. Only this was one cat, very big, and as the
energy grew and took on a deep, rumbling laughter in my
mind, I realized it was not at all interested in being controlled. It began pulling on me, and I slipped into the maelstrom, feeling the joy of destruction rise within me.

The power to destroy, to tear foundations from moor-
ings, to rip and shred and bring the winds to conquer all
who stood in their path . . . I leaned my head back, relish-
ing the destruction as I brought the twister down on the
Shadow Hunters, who were scrambling to get away. They
would not escape me, would not be able to run far and long
enough away from my reach.

I sent the winds reaching out to embrace the Vampiric
Fae, catching them up with the storm, tossing them about
like a flurry of autumn leaves. They tried to hide, tried to
bury themselves behind rock and stone, but in my fury, I
sought them out, sucked them from their hiding places as
their voices blended with the keening of the winds.

I rocked them in the twister, slamming them against
rock walls and ceiling, enjoying the hunt. And then, when

I was growing bored, wondering where there might be other quarry, Ulean reached in, dancing with me in the cacophony of my storm.

Cicely, bring it back. Or let it go. But it's time to disengage yourself from the vortex, let go of the storm now. Let it be.

At first I resisted, but then a little voice of reason—that sounded suspiciously like Lainule's voice—echoed in my head, warning me to bring the storm home, to put it to rest. I pushed aside the passion of the storm and found my core and center. And there, I was able to take control once again and slowly reel in the power, pulling it back to myself. A moment later, the winds abruptly died, and I was back to myself, standing in the aftermath.

I turned, almost afraid to see what I'd done. Mostly, I feared that any of my men might have been caught up in the mayhem . . . or worse, killed. But they were there, scattered behind stalagmites and in rock crevices, and they slowly emerged. Ysandra was staring at me, her eyes wide. Luna and Peyton gave me brief smiles, but they, too, looked worried. Grieve slowly walked over to me.

"Are you all right?" He took me in his arms, examining my face like he might be searching to see if it was truly me.

I nodded, breathing deeply. "No one was hurt, except the Shadow Hunters?"

"Yes, love. Everyone came through. Well, we lost three of our men before you raised the storm. They were dead the minute the Vampiric Fae broke ranks."

"Was Check . . . ?" A sudden fear that my favorite guard might have been caught in the slaughter raced through me, but Grieve calmed my fears.

"No, no . . . Check is all right."

"I'm here, Your Majesty." Check stepped forward, looking bruised and battered, but still very much alive. "The Shadow Hunters are all dead." He sounded worried, and I wondered why everybody was so concerned. I'd been able to control the storm.

This time, Cicely . . . but there may come a day when

*you won't be able to control the winds. And that day would
be tragic for so many reasons.*

*Lainule managed to control them. I have to learn how,
too.* I sighed. "Well, then. Let's get in there and find Leo
and Geoffrey before they wake."

"A little late for that, lovely." The voice to my left chilled
me to the bone.

There, within arm's reach of me, stood Geoffrey, and
beside him, Leo. And behind them, what looked to be a
good dozen other vampires, all looking ready to rumble.
Geoffrey was holding one of my guards, who was slumped
forward, and it was obvious he was dead.

As I stared at Geoffrey, Peyton let out a scream and
rushed toward him. Although Check caught her before she
was in reach of the vampire, that did it. The rumble was on,
and we were all in the fray.

Chapter 20

Ignoring Peyton's rush, Geoffrey tossed the guard aside and turned to me with a wicked grin on his face. He was too close. As I stumbled, I felt—rather than heard—Check deposit Peyton behind him, then race back toward me, with Grieve strong on his heels. But the vampire was too close, and I was still drained from raising the storm. Geoffrey grabbed me by the wrist, dragging me toward him, his fangs flashing in the light of the Faerie fire.

His long dark hair pulled back in a ponytail, he was handsome and mesmerizing and I couldn't pull my gaze away from him. He was bringing all his charm to bear and, as hard as Lannan was to resist when he pulled out all the stops, Geoffrey was even harder. He was more disciplined than Lannan, and there'd been a good reason that he'd been chosen as Regent.

I wanted to run, but couldn't, wanted to fight, but my will slipped away. I leaned into him, smelling the dust and the age and the power that emanated off his clothes, his body, his very aura. At that moment, I saw what Myst had seen—brilliance and ruthless ambition, and a charisma hard to ignore.

As he pulled me back, holding me in front of him with his teeth poised above my neck, the other vamps moved forward, with Leo in the lead. Rhiannon let out a low growl as he laughingly turned to her.

"Well, I see your lover welcomed you back. Used goods, Chatter. I hope you remember that every time you fuck her. But *wait*—there won't *be* another time. This time, I'll kill you and turn her and we'll *all* be good."

And with that, he lunged, lashing out at Rhia. She jumped back, and her eyes began to glow. I couldn't move, and I couldn't look away, so tight within Geoffrey's embrace.

"You signed your final death warrant when you fucked with me, lover boy." A glow began to surround her and she raised her hands, the flicker of flame springing to life.

The vampires, including Leo, stopped in their tracks. Geoffrey shifted, pulling me back away from the group. And then Leo jumped toward her, meeting her outstretched hand. The flicker of flame became a blazing jet, and the fire struck Leo straight in the face. As the other vamps swarmed around him, taking on the guards, Leo began to burn, bright and hot, and his screams filled the cavern. Rhia had gotten to him before Chatter or I could.

Geoffrey took that moment to drag me away, all the while whispering, "Since I have you, I might as well use you."

I knew what he meant. I knew what he wanted, and I wasn't about to allow it. He couldn't keep his fangs poised on me now that we were in motion, and I took advantage to struggle against his hold. And then an idea hit me. He wouldn't be expecting it at all. I began to shift.

The transformation was uneven, but I had been right. Startled, Geoffrey let go of me in order to get a better grasp, still not comprehending what was going on. At that moment, I pushed the transformation, hurrying it as fast as I could, and the next second, swooped up toward the high ceiling of the chamber, out of his reach. He thundered, and the next thing I knew, he had changed into a bat and was headed my way.

I swept toward him. In bat form, I had no clue if he was

as impervious to damage as he was when he was a vampire, but we were going to find out. As I barreled toward him, talons first as if I were picking a rat off the snow, Geoffrey veered, circling out of the way. But he must have been off his game, because I turned on the wing, a sharp turn, and cut him off. I clipped him a hard one, talons nicking his wing, and—disrupted—he plummeted to the ground, shifting as he fell. I knew I couldn't damage him while I was still in owl form, so I retreated to a safe distance to transform back into myself.

As I landed, shifting, everything seemed like it was on fast-forward. The vampires and Fae were fighting so quickly, moving so fast, it was a blur of motion, and there was nothing I could do. I couldn't even tell who was winning.

Leo was burning as Rhiannon pelted him with yet more fire. She seemed to source it out of an endless well of anger and fury. He crisped as ashes flaked off him. And yet she went on, a flamethrower on legs. A moment later, with a last shriek, he turned to dust, and the flames fell silent.

Meanwhile, Geoffrey tangled with Grieve. They were rolling on the floor, and Grieve had a huge wooden stake in his hand. Geoffrey slashed at Grieve and the stake went flying. My love was pouring blood from where the vampire had raked him.

Before I could move, Peyton dove into the fray, somersaulting over the both of them to roll and come up with the stake in hand. Grieve pulled back, and she landed, hard, on Geoffrey, impaling him through the heart. A hushed pause in the cacophony and Geoffrey turned to dust, scattering to the floor.

A few moments later and all the vampires were dead, along with ten of our guards. I pressed my lips together. It was over. We had won, at a cost. Wearily, we all slumped on the floor, staring at one another. Another moment saw Lannan and his men enter the cavern. As I looked at him, I realized there was no turning back. Life would never be the same.

It was time to go home to my icy realm.

Chapter 21

The aftermath of battle is never easy. I could talk about how we made our way back to the Barrows . . . how we burned our dead on the sacred pyres. . . how, shell-shocked and tired, we were too weary to even speak. But I won't. It's impossibly dreary, and sad, and the cleanup after war isn't much fun to reminisce over. Lannan and I said very little to each other, and Grieve avoided him, too.

But two days later, sitting in my chamber in the Eldburry Barrow, I began to feel halfway normal again. My leg was healing up—the scabs were starting to flake already, a by-product of drinking vampire blood and being the Winter Queen—and I had slept for hours upon hours.

Now, with the immediate crisis over, and Myst still in hiding, my new life was staring me in the face. I imagined Rhiannon was feeling the same way. I missed her being near. Missed Peyton and Luna, who were staying at the Veil House, with plenty of guards patrolling the borders.

Grieve entered the room as I slid from beneath the covers, yawning and stretching. He glanced at my legs, then at my thighs where the bruises were fading. After a moment, he motioned for Druise to leave the room and crossed over to sit next to me.

Silent, I brought my knees up, wrapping my arms around them, careful not to jar the flaking skin on my shins. I waited.

"I told you, not long ago, that I realized that someday you might end up bedding the vampire, and that I would accept it if necessary. When I saw you bleeding . . . the blood—there was so much blood coming so fast that I knew the only way to save you was to let you go into his arms."

I pressed my lips together, nodding.

"And once you drank his blood, I knew the Blood Fever would catch you up." He paused. "I don't care what happened between you. I see the bruises on your thighs, but I hear a new respect in your voice for Altos, so I can only pray that he didn't put you through hell."

I stared at my feet. Lannan had been rough, but I had needed it rough—hard and wild and feral and without any prettiness attached to it. That was who Lannan was, and that was the part of me who used to be Cherish coming through.

"He gave me what only he could give that night. What I would never want from you, because it's *not who you are*. What he gave me wasn't love, Grieve. It was raw release. It was . . . freedom. But the trouble with freedom? There isn't much to lose if you don't have anything—or anyone—to protect." I glanced at him then, and he opened his arms and I slid into them.

His lips sought mine, and then we were on the bed, and he was running his hands over my body, kissing me deep. The passion between us flared, not sweet, not romantic, but sensuous and dark and deeper than any connection I had ever known. Grieve was my heart-mate; Grieve was my prince. Flawed, the Wounded King, and yet he was my everything.

I pulled him to me, opened my legs, invited him into the depths of my body, and we moved in unison, with him riding me hard, insistent. He reclaimed me, laid his mark on me, and in turn I covered his face with kisses, drank deep from his well, reveled in his cock that drove ever deeper into my cunt. We were a fit, we were, and our bodies knew it as well as our souls.

As we renewed our bond, my thoughts quieted themselves, and for the first time in days, I felt at home.

The court was gorgeous, lit with the Ice Elemental lanterns, a swath of indigo and silver curtains and drapes lining the wall. And, to honor Rhiannon and Chatter—panels of green and gold. The entire court of the Marburry Barrow had crowded in to join us in celebrating our double wedding, since the Court of Snow and Ice had a much bigger throne room. The Wilding Fae were also here, and everyone was decked out in colorful costumes that marked their connection to the realms of Summer and Winter.

I stood in my chamber, along with Rhiannon, as our lady's maids dressed us. Our wedding gowns had come in on time and fit perfectly.

As Druise slid the sheath over my head, the wash of pale gray chiffon and lace floated down to my ankles. I was wearing a silver corset beneath it, form-fitting and snug. The brilliant splash of the royal blue straps set off the gown perfectly, and the matching sash fit snugly around my waist. As Druise fastened the train to my dress, then helped ease my circlet with the veil attached onto my head, the change in my eye color still struck me. I no longer just lived in the frost-ridden land, I was part of it.

I turned to Rhiannon, a vision in gold and green, and held out my hands. "Amber and jet."

"Fire and ice." We stood for a moment, no more words necessary. We had come through hell for this moment, and now we were here. Somehow, this seemed to cement matters more than even our initiations.

"I just wish Lainule could be here." I stared around the

room. This was my home. This was my life from now on. What a long and twisted route it had been since my mother first swept me away from the Veil House.

"I wish my mother could be here," Rhia said softly. "I suppose this means . . . we've grown up. We're on our own now."

There was no more to say, which was probably good, because at that moment, Peyton and Luna entered the room. Peyton was dressed in royal blue, Luna in rich summer green. They looked at us, both smiling for a change, though the past weeks had worn thin on all of us.

Check and several of the guards were outside the door to escort us down in their dress uniforms. We moved silently, solemnly, through the crowded halls of revelers who could not fit in the throne room but wanted a vision of the Queens of Winter and Summer as we passed by.

The crowd was held back by guards, and as we glided through the halls, they moved in a collective bow-and-curtsey. As we waved to them, I felt odd, not at all excited like I imagined I would if I ever got married. I'd always pictured a small wedding, maybe by a brook, or the side of the ocean . . . not all this pageantry and pomp. But it was what it was, and I was marrying Grieve, and Rhia would marry Chatter, and we would serve our people as best as we could.

We entered the throne room, and near my throne, the Elder Shamans from both of our realms waited, side by side. Grieve was to the left, Chatter to the right, and the looks on their faces washed away the melancholy feel that had crept over me. They were there, waiting for us, ready to spend their lives with us.

Grieve, magnificent in his black tunic and pants, with a long silver cape flowing behind him and platinum hair that fell softly, loosely around his shoulders, kept his gaze on me as I processed down the aisle, the starry night of his eyes shining. And Chatter, in gold and brown, watched Rhia with the same devotion.

We approached the altar and the Shamans began the ceremony, which lasted late into the night, the exchanging of promises to guard and to love winding their way through the midnight hours. As befitting the Fae, there were no promises of sexual fidelity—but of heart-connection and honor and respect and duty.

In the crowd, Kaylin and Ysandra sat, watching, and Lannan and Regina were there, representing the Vampire Nation. The Consortium had not gotten back to us, yet, and I was ready to write them off if they weren't going to do any better than they had when we'd gone to them for help.

I made my vows—to honor, to love, to respect, to cherish—quietly, simply, and with all my heart. At one point, I glanced to the side. Lannan was staring at me, his face a blank mask, and I could not read what he was feeling, but it didn't matter. I turned back to my future as Grieve took his place as my husband. After the vows were sealed, Grieve and Chatter were crowned as Kings of the Realms, and then it was done, and we were married, and the party began.

⚹

Late, late into the night, I slipped from the revelries and wandered outside. The moon was high, it was clear and icy, and the snow-covered land sparkled with frost and brilliance. A cold fire spread through my heart. This . . . this was all mine to command, and yet I felt so insignificant.

Was I ready? Could I handle this?

Within the space of a month, I'd uprooted my transient lifestyle, staked my aunt as she begged for release, learned to murder and kill, found my father and lost him again, and now . . . now I was the Queen of Snow and Ice, married to my love who had been with me through lifetimes. The future stretched in front of me, unending and relentless, but I welcomed it—welcomed the challenge.

Ulean swept around me, gusting gently. *You are ready for this, Cicely. You are ready.*

Her simple encouragement cheered me to no end, and I gazed up at the stars. But then, as the clouds began to come in, I heard a distant laughter on the slipstream—Myst's voice.

You may be ready to lead your people, she whispered, *but are you ready to fight me? I am returning, and I will take you down and destroy you and everything you love. Fear me, for I am fear and cruelty incarnate, my turncoat daughter.*

I shuddered as the clouds blotted out the moon and the stars. The snow began again, furious, thick flakes. As I turned back to the Barrow, I knew the Queen of the Indigo Court was on her way. And this time, one of us had to die.

Character List

CICELY AND THE COURT OF SNOW AND ICE

Check: Cicely's personal guard.
Cicely Waters: A witch who can control the wind. One of the magic-born and half-Uwilahsidhe (the Owl people of the Cambyra Fae). Born on the Summer Solstice at midnight, a daughter of the Moon/Waning Year. The new Queen of Snow and Ice.
Druise: Cicely's lady's maid.
Fearless: Cicely's personal guard.
Grieve: (See also Indigo Court) Prince of the Court of Rivers and Rushes, one of the Cambyra Fae (shapeshifting Fae) now turned Vampiric Fae. Cicely's fiancé and the King-Elect of the Court of Snow and Ice.
Silverweb: The Treasurer of the Court of Snow and Ice.
Strict: Cicely's Chief Advisor.
Tabera: The late Queen of Snow and Ice.

RHIANNON AND THE COURT OF RIVERS AND RUSHES

Chatter: One of the Summer Court. Grieve's best friend and Rhiannon's fiancé. King-Elect of the Court of Rivers and Rushes.

Edge: Rhiannon's Court Advisor.

Lainule: The former Fae Queen of Rivers and Rushes, Grieve's aunt and Rhiannon's aunt. The former Queen of Summer. Destined to fade back to the Golden Isle.

Rhiannon Roland: Cicely's cousin, born on the same day as Cicely, only at daybreak, a daughter of the Sun/Waxing Year. Rhiannon is also half Cambyra Fae and half magic-born, and she controls the power of fire. The new Queen of Rivers and Rushes.

Wrath: Cicely's father—one of the Uwilahsidhe (the Owl people of the Cambyra Fae). Lainule's Consort.

PEYTON AND THE COURT OF THE MAGIC-BORN

Anadey: Traitor; was a friend of Heather's and mentor to Rhiannon. One of the magic-born, Anadey can work with all elements. She owns Anadey's Diner and is Peyton's mother.

Kaylin Chen: Martial arts sensei, a dreamwalker, has a Night Veil demon merged into his soul.

Luna Saunders: Yummanii bard.

Peyton Moon Runner: Half werepuma, half magic-born, she's Rex and Anadey's daughter.

Rex Moon Runner: Werepuma. Peyton's father.

Ysandra Petros: Member of the Consortium. Yummanii and powerful witch who can control sound, energy, and force.

THE INDIGO COURT

Myst: Queen of the Indigo Court, mother of the Vampiric Fae, the Mistress of Mayhem. Queen of Winter.

Heather Roland: Rhiannon's mother and Cicely's aunt. One of the magic-born, an herbalist, first turned into a vampire by the Indigo Court, now truly dead.

THE VEIN LORDS/TRUE VAMPIRES

Crawl: The Blood Oracle; one of the oldest Vein Lords, made by the Crimson Queen herself. Sire to Regina and Lannan.

Geoffrey: Former Northwest Regent of the Vampire Nation and one of the Elder Vein Lords. Two thousand years old; from Xiongnu.

Lannan Altos: Professor at the New Forest Conservatory, Elder vampire, brother and lover to Regina Altos, hedonistic Golden Boy. New Northwest Regent of the Vampire Nation.

Leo Bryne: Was Rhiannon's fiancé; a healer and one of the magic-born. Leo was a day-runner for Geoffrey and now is a vampire.

Regina Altos: Emissary for the Crimson Court/Queen. Originally from Sumer with her brother and lover, Lannan. Was a priestess of Inanna. Turned by Crawl.

Playlist for *Night Vision*

I write to music a good portion of the time and have been sharing my playlists on my website. I finally decided to add them to the backs of the books for my readers who aren't online.

—Yasmine Galenorn

The 69 Eyes:
  "August Moon"
  "Some Kind of Magick"
  "Angels"
A. J. Roach:
  "Devil May Dance"
Aerosmith:
  "Walk This Way"
Air:
  "Astronomic Club"
  "Seven Stars"
  "Moon Fever"

"Napalm Love"
"Playground Love"
The Alan Parsons Project:
"You Lie Down with Dogs"
"Children of the Moon"
"Breakdown"
Android Lust:
"Dragonfly"
"Stained"
"Saint Over"
"A New Heaven"
The Asteroids Galaxy Tour:
"Lady Jesus"
Black Mountain:
"Wucan"
"Queens Will Play"
"The Hair Song"
"Druganaut"
"Wild Wind"
Bon Jovi:
"Wanted Dead or Alive"
Brent Lewis:
"Beyond Midnight"
"Wild Wood"
Buffalo Springfield:
"For What It's Worth"
Cobra Verde:
"Play with Fire"
Dave & Steve Gordon:
"Shaman's Drum Dance"
"Four Direction Ritual"
"Empowered Fire Groove"
David Draiman:
"Forsaken"
Eels:
"Souljacker Part I"
Faun:
"Sieben"

"Deva"
"Punagra"
Foster the People:
    "Pumped Up Kicks"
Gabrielle Roth and The Mirrors:
    "The Calling"
    "Raven"
    "Mother Night"
    "Rest Your Tears Here"
Gary Numan:
    "When the Sky Bleeds He Will Come"
    "The Fall"
    "Hybrid"
    "Dominion Day"
Godhead:
    "Penetrate"
Gorillaz:
    "Stylo"
Gotye:
    "Hearts a Mess"
    "Somebody That I Used to Know"
In Strict Confidence:
    "Silver Bullets"
    "Something to Remember"
    "Snow White"
Julian Cope:
    "Charlotte Anne"
King Black Acid:
    "Rolling Under"
    "Haunted"
Lady Gaga:
    "Teeth"
    "I Like It Rough"
    "Paparazzi"
    "Paper Gangsta"
    "The Fame"
Ladytron:
    "I'm Not Scared"

"Ghosts"
"White Elephant"
"Ritual"
Lindstrøm & Christabelle:
   "Lovesick"
Lord of the Lost:
   "Sex on Legs"
Low with Tom and Andy:
   "Half Light"
Madonna:
   "4 Minutes"
Marilyn Manson:
   "Godeatgod"
   "Tainted Love"
   "Personal Jesus"
   "Sweet Dreams (Are Made of These)"
   "Redeemer"
Mark Lanegan:
   "The Gravedigger's Song"
   "Phantasmagoria Blues"
   "Riot in My House"
   "Wedding Dress"
   "Methamphetamine Blues"
   "Riding the Nightingale"
   "Judas Touch"
Nine Inch Nails:
   "Closer"
   "Down in It"
   "Sin"
   "Deep"
Nirvana:
   "Heart-Shaped Box"
   "You Know You're Right"
Notwist:
   "Hands on Us"
Orgy:
   "Social Enemies"
   "Blue Monday"

"Fiend"
"Dizzy"
"Pantomime"
A Pale Horse Named Death:
   "Pill Head"
   "Meet the Wolf"
   "Heroin Train"
People in Planes:
   "Vampire"
Puddle of Mudd:
   "Famous"
Red Hot Chili Peppers:
   "Blood Sugar Sex Magik"
   "Sir Psycho Sexy"
Saliva:
   "Ladies and Gentlemen"
Sarah McLachlan:
   "Possession"
Screaming Trees:
   "All I Know"
   "Look at You"
   "Dying Days"
   "Witness"
   "Dime Western"
   "Gospel Plow"
Seether:
   "Remedy"
Soundgarden:
   "Let Me Drown"
   "Black Hole Sun"
   "Fell on Black Days"
   "Fresh Tendrils"
Susan Enan:
   "Bring on the Wonder"
Verve:
   "Bitter Sweet Symphony"
Warchild:
   "Ash"

Woodland:
 "Will o' the Wisp"
 "Lady and the Unicorn"
 "First Melt"
 "Winds of Ostara"
 "I Remember"
 "Gates of Twilight"
Zero 7:
 "In the Waiting Line"

Dear Reader:

I hope you enjoyed *Night Vision*, the fourth book in the Indigo Court Series. I truly love losing myself in this mystical, icy world I've created, and the last book in this series will be *Night's End*—coming in July 2014.

But before then, we revisit Otherworld, with *Autumn Whispers*, book fourteen, coming in October 2013, and *Crimson Veil*, book fifteen, in early 2014, plus a few smaller projects along the way (see my website for further information).

I'm enclosing the first chapter of *Autumn Whispers* here, to give you a taste of what's coming up for Delilah and her sisters in Otherworld, as they take on increasing odds in the demonic war.

For those of you new to my books, I hope you've enjoyed your first foray into my worlds. For those of you who have followed me for a while, I want to thank you for once again revisiting the world of Cicely and the snowy world of New Forest, Washington.

Bright Blessings,
The Painted Panther
Yasmine Galenorn

Following is a special excerpt from

AUTUMN WHISPERS

the next book in the Otherworld series
by Yasmine Galenorn

Coming October 2013!

I stood at the top of the ravine overlooking the waterfront below. Nestled on the front of Lake Sammamish, my destination was—like many in the greater Seattle metropolitan area—a sprawling behemoth of a house jokingly referred to as a McMansion. Cookie-cutter design along with all its neighbors, the monster was a tribute to the high wages and high cost of living that came with this area.

Only tonight, all the money and success in the world wouldn't help the owner of the palatial estate. Tonight, the man who owned this house was going to die—and he was going to die the final death.

Behind me, in a sheer flowing robe that mirrored the twilight sky, stood Greta, my mentor, the leader of the Death Maidens. Petite, with hair the color of burnished copper, Greta and I bore the same tattoos, only hers were far older and more brilliant.

Emblazoned on our foreheads were onyx crescents, hers burning with a vivid flame. Mine sparkled a glistening black most of the time. An intricate lacework of black and orange leaves wound up our forearms. Hers were vivid.

Mine had started as a pale shadow but now were nearing a similar intensity.

Patiently standing a few steps behind me, Greta waited as I contemplated the house. I was dressed in a flowing robe similar to hers, though mine wasn't sheer, and now I absently toyed with the tasseled belt girding my waist as I gauged the timing. This would be my fifth kill in the past month—or *oblition*, as it was called in Haseofon—and this time, I was on my own. Greta was only supervising.

I'd been on a fast track the past eight weeks, spending a lot of time in Haseofon, the temple of the Death Maidens, learning to fight on the astral where we worked. And I'd been taking a high dose of the *panteris phir*, or Panther's Fang, to gain better control over my shifting into the black panther side of myself.

I was surprised the latter had been working so well, considering how little control I had over shifting into my Tabby self, but Greta had said that because Panther was a gift from the Autumn Lord, my half-human heritage wasn't a stumbling block to controlling the ability.

Now I closed my eyes, listening for that internal sensor that would tell me the exact moment in which to move in. A pause, as I lowered myself below my conscious thoughts, deep into my subconscious. And then I heard it.

Five . . . four . . . three . . . two . . . one . . . There, it was, echoing in the corner of my mind. The gentle chiming of a clock as it counted down the last moments of Gerald Hanson's life. The clock—or sensor—was my guide, urging me on, directing me when to move in and at what precise moment I was to grapple with Gerald's soul and send it spinning into oblivion.

The only thing I knew about Gerald at this moment was that he was a lawyer, and his life was forfeit to keep the balance. Grandmother Coyote had called in a favor from the Autumn Lord, and Hi'ran had specifically directed that I be the one to take care of this. For whatever reason, I was to be the Death Maiden who attended his death.

I glanced back at Greta. She remained impassive, waiting

for my move, so I set out for the ravine and she followed me. We raced through the etheric winds as if we were meteors, shooting through the sky. Movement on the astral was still confusing to me, although I'd been here a number of times, but I was slowly getting used to it. And here it was that the Death Maidens paid their victims their last visits—on a tiny sliver of the astral plane reserved for our work, and our work alone.

We were the last people our chosen victims would ever see, the last faces they would know. Some we escorted to glory and to great rewards for their courage and bravery. For others we were the harbingers of doom, the final hand of judgment who could not be denied. We sent them into the churning pool of primal force in which their soul-force was cleansed, purged, and reborn as pure energy ready for use.

Gerald Hanson was among the latter.

As the clock ticked down the last minutes of Gerald's life, I walked through the walls of his house, followed by Greta, and stood beside him. He would not see me until it was too late.

To the outer world, it would appear that Gerald Hanson had died of a sudden, massive stroke. In reality, the Hags of Fate would cut his cord of destiny, triggering that stroke. Whatever sins against the balance Gerald had committed, they were great enough to earn him a one-way ticket into oblivion. His soul was so tainted that it could not be allowed to continue on the eternal cycle.

I stood beside him, waiting. There was no one else in the house, except a little dog who was asleep on the sofa. The pup would be well cared for. I'd call Chase after I finished and was home, to make certain he knew the dog, because this case—along with whatever notifications were necessary—would fall under the jurisdiction of the FH-CSI. The Faerie-Human Crime Scene Investigation unit would be involved because Gerald Hanson wasn't human. He was a werewolf.

As the final seconds ticked down, I stepped forward, standing in front of him. A pause, then *three . . . two . . .*

one . . . and Gerald clutched his chest, looking confused. I waited until he spasmed again, then went limp. As his body slumped on the sofa, his spirit rose to stand in front of me. At first he looked confused, but then he saw me and jumped back.

"Where . . . who are you? What . . ." He glanced back at his body and a slow look of understanding crossed his face. As he turned back to me, I moved in.

I reached out and laid my hand on his arm, and we vanished into a place where there existed only the swirl of mist and fog, as a thin silver crescent hung high overhead against the backdrop of stars. There was nothing familiar here, at least not to Gerald. There was nothing to comfort, nor to soothe the fear or offer hope. Here, there was merely the stark whisper of vapor that flowed around us and the cold shimmer of the stars. We stood there, in spirit, between the worlds, and before he could speak I reached out and placed my hands on his shoulders, and his memories flowed into my own, and I saw through his eyes.

Flash . . . A long hall stretched out in front of Gerald; on either side stood rows of cells. Cages with iron bars. The hallway was dimly lit and smelled like urine and feces. The faint sound of whimpering echoed through the air, but the smile on Gerald's face belied the blackness in his heart. As he started down the passage, a lovely Fae woman knelt in the center of one of the cells, her hands pressed over her face. As she heard Gerald's footsteps, she looked up, a pleading look in her luminous eyes, but he snorted, and moved on. The woman would fetch a pretty penny, and there were plenty more like her out there. And plenty of men waiting to buy them . . .

Flash . . . Gerald sat behind a desk—a large oak affair that dripped with money and prestige. He was fiddling with a brief, but as he looked out the window, his cell phone rang. A man's voice on the other end of the line let out a rough laugh.

"Number sixty-five needs a replacement. He broke his toy, again, and is willing to pay an extra fifty grand to find one who can take the extra wear and tear. You have one week."

As Gerald pressed the End Call button, he stared out the window, a faint smile crossing his lips . . . he loved his work. He truly loved his work.

Flash . . . Two men climbed into the limo, taking the seat opposite Gerald. One of them looked sullen, the other afraid. Gerald rolled up the window behind him, separating them from the driver, then offered them a drink. As the men eagerly accepted the glasses and sipped, he leaned forward, waiting.

After a moment, he spoke, his voice steely. "I told you to handle the entire family. You didn't handle the entire family, and now you've compromised our work."

The taller of the pair shifted uncomfortably. "We don't do kids. I told you that in the beginning."

"And *I* told you what was at stake." As Gerald spoke, the smaller man began to shake and dropped his drink as he collapsed. The other man looked at Gerald frantically, but within seconds he followed suit.

The limo stopped, and Gerald opened the window again. "Take us to the Cove. We've got a delivery to make." And with that, he settled back, opened a new bottle of bourbon, and carefully poured himself a glass as the car silently glided through the night.

I pulled myself out of his mind. The images were confusing, but the feeling behind them was a darkness driven by avarice. The desire for money, the desire for power. And the willingness to do anything to get it. Repelled, I gazed into Gerald's eyes. He was scum, worse than scum, and while I wasn't sure of everything he had done to reap such a sentence, I'd seen enough to know he'd buy and sell people without a second thought.

Nervous, he looked over his shoulder. "Where am I?"

Ah . . . so he still didn't realize he was dead.

"On a one-way trip, Gerald. Consider me your angel of death." Before he could do more than whimper, I laid my hands on him—holding him so firmly that he couldn't get away.

He struggled, pleading, but his words fell useless. This

was my mission, and whatever mercy or empathy I had vanished as my training kicked in. His spirit was no match for my strength.

"Fires of the void, come forth to do my bidding. Cleanse this soul and pass it through your center." The rite was second nature now—the ritual ingrained in my being by this point. While Greta had taken me through the rites again and again, this time I was doing it on my own, without any help from her.

Gerald let out a sharp scream. "Please, don't—I don't understand."

"Gerald Hanson, you sealed your destiny by your actions. The Hags of Fate have made their decree. The Harvestmen have agreed. Prepare to face the darkness of the abyss."

I closed my eyes, summoning the karmic fire. A purple flame washed over us, raging through his soul, crackling through the mist and fog to electrify his energy. A wisp of ash flew up from his aura, and then another, and then—with a loud chatter of static—the karmic flames raced through his spirit, reducing it to harmless dust. Another moment, and Gerald Hanson ceased to exist, forever. His soul consigned to the final death, only a fine layer of ash remained poised for a second, and then it, too, blew away into the night.

I watched the etheric wind sweep away the remnants of everything Gerald had ever been, throughout all of his lives, all of his cycles. The only thing left was a harmless, benign energy. No trace remained of the person he'd been, no sign of the lives he'd lived. And then, with a final, silent *whoosh*, the lingering energy spiraled up and then returned to the central pool from which all things sprang.

As always, I felt oddly hollow, like a reed in the wind, bending but not breaking. Mournful, plaintive, but accepting of my place in this world.

I closed my eyes, willing Gerald's memories to fade, although I knew I wouldn't forget them. While they didn't make much sense to me now, there had to be a reason the Autumn Lord had commanded me to be Gerald's doom. I wasn't sure what it was yet, but I had the feeling I'd find out.

But for now, I was stick-a-fork-in-me done for the night. Turning my back on the ever-present mist and fog of this realm, I leaped back to the astral where Greta waited. I hoped to hell we were done for the night.

※

Greta slipped her arm through mine as we journeyed back to Haseofon, the abode of the Death Maidens. She was so much shorter than me that it gave us a Mutt-and-Jeff look, but there any resemblance ceased.

"You did very well. You've adapted quickly." She smiled up at me, and I felt a tinge of pride.

"I've tried." I pressed my lips together.

At first, the concept of being a Death Maiden had freaked me out, but over the past couple of years I'd wavered, feeling my naïveté slip away little by little. At first I'd clung to my eternal optimism, to the little girl/kitty cat who didn't want to grow up. But when Shade—my fiancé—had come into the picture, things began to shift. Half shadow dragon, half Stradolan—shadow walker—Shade existed in the realms of spirits and ghosts, and I'd grown used to the energy.

Over the past few months, I'd made the decision to embrace who I was becoming, rather than fear it.

Truth being: I was proud of being pledged to the Autumn Lord. I was his only living Death Maiden, and I'd never again be the Delilah who first came over from Otherworld. And that . . . that was okay. I realized that I didn't have to give up believing in people; I didn't have to give up simple joys and happiness. Instead, I found myself falling into a comfortable balance.

"Are we done for the night?" I glanced at the cityscape that unfolded in front of us. Though we were traveling on the astral, we were close to my own world, the streets of Seattle, and both realms were superimposed on one another. I'd gotten used to that, too.

Greta nodded. "Did you want to come back to Haseofon to say hello to Arial?"

I thought about it, but Camille and Menolly were waiting

for me to return, and the promise of a cup of hot milk and some cookies was enough to make my decision for me.

"Not tonight, but tell her I love her and I'll see her soon." I paused. "Greta, do you know why I had to be the one to annihilate Gerald?"

She shook her head. "That information was not given to me, but the Autumn Lord was insistent. It had to be you. Grandmother Coyote had specified so. And the Harvestmen, they bow to the whims of the Hags of Fate—as does every creature."

Pulling away, she reached up and stroked my face. "Your crescent—it burns with fire tonight. You made your first totally unassisted, assigned kill. And so your crescent has shifted and now the fire will forever burn brightly within it."

I reached up to finger the tattoo. I couldn't feel much change, but then again, I was used to wearing the Autumn Lord's sigil on my forehead by now. But an odd sense of pride swept through me and I nodded.

"Thank you, Greta. For your help and your friendship."

She laughed, sounding like a schoolgirl rather than the ancient and fearsome force that she was. And then, without another word, she vanished, and I willed myself home and opened my eyes to find myself curled in my cat bed.

❦

Blinking, I realized that I'd gone out of body while still in my Tabby form. I yawned, arching my back up into Halloween-cat pose. I was in my tiger-cat bed—it was striped like a tiger, with a tiger face and tail. Iris had bought it for me and I loved it.

From my vantage on the living room floor, I could see her sitting in the rocking chair, looking like an angry beached whale. Iris was more than two weeks overdue, pregnant with twins, and we were all tiptoeing around her. Roz was sitting next to her, trying to make her smile.

Camille was curled up on the sofa, next to Trillian, her alpha husband, and behind them, Smoky—yet another husband (out of three) leaned over their shoulders. They were poring over the pages of one of those huge coffee-table books, but in cat form, I couldn't read the title.

Vanzir was huddled over the controls to the Xbox, and other than that, the room was empty. Menolly was off at work, I knew that much, but I didn't have a clue as to where Morio, Hanna, Nerissa, and Bruce were.

I crept out of my bed, stretched again, and flipped my tail high into the air. I loved the luxuriousness of being *cat*. My fur was long and silky, golden with faint stripes running through it, and when I shifted form, my clothes transformed into the blue collar around my neck. Iris had hung a bell on it, which annoyed the hell out of me and put an end to my bird chasing. Well, bird *catching*. I still chased. I couldn't help it, it was my nature.

I stopped in front of the fire to lick one of my paws, then shook my head and stepped delicately away from the nearest chair, giving myself room to transform. As I shifted, paws lengthening into arms, back arching, shifting, changing, transforming back to my two-legged state, I became aware of a faint ache in my lower back where I'd been training hard during the week. And the bruises throbbed where I'd tripped over a log in the forest while out on a run with Shade.

As I took my natural form and slowly stood from the crouching position in which I'd been, Iris gave me a weary smile.

"Did you have a good nap, Kitten?" Camille asked, setting the book down. Now I could see that it was a book of photographs from Finland, one that Iris had received as a wedding present back in February.

I yawned, then sat on one of the ottomans, pulling my legs up to wrap my arms around my shins. Leaning my chin on my knees, I frowned. "I didn't exactly nap. Greta came for me."

Camille perked up. "She took you out again? That's five times in the past two weeks. Did you see Arial?"

I shook my head. "No, I decided to come back here instead. I was assigned a target tonight on my own. Greta stood back, and this time it was all up to me."

I glanced at her. If anybody understood, it would be

Camille. She'd been through hell over the past year, and she'd also been delving deeply into death magic with her other husband, Morio. She'd been playing in the dark a lot lately.

"On your *own*? How did it go?" Her violet eyes were flecked with silver and I realized they'd been that way a lot lately, the further she dipped into the magic and into her training as a Priestess of the Moon Mother.

"I did what I needed to. But there was something odd. I don't understand yet, but I think you guys should know." And so I told them how I'd been specifically assigned Gerald's kill and what I had seen when I looked into his mind.

"That's disturbing, but I don't see how it affects us, to be honest. We don't know where all of this happened, or who the woman was, or even what the hell was going on." She paused. "File it away for future reference. Meanwhile, I got a call through the Whispering Mirror from Father. We've been summoned back to Otherworld tomorrow night for a meeting about the war. We leave here as soon as Menolly wakes up. And we're to bring Chase along. And Sharah."

I frowned. "Why can't they just tell us through the Whispering Mirror?"

"Because something's up. I can tell. No, we have to go, and they want all five of us there. Smoky said he'd come, and Trillian. The others will stay here to guard the house." Camille frowned.

"We really have to do something about the security situation here." It had become problematic, especially as our enemies grew more powerful.

"I agree. It's fine to leave some of the guys at home, but we need to be able to head out in full force, especially now that Iris is about ready to pop." Even though Camille said it affectionately, Iris flashed her an irritated look.

"Girl, if I don't pop soon, I'll be ballistic enough to protect the entire city. I swear, these children are already plaguing me and they aren't even born yet." Iris rubbed her stomach, letting out an exasperated sigh. "I'm two weeks overdue and these young ones are kicking up a storm. If they don't birth themselves soon, I'm going to forcibly evict them."

I stifled a laugh. During Iris's pregnancy, she had become a volatile bundle of hormones. Everybody was crossing fingers it would be over and done with soon, but I suspected Bruce was the most anxious.

Their house was snug as a bug. The guys had put the finishing touches on during the late summer months, and it was a hop and a skip away from ours. Iris and Bruce were firmly ensconced within it, but several times a week, both of them—or sometimes just Iris when Bruce was preparing for a lecture the next day—would join us for the evening.

I kissed her on the forehead. "It won't be much longer."

"And what do you know about babies? How many have you had?"

Oh, she was grumpy, all right. I backtracked, fast. "You're right. I just hope for all our sakes that it happens soon."

That brought a smile to her lips, and she ducked her head.

"Bruce has taken to hiding in the study after dinner, so I know he's feeling it, too." She let out a long sigh. "It will be over soon. Then I'll just have two babies to raise and I'll get irate about other things." With a rueful smile, she leaned back in the rocker and closed her eyes.

I reached out and brushed the hair from her face. "Would you like me to brush your hair?" When I was in Tabby form, I loved having my fur brushed. It was relaxing and I had the feeling, with the amount of hair our sprite had, she might just like it, too.

Iris gave me a quizzical look, then nodded. "Thank you. I'd like that."

Camille fished through her purse and handed me a brush as I gently removed the numerous pins and clips holding Iris's ankle-length golden hair in the coils that wrapped around her head.

"Sit, little mama." I pointed to the ottoman. She settled herself, with a little help from Camille, and I sat in the chair behind her and softly began to brush the long strands. After a moment, Iris let out a long, slow breath and her shoulders slumped gratefully. I took my time, sleeking over the glimmering tresses that were soft as silk, thinking about my own hair. It had been long once, down to the middle of my back.

Should I grow it out again? But I'd changed so much, and my new style—short and spiky—fit the new me. No, there was no returning to the woman I had been. So long hair would be reserved for when I was in Tabby form and my tail plumed out in a delightful puff. Content, I returned my focus to Iris and gave her a little scalp and shoulder massage in addition to the brushing.

After about fifteen minutes, I gathered Iris's hair back in a ponytail, looping it up so that it wouldn't trip her when she walked. She sighed, leaning back with a grateful smile, and I hugged her.

"That felt marvelous. Thank you, Kitten. I really appreciate it." As she stood, ready to head back to her house, the doorbell rang.

Camille answered. When she returned, she had a strange look on her face. Behind her followed a cowled woman in a long gray cloak. My blood chilled. Grandmother Coyote, and she had come to *us*.

The Hags of Fate wove destiny, and they unraveled it. They measured out the cords, and they cut them. They balanced good with evil, evil with good, order with chaos, and chaos with order. And, along with the Elemental Lords and the Harvestmen, they were the only true Immortals. They had been here long before the world had begun, and they would be here long after it ended.

Iris paused, staring up at the elderly woman with a hint of fear in her eyes. "Grandmother Coyote—what brings you here?" The fear was palpable in her voice.

Grandmother Coyote rested her gentle—yet not merciful—gaze on Iris's face. "Be not afraid, young Talon-haltija. I am not here on your account. There is nothing to fear from me. Run now, to your home, and rest. The destinies of those who lie within your womb are only beginning, and you must have the strength and energy to run after them as they grow. There is greatness within you, and you are as yet unrealized in your place in the world. Be at peace."

A look of relief washed over Iris's face, and she curtseyed, then glanced at Camille and mouthed *Later* before
waddling out of the living room.

Camille motioned to a chair. "Won't you sit down?"

Grandmother Coyote lowered herself into the chair,
leaning her walking stick against the arm. "I will not
bother myself with chatter—it is not my nature." A crinkle
in her face substituted for a smile. "But I will drink a cup
of tea. Camille, fetch me one."

Camille curtseyed, then hurried to the kitchen. I heard
her fumbling around with the china and realized she was
as nervous as I was. Grandmother Coyote never paid social
calls, so whatever brought her to us had to be serious.

"Where is my grandson—so to speak?"

"Morio's off training." I waited. The Hags of Fate spoke
on their own time, according to their own agendas. It would
do us no good to ask why she was here and I knew it. Like
all cats, I could be patient.

Smoky also seemed alert, on his guard. Trillian stood
near the door, waiting for instructions. Vanzir put down the
game controller and pushed himself off the floor, dusting
his hands on his pants as he leaned against the arm of the
sofa and nodded to Grandmother Coyote.

As Camille brought the tea in, Trillian took the tray
from her and set it on the coffee table. He poured as we
gathered around. Grandmother Coyote accepted the cup
and sipped the steaming liquid. Then, with a deep breath,
she inhaled the fragrance. Finally, she set the teacup on a
coaster on the table next to the chair and looked around the
room, her gaze falling on Camille.

"You cannot get rid of Rodney, my girl, as much as you
want to. He's important. I know how much you hate him,
but you have no choice. Unleash him at the right moment
and he may save your life."

Camille gulped. I knew how much she hated the freaka-
zoid bone golem who thought of himself as a budding
Howard Stern—we all did—but she said nothing, merely
nodding.

Another moment, and Grandmother Coyote cocked her head, turning slowly to look at me. "Delilah, I have come for you tonight."

Oh joy. "Me?"

Usually, when Grandmother Coyote had something to say, it was to Camille, but apparently she'd said all she had to say to my sister with the warning about Rodney. At least for the night.

"Yes, *you.* I have brought visitors. And while this matter will concern all of you, Delilah, you are the one who stands at the fulcrum this time. A balance has been upset and must be righted."

As she paused, a scratching sounded at the front door.

"What the fuck—" Camille moved toward the foyer, but Grandmother Coyote stopped her.

"Halt. I brought visitors here on my summons. I shall reveal them in good time." She paused again, then yawned. Her teeth were steely, cold and metallic, sharp as blades, looking like they could gnash bone into shrapnel. And I had no doubt they could—and perhaps they had.

A chill ran down my spine, and I had the feeling that my work with Greta tonight had something to do with what Grandmother Coyote was talking about.

"What do you need me for?"

Grandmother Coyote touched her nose. "That cannot be discussed without me introducing my comrades. But first, you are correct in your silent surmise. This matter relates directly to your training as a Death Maiden. Second, this matter involves demonic energies in the city *not* related to Shadow Wing." At with that, she nodded to the hallway. "Go now, let in my pets."

I moved to the door, wondering who was waiting outside. It could be a troll or a goblin or a centaur or—who knew what. Knowing Grandmother Coyote, *anybody* could be on the other side. My stomach lurching, I yanked open the door.

There, on the porch, like stone statues come to life, stood two gargoyles. And they didn't look happy.